Praise for

THE GATES OF TWILIGHT

"Excellent . . . tightly woven, exotic,
tense, atmospheric . . . I rarely get to read
something this impressive."
—Melanie Rawn

"A captivating novel whose appeal should
extend well beyond fans of the genre."
—*Publishers Weekly*

"Detailed, exotic . . . A realistic portrayal
of another society; highly recommended."
—*Library Journal*

"No one can create a fantasy world like
Paula Volsky. She just keeps getting
better and better."
—A. C. Crispin

Also by Paula Volsky

Illusion
The Wolf of Winter
The Gates of Twilight

Bantam Books

New York
Toronto
London
Sydney
Auckland

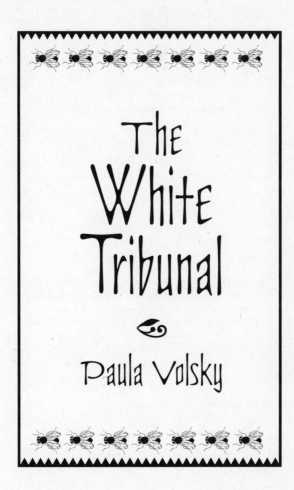

The White Tribunal

Paula Volsky

THE WHITE TRIBUNAL

A Bantam Spectra Book/September 1997

SPECTRA and the portrayal of a boxed "s" are trademarks of
Bantam Books, a division of Bantam Doubleday Dell
Publishing Group, Inc.

BOOK DESIGN BY ELLEN CIPRIANO.

Library of Congress Cataloging-in-Publication Data

Volsky, Paula.
　　The white tribunal / Paula Volsky.
　　　　p.　cm.—(A Bantam spectra book) .
　　ISBN 0-553-37846-5
　　I. Title.
　　PS3543.0634W48　1997
　　813'.54—dc21　　　　　　　　　　　　　　　　　　97-12378
　　　　　　　　　　　　　　　　　　　　　　　　　　　　　CIP

Published simultaneously in the United States and Canada

Bantam Books are published by Bantam Books, a division of Bantam
Doubleday Dell Publishing Group, Inc. Its trademark, consisting of
the words "Bantam Books" and the portrayal of a rooster, is Regis-
tered in U.S. Patent and Trademark Office and in other countries.
Marca Registrada. Bantam Books, 1540 Broadway, New York, New
York 10036.

PRINTED IN THE UNITED STATES OF AMERICA

BVG　10　9　8　7　6　5　4　3　2　1

The White Tribunal

Oπe

The old mansion was haunted, beyond doubt. The offended ghost of its slaughtered master still loitered upon the premises. Yurune the Bloodless, sorcerer and deviant that he was, had surely deserved his fate at the hands of an outraged mob. The ax stroke that parted his head from his body should in all justice have dispatched his soiled spirit straight to the malevolences that he served. But justice had proved characteristically capricious, and Yurune's essential self lingered yet to guard his domain and secrets against his killers' descendants. Or so the story ran.

Was it true, was any of it true? Tradain liMarchborg was determined to find out.

There would be no shrinking and no cowardice—not today. How many times in the past few years had he approached the gutted building only to retreat, cowed by a shivery shadow, by a whisper or a gleam; by nothing at all? How many times had he slunk ignominiously away, throat constricted and heart hopping? Too often—but not this time. He was thirteen, and far too old for childish terrors. This time, he was going in.

He lay concealed in the tall yellow grasses that rustled at the crest of a rise overlooking the house. His caution was redundant, for the place was deserted as always. Humans wisely shunned the spot, had shunned it since the days of Yurune. But the pressure of invisible eyes was all but tangible, and instinct clamored a warning. The gooseflesh rose along his arms, the weedy adolescent figure stiffened, and he glanced back quickly over his shoulder.

No one there, of course. Pressing himself flat to the ground, he held his breath and listened. No voices, no footsteps, nothing beyond the ceaseless papery rustle of the wind amidst dead grasses. Nothing audible or visible to justify the chilly, oddly enjoyable trepidation that now possessed him.

Releasing his breath, he lifted his head to peer once more through the fringe of pallid vegetation. Down below bulked the mansion, at once familiar and immensely alien, silent and sinister even in the harmless daylight of late autumn. The walls were charred, but whole; shutters cracked but still barred, still defensive, even after all these years. The four eccentric turrets, twisted and misshapen, presumably reflected the bent nature of the architect/owner. The house was ringed with ancient trees. Their branches, dark and elaborate as wrought iron, arched above the spiral towers. Although those branches were bare, save for the occasional clinging scrap of brown parchment leaf, little light struggled through to touch dead Yurune's dwelling. The place was a natural home of shadows.

Beyond the house, beyond the iron trees, rippled the leaden waters of Lake Oblivion, an aqueous mass grave embracing countless casualties of the last century's Sortilegious Wars. The great rock rising from the grey waters at the lake's center, and the ancient fortress crowning that rock, were veiled in fog, as usual—and just as well. Fortress Nul, that prison reputedly inescapable and purgatorial, was best left hidden from sight and mind. Likewise best forgotten or ignored—the myriad restless ghosts said to haunt the lake and its environs; ghosts that watched and waited, ghosts that dreamt cold dead dreams of vengeance, ghosts that laid weightless frigid fingers upon the eyes of intruders . . .

Tradain shivered pleasurably, and his own living fingers sought the medallion that hung at his neck—a small silver disk, stamped with the potently protective image of immortal Autonn. The talisman seemed meaningless now, its lifeless weight no source of courage. He let it fall, and his full attention returned to Yurune's mansion.

The shuttered windows disclosed nothing. His own face was far more revealing—expressive, perilously ingenuous, with clear-cut features and keen eyes too blue and thickly lashed to waste on a boy—a youthful, unfinished face, saved from prettiness by the boldness of straight black brows, the strength of a well-defined jaw, and the carelessness of raven's wing hair.

Belly to the ground, he inched himself a few feet down the slope, then paused. His precautions were ridiculous. If ghosts or malevolences guarded this place, his presence was not about to escape their notice. He might just as well stand up and march straight on. Rising to his feet, he paused a breathless moment, during which lightning failed to strike. The sun shone dimly through the perpetual mists, the breeze whispered, the mansion brooded, and that was all.

Nervous tension mounting with every step, he resumed his advance. The meadow behind him was empty, and the heat of hidden eyes singeing his back was no doubt imaginary.

On he went, to the bottom of the hill where the iron trees grew, through a crackling sea of fallen leaves, and now the house of Yurune rose before him as it had risen so often in the past, but never before so close, and never so unequivocally threatening.

Through the leaves he waded, to the foot of the black basalt stairway—nothing so mundane as marble or sandstone for Yurune. A quick glance right and left—no sign of life or motion beneath the trees—then up the steps to the great portal, broken and shattered by that long-ago mob. The oaken remnants swung yet on ruined hinges. The entrance was unobstructed and apparently unguarded, but the sense of a vigilant, inimical presence was strong enough to freeze him on the threshold.

The hesitation was minimal, for the excesses of imagination were not about to break his resolve at this point. Taking a deep breath, he stepped over the threshold into dimness.

Muted light sliding in through the chinks in the shutters revealed a scene of devastation. Yurune's possessions—the heavy, plain furnishings, the scanty ornaments, sconces, and lamps—lay battered, hacked, and scorched. The hangings had been ripped from the walls, piled in a heap, and ignited. They had not burned well—a blackened mound remained, and soot grimed the ceiling above the spot. The cast-iron chandelier had been torn down to shatter upon the stone floor. Fragments lay strewn across the flags, and a few of the sockets still held the waxen stumps of ancient candles. It seemed that nothing had been stolen. The undisturbed dust of a century or more shrouded all. The invaders had been desperate enough to face Yurune the Bloodless, deadliest of black magicians, and they had destroyed him; but they had not dared to loot his house.

Through the ravaged chambers stole Tradain, encountering neither marvel nor menace. Presently he found his way to a windowless corridor thrusting darkly into the heart of the house, and there he stopped to draw candle and tinderbox from his pocket. He lit the candle, and the yellow light quivered upon the blackened stones, the dust and cobwebs, the ruby eyes of the fugitive rats. A dry puff of air gusted along the hallway. The flame shook, the light bounded, a quiet footfall echoed softly. Tradain's vivid glance shifted this way and that. The house was inhabited and empty, asleep and aware. He did not know what it expected of him. What he himself expected and needed was revelation. So far, he had not found it, but Yurune's mansion would yield its secrets yet.

On along the corridor he prowled, to an antechamber illumined only by a skylight four stories above—the room wherein, as legend had it, Yurune the Bloodless had met his end. Here, the parents of the countless murdered and violated children had hacked their tyrant to pieces.

Were there stains on the floor to confute the sorcerer's appellation? Tradain saw none. The porous stone was clear. Despite the gruesome celebrity of the place, he hardly paused to wonder, for the tapestry at the far end of the room, that would have thoroughly covered the wall in Yurune's time, was now hanging in rotten shreds, behind which he descried the outline of a door. Crossing the room, he thrust the woolen tatters aside and opened the door, to behold a stairway plunging into darkness.

He set his foot upon the first tread, and thought he felt the house peering over his shoulder, and breathing silent threats in his ear.

Silent?

Behind him, clear and unmistakable, a footstep crunched upon broken glass. In the haunted stillness of Yurune's mansion, that faint pop was startling as the bang of a firecracker. Heart contracting, he spun in time to catch sight of a small, dark form diving for cover behind a mound of broken furniture. He carried no weapon, and if he had stopped to think, he would have retreated. Instead, three long strides took him around the pile, where he stooped, grabbed, and dragged forth a wriggling figure by one ankle. When he saw who it was, he released her at once.

"Glennian." He couldn't decide between annoyance and amusement.

"Herself," the child answered with characteristic impertinence. Sitting up, she tossed back her long mane of chestnut hair.

"Might have guessed." He seated himself on the floor, facing her, and the perpetual cold of the mansion's stones at once began to work its way through his clothes.

"Didn't, though. You were scared, weren't you?"

"Do you have to follow me around, all the time?"

"I don't!"

"Yes you do. Everywhere I go, you turn up."

"You're really conceited."

"Why don't you find some little girls your own age to play with?"

"Girls my own age are like *babies*. They're *boring*. They're—they're *ignorant*. They don't understand Rhizbaut's Fifth Theorem, or the Chorkan Variations, or Fantollio's Principle of Sequential Progression."

"Neither do I."

"They won't solve equations, they can't follow the simplest proofs, they don't even like chess. Besides—" Her face altered slightly. "They don't want to play with me."

"Well, can you blame them, if they know you think they're boring and ignorant?" he inquired reasonably.

"They don't know. I've never said it out loud."

"Sometimes you don't have to say things out loud. People can just tell."

"They can't know what I'm thinking. They're too silly. All they like to do is giggle all the time, and make faces behind my back, and whisper secrets to each other, right in front of me, so as to make me wonder what they're saying. And then when I ask, they just giggle harder."

"Have you ever tried to—" His voice trailed off. She was gazing at him expectantly, awaiting wisdom, of which he had none. The general attitudes and behavior of prepubescent females—or any females, for that matter—were entirely incomprehensible to him. As for the problem itself, it was not one he'd personally experienced. Blessed with a sanguine nature, an active and well-coordinated body, and a healthy measure of confidence, he had never lacked friends. He could sympathize with the quirky, lonely child excluded by her peers, but he hadn't the least idea what to say to her.

"Ever what?" Glennian prodded. Receiving no reply, she gave her hair another defiant flip. "Well, I don't care. I don't care anything at all about those girls. Papa says they're not on my mental level."

"Papa does, eh? And you call *me* conceited?"

"It's not conceited when I'm only telling the truth. Like it's true that my memory is just *amazing*."

"Famed far and wide, no doubt."

"Papa says I have more in common with older, very intelligent people."

"Like me, for instance?"

"Well—" She considered. "You're older, anyway."

"Which is why you follow me around. If not—" He forestalled her
indignant rejoinder. "If not, then what are you doing here today?"

"I go where I like."

"Really? Wonder what Papa would have to say about that?"

"If you tell my parents I was here, you stink like a dead rat. Informers
are lower and slimier than maggots."

"That bad, eh? All right, I won't tell."

"That's better. Anyway, they've got enough to worry them already."

He knew her well enough to pay attention to that. "Something the
matter at home?"

"Maybe." Her air of impudence faded at his tone of genuine concern.

"What's the trouble, Dwarf?" Even as he spoke, Tradain recognized
the misnomer. Glennian was no longer dwarfish. She was tall for her years,
and the body beneath the comfortable childish garments was slim and colt-
legged. Her eyes—wide, grey-green, and plentifully speckled with brown—
were beginning to acquire depth, and the subtle tilt at the outer corners was
emphasizing itself as her face shed its baby roundness.

"I don't want to leave, that's what's the trouble. This is our home,
where our family's always lived. It's where we belong. You think I should tell
them I just won't go?"

"Go where?"

"Away. We're not just leaving the city, but going to a whole other
country, where no one will know our name, and we won't even be able to
speak the language. I hate it. I'm not supposed to be talking about it, but I
don't care. I wanted to tell you."

"Your family's traveling? Or temporarily taking up residence
abroad?"

"Not temporarily. We're going for good. Forever. We're leaving soon,
maybe in the next day or so, unless I can think of a way to stop them—my
parents, I mean. Everyone says I'm a veritable child prodigy—"

"Your vanity's prodigious, all right."

"So I ought to be able to figure out how to do it. If you look at it the
right way, it's only a problem in logic, like any other. Like chess. Only the
variables are different, but I know there has to be a solution, somewhere.
I've just got to find the right approach. You'll help me, won't you?"

"Slow down. You're sure of all this? Remember, your family's important. You've had ancestors living in Lis Folaze since the founding of the city. Your father is titled, famous, master of liTarngrav House. He can't mean to chuck all that on a whim. You must be making some kind of mistake."

"I'm not. Don't treat me like some drooling infant. I'll turn eleven in just three months, you know."

"Forgive me, madam. All right, if what you're saying is true, then there must be a reason. What's your father thinking of? Why would the High Landguardian Jex liTarngrav depart Upper Hetzia?"

"He's not about to tell me, is he? Anyway, it doesn't matter, because the point is, I won't go. I've been thinking—what if I hide out in the woods? They'd never find me. All I'd need would be someone to help me build a hut, and I could hunt and kill my own food. Tradain, do you by any chance own an ax?"

"Afraid not."

"Bow and arrows?"

"No. Come on, Dwarf. Think. Why would your father want to leave? You say nobody's explained, but I know you—you've seen something, or overheard something." Her eyes evaded his, and he commanded, "Talk."

"Well—" She studied the floor attentively. "They won't tell me anything, but I've got eyes and ears, and me, I think Papa's scared of the White Tribunal."

He was silent, momentarily chilled at the mention of that name. At last, carefully excluding any tone of accusation, he inquired, "Your father hasn't been messing with sorcery, has he?"

"No! Don't talk that way about him!"

"Sorry. Just asking."

"Well it isn't true. My father wouldn't dirty his hands with magical muck! He's not like that! Only, maybe—I wonder—if that's not all there is to worry about. You're right about me listening, and I heard them talking when they thought they were alone, and he said—" Shutting her eyes to assist memory, she repeated, " *The plague of sorcery supposedly ravaging Upper Hetzia will never abate, so long as the wealth and worldly property of the condemned magicians are forfeit to the White Tribunal. The very zeal of the self-proclaimed physicians para—para'* "—Glennian stumbled over unfamiliar words—" *'zeal of the self-proclaimed physicians* paradoxically *feeds the fury of the imaginary ep—epidemic.'* " She opened her eyes. "That's just what he said. I wasn't in the room, and I couldn't see his face—well, all right, so I was eavesdropping—but I could tell from his voice that he was using the sort of smile that makes you feel about the size of a gnat—"

"He was sneering," Tradain suggested.

"That's it. And I think he meant—he was saying—"

"That the White Tribunal will hunt him for his money."

She stared at him, astonished for a moment, then folded her arms and replied with an air of certainty, "They can't do that."

"That's all you know, little one," Tradain observed from the heights of superior wisdom.

"Don't call me little! You don't know everything! You don't even know Rhizbaut's Fifth Theorem—and you don't know anything much about the White Tribunal, either, Master Big Noise."

"I know enough to tell you that a convicted sorcerer stands to lose his whole fortune, and everything he owns, to the court. So those thirteen jurists have good reason for going after rich men, like your father. That's what you overheard him talking about when you eavesdropped."

"Well, I don't believe it. You know why? Because the Dhreve wouldn't allow it, that's why. This country's ruled by the Dhreve Lissildt, not by the White Tribunal."

"Is it?"

"Yes, and he's a good Dhreve, and a good person, just ask anybody."

Lissildt—well intentioned, but ill-informed, inexperienced, and weak in character, luckless inheritor of disastrously undermined authority. The possibly compromising words of his own father rang in Tradain's mind, but he knew better than to repeat them aloud before little Glennian liTarngrav, whose own precocious tongue was unguarded at best.

"A good person," he agreed absently.

"Yes, and even if he weren't," the youngster chattered on, "there'd be plenty of others to stop the White Tribunal from hurting people who don't deserve it. Others to set things right. Because that's what a good person really *is*—someone who sees what's wrong, and then doesn't just sit there crying, but gets up and *does* something about it. Don't you think?"

"Ummm." He scarcely heard her. His mind was speeding along its own track. So the High Landguardian Jex liTarngrav, despite all his wealth or because of it, had grown so fearful of the White Tribunal that he meant to flee his homeland. The revelation was startling enough in itself, and from a purely personal standpoint, the implications were unsettling.

"So I don't believe that we really need to go at all," Glennian continued, blind to his abstraction. "In fact, I think Father's being sort of chicken-hearted about it. But you won't tell him I said that, will you? Tradain?"

It took him a moment or two to answer, and when he spoke, his advice was not to her liking. "Go home, Glennian. Go home right away."

"I don't want to." She scowled. "I won't let them drag me off to some stupid foreign place, just because they're scared. I'm going to stay right here.

I can hide out in the woods, and I'll build a shelter, and I'll be a mysterious hermit, living on berries and rainwater—"

"That's ridiculous, and you know it."

Her scowl deepened.

"If your parents leave, then you go with them. End of discussion. You should be with them right now, not skipping off on some silly lark. They're probably looking for you, and they don't need extra trouble at a time like this."

"Nobody knows I went out. Not even Pfissig, that nosedrip."

"Who?"

"Pfissig. You know, Kwieseldt's barfable boy."

"Oh, yes." Kwieseldt, he remembered, was the liTarngrav household steward. The vomitive lad in question was the steward's son, object of Glennian's particular detestation.

"He's always trailing around, sneaking and spying, Pfissig is," the child continued. "He's always watching and prying, and sticking that long, red, snuffly nose of his into other people's business. And then he carries tales back to his dad. He thinks he's clever, but today I gave him the slip."

"Congratulations. I hate to burst your bubble, but by this time, somebody's probably noticed that you're gone. And if they knew you'd come here—"

"Well, I haven't seen anything so particular about this old pile, for all the stories they tell. It's nothing so much, in *my* opinion. But you've got to promise you won't tell anyone I came here."

"Word of honor."

"And promise you won't repeat a word of what I've told you."

"That's something else again. I'm going to have to tell some of it to my father."

"You can't! I hope your tongue falls out!"

"Listen, this is important. Your father and mine have been best friends all their lives. They're close as brothers, partners in business and politics, blood-connected by the intermarriages between our two families, allies forever, and all the world knows it. If suspicion falls on one, the other's in just as much trouble. If that's true, then my own father needs to know about it."

"How do you know he doesn't already? If they're such good friends, my papa would have told him, long ago."

"That may be true, but I have to make sure of it. You understand that, don't you?"

She nodded unwillingly.

"Then I want you to come back to the city with me." He saw her chin go stubborn, and added, "You asked me not to treat you like an infant. Now show me I don't need to."

"Oh, all right." She stood up, shaking the dust and cobwebs from her skirt. "Anyone would think you were my uncle, or something."

Rising, Tradain cast a last uneasy but longing glance around him. The sense of inimical surveillance had subsided, perhaps repelled by Glennian's bright presence, but it was not gone. He could still feel it, faint and distant now, but vigilant as ever.

Glennian noted his expression. "Did you want to look around before we go?" she asked. "Are you here chasing Yurune's ghost? Don't stop on my account. If the old boy's still floating around, I don't mind saying hello."

"Another time. Come on." He extended his hand, and she took it. As he led her from Yurune's death chamber, and out into the long, windowless corridor, he felt her grip upon him tighten. The air was chilly and dank, but her palm was sweating. Her breath was quick, and her eyes darted everywhere. So much for her bravado.

Back along the drafty corridor they hurried, at the swiftest pace that dignity allowed, and back through the silent, ruined chambers. Not quite so threatening now, with Glennian beside him, and the house, or whatever guarded it, apparently mollified by their retreat, but still he felt the pressure of invisible regard. Back along the pathway of their own fresh footprints in the dust, past the wreckage of the great chandelier, out at last through the broken front door, and down the basalt stairway to the leaf-littered grounds, where the shadows always lingered.

Tradain wavered between relief and regret. "I'll come back," he promised the house.

"Me too. Spit twice on it," said Glennian, and did so.

She had a way of sabotaging solemn moments.

Turning away from Yurune's mansion, they struck off across hills mantled in forest and veiled in mist. As they went, the dark aura faded behind them, the sense of uncanny menace vanished, and the woods resumed their accustomed unpolluted beauty. A few of the trees still flaunted rags of scarlet and gold. The brambles bore polished clusters of orange berries, feathery tufts of amber vellius sprayed from blackened pods, and a few late-blooming jisterix glowed like miniature suns. The dead leaves crackled gloriously underfoot, and the air was rich with the scents of moist soil and flora hovering on the verge of winter sleep.

Amidst such surroundings, it was hard to believe in ghosts or malevolences. That malignant intelligence inhabiting Yurune's mansion—had it been real or imaginary? Someday, Tradain inwardly vowed, he would find out, but now was not the time to address such issues—Glennian's information suggested far more immediate concerns, and her news should be relayed as quickly as possible.

It was a long hike back to the city, and he unconsciously lengthened his stride, forcing his companion into a trot to keep pace. He slowed when he noticed, for he knew she would rather have died than complain. Thereafter, they proceeded at moderate speed, pausing just once to rest briefly at the summit of Ziehn's Tooth. From that high vantage point, they could gaze out over miles of wooded countryside, blurred with the ever-present mists. Today, visibility was comparatively good, and they could see as far as Lis Folaze, with its tripartite domes and its distinctively triple-forked spires. Through the city curved the silver Folaze, spanned by a multitude of red stone bridges. Tallest and sharpest of pronged towers crowned the Heart of Light, that dire stone pile housing the White Tribunal and occupying its own small island in the middle of the river. Slightly to the north, the tremendous dome of the Dhreve's palace dominated the skyline. Beyond the palace, where the mists thickened, a telltale glow marked the site of the Melt—a vast, amorphous heap of luminous stone, remains of a sorcerously dissolved block of warehouses and tenements—one of the city's more spectacular mementos of the Sortilegious Wars.

Descending from Ziehn's Tooth, Tradain and Glennian walked the hills for another hour or more, and as they walked, she hummed to herself. Her voice was childishly piping and unremarkable, but the tune itself was beguiling, and presently he asked her, "What's that?"

"What's what?"

"The music."

"Nothing. Just one of my things."

"You mean, you made it up?"

She nodded.

"How d'you do that?"

"Well, I don't exactly *do* it. They're just there, in my head, sometimes. Once they come, they don't go away until I sing them, or write them down, or something."

"That's all there is to it?"

"Of course not. If it's a good one, worth the bother, I sort of poke and prod it until it's better. Don't you?"

"No. There are no tunes in my mind to poke and prod."

"There aren't? None? You mean, never?"

"Well, of course I think of music, sometimes. I whistle, but it's always what I've heard somewhere else—nothing I've made up myself."

"Doesn't that get kind of boring?"

"Not so far."

"But they're not yours. Isn't it sort of like talking, and just saying someone else's words, instead of thinking up your own?"

"No. Because not everyone's like you, not everyone thinks up music."

"That's sort of sad."

"You wouldn't think so," Tradain loftily countered the implied deprecation, "if you weren't such a chit."

"I am not a chit!"

"Do you know what it means?"

"I don't care what it means!"

The shadows were lengthening by the time they emerged from the woods to continue along the wide Dhreve's Highway, arrowing its way over field and farmland. Cottage and farmhouse gave way to the brick and stone dwellings of the city. The ground leveled. The houses grew taller, grander, and closer. Most of them were painted or stuccoed white, their pale exterior walls boldly ornamented with black geometric designs, visible through all but the heaviest fogs.

The Conquered Malevolence inn appeared, with its horrific hanging sign, and its hundred fanciful lanterns dangling from the eaves. Beyond the Conquered Malevolence rose Ausleeb's Haven, celebrated for its monster fleas, and then came a stand of stalls, occupied by merchants vending protective charms and amulets, images of Autonn, and ghost wards of every description. Among the stalls stood the varnished red booth of a professional litanist, willing to utter protective chants and invocations on behalf of a paying client for minutes, hours, or days on end. Upon this particular day, the litanist's trade was brisk, and the singsong syllables gushed from his booth.

Beyond the stalls, the road narrowed, the crowds thickened, the noise increased, and presently the anachronistic old city wall loomed before them, its huge gate perpetually open and unguarded. Above the portal hung a talisman affixed in recent years, a tangle of interwoven spikes whose complex structure theoretically mitigated the power of sorcery. Passing beneath the talisman, they found themselves on familiar cobbled streets, crowded as always with carriages, sedan chairs, and pedestrians.

It was late. The fog was beginning to thicken, the lamplighters were already at work, and the merchants were starting to close down for the night. Near at hand, a draper sprinkled his threshold with Gref's Potent Powder to repel the nocturnal intrusion of ghost and malevolence. His neighbor, a tailor, performed ritual warding gestures, and the air buzzed with the declamation of the ubiquitous litanists.

Inured to these sights since earliest childhood, Tradain and Glennian paid little heed. Together they walked as far as the Statues—human in form, granite in substance, wont to drip blood at irregular intervals—another souvenir of the Sortilegious Wars. There, their paths diverged.

"I won't say good-bye." Glennian faced him. "Because I'm not going away. If my parents leave, they can go without me."

"You know, you're acting like a baby. You're—"

"So what about the both of us going back to Yurune's mansion tomorrow?" Glennian cut him off in mid reproof. "I want to see all the rooms. I want to go down those stairs you were sniffing around."

"Run along home, Dwarf."

"You're not *scared*?"

"Tomorrow, I'll have no time for playing games with little children," he informed her.

"Go eat a cow flop, with boiled carrots."

"Did you get that out of one of your mathematical treatises?"

"I'll go back there by myself, then."

"No you won't."

"Yes I will, unless you come with me. Come on, Tradain, *please*."

"Listen, what about this?" he appeased her. "In a little while, maybe a few days, if you're still in the city—"

"I will be!"

"Then we'll go back to that mansion, and together we'll see what lies at the bottom of those stairs."

"You promise?"

"Word of honor."

"Spit twice on it."

He complied. "Now, go home."

"Anything you say, Uncle. See you soon, then. Remember, you've promised." Turning away from him, she walked north, toward the Dhreve's palace, with its satellite aristocratic mansions, among which numbered enormous liTarngrav House.

Tradain hurried east, pausing only once to look back at her. The image of her slight, colt-legged figure, long hair swinging with each bouncy step, would remain with him for years. She vanished into the crowd and the mists, and he continued on alone through the streets, to the region of wealthy lanes and squares clustering at the foot of Brilliant Bridge; so named for its lanterns of cunning design, equipped with mirrored reflectors curved to catch and concentrate the light. Here, the grand dwellings were neither painted nor stuccoed, but constructed of lustrous white marble, with geometric designs picked out in black stone or in black squares of the famous

Hetzian porcelain. Soon he came to his father's house—not huge or splendid enough to merit the title of mansion, but imposing and very handsome, with its tall white columns, its minimal ornamentation, and its perfect proportions, pure and restrained to the point of austerity. Alone among its neighbors, Ravnar liMarchborg's house displayed no protective amulet above the door—an omission counting among its master's many minor acts of social heresy.

Tradain had sometimes found himself wondering, in the last year or so, whether such acts went unnoticed.

He entered through the front door and, dodging the inquiries of the servants, went straight off in search of his father. Bypassing the formal ground-floor chambers, he made directly for the private apartments above, where, just possibly, Ravnar might sit alone, for once relieved of the grating presence of—

No such luck, however. Long before he reached the door of Ravnar's suite, he heard the voice of his stepmother, uplifted in passionate accusation. She was a noisy one, the Lady Aestine. She had a clear soprano voice that could, in moments of stress, drill eardrums. Such moments were all too frequent. Cursed with ungovernable emotions and a host of gnawing suspicions, Ravnar liMarchborg's highborn, high-strung second wife was prone to alternating fits of gloom and screaming outrage. The gloom was dreary and pathetic; the rage, groundless and offensive. The woman's misery infected all the household, and Tradain wholeheartedly loathed her—a sentiment shared by his two older brothers. Now he heard the shrill voice jittering up the scale, heard the string of angry reproaches, and he stopped outside his father's door.

"You never have time for me. You don't *make* time for me."

The usual whining belligerence. A truly objectionable woman.

"Doesn't it make any difference at all that I—that I'm so unhappy—"

Ravnar liMarchborg's voice came, soothing, reassuring.

"Did you marry me just to ignore me? Do you wish you hadn't married me at all? Well, do you?"

Again, a forbearing reply.

"Life would be better without me, wouldn't it? Those boys of yours, your three cherished darlings, make it clear enough how they feel. I suppose you agree with them—you always agree with them—so I'll do you a favor. I'll remove myself from your sight. That will please you, won't it? I only invaded your precious sanctum because there was something I wanted to tell you, but I see you're not interested in anything I might have to say."

A polite denial, a query.

"No, I've changed my mind. And I am going to make you very happy now, by leaving you alone. I won't waste another moment of your valuable time. Not another single, solitary, priceless instant!"

A tremendous crash of shattering glass terminated the conversation. The door banged open and Aestine emerged, flat chest heaving, narrow face flushed an unbecoming shade of carmine. Her furious eyes were swollen and bloodshot. Tears dripped down her cheeks, and her nose was running. Her mouth was stretched tight and quivering, the lines from nostrils to lips etched unnaturally deep. She looked ghastly—at once wretched and oddly venomous—and Tradain observed her with detached distaste.

She looked up to meet his analytical regard, and for a moment her expression alarmed him. The animosity between Lady Aestine and her three stepsons, there from the first, was ordinarily veiled in mutual careful courtesy. Now, the naked loathing glittered in her eyes.

"Go in, my little princeling." Her voice was all but choked with tears and rage. "He'll find time for you, he always does. After all, you come first, don't you? Well, what are you gawking at? Go on in!" Without awaiting reply, she flung off down the corridor.

Tradain stared after her a moment, then shrugged and entered his father's apartment to find Ravnar liMarchborg there alone, inspecting the wreckage of a glass curio cabinet. In the midst of the vitreous shards and broken keepsakes lay a silver candlestick, presumably hurled by the irate lady of the house.

Ravnar glanced up at his son's entrance, and Tradain met eyes as blue and vivid as his own. Similar in character as well as appearance, father and son shared the same perilous ingenuousness.

How can you stand it? The words almost slipped out, but Tradain caught them in time. Ravnar, with his well-developed sense of duty, did not tolerate criticism of his second wife. Complaint was useless. Aestine was a permanent addition to the family, and much as Ravnar might now regret a hasty choice, his decision was irrevocable. The bonds of marriage were unbreakable.

Rather than voicing pointlessly painful queries, Tradain confined himself to an innocuous, "What's that in your hand, Father?"

"A memento. I haven't looked at it in years. Until just now, I had quite forgotten it." Ravnar's expression reflected nothing but thoughtful tranquillity. Whatever unquiet emotions seethed below the surface—and they must surely have been there—the High Landguardian liMarchborg held them in check. He extended an open palm, upon which lay a miniature painting in an ivory frame.

Tradain beheld the finely executed portrait of three very young men or, perhaps, three boys poised on the verge of manhood, all attired in a fashion some thirty years out-of-date. Two of them he recognized without difficulty. There was his own father Ravnar liMarchborg, the blue eyes and strong black brows unmistakable. Beside Ravnar stood a red-haired, broad-shouldered, stocky youth, sporting jeweled knee-sparklers: Jex liTarngrav— Ravnar's friend, and Glennian's father. The third was harder to identify, but there was something familiar about the starkly white, studious face, framed in straight, fair hair; perhaps something in the line of the thin, high-bridged nose, or perhaps the long, narrow jaw, with its deeply cleft chin. He frowned, trying to remember.

"Can't place him?" Ravnar liMarchborg smiled. "Think of an older man. It's Gnaus liGurvohl."

Startled, Tradain glanced at his father, then back down at the painting, trying to correlate the youthful image before him with the face of the man known to the intimidated citizens of Lis Folaze as liGurvohl the Incorruptible, Premier Jurist of the White Tribunal. Same tall and pale brow, same features, same bony structure in general. As for the mouth—difficult to judge. The young man in the picture was smiling faintly, and few if any had witnessed the tight, straight lips of the Incorruptible curve in so genial an expression. And the eyes? Uncertain. The all but colorless rainwater eyes of Gnaus liGurvohl were deep-set, hooded, ringed with line and shadow. The pictured orbs were very different—and yet it was the same face, surely.

"What are you doing sharing portrait space with old Rack and Fire?" Tradain inquired. "I thought you and he hated each other."

"Not always. We were great friends once."

"You and that old blood-boiler?"

"It was a very long time ago, and Gnaus was different in those days. There were three of us, back then—Jex liTarngrav, Gnaus liGurvohl, and I. Children together, grew up together, best friends—all of that. Jex and I are friends to this day—"

"That's what I need to talk to you about, Father. I—"

"But Gnaus went another way. Got caught up in the malevolence hysteria, made a career hunting the so-called sorcerers. Gave him some sense of significance, I suppose."

"Significance?"

"Jex and I stood to inherit, but Gnaus was a younger son. He'd never own great wealth, or a title. What else did he have?" Lost in his memories, Ravnar seemed almost talking to himself. "And so he hunted magicians. Discovered and destroyed them. Grew famous, and assumed leadership of the White Tribunal, which thereafter required an unfailing supply of sorcerers to justify its continued existence."

"Are you saying that the Incorruptible is a fraud?" Tradain managed to make himself heard. "That he's Disinfecting innocent people, just to keep his job?"

"Oh, not consciously, not deliberately. I'm certain he's quite convinced himself that the danger is real."

"But you're not convinced, Father? You don't believe in magic, malevolences, or sorcerers?"

"I certainly concede the reality of forces and phenomena existing far beyond the present level of human understanding. These powers are called magical, and regarded as supernatural, therefore malignant. But I must wonder if the term 'supernatural' possesses any real meaning. Nature, by definition, includes all of existence. What can lie outside of that?" Again, Ravnar seemed almost to speak to himself.

"What about malevolences, Father? Aren't they outside of natural existence, and opposed to natural order? Don't you believe in that?"

"I don't know, son. I'm not altogether convinced that malevolences are real. If they are, then we know nothing of them beyond the legends generated by our own fears. If they're present among us, and hostile to man, that doesn't necessarily make them unnatural."

"Evil, then."

"Another of those colorful but vague expressions. Let's say potentially dangerous."

"Potentially dangerous." Tradain nodded thoughtfully. He enjoyed these philosophical exchanges with his father, and always strove to prolong them. "They say that a sorcerer receives his magical powers as the price of the human life-force that he sells to malevolences. Do you believe that?"

"What, exactly, is this 'human life-force,' you speak of? Where is it located, what does it do, how is it transferred to its purchaser? Speaking of which, why should a being as powerful as a malevolence bother to purchase what he wants from humans? Why not just take?"

"Because Autonn prevents the theft?"

"Prevents the theft, but not the sale? What is the point? And why should Autonn, whoever that is, concern Himself at all?"

"Are you saying you don't believe in Autonn, either?" Tradain was intrigued. The discussion was drifting into interestingly dangerous realms.

"I only voice questions."

"Here's another, then. If it's true that malevolences are real, and if it's true that they're enemies of man, and if it's true that these enemies are the source of magical power, then doesn't it follow that magical power must be destructive? And if it's destructive, then isn't the White Tribunal right in Disinfecting sorcerers?"

"A great many ifs in that, and a lot of room for question. Until some of those assumptions have been confirmed, there's no justification in prohibiting investigation, in my opinion. Even were the danger proved beyond question, I'd oppose the Tribunal's methods. Terror accomplishes little beyond self-perpetuation. Perhaps Gnaus liGurvohl will discover that one day—but I doubt it." Ravnar studied the portrait with a kind of condemnatory regret for a moment, and then recalled himself to present reality. He looked up sharply to observe, "You understand that what I've said is meant for your ears alone."

"You can trust me," Tradain promised, immensely flattered to merit his father's confidence.

"I know it. But you're looking serious, son. I suspect you didn't come in here to discuss social issues."

"I came because I learned something today that I think you should know. Little Glennian liTarngrav told me that her whole family is about to leave Upper Hetzia for good. Her father is worried about the White Tribunal, so they're going in the next day or so. Glennian doesn't even know where."

"Lanthi Ume, I believe. Pleasant climate, marvelous architecture."

"You already knew?"

"My dear boy, Jex liTarngrav shares your concern. He informed me of his plans weeks ago, urging me to accompany him."

"You said no?"

"I will tell you now what I told him then. Lis Folaze is my home, and I've no desire to leave it. Beyond that, I see no need. Unlike Jex, I possess no wealth great enough to excite envy or inflame greed. Moreover, I've done nothing wrong. I most certainly haven't dabbled in sorcery, and so there can be no proofs or evidence against me. Without proofs, there can be no case, and thus I've little to fear from the White Tribunal."

"But, Father—" Tradain struggled uncomfortably for words. "Can we depend on that?"

"If not, then what can we depend on?"

"But the White Tribunal seems to do whatever it wants, and nobody dares to complain, not even the Dhreve."

"I will complain," Ravnar observed mildly, "if they attempt to deprive me of my legal rights. But I hardly think they would presume so far. The liMarchborg name is noble, ancient, respected. I am not without friends and influence in this city."

"But what if your friends were afraid to stand by you? What if you were accused and didn't even get the chance to speak? You could be buried alive in some dungeon, with never a fair trial. I've heard of such things happening, even to noblemen."

"Ah, you sound exactly like Jex, but you and he are both mistaken. Tradain, you must not lose sight of the fact that we live in a civilized land, governed by a well-conceived and well-established system of law. The system is far from perfect, yet it is our most valuable possession, our strongest defense against chaos, the very foundation of the city. That being the case, we must trust in the power of the law, and believe in its promise of justice. For me to leave the city now is a violation of that trust, a repudiation of all that I believe in, and I will not do it. Do you understand me?"

"Yes, Father." Tradain responded, all doubts dying, as usual, in the face of his father's faith. A man so honorable, so high-minded, and manifestly good as Ravnar liMarchborg had to be right.

"You'll see. When this sorcery nonsense is finished, and the White Tribunal nothing more than an unpleasant memory, we shall still be here in Lis Folaze, where men of sound judgment will be needed to set things right. Mark my words."

Tradain found himself smiling, caught up in Ravnar's vision of the future. He felt at that moment as if he and his father might be the only men of sound judgment needed to set things right. They would do it alone, the two of them, for there was nothing in the world they couldn't accomplish together. Just then, he came within a breath of embracing his father, but sensibly controlled the sentimental impulse. Often, in years to come, he would recall the moment and regret that restraint.

Manly reserve notwithstanding, his emotions showed on his face. Ravnar saw them, and his own smile, so infrequent of late, flashed in response.

Leaving his father's apartment, Tradain went off in search of his two brothers. The oldest, named Ravnar for their sire but always called Rav, was skinny, scholarly, and usually a friendly source of sound advice. The middle son, Zendin, was mischievous, mercurial, and charged with unholy charm. A little harebrained, but always full of ideas, some of them worth listening to. It often paid to consult Zendin.

He found that both brothers were out, and unlikely to be home for dinner. Someday, he too would enjoy such freedom. Tradain repaired to his own room, where he occupied himself with a history of the Strellian Debacle. Two hours later he emerged with reluctance to take his place at a predictably cheerless table.

He had hoped that Lady Aestine might convey her sentiments by means of pointed absence, but she had not obliged. There she sat in wounded, wrathful silence—spine rigid, face still tearfully puffy. She was, quite conspicuously, drinking too much wine. *See what your cruelty is driving me to*, the message seemed to be. Each gulp was laborious, as if the liquid forced its way past some constriction in her throat, and her brooding stare pressed upon her husband like a hot branding iron.

Ravnar appeared to notice nothing. When his courteous overtures to his wife went unacknowledged, he turned to his youngest son, who would ordinarily have enjoyed the attention. Now, however, with Lady Aestine's bloodshot eyes boring into him, and her hostile emanations all but fogging the atmosphere, Tradain longed only for escape. Excusing himself as early as decently possible, he once more sought the sanctuary of his chamber, and there he remained for the rest of the dreary evening.

By midnight, neither Rav nor Zendin had returned. They had broken their own curfew, and would smart for it, should Ravnar find out. Sleepy and unaccustomed to late hours, Tradain abandoned his vigil. There was much that he wanted to tell and ask, but it would have to wait until morning. Now, without troubling to summon a servant, he undressed, extinguished the lamps, and climbed into bed. For a little while, the turmoil of his thoughts kept him wakeful, but soon natural fatigue triumphed, and he sank into a slumber undisturbed by dreams or dire visions.

No premonition of disaster came to warn him. He was deeply asleep when the door of his chamber crashed open. The noise woke him, and he sat up in bed. An instant later the bed curtains were wrenched apart, and the sudden glare of lantern light forced him to turn his face away, but not before he had glimpsed four broad figures looming over him. Dazzled and confused, he scarcely noted the details of their appearance, but two points registered: all four hid their faces beneath conical hoods, and all four were armed.

Their identical facelessness lent the intruders an air of fantastic unreality. But they were real enough, as he discovered when one of them flung him violently from the bed to the floor. The impact drove the sleepy fog from his mind, but confusion remained, and the fear was already sizzling along his veins.

Thieves?

He jumped to his feet, and his eyes darted left to the door, where two of the hooded figures stood blocking his escape. The window to his right was unguarded, but it was a straight drop of three stories to the ground.

A call to the servants might summon assistance. Even as his lungs expanded, his eye caught the gleam of lamplight on naked steel, and the cry died unuttered.

Flight and fight, equally impractical.

Words?

"There's no money here," said Tradain. His voice came out miraculously firm and steady.

Nobody troubled to answer that. The garments he had worn the previous day still lay on a chair beside the bed. One of the intruders took up the clothes and tossed them to the floor at Tradain's feet. The unspoken command was clear.

"What do you want?" His eyes, voice, and hands were all steady.

No answer. Four blank nonfaces, featureless in the jumping light.

Kidnappers, snatching him clean out of his own father's house. Their boldness was unbelievable, and therefore more than likely to succeed, unless they could be stopped now, before they got him away, beyond the reach of family and friends.

As he struggled into his clothes, pulling them on hurriedly over his nightshirt, Tradain's mind raced. Half a dozen schemes were conceived and rejected within the space of seconds. Then he was dressed, and there was no time left for further thought, no room for anything beyond jumbled alarm and incredulous outrage, as they grabbed his arms and hustled him to the door.

Their booted feet clattered on the parquet floor. They made no effort at stealth or concealment. Even as he marveled at their insolence, he took note for the first time of the identical white cockades adorning each of the kidnappers' hoods, and recognized there the emblem of the White Tribunal.

TWO

Such midnight visitations by the Soldiers of the Light were notorious, and not uncommon. He had known that noble households enjoyed no immunity, and yet, this armed quasi-military presence within the very home of Ravnar liMarchborg was inconceivable.

"There is some mistake," Tradain informed them.

No answer. Out of the bedchamber, along the hall, and down the central stairway they wordlessly hurried him, down to the marble foyer now alive with invaders. Some nameless official, somewhere, had dispatched a round dozen Soldiers of the Light to the liMarchborg residence—a number sufficient to overcome considerable civilian resistance. There was no resistance, however. None of the servants were in evidence; presumably, all had hidden themselves, or fled. The master of the house was present, but under restraint, his wrists shackled. Similarly fettered were the captive Landguardian's two older sons.

Ravnar liMarchborg—in chains. Almost it seemed sacrilegious, and Tradain's indignation flared. Instinctively he started toward his father, only to find himself forcibly halted. For a moment he struggled, then subsided. His eyes sought his father's face, and what he saw there reassured him.

Ravnar wasn't afraid, not in the least. When he spoke, his tone was civil but crisp, as if he addressed craftsmen of questionable competence. "You've a properly sealed warrant for my arrest, I presume?"

No answer from the Soldiers of the Light.

"You are aware, are you not, that the law requires presentation of a warrant prior to your entry upon the property of a private citizen?"

No answer.

"Who is the commanding officer?" Ravnar inquired.

There was an empty pause, then the slight, silent inclination of a hooded head.

"Be so good as to specify the charges that you bring against me." There was no response, and Ravnar added, "It is my entitlement under the law to an immediate, full disclosure of the charges. In the absence of such disclosure, my forcible removal from the premises, together with the restraints you impose upon my person, constitute a violation of my rights—a violation for which you may find yourself held accountable. You will recall that I am a High Landguardian of Upper Hetzia, and you will conduct yourself accordingly. Now I ask you again—what charges are preferred against me?"

Tradain thrilled with pride. Even in chains, his father possessed unassailable courage and dignity. Surely these intruders, these criminal louts afraid to reveal their own faces, must sense the natural authority of a hereditary nobleman.

Perhaps they did, for their commanding officer spoke at last, from behind his mask:

"*Sorcery. Traffic with malevolences. Supernatural abominations of varying degree. Crimes against humanity. Crimes against the state. Crimes against nature. Magical perversions, occult contamination, distortion of normality, and significant disruptions of reality. Thus are you charged.*"

The incredible words dropped like stones. Astounded, Tradain glanced from face to face. His father's remained tranquil. Similarly untroubled appeared his brothers Rav and Zendin. His own young visage was not so perfectly controlled. The angry blood heated his cheeks, and he heard himself blurt, "Those are lies." The soldiers seemed deaf, and he added, "Ridiculous lies." Still they ignored him, as if he were invisible and inaudible, and he raised his voice to declare, "The High Landguardian Ravnar liMarchborg is innocent, and anyone short of an idiot can see it. Father, tell them." Still there was no answer, and he shook himself free of restraining hands, to advance upon his sire. "Father, tell them how stupid they—"

The hands were back again, and the restraint was insupportable. He fought back then, driving a clenched left straight for the center of the nearest conical hood.

The blow was effortlessly deflected, and then his own wrist was caught, immobilized, and the steel bracelet appeared out of nowhere to close upon his astonished flesh. Expertly they bent and turned him, suppressed his amateurish struggles, and secured the second wrist.

He could hardly believe it. Such things did not happen, not in the very home of a nobleman. The fetters did not pain him, but the indignity burned. He found his father's eyes, and for the first time glimpsed perturbation there.

"Release the boy," Ravnar commanded. "He is underage."

The invaders had gone deaf and mute again.

"Your warrant cannot include a legal minor," the prisoner observed. "That is assuming you possess a warrant at all—a small detail that you, in the heat of your righteous zeal, have perhaps overlooked. Does the White Tribunal's wizard hunt now extend to the schoolroom and the nursery?"

No reply. The commander signaled, and the Soldiers of the Light herded their prisoners toward the door. Tradain marched mechanically.

A mistake, an incredible blunder. But Ravnar liMarchborg would soon set things right.

Nothing to be afraid of.

"Wait. Stop." The thin, almost gasping voice from above turned every head.

Tradain looked back to behold his stepmother, in her shift, poised halfway down the stairs. Aestine, ashen and unsteady, clung to the banister, whose support seemed all that kept her upright. Her face was stiff with horror, and the glazed fixity of her white-rimmed stare recalled the taxidermist's art. For once, he genuinely pitied her.

"Stop. Let him go, you must, this is wrong—" Aestine's faint voice trailed off into air-gulping nothingness. Just as well. She looked as if she would have screamed if she could.

"Do not concern yourself, madam," Ravnar advised. "The charges against me are absurd, the arrest is improper, the legalities have not been

observed—Tradain's detention, in particular, is outrageous—and I anticipate immediate release. You may notify or consult whom you please, but I
hardly think it necessary. I expect to return home, with my sons, by early
morning, if not before. Take heart, there is nothing to fear."

At that moment, Tradain fully believed him. Impossible to know,
however, if Lady Aestine did likewise. She swallowed hard, and nodded
once. Her face, even in the warm-colored lamplight, was grey.

Then he turned away and saw her no more, for the Soldiers of the
Light were leading their prisoners from the house, out into the chilly damp-
ness of the autumn night. As always, at such an hour, heavy fog veiled and
disguised all the world. The light of lamp and lantern skimmed the contours
of opaque clouds without achieving penetration. The marble townhouse of
Ravnar liMarchborg, white as some ghost palace, seemed to float weight-
lessly amidst the pale mists. Already the house appeared unreachably distant, almost unreal.

They hurried the few yards down the short walkway to the street,
where a conveyance awaited; something akin to a graceless cross between a
carriage and a wagon, with a tall, strongly constructed wooden box mounted
on four wheels, a perch for the driver at the front, and a pair of draft horses
to draw it. Into this box the four prisoners were efficiently loaded. The door
closed behind them, and an iron bolt scraped home. The Soldiers of the
Light deployed themselves, the driver's whip cracked, and the vehicle rattled
off into the fog.

It was astonishingly dark inside the box. The air was heavy and close.
If ventilation holes existed, they were invisible and inadequate. But then the
danger of suffocation was slight, as their destination lay not far distant.

*The Heart of Light. Has to be. Torture chambers in the cellar, they
say*—

But he would never see that cellar, nor would anyone else of his
family name, for Ravnar liMarchborg's eloquence, civilized rationality, and
patent integrity were certain to prevail. . . . *return home, with my sons, by
early morning* . . . he had said, and Ravnar never broke his word.

Nothing to worry about, really. Even an exciting experience, of sorts,
or would seem so in hindsight, when it was over. He would have remarkable
stories to tell his friends, when next he saw them. Tomorrow, perhaps.

In the meantime, he sat wedged into a corner at the rear of the
moving box. Devoid of springs, the thing clattered and jounced horren-
dously over the cobbles. Only the pressure of his feet braced hard against the
floor kept him in place. There had been ample time for his eyes to adjust,
but the darkness remained absolute. For all practical purposes he was blind,
but his hearing remained acute. Not that there was anything much to hear,

for nobody spoke a word. He would have welcomed the sound of his father's voice, but Ravnar maintained silence, and surely not without reason. Best to follow that example. To his right, Zendin's quick, distressed breath rasped, and briefly Tradain wondered, for it was clear that his brother failed to share their father's optimism; that Zendin was, in fact, terrified. But Ravnar's middle son was of an excitable disposition, and his present agitation need not be taken as a sign of—anything in particular.

In the dark, however, suppressed panic was contagious. His own nerve would fail if he listened much longer to his brother's gasping breath, and so he focused elsewhere, straining hard to catch a sound or scent that might tell him where he was. But the groaning rattle of the wagon, the clop of the horses' hoofs on stone, and the tramp of booted soldierly feet flanking the vehicle effectively excluded the world.

The trip seemed endless. He had no idea how long he sat there in that black void, drawing increasingly deep draughts of decreasingly breathable air. Darkness annihilated all sense of time and direction. Presently, an alteration in the quality of the vehicle's motion, together with a diminution of creaking wooden complaint, suggested unwontedly level pavement beneath the wheels, and he judged they were crossing Immemorial Bridge, which spanned the waters of the River Folaze between Lisse Island and the western bank.

The rattle resumed. They were over the bridge. An indeterminate interval of jolting progression ensued, and then the wagon halted with a shudder. The metallic screech of the bolt repeated itself, the door swung wide, and military figures stood framed in the misty opening. The four prisoners emerged into a small granite courtyard soft with fog and diffuse lantern light.

Tradain blinked. Before him loomed the Heart of Light, its famous or infamous pitchfork-towered summit lost in cloud and darkness. He had never thought to observe the stronghold of the White Tribunal at such close range. Viewed objectively, the old courthouse-gaol was a rather handsome, distinctly impressive edifice, with its walls of red sandstone, its somber leaden roofing, and its deeply recessed, arched windows. Tradain, however, perceived nothing beyond gloom and menace. But there was little time to look, for the Soldiers of the Light were there, tall forms blocking his sight, as they shepherded their charges toward a featureless little door sunk like a secret wound in the nearest wall.

He slanted a sidelong glance. His father radiated tranquil confidence. *Nothing to worry about.* Zendin's face was achingly rigid. Senior brother Rav was composed, scholarly white countenance serene. Rav might be a bookworm and an eccentric, but he didn't lack courage.

Through that anonymous door they marched, into a grim little vestibule with bare stone walls, bare stone floor, and no furnishings other than a plain oaken table and chair, the latter occupied by a bored official clad in a uniform bearing the blanched insignia of the White Tribunal. The captain of the squad conferred inaudibly with the official, who marked an entry in his ledger. Their colloquy was interrupted by the courteous but very clear voice of Ravnar liMarchborg:

"For the second time tonight, I ask to examine the warrant authorizing my arrest, and the arrest of my sons, one of whom is a minor. Assuming such a warrant exists, I invoke my right as a High Landguardian to confront the owner of the validating signature. I wish to meet with him immediately, in the presence of witnesses, and in the company of the legal counsel to which I am entitled."

The seated official, his ennui undented, gestured minutely, and then the unthinkable occurred. Soldiers of the Light led Ravnar liMarchborg and his two older sons off in one direction, while a couple of them dragged the youngest, underage son off in another.

Tradain curbed the impulse to fight. Likewise he suppressed verbal protest. His father would hardly respect such a childish display. Thus, he walked straight-spined between his captors, as if willingly. Only one backward glance did he permit himself, and caught a last glimpse of Ravnar, Zendin, and Rav, dignity intact, disappearing through an archway. Then they were gone, and he himself was hurrying from the room, swept resistlessly along a gloomy corridor, around a corner, then up a spiral stairway, and up, and up—

He guessed they were ascending the great central tower, climbing toward the triple-forked summit. But they stopped far short of the top, upon a circular landing, with anemic lighting and five identical doors. Opening one of the doors, his captors deftly freed the prisoner of his manacles before thrusting him through into the black space beyond. The door slammed behind him, the bar dropped into place, and the darkness crashed down on him.

Tradain stood encased in black ice. There was a curious roaring in his ears, which took a moment to identify as the rush of his blood. Other than that, he heard nothing. His nerve endings told him that he was alone in this place, but he needed confirmation.

"Is anyone here?" He didn't know how long he had stood motionless before attempting utterance, and then it was extraordinarily difficult to speak. The words emerged a feeble, high-pitched, childish squeak. He waited a moment, then repeated the query in recently acquired, deeper tones.

No answer, which was no surprise. He was indeed alone in the dark. Stretching his arms, he groped the void.

Nothing. No sight, no sound, no information of any kind.

Wrong.

His skin told him that the air moved. His nose and lungs told him that it was fresh. The chilly currents directed his sightless senses, his vision altered, and presently he discerned a small, square opening before him, a little above his head. He stumbled toward it, reached up, and his hands closed on iron bars. The chill upon his flesh deepened as he hauled himself up and gazed out the unglazed window, straining his eyes to penetrate the fog.

He could see nothing beyond the mists, lightened to pearlized orange here and there by the glow of scattered lanterns. He could not judge which section of the city his window overlooked, and it didn't matter. His eyes stung. He was on the verge of weeping, and that was unacceptable. His father and his two brothers would not be weeping.

Torture chambers in the cellar—

It wasn't easy, but he managed to swallow the tears. The image of his father's calm face helped. He was a liMarchborg, after all. Turning from the window, he spread his arms wide, to press stone with his fingertips, left and right. He let his arms drop, and walked forward, placing his feet with care. Half a dozen paces across the straw-littered floor brought him to the door, closely flanked by converging walls. They had locked him up in a wedge-shaped compartment not much larger than a coffin. The sense of constriction was inordinate. He imagined himself caught in a vise.

The next sensation he recognized was that of pain in his right hand. He realized that he was beating his clenched fist against the locked door. Useless. He ceased, and the ache subsided.

Nothing to see or hear, nothing to do.

Sleep.

Unconsciousness. For the first time in his young life, Tradain appreciated the lure of deep oblivion. He would close his eyes, and when he opened them again, his father and brothers would be there to take him home.

. . . home, with my sons, by early morning, if not before.

Soon, very soon. Sleep until then.

He lay down on the straw. The thin, scratchy layer beneath him could not exclude the chill of the stone floor. Moreover, the straw was damp. Verminous, too, as he shortly discovered. The dank wisps were alive with hopping, stinging creatures. In vain he thrashed and slapped. They were everywhere.

But the tiny, invisible assault served to divert his mind from infinitely greater horrors, for a little while. Presently, however, some dim, unacknowledged corner of his brain assumed automatic control of the physical defense, and his liberated awareness flew back like a homing pigeon to the images of recent outrage. Armed ruffians within the liMarchborg home. Their hands, upon the residents. Iron fetters. The words, impossible words . . . *Sorcery* . . . *supernatural abominations* . . . *crimes against humanity* . . . *magical perversions* . . .

Unbelievable. Lunatic as a nightmare—but just as evanescent, no doubt.

No doubt.

His brain buzzed. He would never find sleep in this place, he was certain.

But consciousness must have lapsed at last, for the next thing he knew, the grey dawn light was poking in through the little window to reveal a tiny stone closet of a cell, devoid of furnishings other than a bucket in the corner.

. . . *home, with my sons, by early morning* . . .

His skin itched ferociously. The insects had made a banquet of him. A rinse with cold water might have helped, but there was no water.

Did his father and brothers fare similarly, in some other cell, somewhere? Had the three of them remained together? He hoped so; he hoped none of them were alone.

Tradain looked around him. Nothing to see. Stepping to the window, he grasped the bars, lifted himself, and peered down through the matinal mists at a very large, very white courtyard, square and spotless at the base of the tower. Abutting the tower wall, a raised platform of white stone decorated with geometric designs in black formed a sort of a stage. Atop the stage stood a vast cauldron of black iron, large as a merchant's booth, supported and raised above the stone flooring by three legs as thick as saplings. He recognized the courtyard at once, although he had never before seen it—for this was the famous Radiance Square, usually closed to the ordinary citizenry, but open to all upon the fairly frequent occasion of public Disinfection. The courtyard, nearly deserted at the moment, looked harmless enough. Except, perhaps, for that gigantic cauldron.

Averting his eyes from the vessel of infamy, he gazed out over the city, just now stirring to life beneath its opulent blanket of fog. Here and there, smudged lights beamed weakly through the mists. The small, erratic luminosities flitting through the streets betrayed the presence of linkboys. The gliding glows upon the River Folaze suggested the progress of boats and barges, their existence otherwise undetectable. The tenements and warehouses edging the water were visible in hazy outline; those on the far bank faded out of existence. The distant clang of a bell sliced the fog, and the echo of human voices carried faintly upon the chilly, semi-opaque air.

All of it looked entirely normal. There about and below him spread the city of Lis Folaze, wakening to the morning, the citizens going about their mundane business, their ordinary little routines, and all without the slightest inkling that anything was wrong—

Smug fools.

He hated them all, for their ignorance, their comfort, their unthinking safety—hated them for their good lives, and their good luck.

They didn't know what was happening almost under their noses, inside the Heart of Light. Didn't recognize the outrage, didn't comprehend the danger, or else, incredibly, didn't care—so long as it didn't affect them, personally and immediately.

Sheep.

His hands, clenched on sharp-edged iron bars, were cold and sore. Nothing to see down there, anyway. Allowing his grip to slacken, he let himself slide back down to the straw-strewn floor.

The minutes crept. He tried not to let himself think of his father, or his brothers, but their faces refused to vanish, and their voices echoed in his head. There was nothing he could do for them, and nothing to rid himself of the sense that he should do something.

They were probably thinking exactly the same about him.

Fix your mind on something else.

Something demanding concentration. Chorkan Variations, perhaps. But the thought of Chorkan Variations put him in mind of little Glennian liTarngrav, who had mentioned them—only yesterday, had it been? Glennian, whose family, fearful of the White Tribunal, hovered upon the verge of flight. He wondered if they'd actually gone. Were the liTarngravs safely clear of Lis Folaze, or did Jex liTarngrav, like his close friend Ravnar liMarchborg, presently languish somewhere nearby, within the Heart of Light?

He didn't want to think about it.

Chorkan Variations. He focused his thoughts, and for a time, the questions and fears receded.

His mental self-discipline was far from perfect. Concentration flagged periodically, and broke altogether around midmorning, when a scrape and a clank at his cell door announced human presence.

Father?

Rising to his feet, he turned to face the sound. A small panel at the bottom of the door opened. A tray laden with a pitcher, a bowl, and a small loaf of dark bread slid into the cell. A human hand, dirty under the finger-nails, was briefly visible. The hand withdrew, and the panel closed.

An instant later Tradain was on his knees beside the door, pounding the panel and calling to the invisible turnkey.

No response. The turnkey was deaf, or indifferent, or both. Ceasing his useless outcry, he turned his attention to the tray. There was water in the pitcher, thin grey gruel in the bowl, and the loaf was elderly, but of a respectable size. The prisoners in the Heart of Light might harbor a variety of legitimate fears, but it seemed that starvation did not number among them.

Nothing in the world could quell thirteen-year-old voracity. He emp-tied the bowl within seconds, gulped a few mouthfuls of water, and tore into the loaf, devouring all save a couple of crusts. These last, he supposed, would easily tide him over, should he hunger again before lunch.

Probably he would be free, and home again, before then. Release inexplicably lagged, but couldn't for much longer. In the meantime—what? More Chorkan Variations?

He couldn't fix his mind on them. The sequences jigged crazily through his head. Try as he would to exclude them, the doubts and fears kept working their way back into his thoughts. The wretched minutes ex-pired one by one.

Where is he?

Detained, evidently. But not for much longer.

The Chorkan Variations were no good. Mentally shrugging away from them, he rose to pace the tiny confines of his cell. Back and forth, no more than a few meager steps in any direction, stone walls closing in on all sides. He stepped to the window, pulled himself up, and peered out through the bars.

The mists had thinned a little. He could now distinguish the small crafts plying the silver Folaze, the buildings on the far bank, the curve of the dome topping the Dhreve's palace, and the thrusting spire of the Long-shanks, tallest clock tower in the city. He could also see the citizens hurry-ing along the streets, and some of them were not so very far away. Had he shouted, he would certainly have been heard.

He let himself drop away from the window. Already hungry again, he wolfed his remaining crusts of bread, then sat, back pressed to the damp wall, and composed himself to wait.

The hours limped.

By the time the ringing voice of the Longshanks announced the hour of two, his stomach was growling again. It occurred to him, for the first time, that the morning's rations were intended to last until dinnertime.

But he would be free of this place and back at home long before dinnertime.

He occupied himself as best he could with mental and physical exercise, with memory games and calisthenics, and even, in desperation, with plaiting and knotting of dirty straw, and with strenuous efforts to duplicate Glennian liTarngrav's trick of making music out of nothing. But there was no music in him.

The sounds of the city reached him through the window, and yet it seemed extraordinarily quiet, for he was unaccustomed to solitude. Always, there had been people around him—family, friends, servants. Conversation, light or serious, jovial or acrimonious, but always human voices. And now—

The air outside was darkening, his insides were twisting, and the unacknowledged terrors were pressing heavily upon his mental defenses by the time the door finally opened. The turnkey—a burly lout, afflicted with scabies—hulked upon the threshold.

"Traynbuk't," the turnkey barked, his accents imperative.

Tradain stared uncomprehendingly.

"*Traynbuk't.*" There was no response, and the turnkey repeated with exaggerated clarity, for the benefit of a deaf or simple-minded prisoner, "Tray. And. Bucket. Give me your TRAY and your BUCKET, right NOW, or see what you GET. You understand simple HETZIAN?"

He understood simple Hetzian. Tradain surrendered the specified articles. Only when the transfer was complete, did he think to demand, "My father, the Landguardian liMarchborg—where is he? What's happened to him? And my two brothers, what have you done with them?"

Too late. The door was already swinging shut. It closed with a bang, and he sat staring, with all that he should have said reverberating through his head. He had missed his chance, and who could say when the turnkey— or anyone else, for that matter—was likely to return? He had no information—and no food, for it seemed that prisoners were fed but once a day— and all because he'd lacked the presence of mind to exploit his best and perhaps his sole opportunity.

Even as he sat mired in self-reproach, the door reopened, and the turnkey reappeared to return the empty bucket, its contents presumably dumped down some chute, descending to some cesspool stinking like a hidden crime at the bottom of the Heart of Light.

Unwilling to repeat his error, Tradain jumped to his feet.

"Tell me what they've done to my father," he commanded.

There was no answer, and his fear-fueled, hunger-honed anger flashed. The turnkey was mechanical in his labors, oblivious to the juvenile prisoner's meaningless noise, and thus off guard. His own head suddenly ablaze with Zendin's never-before-used illicit advice, Tradain drove his clenched fist straight at the turnkey's jaw, and then, when his victim's head snapped backward, chopped the stiffened edge of his right hand into the offered windpipe.

Had he possessed adult strength and skill, such a blow might have killed his opponent. As it was, the turnkey sat suddenly, coccyx jarring on the stone floor, breath creaking along a shocked throat. Leaping the prostrate form, Tradain flew through the door, out of the cell, and onto the landing, and there before him was the stairway spiraling down the tower, down from the realm of nightmare, and back to the real world of family, friends, light, freedom—

Life.

All within reach. No sooner had he set his foot upon the first tread, however, than the turnkey, damnably resilient, was there with him again. A big arm locked around his neck, and then he was paralyzed, all but breathless, drawn backward into the dead space he had thought to escape.

His struggles were ridiculous, and painful. He was no match for the turnkey.

Back into the cell, down hard on the straw, the breath slamming out of him, and then the final crash of the door.

He wanted to kill the turnkey, wanted to kill someone, but he wasn't big enough, old enough, strong enough.

The tears were welling again, and he couldn't stop them.

The light died, and the air chilled. Night had fallen again, and he was still here.

. . . *return home, with my sons, by early morning* . . .

Ravnar had been wrong, for the first time. Ravnar could be wrong.

He was shivering. The autumn evening was uncomfortably cold, but neither fear nor physical discomfort could keep him awake. Despite the misery, hunger, and vermin, or perhaps because of them, he escaped swiftly into sleep.

∾ ∽

The clatter at his door woke him early in the morning. The tray slid into the cell, and the sliding panel closed. No chance to question the turnkey, and what good would it have done, anyway? This time, he approached his dreary rations with restraint, knowing they would have to last the entire day.

But he would be free of this place, before the day was done. So he assured himself.

At dusk, the turnkey reappeared to collect the tray and bucket. Tradain's questions went unacknowledged, perhaps unheard.

The third day witnessed no change; neither did the fourth, nor the fifth, or so it seemed.

Early evening, almost no light left in the coffin of a cell, and he sat listening to the rain battering the Heart of Light. Water slanted in through the window, and the wet breeze chilled him to the bone. His arms were wrapped about his bent knees, his head sunk on his breast.

There was a slight commotion at the door, and Tradain looked up. The turnkey had already collected traynbuk't; there was no reason for him to return before the morning.

Father. Late, very late, but here at last. Heart pounding, he scrambled to his feet.

The door opened, and lamplight filled the tiny chamber. Tradain squinted against the dazzle. He caught a blurred glimpse of three figures— their features momentarily indistinguishable, but he knew on instinct that his father did not stand among them. One of the men stepped into the cell, closing the door behind him. The others remained outside.

Setting his lantern aside with care upon a clear space of floor, the newcomer straightened, then turned deliberately to study the prisoner. Tradain gazed back with equal attention. He beheld a tall, very spare figure, clothed in charcoal woolen garments of sober simplicity. His eyes rose to anchor on the face, which was narrow, morbidly pale, long of jaw, and framed in straight, scanty grey hair. In the low light, the deep-set eyes appeared colorless as rainwater. It was an arresting countenance, starkly beautiful and inhospitable as a glacier. *Beautiful?* He must have meant ugly— certainly it was ugly, with those dark, storm-cloud shadows beneath the eyes, those harsh lines, and sunken cheeks. *Old, worn, used.* And yet, the lips beneath the thin, high-bridged nose were beautifully drawn, and the voice that emerged from between those lips was astonishing; sonorous and solemn as a great bell, yet charged with the lightning force of absolute conviction.

"You are very like your father."

The sound of that voice confirmed his immediate impressions, and Tradain knew whom he faced. Inclining his head, he spoke with courtesy carefully devoid of deference: "Premier Jurist liGurvohl."

He hoped it came out sounding right, untinged with fear or awe. Difficult to speak well, however, with a mouth so dry, for he stood before the master of the White Tribunal, whose mind and will decreed the destiny of the doomed. He couldn't imagine why such a personage as Gnaus liGurvohl had come to call on him.

"I wish to offer you an opportunity," liGurvohl announced, as if in answer to his unspoken question. "Do you desire to serve your city, your family, and yourself?"

"Where is my father?" Tradain demanded. "And my brothers? What's become of them?"

"They are close at hand."

"Unharmed?"

"It is not your place to ask questions."

"When can I see them?"

"You forget yourself."

"Why have we been brought here?"

"You are ill-trained. Further instruction is indicated."

"We've done nothing wrong."

"I am willing to entertain the possibility that you yourself have not." Gnaus liGurvohl's colorless eyes appeared to probe the prisoner's mind. "And I will permit you the chance to convince me of it."

"How shall I convince you?"

"Prove yourself a friend to the White Tribunal, and I am ready, in view of your extreme youth, to judge you free of the sorcerous infection poisoning the House of liMarchborg."

"That's ridiculous. There is no sorcerous infection poisoning our House."

"Understand that I do not tolerate impertinence, and govern your tongue."

"It's no impertinence to deny a falsehood!"

"It is more than impertinence—it is an insult to my intelligence, an insult to the Tribunal itself—to deny an obvious truth. Listen. Your father's guilt has been established beyond question. The High Landguardian Ravnar liMarchborg—together with his older sons, and with the assistance of his friend, the High Landguardian Jex liTarngrav—has engaged in magical abominations, loathsome in the sight of Autonn."

"That is a lie."

"Already, I hold proofs against him more than sufficient to justify recourse to the Grand Interrogation."

"What are these proofs?" Tradain fought hard to maintain his self-command, or at least the appearance thereof. The term "Grand Interrogation," which he recognized all too readily, had set his pulses to racing, but he would do justice to his training. "Has my father had a chance to examine them? Has he confronted his accusers? Has he legal counsel? These are all his rights under the law, aren't they?"

"Ah." LiGurvohl's lips bent in a smile almost kindly. "You are truly the son of Ravnar liMarchborg. I see it more clearly with each passing moment. You have inherited his face, his mind, and his proud, unregenerate character. And yet it may be—and I hope it is so—that you have been spared the worst of his moral deformities."

"He has none."

"He is guilty of monstrous crimes. He and his confederates have trafficked with malevolences, allying themselves with the enemies of Autonn. Do you begin to comprehend the enormity of that betrayal?"

"He—"

"You do not comprehend. You do not recognize the vileness of sorcery, you do not catch the stench in the air around you, the foulness of pervasive decay, the filthy secret heat hidden in a host of putrid hearts. You perceive none of this, and your brute ignorance endangers all our race." The Premier Jurist's lucent gaze turned inward for a moment. "These people must be educated," he murmured.

"I know the history of the Sortilegious Wars." Tradain forced himself to meet the rainwater eyes squarely. "I know about the havoc and destruction, I know about Yurune and the others, and all the misery they caused. I understand why sorcery is the worst crime. I learned all that from my father, and that's how I know he couldn't be involved."

"Your allegiance is misplaced. There remains only to secure the High Landguardian's confession, before he is bound over for trial."

"My father has committed no crime, and he will never confess wrongly."

"Nor should any man. And yet, here within the Heart of Light, the truth cannot cloak itself in darkness." Gnaus liGurvohl's colorless eyes, luminous as the Melt, seemed to glow with their own internal fires. "For our interrogators are gifted with the power to draw the truth from the closest of sealed lips, and the darkest of hardened hearts."

Tradain was silent.

"This process of interrogation," liGurvohl continued, sonorous tones waxing in richness and warmth, "whereby the truth is gradually brought to the light, is frequently prolonged, often taxing, educational, and invariably successful. In the end, your father will reveal all that he conceals—he will do so gladly, and he will hold nothing back."

"What will they do to him?"

"That is as their wisdom and skill shall dictate. You hold it within your own power, however, to spare your father all of this."

"What do you mean?"

"A sworn statement from you, a male of the liMarchborg blood, affirming that you have witnessed Ravnar liMarchborg engage in sorcerous

rites, will suffice to secure conviction. The High Landguardian's own confession may then be dispensed with as redundant."

It took a fraction of a moment for the other's meaning to sink in, and
then Tradain asked slowly, "You are asking me to help you convict my
father of sorcery?"

"Your father's conviction is already assured. The proofs against him,
as I have mentioned, are very strong. Your assistance is not required, but
may serve to spare the High Landguardian considerable inconvenience. In
view of your youth and noble lineage, I grant you the privilege of demonstrating your good faith and good character."

"By swearing to lies?"

"Do not try my patience with insolence. Here in this place, we seek
only the truth. Come, reflect. Stretch your memory. Surely at some point
you have witnessed questionable incidents in your father's house. There
have been sights and sounds—inexplicable odors—disturbing manifestations—which you, in your childish innocence, did not comprehend at the
time. Only recall them now, and the situation will clarify itself. Think. One
such episode is all you need relate, for your father's sake, as well as your
own."

Tradain gazed up into the Premier Jurist's eyes, in search of guile,
but encountered only a blazing sincerity, impossible to doubt.

"There was nothing," he told the fervent colorless eyes, and watched
the Premier Jurist's face change.

"I am too late." Gnaus liGurvohl bowed his head. "This one is already lost. The young serpent is venomous as its sire."

"Premier Jurist liGurvohl, please believe me, my father is innocent,
and so are my brothers. They—"

"Enough. Your voice, fouled with falsehood, offends my ears."

"He has friends to vouch for him. You yourself were once his
friend—"

"Silence. Not another word."

LiGurvohl did not raise his voice, but somehow the prisoner found
himself struck dumb with sudden terror. The Premier Jurist lifted one skele-
tal but oddly elegant hand to strike the door, which opened at once. His two
uniformed subordinates waited in the corridor.

"Bring him," liGurvohl commanded, and stalked from the cell without a backward glance.

They hurried him out onto the landing, then down the spiraling
stairs to the bottom of the tower, along a reeking corridor, and down again,
lower and deeper than he could keep track of, surely many levels underground. At last they came to a worming passageway so airless and dank that

the dirty moisture pooled in the hollows of the ancient stone floor underfoot. At the end of the corridor, a black iron door, and beyond the door—

All that he had feared, and more.

The subterranean place was windowless. A few scattered lanterns cast
their weak reddish light upon the unexpectedly lofty ceiling, stone floor, and
walls of a sizable chamber filled with far more than he wanted to see. He
didn't want to look at the braziers, the irons, the blades and cords, or the
many instruments whose function he did not know, and did not mean to
guess. He did not want to study the various machines and mechanisms,
ingenious though these devices undoubtedly were. He did not want to see,
or hear, or smell the resident beasts in their cages and their tanks. (*True,
then*. Whispered tales of a nightmare zoo at the bottom of the Heart—all
true.) Above all, he did not want to see his father and his brothers, all three
bound, naked, and shockingly vulnerable, but see them he did.

Ravnar liMarchborg occupied a great oaken armchair, to which he
was attached by leather straps at wrists, ankles, and neck. He was unclothed,
but portions of his anatomy were closely wrapped in linen bindings. *Ban-
dages?* The exposed areas of his flesh were blotched with raw sores, the
source of which was not immediately apparent. His head turned to the door
as his youngest son entered the room. His colorless lips moved, but no
sound emerged.

Ravnar's oldest son, Rav, hung suspended by his wrists above a great
glass aquarium, through the murky depths of which glided schools of mud-
colored, palm-sized fish. Laxity would have immersed his body to midthigh
level. But Rav had drawn his legs up out of the water, to hold them poised
several inches above the surface. The bare calves and thighs were streaming
with blood from dozens of lacerations. The flesh along his right ankle was
eaten away clear down to the bone. The frenetic swirl of fish about the
blood in the water explained all. The quivering of Rav's limbs hinted at the
torturous muscular exertion required to maintain elevation.

Middle son Zendin crouched in a wire cage shared by a pair of large
constrictors. The snakes were aggressive and energetic, strong enough to kill
by strangulation, should one or the other succeed in looping about the
prisoner's throat. Self-defense demanded constant vigilance, and Zendin's
face and movements already betrayed exhaustion.

All this Tradain took in at a single glance, and all of it was insupportable. Instinctively he sought his father's eyes, to encounter there a look of
unequivocal horror. *Because he sees me here.* Then his view was obscured as
one of those anonymous fleshly automata belonging to the Heart of Light
stepped forward and bent to tear one of the linen bindings from Ravnar
liMarchborg's chest. The linen came away reluctantly, and with it came a

bloodied band of flesh, evidently softened and loosened by the caustic chemicals impregnating the fabric.

Ravnar's gasp of pain lost itself in the cry of his watching son. Tradain started toward his father, and one of the guards at once arrested his progress. He struggled vainly.

The Premier Jurist Gnaus liGurvohl advanced to the seated victim's side.

"Will you cleanse yourself?" liGurvohl asked, with the air of a physician offering an enema.

Ravnar declined to acknowledge the question. Presumably he had heard it before. One of the automata tore another rag of linen and flesh away, and the prisoner's breath whistled through his teeth.

"May we not put an end to this sorrow? May we not find peace?" liGurvohl inquired, in tones of extraordinary beauty. There was no answer beyond the rasp of stertorous breath, and the Premier Jurist turned to face Tradain. "Come," he encouraged. "A single word from you will end it. Prove your mettle. Help him."

Help him. Tradain shuddered. There could be but one conclusion, after all, or so liGurvohl had carefully explained, but it couldn't be true, it was too monstrously unjust, too evil to be real. Surely he would wake to find himself at home, in his own bed—

He could sign a false denunciation, that amounted to a death warrant; else stand and see his father flayed alive, here and now.

He knew, beyond question, which choice Ravnar would prefer. The High Landguardian liMarchborg would never smirch his honor with a lie, or suffer his son to do so. He would, literally, prefer death by torture.

But then Ravnar lost another broad strip of raw flesh, and could not repress a cry, and the right decision, which had seemed so obvious moments earlier, was no longer clear. Horribly helpless, he stood watching the blood course down his father's body.

"Grant him respite," liGurvohl appealed softly.

An assent struggled to escape him. He turned his face away from his father, and one of the guards moved as if to restrain him, but liGurvohl gestured minutely, and the man let him be.

A low groan intruded upon his mental agonies, and he looked up in time to see oldest brother Rav, strength exhausted, slump limp in his shackles. Rav's legs hit the water with a splash, and the tumult was tremendous as every fish in the aquarium darted for the fresh meat. Through the walls of the glass tank Tradain could see them, hundreds of quick, mud-colored forms, swarming more like insects than fish about his brother's thrashing limbs. Rav's struggles to lift himself clear of the tank were violent but ineffectual. He was screaming, and Tradain was screaming as well, pleading with them to stop, offering anything, if they would only stop.

Gnaus liGurvohl gestured, an assistant cranked a winch, and Rav was drawn up into the air to dangle slackly above the tank, water and blood streaming from his torn legs.

"You do right to spare them further suffering. You are their benefactor." LiGurvohl crooked a finger, and an underling conducted Tradain to a small table upon which lay inkpot, quill, and a sheet of paper closely covered with writing.

"Sign," the Premier Jurist instructed. "Come, let us make an end."

The writing was very clear. Even in the low light, Tradain read without difficulty. As he had expected, the document contained a statement describing the various sorcerous practices he had supposedly witnessed in his father's house. The High Landguardian Ravnar liMarchborg was identified as chief culprit, aided and abetted by a circle of accomplices that included the two older liMarchborg sons, the High Landguardian Jex liTarngrav, and several household servants.

Fantastic tales. Insane, really. Under other circumstances, laughable. Surely he would wake, now.

Tradain studied the incredible document. He was thirteen years old, and fearfully uncertain. His confused eyes flew again to his father's face, and he saw Ravnar, bathed in crimson, but perfectly composed, shake his head.

And oldest brother Rav? Hanging motionless, pathetically skinny and white, seemingly unconscious.

Zendin? One foot planted upon a constrictor's spine. Both fists clenched upon the other serpent's head. Holding his own, for now.

Courage, and speak the truth. He could hear his father's voice in his mind.

Tradain looked up to meet liGurvohl's eyes. Tossing the paper back down on the table, he declared, "These are all lies."

"Facts. Realities. Difficult for the youthful mind to encompass, but undeniable." LiGurvohl's expression communicated somber pity.

"I do deny them." Tradain—wanting to yell, wanting even to weep like a girl—forced himself to speak calmly. He had discovered long ago that composure, hard though it sometimes was to maintain, generally drew the best results, especially with adults. Flicking the paper briefly with his gaze, he declared, "These things in there are made up. They never happened."

"They did happen," liGurvohl informed him. "For the moment, perhaps, you have truly forgotten. The human memory is a sadly flawed instrument."

Astounded, Tradain looked up to encounter total, unwavering conviction. And he knew, to the endings of his nerves, that the Premier Jurist believed utterly in the truth of the accusations.

"Your memory has been smothered by magic, or by vile chemical concoction," liGurvohl continued. "For your own sake, I urge you to fight the destructive influence—fight for clarity, and for truth. Truth, young liMarchborg. It is your only hope to save yourself, it is the only hope that any of us owns. Understand, I am trying to help you. Accept assistance, while yet you may, and profit thereby; for young though you are, it is your final opportunity. Search your memory, your dreams, your visions. Sift through all the recollections, concentrate your will, and—believe me—you will find what you seek. Sooner or later, you will recover the words and images, preserved deep within your mind. Recall the truth—grasp and behold the truth—and then sign the statement with a clear conscience."

Tradain, momentarily speechless, allowed his gaze to travel slowly about the room, passing over unendurable sights, lingering upon harmlessly blank expanses of stone wall, and at last returning to the Premier Jurist's brilliantly expectant eyes. When he found his voice again, he told the eyes, "You wouldn't recognize the truth if you were drowning in it."

Nobody spoke so to the Premier Jurist of the White Tribunal. Tradain braced in anticipation of a thunderbolt, which did not strike. The dreadful silence seemed endless.

"Drowning in truth." When he finally used it, liGurvohl's beautiful voice expressed nothing but grave sorrow. "It can be no accident, and it is scarcely without meaning, that you yourself have chosen that term. I have striven to save you, and I have failed, for you are lost beyond redemption. That being so, another course is indicated for Ravnar liMarchborg's youngest and best-loved son."

LiGurvohl inclined his head almost imperceptibly, and his minions came alive. Tradain was seized and hustled across the room to the foot of a roughly constructed flight of narrow wooden stairs. Up the stairs they pushed and dragged him, handling him like some unwieldy parcel, up to a platform of unpainted boards, shaped to hug the lip of a great glass vessel, cylindrical in shape.

Another aquarium? No, the thing was empty, its function unrevealed by its form.

No time for cogitation as a firm shove sent him over the edge of the platform. He fell an alarming distance, to land unhurt at the bottom of the glass cylinder. Bewildered and shaken, he looked around him. Through the surrounding transparent wall, he could see his father, sitting only a few feet away, staring straight at him, and the look in his eyes—the dreadful look in those eyes all but identical to his own—

The guards and assistants were clustered about Ravnar liMarchborg, and the Premier Jurist was there beside him, overpoweringly intent, lips moving, but the words were inaudible. Ravnar was shaking his head, very emphatically, each directional shift causing the leather strap to dig deep into his neck, an inconvenience of which he seemed unaware.

Insistence from the torturers, resistance from the victim, all of it in pantomime. Strain though he would, Tradain caught nothing beyond an indistinguishable mumble of voices.

He wondered, with a certain sense of sickness, what would happen to him, should his father refuse to yield. Unworthy thought, contemptible concern. He shouldn't care what might happen, he shouldn't care for anything beyond the preservation of perfect liMarchborg integrity. Nevertheless, he wondered what they would do to him.

He didn't have to wonder long.

Freezing droplets rained down on his head. Tradain looked up. A small pipe protruded over the lip of the cylinder, and from that pipe dripped arctic moisture. Even as he watched, the stream of droplets swelled to a steady trickle.

Water, nothing but water. It came from the big cistern poised on the buttressed stone ledge just beneath the vaulted ceiling. Water, quite clean, innocent of carnivorous fish, but intensely cold, beyond doubt chilled with ice or mountain snow. He stepped aside, avoiding all save a few small, random splashes about his ankles. So far, not so bad, but worse things must inevitably follow.

Already, the water was pooling at the bottom of the great vessel. Already, he could feel the profound cold of it soaking through the soles of his shoes. Unlike his father and brothers, he still had shoes, which were growing heavier by the moment.

He looked up again, and now the water was gushing freely from the pipe overhead. The glass floor was covered to a depth of a couple of inches, and the level was rising at an unhurried but steady rate.

Drowning in truth. LiGurvohl's words rang in his mind, their meaning belatedly clear. Drowning. But that was absurd, Tradain reasoned, for he couldn't drown in such a place as this. If the water rose above his head, then he would simply float, remaining buoyant indefinitely. If the vessel continued to fill, the rising water would eventually bear him to the top of the cylinder, where he might catch hold of the edge, and climb to safety; for they hadn't thought to tie his hands. In the meantime, Ravnar liMarchborg's son would endure.

But the water was really ferociously cold. It was halfway up his calves now, and already his feet were numb. Tradain shifted his weight from side to side, jigged and shuffled in place, without restoring sensation. He seemed to stand upon a pair of wooden blocks.

Through the glass he could see his father watching; the terrible look of horror and anguish intensifying by the moment. He couldn't bear to see that look, and he closed his eyes, which only seemed to concentrate the power of the cold that was sucking the sensation from his body.

The water lapped at his knees, and now his lower legs were numb, a condition more alarming than the worst sort of pain. He was shaking, and his teeth chattered. He hoped his father wouldn't take these tremors as signs of cowardice.

Frigidity rising inexorably, and nowhere to escape it, nothing to stand on, curved glass walls offering no handhold for climbing—

But he didn't need a handhold, he realized. The glass cylinder was relatively small in diameter. He could brace his shoulders and upper back against one side, his feet against the other, lift himself clear of the water, then work his way straight up the vertical vitreous shaft. Why had it taken him so long to think of it?

Escaping the water proved easier than he had expected, so much so that he anticipated opposition from the guards. But no. The minions of the White Tribunal were observing his ascent closely, yet nobody moved to restrain him.

He couldn't feel anything in his feet, they were dead, but he retained control of the muscles maintaining pressure against the glass. For some moments he stayed where he was, eyes fixed on the swift stream plummeting from the pipe overhead, and then he looked down to find the icy water lapping at his garments, and he worked his laborious way up another several inches.

Hard work, but he could do it.

Visible through the glass, the eyes watching, indecently interested. Premier Jurist Gnaus liGurvohl's cadaverously beautiful countenance, attentive, impassive. Ravnar liMarchborg's face—but no, he couldn't look there.

Time must have elapsed, for the coldness was slapping his back again. The water had risen. He needed to push himself higher up the tube.

He did so, and found himself drawing near the top of his prison. The stream from above was splashing his face and chest, freezing him to the marrow.

Higher yet, and he noticed a subtle alteration in the reflection of light off the curving walls, but thought little of it until he suddenly lost all purchase on the glass and felt himself slipping. There was only a moment to register the fact that the tube had been oiled and then he fell, hitting the water on his back. The shock of the cold momentarily paralyzed him, and he sank almost without a struggle through water deeper than he was tall, until his feet found the bottom, his wits returned, and he pushed himself vigorously to the surface.

His head emerged, and he could breathe again. He gulped air, and automatically began to tread water, an exercise he was ordinarily capable of continuing almost indefinitely.

Not today, however. Today, his limbs were leaden, stiff, and clumsy with cold. But he could fight the cold or, better yet, escape it. He could lift himself out of the water. He had done so once, he could do it again.

But the freezing little cataract poured from the cistern overhead, the water rose inexorably, and now the only section of curving wall that he could reach was heavily oiled, impossible to brace against. Three times he tried and failed, then ceased, for the effort was useless and exhausting.

No matter. He could still tread water.

For a time he did so, pumping his arms and legs grimly, trying not to watch his own observers, who stood waiting to see him give up and give in, waiting to see him sink—

He wouldn't. He could tread water forever, if he had to.

But his arms and legs weren't working right, they were no longer his to command. The mental directives went disregarded, his kicking insensibly slowed, and he went under, inhaling water as he sank.

He beat his way back to the surface. Choking and frantic, he forced his numb limbs into action.

Just another three or four minutes.

That was all he needed, and then the rising water would bear him to the top, where he could reach the lip of the cylinder. He was almost there.

Tradain looked up. Even as he watched, the icy flow from the cistern dwindled and ceased. The lip of the cylinder was far beyond reach.

He was going to drown. It was happening even now, he realized, as he went down a second time. He managed to hold his breath, but he couldn't hold it for long. He needed to fight his way back to the air before his burning lungs burst, but his body seemed already dead, rigid and lead-weighted, with no more fight left in it. Then somehow his head was above the surface again, only for an instant, and he didn't even realize that he used that instant to call for his father's help.

He could no longer see, hear, or feel much. There was only a peculiar sense of something unfamiliar happening to him, something mercifully unaccompanied by pain or terror, but nevertheless untoward. He didn't want to know what it was. He didn't want to know anything, and presently he did not.

Three

Cold. He was unbearably cold, and sick, and therefore still alive. He lay prone upon a hard, flat surface, and there was water all around and beneath him, a sizable puddle, but he was no longer submerged. There was a sense of intense pressure upon his back— something or someone was all but crushing his rib cage—and then a jet of water burst from his mouth. He coughed the last of it out, and instinctively gasped the air down into his starving lungs.

For a moment he didn't know where he was, or what had happened. The embers of horror and desperation glowed yet through the clouds blanketing his mind, but he didn't want to see them. For now, he wanted only to lie still, devoid of thought.

But the respite was already over.

Someone had him by one arm and by his hair; someone was forcibly dragging him to his feet—

No good. He couldn't stand upright. He caught a confused glimpse of faces, and other things—too fast for the images to register—then the room and everything in it blurred and spun. His legs buckled, and he would have gone down again, had not anonymous hands caught him.

He was slung over somebody's wide shoulder. For a moment he regarded the stone floor, and then there was movement, a jerk and a jolt so sickening that his cold face flamed, his stomach roiled, and a thin stream of warm water spewed from his mouth and nose. He heard his porter curse, then something struck him a tremendous blow, and awareness once again obligingly fled.

Not for very long, however.

He was back in his cell, again. Same cell—he recognized the wedge shape, the distinct depressions in the straw created by his habitation, and, above all, the view from the window, as he confirmed within moments of his awakening. He was weak, dripping wet, cold, and miserable, but essentially whole.

Could the same be said of his father and brothers?

The red wounds marking Ravnar's body. The white bone showing along Rav's leg. The constrictors, angling for Zendin's neck.

Cold, so intolerably cold. He was shaking, and his teeth chattered. He tried to burrow down into the straw, but there was scarcely enough to cover him.

Outside, dawn was starting to paint the mists. The turnkey would shortly arrive with his tray of provisions, and there had to be some way of milking facts from that source.

Roseate light kissed a frisky verminous throng. Tradain, inured to insect enthusiasm, sat waiting.

The light waxed, the panel in the door slid aside, and the familiar tray slid into the cell.

He went at once to the opening. Ignoring the gruel and the petrified loaf, he knelt and spoke into the fleetingly visible scrap of shadowy landing: "Tell me what's happening."

No reply. The panel slid shut, the footsteps outside retreated, and silence fell. The vermin cavorted. Surrendering to impulse, Tradain flung his bowl of gruel against the wall. The bowl shattered, and slow grey rivulets descended the grey stones. The destruction afforded a minor, fleeting satisfaction, for which he would pay with hunger.

He wasn't hungry, anyway.

The hours crept. In the midafternoon, movement in the courtyard below drew his attention, and he went to the window to look down into Radiance Square, where a bucket brigade was filling the vast iron cauldron that stood at the center of the black and white stone stage. A line of workmen stretched from the ladder propped against the flaring lip of the cauldron, along the stage, down to the ground, and around one corner of the Heart of Light, presumably to terminate at the nearest pump. The workmen toiled with a will, and the buckets all but flew from hand to hand, but the task was considerable, and would take hours to complete.

While the cauldron filled, a second group of laborers piled wood and coal beneath the great vessel.

Such activity unmistakably signaled the imminence of a public Disinfection.

Tradain allowed himself to drop away from the window. He was light-headed again, perhaps feverish, and unable to stand upright. In any event, he did not wish to view the preparations, and certainly did not want to contemplate their significance. He would start howling like a lunatic if he let himself think about it.

Ravnar liMarchborg was a High Landguardian of Upper Hetzia, possessed of wealth, friends, and influence. He was entirely innocent of wrongdoing. If justice existed in the world, Ravnar would be exonerated and freed.

. . . *expect to return home, with my sons, by early morning, if not before.*

By late afternoon, the cauldron was filled. At sunset, they lit the fuel, and the eager orange flames echoed the tones of the western sky. The fire would burn, and the water would heat all through the night, attaining the requisite rolling boil—

. . . *by early morning, if not before.*

The scrape of the bolt caught his notice. The door opened and the turnkey appeared to demand traynbuk't. In silence, Tradain obeyed, curbing the impulse to toss the contents of the bucket straight into the other's face. Interrogation, he had learned, was useless. No point in attempting it.

Thus he was taken by surprise when, for once, the turnkey spoke first, to observe with a congratulatory air, "Eh, but you will have a good view, from here."

There was no reply, and the turnkey added by way of explanation, "The Disinfection, boy—the ceremony."

Tradain was mute, and the turnkey, piqued by the prisoner's lack of appreciation, added, "You know, there are plenty would pay a bundle for such a good perch as you've got. Believe me, I know." Ungrateful silence, and he continued, "They come at me, jingling coins in my face, begging for a good spot to watch from—*begging*, I tell you, and you wouldn't believe who some of them are, really high up—and I've got to tell them no, sorry, can't do it, really sorry. Then they pump the pot, and I still can't do it for them. My hands are tied, you see. It kills me when I think what I've had to turn down. And here you are, just a pup, with the best view in town, for free. It really says something, doesn't it?

"You're quiet this evening," the turnkey continued. "That's funny, usually you pester me to death with questions. What's the matter, you scared? Don't you know that you're all right? It's true, boy, you're all right. Your dad's confessed and signed, and that means you're fine, because old Boil-the-Blood liGurvohl never breaks his word. If he promised your dad that you'd live, then depend on it—you will. So buck up, you're lucky. Daddy liMarchborg wouldn't bend to save either of your two older brothers, but he caved in for you. Has a soft spot, eh?"

"Confessed and signed?" Tradain asked.

"Sure as nightfall."

"No. He wouldn't."

"Would and did, thanks to you, boy. But for you, he might never have broken. He did though, and the trial's already over, so relax and get a good night's sleep. For you, everything is fine."

Fine.

In his mind, he drove a fist into the smirking mouth, and felt teeth yield under the impact. In reality, the turnkey retired, the door closed, and he was alone again.

He wondered if holding his breath might induce unconsciousness. He had gathered, from some source or other, that this avenue opened to the truly determined.

Darkness swallowed the world. Down below in Radiance Square, the flames licked at the iron cauldron, and the water heated.

❧ ❧

He must have slept, for dawn was breaking, and the muted light of morning slanted in through the bars to diffuse through the fog filling his cell. His clothes remained damp, and he was chilled to the core. Sick and dizzy, too, as he discovered when he dragged himself to his feet. Tradain stepped to the window. Still early. Down below, Radiance Square was empty save for a couple of lounging Soldiers of the Light, just finishing their nightly shift. The fire blazed beneath the cauldron, and now the water boiled vigorously. A double row of massive chairs had been set out upon the raised wooden platform presently occupying one end of the stage.

Even yet, it seemed unreal.

The mists thinned, the light waxed, and fresh Soldiers of the Light came to relieve their comrades. The skies paled to a uniform, featureless grey, and the citizens began to enter Radiance Square. At first there were only a few of them, the truest devotees, isolated figures muffled in woolens against the raw morning air, arriving early to secure the best positions at the foot of the cauldron. Others followed at a more leisurely pace, and presently the area about the stage was crowded with attentive humanity. Still they came, to fill the white square with color—for even the most modestly prosperous of citizens were wont to garb themselves in bright hues, visible through all but the heaviest mists.

Time passed, and the pallid pavement disappeared from view, but the bleachers flanking the stage remained almost unoccupied, for space there was reserved for the noblest of titled spectators; for High Landguardians, Landsmen, and their ilk, and even, upon occasion, for royalty. The Dhreve himself graced particularly noteworthy Disinfections with his presence—though never willingly, it was said.

And now they were arriving, those noble and those titled, those gorgeous figures in their polychrome splendor of fabric and embroidery, of plumes, lace, glittering garniture, and scintillant gemstone, attended by their almost equally vivid servants and retainers. The bleachers were filling, but the central section, redundantly shaded against a nonexistent sun by a cloth-of-silver awning, was still empty.

He could only hope it would remain so.

Surely the Dhreve would not lend his tacit implied approval to—?

No.

There was music nearby, the earnest idiot blare of a brass band, scraping his nerves.

Is this supposed to be some sort of a festival? Public entertainment?

Impotent rage quickened his blood, restoring sensation to numb extremities. His grip on the bars tightened as the music changed, and the band struck up the Hetzian national anthem to mark the arrival of the Dhreve Lissildt. All present rose briefly as the Dhreve, in the midst of his attendants, took his seat beneath the silver awning.

The anthem concluded, and the band fell mercifully silent. An expectant hush enveloped Radiance Square, and during that brief lull, Tradain studied the face of Upper Hetzia's titular ruler. Lissildt was young, no more than nineteen or twenty, his youth accentuated by a short, slight frame, very fair complexion, and regular, almost delicate features. A melancholy demeanor bespoke resignation, well in keeping with his known dislike of the ceremony that political exigency obliged him to witness. It was the hope of the zealous that increasing maturity might gradually cure young

Lissildt of his squeamishness. In the meantime, reluctant or no, the Dhreve did his duty, and wisely so; for his absence upon so significant an occasion might have suggested an unspoken criticism of the White Tribunal—a body not to be publicly slighted with impunity, by anyone, ever.

Tradain's eyes left the Dhreve to travel the crowd, whose component faces reflected a certain focused intensity. He saw widespread curiosity, trepidation, and, in some cases, pleasurable anticipation. But nowhere, not even among the standing commoners, did he witness merriment, drunkenness, pugnacity, or obvious unseemliness of any sort. For the Disinfection was an occasion of gravest moment; a ritual moral cleansing, a demonstration of patriotic solidarity, an expression of gratitude to the ineffable Autonn—mankind's lone protector, bulwark against a host of malevolences. In short, the Disinfection warranted respect amounting to reverence, any omission of which was apt to draw the close attention of the White Tribunal, whose Soldiers of the Light stood ranged conspicuously before the stage.

Thus popular avidity was judiciously restrained, but quite perceptible.

A door at the center of the wall backing the stage opened, and a file of men issued from the Heart of Light. All of them were robed—two in the ocher and black of city magistrates, the rest in the sweeping snowy vestments of the White Tribunal. Tradain's glance rested the longest upon the tallest, central figure among them—that of Gnaus liGurvohl. The Premier Jurist, imposingly glacial in his robes of office, appeared all but impervious to external stimuli. His nonexpression was serenely remote as he advanced to the largest and highest thronelike chair among those grouped at the side of the stage. His companion judges were almost equally composed, although less icily awesome.

The magistrates seated themselves. The door opened again, and a small procession emerged. At its fore walked the Governor of the prison, spruce in his quasi-military uniform, plumed hat bearing the white cockade. Behind him came Soldiers of the Light, herding a gaggle of wretched scarecrow prisoners, who tottered, and faltered, and squinted against the dull morning light. One of the prisoners, unwilling or unable to walk, was half supported, half dragged by a brace of his captors.

Rav.

Rav, a cripple, his ruined legs wrapped in filthy bloodstained rags, but his bruised white visage tranquil and apparently untroubled as always. And there was Zendin, jaw set, defiant eyes ablaze. Behind Zendin tottered a quartet of visibly terrified liMarchborg household servants, and then there were five others Tradain had never seen before, menials clad in the remnants of the liTarngrav livery, their faces swollen and black with bruises, their hands—

Crushed. Shapeless chunks of raw meat.

There was no sign of his father.

Even now, Ravnar liMarchborg's execution seemed an impossibility. Surely, someone would intervene. Tradain's eyes flew to the Dhreve Lissildt, who sat motionless, voiceless, powerless—

Useless.

The Governor stepped forward to read off the names of the prisoners, the long list of their gaudy crimes, the record of conviction and condemnation, and finally the collective order of that Disinfection designed to rid the world of sorcerous poison. To all of this, the assembled citizens listened devoutly. There was no particle of impatience visible upon any face in the crowd, but only an unobtrusive shifting of weight and shuffling of feet, to mark the eager restlessness of those who had heard such lists and orders time and time again.

The Governor concluded. The prisoners were conveyed up the makeshift stairs to the rough wooden platform overhanging the volcanic cauldron. From that height, in swift succession, they were flung down into the boiling water. Tremendous splash followed splash.

The victims were unfettered; by no means was it deemed desirable to hamper the desperate freedom of their movements. Nor was solitary death an element of the grand design, for the executioners cultivated an efficiency capable of plunging the last of the condemned into the boiling bath before the first to hit the water had died. Ideally, there existed some brief span wherein all the living, conscious victims shared the pot. Then, the frenetic interaction among the dying—the grappling, flailing, clinging, and, above all, the ludicrous efforts to escape the heat by climbing atop one another's bodies—these ridiculous displays were widely believed to enhance the edifying nature of the spectacle.

Likewise noteworthy—the conflict raging about the edge of the cauldron, where Soldiers of the Light, armed with long poles, stood poised upon the scaffolding, ready to thwart the efforts of the condemned to drag themselves from the water. In most cases, the pain-crazed victims found no handhold upon the smoothly curving iron, and for them, the single firm thrust of a pole sufficed. Sometimes, however, a particularly hot spot in the metal wall served almost as a grill, to which the naked flesh of an outstretched hand would instantly adhere. Then there were flamboyantly frenzied, skin-tearing efforts to disengage; sometimes pointlessly successful, sometimes not, but always wonderful to behold.

Not everyone in the audience enjoyed an unobstructed view. Those positioned at the very foot of the cauldron sacrificed some spectacle for the sake of exciting immediacy. Others, farther off, often witnessed more, with the best of visual, aural, and olfactory experiences naturally belonging to those exalted personages occupying the bleachers.

But Tradain's view from the tower cell was better yet, surpassing even the Dhreve's. From his vantage point, he could see the entire stage and everything on it: soldiers, Governor, jurists, scaffolding and cauldron, violently boiling water, and violently struggling victims.

They didn't struggle for long, however.

Rav liMarchborg died almost at once. Already much weakened, he succumbed swiftly, losing consciousness within seconds of his immersion. Zendin, hitherto nearly undamaged, fought with a vigor that might actually have won him escape, but for the opposition of the soldiers. Half a dozen thrusts of assorted poles were required to foil Zendin's remarkably persistent efforts to climb out. At last, a well-placed blow thwacked the boy's temple, and thereafter, all resistance ceased. For a while the assorted servants shrieked and thrashed energetically enough to satisfy the most demanding connoisseurs of agony, and then their cries faded, and their bodies went limp. Presently, eleven flaccid forms tumbled in silence through the churning water.

Tradain's hands were locked on the iron bars. He couldn't release his grip, which was curious, because there was nothing more to see. It was finished, entirely finished—

Why, then, were four Soldiers of the Light straining to lift the great, rectangular flagstone at the center of the stage? Why did the area uncovered by the displaced stone gleam black and smooth as polished nothingness? Why was the audience so intent and unmoving, and why was the Premier Jurist Gnaus liGurvohl rising from his throne to stand unfathomably fearsome as the tribunal whose embodiment he was?

"Citizens of Lis Folaze." LiGurvohl's magnificent tones filled all of Radiance Square, effortlessly rising to the tower cell window. "You have witnessed the justice of mankind visited upon those who chose to serve our enemies. You have participated in the great communal cleansing, and you are elevated thereby. Eleven sorcerously contaminated criminals have been destroyed, their moral blight boiled away, and the world benefits by that purification. Yet the task remains unfinished. The injuries inflicted upon our great Defender have scarcely been purged of infection. Deep within the wounds of Autonn, the deadliest of poison lingers. We are here today to right that grievous wrong. We are here today to heal our Benefactor, thus confirming our worthiness in His eyes. His enemies are our enemies, and

today those furtive magicians, those secret servants of malevolence and darkness, are brought at last unto the light that reveals all things. In the splendor
of that huge radiance, the evil that festers in shadow is exposed and consumed, and Autonn is once again made whole."

LiGurvohl fell silent, and for a moment stillness encompassed Radiance Square. Then, despite the military presence, a hum of excited conversation arose, for the Enlightenment announced by the Premier Jurist was
reserved for the very cream of criminals—those convicted of grand sor-
ceries—and thus, infrequently witnessed.

The door opened again, and half a dozen Soldiers of the Light led
forth the last and greatest of the prisoners—the High Landguardians Ravnar
liMarchborg and Jex liTarngrav, convicted sorcerer and accomplice. Both
men were heavily shackled. Both, though clearly suffering the effects of
torture, were able to walk unaided. Both affected identical expressions of
untroubled indifference.

The soldiers brought them to the rectangular void glinting at the
center of the stage, and there left them closely chained to staples sunk in the
stone. The spectators buzzed. The victims appeared serenely unaware.
Ravnar said something to his companion, and both prisoners smiled. A low
muttering, half indignant, half astonished, rumbled through the audience.

Once again, the Governor stepped forward to read off the names and
titles of the condemned, the list of crimes, and at last the unusual sentence
of Enlightenment.

Gnaus liGurvohl, statuelike throughout the Governor's address, now
slowly lifted his arms, thereby riveting collective attention upon himself. His
own gaze anchored upon empty air, several feet above the heads of the
prisoners. He spoke, his rich voice impossibly beautiful, grammar and syntax
incomprehensibly archaic, for the famous Invocation that he uttered was
ancient almost beyond reckoning. The audience froze into breathless immobility, and even the condemned appeared spellbound. As the rhythmic syllables poured from the Premier Jurist's lips, the misty air thickened above the
stage, swirled, slowed, and gradually coalesced.

A foreigner or an ignoramus might have mistaken Gnaus liGurvohl
for a practitioner of those same forbidden arts so fatal to so many victims of
the White Tribunal. The Hetzians of Lis Folaze, however, knew better. The
office of Premier Jurist, clothed in mystic sanctity, conferred unique privilege; for the Premier Jurist alone possessed the authority and the right to
conduct the ceremony of Enlightenment, wherein Autonn's relationship to
the humanity He protected expressed itself in visible form. It was a power
jealously guarded and sparingly employed, always to maximum effect.

LiGurvohl spoke on, and the restless mists above the stage gathered and shaped themselves, accumulating density, substance, and color. The forms waxed in definition, the hues intensified, the clouds contracted, trembled, and luminesced. The atmosphere chilled perceptibly, as an image glowed its way into being.

The multitude beheld a lucent head and shoulders, with arms and upper body fading off into amorphous cloud; the whole faintly transparent, ghostly, yet imbued with the triple dimensionality of solid matter.

The face was human but somehow more than human, apparently belonging to a male of indeterminate years and inexpressible experience; a face of strength, wisdom, and benevolence, but scored with the sorrows of the ages, rigid with pain and untold exhaustion. Face and body were marked with countless wounds, many of them bleeding darkness in slow midnight jets. Spreading pools of empty blackness threatened to engulf the luminous form.

A sighing murmur swept the crowd, and many faces were wet with tears. Several spectators actually sank to their knees, and the unrestrained sobbing of the immoderately fervent was clearly audible. While his fellow jurists bowed their heads in attitudes of extreme, almost cringing humility, Gnaus liGurvohl maintained an upright posture. A note of unwonted warmth transformed his beautiful voice, and the rainwater eyes shone with intense emotion, as he observed, "Autonn, our Benefactor, Your servants greet You. Unto You we tender our gratitude, our perfect obedience, and our eternal devotion."

There was no visible response, no sign that the entity known as Autonn had heard or comprehended the salutation. No man actually knew (although many evinced a monolithic certainty) whether the anthropomorphous form visible throughout the Enlightenment encompassed the reality of Autonn, or merely reflected His image, devoid of true life and understanding. The issue was hotly debated among the learned, and opinion remained divided, but no one could question the extraordinary import of the manifestation.

Judging by his demeanor, Gnaus liGurvohl fully believed in the communicative power of the luminous form before him. Autonn might or might not grace Radiance Square with His true presence, but, at the very least, He closely monitored proceedings. Understandably so, for was it not reasonable, indeed inevitable, that humanity's great protector should wish to confirm the duty and loyalty of those mortal creatures in whose behalf He endured such inordinate inconvenience?

"Eternal Benefactor, Your wounds are deep, and Your suffering is great." LiGurvohl eschewed the presumption of commiseration. He merely stated facts. "Those wounds, inflicted by the immortal malevolences whose company You have chosen to abandon, purchase the present freedom and safety of mankind. Upon that plane existing beyond the limits of our human perceptions, the endless battle rages. We owe You our lives, our minds, and our world. Without You, we are lost.

"Yet there are those among us so ungrateful, so twisted, and so vile that they have willingly allied themselves with Your foes. In exchange for the false and fleeting illusory power that men call sorcery, they have sold the life-force that strengthens Your enemies, the energy that blasts Your existence. We are shamed and saddened to acknowledge these traitors as our own. They have abjured the ties and obligations of mankind, they have severed themselves from us, from our world upon this plane, and, indeed, from all save the malevolences that they serve. This so, we equally abjure our ties to them. We disown them, we cast them forth from the race of man, we offer them and all that they are unto You. Take them in reparation, Autonn-Benefactor. Take them in justice, take them in some small payment of our debt, take them and deprive Your enemies of their resources. Take them, Autonn, and use their essence to make Yourself whole."

LiGurvohl bowed his head, and silence shrouded Radiance Square for the space of some seconds. The world itself seemed to pause. Then, an almost tentative light beamed from the hitherto black space beneath the feet of the prisoners, climbed through the misty air, and touched the glowing face of Autonn. Answering radiance descended, disparate energies embraced and joined, pulsing between air and ground, faster and faster, too swift for the eye to follow, at last to climax in a flare of terrible brilliance, a silent searing blast insupportable to the naked eye. Thousands of arms rose to shield thousands of faces, while the white frenzy raged at the center of the stage. Though the effulgence defied observation, there seemed to be no heat, and no sound; only light, unimaginable light.

When the quiescence of countless nerves signaled an abatement of the glare, a host of eyes reopened to behold a stage unblemished, undamaged, and bare of prisoners. The empty fetters and loose iron chains still lay fastened to the staples sunk in the stone, but Ravnar liMarchborg and Jex liTarngrav had vanished without a trace.

The audience exhaled, lingeringly. The events of the Enlightenment, though unvarying, nonetheless never failed to astonish.

It was not yet concluded, however. The luminous presence of Autonn hovered yet above the stage, and now the image was changing. The black wounds that marked the ghostly flesh were fading, miraculously effacing themselves. Presumably, the life-force of the sacrificed sorcerers exerted a powerfully restorative effect. The gaping fissures shrank, closed, and paled, dwindling to meager patches of ashy grey. The pools of spreading shadow evaporated, and gradually the countenance of Autonn altered, intense pain yielding at last to a look of otherworldly peace.

The audience was voiceless, motionlessly rapt. For a moment longer Autonn's image hovered there, cleansed and calm, then slowly faded from view.

"It is finished. He is renewed." Gnaus liGurvohl's voice was at once hushed and profoundly audible. Without another word, the Premier Jurist stalked from the stage, to vanish into the Heart of Light. His fellow judges trailed devotedly in his wake.

The great silence continued unbroken as the audience began to disperse. The citizens departed in awed clumps, and Radiance Square swiftly emptied itself. Up on the stage, Soldiers of the Light had already replaced the great stone block that normally covered the polished blackness whereon victims awaited Enlightenment. The fires burned on, however. The great cauldron boiled vigorously, and would continue for some hours to come — enough time to effect a thorough separation of meat and the human bone that would, when properly cleaned and ground, add strength and translucency to the famous black Hetzian porcelain. As for the by-product of the bone harvest, the rich soup full of criminal meat and fat, even that would not be wasted, but used to nourish the beasts in the zoo at the bottom of the Heart of Light. For it was known to all that wise husbandry of the world's resources gladdened the heart of Autonn.

The soldiers completed their tasks and marched away. The soup boiled on in an empty square. The kitchen aroma infused itself through the misty air. For a very long time, Tradain remained where he was, bonded to the window, gazing down at the cauldron with eyes that were wide, fixed, and blind.

Four

They came for him an hour later. The door
opened and a couple of Soldiers of the Light
entered to pluck him away from the window
bars to which he still unconsciously clung.
In silence, they fettered his wrists behind his
back, then hurried him from the cell, down
the stairs, through the foyer, and out into the
courtyard, wherein waited a closed conveyance of the sort that had carried Ravnar
liMarchborg and his sons to the Heart of
Light, days earlier. It might even have been
the same one.

Into the boxlike vehicle they thrust
him, then slammed the door and locked it.
The driver's whip snapped, and the wheels
turned. It was midmorning, and a few thin
shafts of weak light filtered in through an
X-shaped set of ventilation holes perforating

the low roof. Had he risen, he might easily have applied his eye to an opening and studied—the featureless grey sky.

Why bother? He stayed where he was, indifferent gaze fixed on nothing.

Apathy notwithstanding, he felt it when the wagon passed from the Heart of Light courtyard, and out into the street beyond. He felt the change in motion and air as he was carried over Immemorial Bridge, for something fundamental inside him took note, even while his consciousness armored itself in grief. Then the vehicle was clattering over city cobbles, and he could hear the gabble of human voices in the streets, separated from him only by the thickness of a wooden wall, but inhabiting another world.

Presently the voices died and the clatter subsided, for the ground beneath the wheels was now unpaved. Lis Folaze lay behind. For some measureless span of time, the wagon hurried along a bumping, rutted road, then paused while unrecognizable voices conversed unintelligibly. Progress resumed, very briefly. There was a jerk, a jolt, the hollow thunder of the horses' hoofs upon a wooden surface, and an abrupt halt.

He sensed gliding motion, and heard the lapping of water. Wagon, horses, and all crossed water aboard a barge-ferry.

He knew where he was, then, and he knew where they were taking him. Already cold, he went colder. Deliberately he sought to empty his mind of thought, and reality distanced itself a little.

The barge reached its destination. He heard a solid thunk, and felt a slight vibration as the landing ramp hit the wharf. The wagon descended the short artificial incline. The ground leveled, rose, and leveled again. There was pavement under the wheels once more, and a mighty clattering, as the wagon advanced the last few yards. He heard the clang of a metal gate swinging shut. Another halt, this one unmistakably final.

The door opened, and Tradain squinted against the light. Somebody caught his arm and pulled him forth. He emerged into a small stone space, bounded on all sides by lofty grey walls, and surmounted by a square of grey sky. He stood in some tiny courtyard belonging to a vast, grimly granitic edifice. He had never before observed the building from this particular vantage point, but he recognized the color and stark contours without difficulty. He stood within the confines of Fortress Nul, that prison of gloomy reputation, perched upon its towering rock at the center of Lake Oblivion.

They marched into the building, and along dim tunnellike corridors to a windowless cubicle of an office, where a uniformed functionary slumped lax and bored at his desk.

The officer's look of ennui vanished as they walked in. With a glance at the prisoner, he observed, "Ridiculous. What are we these days, nursery-maids?"

"Wet nurses, more like." So saying, one of the guards handed over a couple of documents, bearing the triple seals of White Tribunal, Lis Folaze Municipality, and Dhrevian authority. The recipient read attentively.

"By what right do you bring me to this place, or hold me here?" demanded the son of Ravnar liMarchborg. The other raised gimlet eyes, and he moistened his lips before adding, "I've been convicted of no crime. I've had no trial."

"Really." The officer's brows rose. "Complaints noted."

"I wish to speak to—to—" Tradain didn't know the appropriate title. "To whoever's in charge here."

"The Governor?"

"Yes."

"Request noted."

"When may I see him?"

"You will be notified."

"Today?"

"Unlikely."

"Tomorrow?"

"Improbable."

"Will it be a long time?"

"Not in the cosmic sense."

"I wish to write a letter, then."

"Feel free."

"I need paper, ink, and quill."

"True."

"Well, may I—?" Tradain eyed the desktop, cluttered with note-books, ledgers, and writing implements.

"Request noted."

"Won't you just tell me—"

"You will be notified."

"But—"

"Enough." Evidently tiring of the sport, the officer relapsed into boredom. Jotting a short entry into the ledger lying open before him, he glanced up briefly, to demand, "Your age?"

"Thirteen. I—"

"Thirteen. Very good. That is your number, then. How fortunate that the number 'thirteen' should prove available at this particular time. The coincidence pleases me. You are now Number Thirteen."

"I don't know what you're talking about. I am Tradain liMarchborg, son of the High Landguardian Ravnar liMarchborg. I—"

"You will learn to accept what cannot be changed, Number Thirteen. The wisest among our residents do so. I would regard such adaptability as a mark of maturity."

"Listen, this is not a joke, or a game. This is—" One of his father's phrases popped into Tradain's mind. "A miscarriage of justice."

"But justice is a very relative term, Number Thirteen, as you will discover for yourself, if you live long enough." Leaning back in his chair, the officer uttered a negligent command. "Pols."

Pols? To Tradain, it meant nothing, but his guards understood well enough. Leading their charge from the office, they steered him through a granite maze to a distant gallery where his manacles were removed and he was surrendered to the care of a small, ferret-faced corridor captain, who led him to a vacant cell, pushed him in, locked the door, and departed.

Tradain looked about him, almost incuriously. The compartment, although tiny, was half again the size of the wedge-shaped space allotted him in the Heart of Light. It contained a straw pallet, bucket, splintery little table, three-legged stool, water jug, and cup. There was a small, unshuttered window overlooking a colorless walled yard, presently empty. No fireplace or stove. No lantern or candle. The door was barred in steel from top to bottom, affording any passerby an unobstructed view into the cell. Here, they could watch him while he ate, slept, or relieved himself—they could watch him night and day.

There had to be a way out. *Manufacture a skeleton key. Overpower the guards. Swim Lake Oblivion.*

Nobody escaped Fortress Nul.

Somebody could. Somebody would.

He needed to focus on that; preferably, to the exclusion of all else.

In the Heart of Light, he had passed the featureless days alone in a tiny cell. Such was not to be the case at Fortress Nul.

In the midafternoon, the corridor captain of the ferret face appeared, unlocked his door, and announced with an air of satisfaction, "Three hours left on Second Shift. Plenty of time to make some use of you. On your feet, Thirteen."

Tradain, supine upon his pallet, regarded the ceiling in silence.

"Up. To work, boy. Today, my gang will exceed its quota."

Tradain studied the stone and mortar.

"I said, my gang will exceed its quota. This month, I'll earn a commendation and certificate, it's all but sure. You know what that means?"

Tradain had no idea. He said nothing.

"It means recognition, boy. It means progress, it means I take a step forward toward my goal. Know what that is?"

Tradain did not.

"Unit commander," the Ferret confided. "I'm qualified. I'm ready. I'm deserving, and it's my turn, now. The big boys know me, so my promotion's in the bag, provided my gang maintains its level. Nothing's going to go wrong now. You understand?"

Tradain was beginning to.

"I expect each of my Pols to pull his weight."

Pols?

"There are other units in this place, remember. You're lucky to be here, but that could change in a wink."

Lucky.

"So make up your mind to it, you're for the Boneworks."

Boneworks?

"On your feet." There was no reaction, and the piqued Ferret advanced a couple of paces to haul his prisoner forcibly from the pallet.

Tradain offered no resistance as the other dragged him from the cell, along the anonymous corridors, through an arched doorway, and out into a chilly walled yard where a glum gang of inmates toiled under the supervision of armed guards. The heavy weaponry of the officers appeared almost absurdly redundant in view of the prisoners' uniform listless emaciation, but Tradain missed the incongruity, for his shocked gaze anchored upon the great iron cauldron boiling at the center of the yard. For a moment, time slipped gears and he gazed once again down on Radiance Square, where the fire blazed, the cauldron bubbled—

A firm shove informed him that he had halted.

"Move," the Ferret commanded. Receiving no response, he glanced sharply into the prisoner's frozen face, noted the horror there, and loosed a comforting cackle. "Don't worry, we don't cook live inmates. At least, not the ones who behave themselves, and work hard to meet quotas, and keep on the right side of the corridor captain. This is just Boneworks, boy, where the carcasses are stripped, their skeletons boiled clean, dried, then ground to powder and vended to the porcelain factories."

Animal bone, plunder of the slaughterhouses and public dumps, used in the manufacture of ordinary plates and cups, washbasins and pitchers. But

*that won't serve for the best, the finest Hetzian ware, that mixes human bone
into the clay, and human blood into the glaze. Nothing less will do.*

"Not much by way of man-meat today." The Ferret must have read
his thoughts. "Only two, from the almshouse."

Today.

"So you see, there's nothing to fear." A forceful push underscored the
reassurance.

Tradain stumbled forward a few paces, and balked.

"Go to it, Thirteen."

No reaction.

"Dull one, eh? All right. I'll make allowances, I can do that. Patience, understanding—these are essential qualities of leadership. I possess
both, in abundance, and I'll prove it now. Your job," the Ferret informed
his slow-witted charge, "is to strip the meat, fat, and sinew from those bits
and pieces heaped up over there. You see that pile there?" The question was
rhetorical. His gesture encompassed a stinking mound of putrefaction, impossible to overlook. "You've got the easy life, the fels have already done the
heavy work of chopping."

Fels?

"Now, you just go get yourself a scraper from Sergeant Gultz,
there—" The Ferret indicated a hulking uniformed individual of morose
demeanor. "Grab a chunk from the pile, sit down somewhere, and get to
work. You deaf, boy? I said, get to it."

Silence from the motionless prisoner, and the Ferret's affability dwindled. "Now hear me, Thirteen. I am the most amiable and evenhanded of
corridor captains, yet I do not lack firmness. You will find me perfectly just
and impartial, but not overly indulgent. You understand me? A nod will
suffice."

The prisoner offered no acknowledgment.

"I fear you do not understand me. That is disappointing, but the
problem is not insoluble. I will overcome this difficulty, as I surmount all
obstacles, for I am endowed with great tenacity of character. Let me put it to
you this way, Thirteen. Apathy will not be tolerated. Laziness and slovenli-
ness are unacceptable. Failure to fulfill your obligations brings punishment
in the form of hunger, thirst, cold, humiliation, extreme pain, possible muti-
lation and/or death. A place among the pols isn't guaranteed, you know.
Things could be a lot worse. Think about it."

Tradain looked away.

"You leave me no choice, Thirteen. Deliberate insubordination in-
vites retribution, and truly you leave me no choice. Gultz!" The Ferret's
voice rose to a shout. "*Gultz!*"

"Sir?" The massive sergeant was there in an instant, broad face a study in repressed disdain.

"Tell Number Thirteen here what happens if he defies Corridor Captain Kreschl."

"I'll take a truncheon to him," Gultz replied casually. "Smash his nose, knock his teeth out, maybe break his jaw. For starters."

"You hear that, Thirteen?" the Ferret inquired.

Tradain nodded. His eyes ranged the yard, picking out several faces battered and broken in just the manner described by the sergeant.

"Speak up, you little rodent," Sergeant Gultz advised.

"I hear you," Tradain conceded.

"Excellent. Negotiation is always the key to mutual understanding," opined the Ferret. "Now, I trust I have made my position clear?"

"Take this." Sergeant Gultz proffered a small wooden implement, like a worn and cracked little paddle, with a wide blade narrowing to a tolerably fine edge. "Don't try playing the genius, I keep track of these things, and I'll want it back at the end of the shift. Now, you grab a haunch of something, scrape it good, and dump it in the pot. Man-meat gets special handling—you bring that kind of work to me for inspection. If it doesn't pass, you keep at it until I'm satisfied. Your quota's ten pieces per hour. Miss your quota, and you make me look bad. Make me look bad, and I'll rip your lungs out. Got that?"

Tradain nodded.

"I didn't hear you," the sergeant observed.

"I understand," Tradain said, and something in the other's air of sinister expectancy prompted him to add, "sir."

"Comprehension. A meeting of the minds. I feel we have accomplished something here." The Ferret nodded, gratified, and both of his listeners shot him identical glances. "There you have it, Thirteen. Ten pieces per hour. Hop to it."

At the far end of the yard loomed the fleshly heap, its blood-caked components resolving themselves as he reluctantly approached. Limbs, haunches, split torsos spilling viscera, necks, and assorted heads mingled with a haphazard disregard of species. He spied fragments of cow, horse, hog, goat, sheep, and dog, all of them black with the flies whose ceaseless buzzing maddeningly filled the air. The stench intensified as he drew near, and his head swam. He glanced back over his shoulder to encounter Sergeant Gultz's unblinking stare.

Holding his breath, he advanced to the mound, averted his eyes, and reached out to grasp some anonymous orphaned member, soft with corruption. Blind selection proved unlucky, and he looked down to find himself clutching a human arm. Revolted, he flung it away, and Sergeant Gultz started for him. Hastily he grabbed another limb, this one of ruminant origin, and the sergeant's advance halted.

Loathsomely burdened, Tradain backed away from the ripe meat, the stink, the flies. Choosing an empty patch of dirt alongside the wall, he seated himself. A few feet away, a gaunt fellow prisoner labored over a putrid haunch of something or other, and experience revealed itself in the skill of his performance. Wielding his wooden scraper with virtuoso precision, he carved meat from bone in long, even strips. The strips fell in a neat pile, and within a minute or two, the haunch was clean. Tradain watched in miserable interest.

Sensing scrutiny, the prisoner raised wary, weary eyes. "Better get cracking," he advised, muted tones scarcely audible above the drone of the flies. His gaze returned to the work before him, and did not shift as he added, "You're under the lens." A minute jerk of one finger in the direction of the attentive Gultz communicated his meaning.

Tradain at once commenced scraping, a task for which he displayed small aptitude. The hoofed and hairy limb before him—probably the hind leg of a goat—carried a considerable quantity of flesh, most of it well advanced in decomposition. The meat crawled with maggots, and the stench was abominable. He gagged, and turned his face away.

"Breathe through your mouth."

The whisper barely reached his ears. His neighbor appeared wholly preoccupied. Tradain gulped air and reapplied himself. The meat was soft as mud, but his hands were unskilled, and the work proceeded slowly.

"Like this."

He turned to watch his neighbor deal the final strokes to a couple of clinging, faintly iridescent scraps.

"It's all in the wrist."

The scraps flew, the naked bones shone white, and the speaker rose to bear his work to the pot.

It looked easy enough. Tradain imitatively plied his scraper, and the gelatinous globules spattered in all directions. Exposed maggots wriggled for cover, and new foulness poisoned the air. His innards rebelled, and he vomited, scant contents of his stomach spewing forth to drench the work before him.

For a moment he paused, breathing deeply, and then Sergeant Gultz was there, and a big hand closed on the back of his neck, pressing his face down into the noxiously sauced meat.

"You can scrape it, or eat it," Gultz remarked.

Tradain responded to this suggestion with a second fit of retching, but there was nothing left in his belly to lose.

"You'll pull your weight, Thirteen," the sergeant promised. "Here, or else among the fels. Your choice. Or maybe—" His grip tightened. "Maybe I'll just snap your little neck like a carrot. Solve the problem fast. I'll have to think about it." Administering a final, expressive squeeze, he straightened and sauntered away.

Tradain forced himself to open his eyes, which had all but glued themselves shut. The work still lay unfinished before him. *Your quota's ten pieces per hour.* The scraper still lay in his lap. He picked it up and shakily resumed his labor, but his hands were clumsier than ever, and progress lagged. In the time it took his neighbor to speed through a pig's shoulder, a horse's foreleg, and a donkey's neck, he barely managed to scrape a single goat's limb clean.

Rising, he made for the cauldron at the center of the yard, but was intercepted by his nemesis.

"Show me," Sergeant Gultz commanded.

Tradain displayed his work.

"You call that pot-ready?" The question was rhetorical. Gultz pointed. "You see that? You blind?"

Tradain followed the pointing finger to the rags of whitish fibrous matter still clinging to the knee joint.

"Get back to work on it. No, not over there." The prohibition forestalled retreat. "Right here."

Tradain sat, in the sergeant's very shadow. Applying wood to bone, he exerted force, but the tough, clinging fibers resisted his efforts. He increased the pressure, and the cracked wood of the scraper split under the strain. The instrument broke in half, and one of its flying fragments struck the sergeant's boot.

Tradain looked up to find the other's face creased in a smile of genuine pleasure.

"Good one." Sergeant Gultz nodded.

"Accident. Sir."

"I can always spot the troublemakers, every time. Knew at a glance that you'd try something, and you haven't disappointed me. Deliberate destruction of government property. Insubordination. Assault on an officer. Good beginning, Thirteen."

Accident, and you know it, you pig-faced bastard. Dread iced along his veins. Tradain said nothing.

"Busy little mischievous hands," the sergeant mused. "What shall we do with them? How to educate them?" He pondered briefly. "I think I have it. Stand up."

Tradain obeyed.

"Give me your paw."

"What for?"

"You want to find out what happens if I have to tell you twice?"

Tradain extended his left arm. Instantly seizing the proffered wrist, Sergeant Gultz dragged his victim a few paces forward to the side of the cauldron, and it flashed through Tradain's mind that he was about to be thrown into the boiling water, to die as his brothers had died. He fought then, his struggles wild and ineffectual.

Gultz subdued him with ease and, when resistance subsided, deliberately pressed the prisoner's clenched fist to the heated iron of the pot.

For a split second Tradain felt nothing, and then the pain shot along his nerves, a cry escaped him, and he pulled back with all of his insufficient strength. For a moment Gultz held him there, and then contemptuously released him. Tradain dropped to his knees, cradling a momentarily paralyzed left hand.

"Get the message, little Thirteen?" the sergeant inquired. "Eh?"

"Yes. Sir." His voice was little more than a gasp.

"That's what I like to hear." Gultz dug in his pocket to produce an undamaged scraper, which he tossed to the ground before the kneeling prisoner. "Then what are you waiting for? Get back to work." Deeming his mission accomplished, he strolled away without a backward glance.

Tradain dully regarded the wooden implement, then picked it up. The bones of the goat's leg, still festooned with clinging strings of fiber, lay a few feet away. He covered that distance on his knees, then halted to cast a covert glance about the yard. Expecting to find himself the object of universal scrutiny, he discovered his fellow prisoners obliviously industrious; while Sergeant Gultz, his attention already focused elsewhere, was busy bullying some luckless emaciated wretch at the far end of the enclosure.

He hardly dared inspect his own left hand. He would find it blackened, charred to the bone . . .

He forced himself to look down. The heel of his hand and the outer edge of his thumb were deeply reddened, but the flesh remained unbroken. He felt little real pain as yet, but the curious sense of paralysis persisted. Not nearly as bad as he had feared.

But bad enough.

Slowly he took up his work again, at last scraping the limb quite bare. This time, the bones passed inspection, and he dropped them in the pot, then returned to the heap of mammalian parts and selected a cow's head, comparatively fresh, brown eyes disturbingly intact. The troublesome resistance of undecayed flesh and skin was offset by the blessed absence of maggots. He was beginning to acquire a certain measure of skill with the scraper, and the cleansing process might have proceeded at good speed, but for the growing hurt in his left hand. Initial paralysis had worn off quickly, and with it went all natural anesthesia. The flushed skin was losing color as it began to puff with blisters. Time passed, the shadows lengthened across the prison yard, the blisters swelled to yellow-white cushions, and the punished nerves protested.

The sun was setting by the time Tradain dropped the cow's naked skull into the bubbling cauldron. A whistle shrilled, a couple of guards collected scrapers, and the prisoners lined up to file from the darkening yard. Back into the fortress they marched in perfect silence, but with an alacrity suggesting the imminence of feeding.

He was hungry, Tradain realized. Even in the midst of these horrors, his young body craved food. In his mind, he scarcely wanted to live, but that message hadn't reached his stomach.

A hand clamped his shoulder. Without looking, he knew who it was.

"Not you," declared Sergeant Gultz.

Tradain halted, but didn't trouble to turn his face.

"Not you," Gultz repeated. "Your quota's ten per hour, and you didn't come close. Did you think I was joking?"

I thought it was all too funny. He had enough sense to keep his mouth shut.

"No work, no food." The sergeant's logic was unanswerable. "But I won't stop you from watching."

Another few steps along the gloomy corridor, with the sergeant's hand on his shoulder. Through a tall doorway and into the ill-lit mess hall, where the grey-faced prisoners, seated upon long benches of greyish planking, drooped over bowls of grey gruel, augmented with greyish beans.

Repellent fare, but his mouth was watering. His stomach growled, and his companion heard it.

"Baby wants its nipple?" Gultz inquired.

Tradain maintained politic silence. The diners did likewise. Evidently, conversation was discouraged at mealtime. Conversation, in fact, seemed to be discouraged at all times.

The meal ended, a whistle sounded, and one of the officers roared, "Pols, OUT."

The prisoners exited docilely, and a squad of guards herded them back to their respective cells. A shove thrust Tradain into his isolated space, and the door crashed behind him. The cold air sliding through the barred window chilled his flesh. His left hand throbbed. Alone in the gathering dark, he traced its altered contours. The blisters, hugely swollen and filled with fluid, begged for experimental prodding. It took a conscious effort of will to keep his fingers off them.

His mind was crammed with ugliness. Extending himself upon the pallet, he escaped for a while into dreamless slumber.

At the break of dawn, the rusty groan of his barred door woke him. Tradain opened unwilling eyes to gaze upon the face of Corridor Captain Kreschl, whom, in his own mind, he had dubbed the Ferret.

"I am displeased, Thirteen," the Ferret declared, without preamble. "Sergeant Gultz informed me of yesterday's events. He spoke at length of your laziness and intractability, and I must confess that I am disappointed, for I had expected better of you. It would appear that you lack the maturity required to function successfully in the Boneworks. Nevertheless, I am not discouraged. Rest assured, I will find the proper place for you. Get up and come with me."

Tradain obeyed, and the Ferret conducted him through the stone labyrinth to a low-ceilinged chamber whose walls were lined with bins containing clean, white bones. About the room stood a number of large mechanical contrivances, each furnished with a cylindrical body, a stout handle, and an open hopper.

"Grinders." The Ferret's expansive gesture encompassed the machines. "Easily operated. You fill the hopper with bone, turn the handle, and the powdered product collects in the drawer at the bottom. When the drawer is full, you empty the contents into a sack from that pile in the corner, and leave your full sacks beside the door to await removal. Your quota is a half-dozen sacks per hour. Understand?"

Tradain nodded.

"Excellent. Then what are you waiting for? Choose your machine and get to work. I will return presently to check your progress. And I trust, Thirteen, you'll not disappoint me again."

The Ferret exited. The door closed behind him, and the bolt scraped home.

Alone. Nobody watching.

Tradain cast his eyes about the room, which was windowless, but furnished with a skylight. Quite out of reach and, in any case, crisscrossed with heavy bars. No escape there. No escape anywhere.

He shrugged and, carefully favoring his blisters, commenced transferring armloads of clean bone from one of the bins to one of the hoppers. His pace was steady and fairly swift, for it wouldn't do to disappoint the Ferret.

When the hopper was loaded, he began grinding, but this task proved unexpectedly demanding. The bones offered considerable resistance, and he found at once that he lacked the strength to operate the machine one-handed. Both hands were required, but his left, sore and swollen, was all but useless.

No telling what they'd do to him if he refused to work.

Jaw set, Tradain pushed hard with both hands. The handle moved infinitesimally. He increased pressure, and his blisters burst wide open. Astonishing quantities of fluid spurted, and for the first time, the real pain of his injury struck.

For the life of him, he couldn't repress a cry. He looked down to behold raw flesh, red and plentifully oozing. The pressure of the air upon it was agony. He couldn't operate a machine with that hand. He probably couldn't hold a soupspoon with it.

Now what?

The door opened, and a couple of guards ushered in a slouching gaggle of paste-faced inmates. The prisoners, apparently veterans, set about their tasks without instruction and without hesitation. Despite their uniform look of malnutrition, there wasn't one of them whose strength did not exceed his own. Scrawny but wiry arms pumped, internal blades rotated, and bone crunched loudly.

Tradain stood watching. His fellow prisoners appeared unaware of his deficiencies and his existence, but the guards owned no such tact.

One of them—no taller than he, but twice as wide—approached to demand what he thought he was doing.

Mutely, Tradain displayed his useless left hand.

"So?" the guard inquired.

The return of the Ferret spared Tradain the necessity of reply.

"Show me what you've accomplished, Thirteen," the Ferret directed. "Make me proud of you."

"Corridor Captain, he's slacked his shift." The guard radiated baleful triumph.

"Malingering again, Thirteen?" demanded the Ferret. "Are you truly determined to squander your every opportunity? I am more than disappointed. I am aggrieved."

"Then your quarrel's with Sergeant Gultz, who burned my hand for the fun of it," Tradain replied. Around him he heard the hiss of sharply indrawn breath. His fellow prisoners were, it seemed, not nearly so unaware as they appeared.

"I am sorry to witness these attempted evasions." The Ferret scowled.

"They are clear evidence of irresponsibility. Thirteen, you are useless, fit only for the work of children, women, gaffers, and idiots. To such, I now consign you. Come with me."

No point in asking where.

Once more, he followed his guide through the granite bowels of Fortress Nul, down several levels to the kitchen, where the hot air smelled of old oil, and the big rats hardly troubled to stir from the path of humans.

Here, some eight or nine prisoners drudged under the supervision of a lone corporal whose patent boredom required no explanation. His charges—all of them grey with age, bent-backed, infirm, and spiritless— appeared equally incapable of aggression or defense.

"Corporal Woenich, I bring you an undersized, sickly, malingering pol," the Ferret announced.

"Yessir," the corporal returned stolidly.

"It is unpromising material, I fear. He has already managed to damage himself, and will no doubt lose his left hand when it festers. Following the amputation, he's sure to die off quickly. In the meantime, you must make whatever use you can of him."

"Yessir."

"I had hoped for better things, Thirteen." The Ferret addressed Tradain sternly. "But your attitude is poor, and you have proved yourself unfit for man's work. Here, you find your own level, and here I am forced to leave you."

The disappointed corridor captain departed.

Moodily, Corporal Woenich surveyed his new acquisition. "I always get the dregs," he observed. "Root cellar's all you'll be good for. Over here."

Tradain followed his mentor to a small, shadowy opening in the kitchen wall. Woenich wheeled, seized his arm, and slung him through into darkness. Tradain stumbled down two or three steps of an invisible stone stairway, lost his footing at the bottom, and sprawled full length. The other's voice floated down the stairs to him.

"Start stripping those lorber clusters," Corporal Woenich commanded. "Even an undergrown juvenile cripple should be able to manage that much. And don't plan on loafing. I'll be back before long to check, and I expect to see some progress, or else."

The voice ceased. The corporal withdrew.

Tradain slowly sat up and looked about him. The root cellar was not pitch-dark, as he had initially supposed. Feeble light filtered in through a single small and deeply recessed window, striped with heavy bars. His eyes had adjusted to the gloom, and now he beheld a low-ceilinged space, with damp stone walls and filthy stone floor. Low wooden partitions separated mounds of turnips, lorbers, parsnips, skeeks, and onions. A drift of dingy rags smudged one corner.

The sight of the vegetables, dirt-crusted and unappetizing though they were, recalled his own hunger. He hadn't eaten since—he didn't remember exactly when. He needed food, anything he could get, and this moment of solitude offered rare opportunity.

Dragging himself to his feet, he lurched to the nearest storage compartment, scooped up a giant among skeeks, brushed the surface soil off, and sank his teeth into the prize. Tearing away a sizable chunk, he chewed strenuously.

Useless. The dense substance of the aged tuber—tough and resilient as gristle, bitter as failure—defied his best efforts. The thing was altogether inedible.

Disgusted, Tradain threw the skeek away. It flew through the air to land in the corner, atop the heap of rags.

The rags stirred, and spoke.

"*I have not troubled you. Why do you attack me?*"

Five

He started, but held his ground, watching in fascination as the ragged mound unfolded itself. Amidst many labored gasps and rasping sighs, a recumbent figure sat up slowly. He had thought the prisoners in the kitchen old and decrepit, but they were vernal by comparison to this one. Tradain beheld a frail and wasted form, decked in colorless tatters. He looked into a face indescribably ancient, worn and savaged by the years. He saw sunken features, eyes filmed with age, lipless mouth drawn in over toothless gums, seamed flesh bleached by time and darkness; the whole framed in long, weightless white hair and beard.

A wisp, a cobweb, a living wraith; probably about a thousand years old.

Astonished, he stood staring, and the wraith repeated its quavering query, "Why do you attack me?"

"I didn't attack you. At least, not on purpose." Tradain found his voice. "I didn't know you were there."

"You are blind, then. That is why you have been assigned to this level."

"No. I'm not blind."

"Nor yet feeble-minded, by the sound of you. What, then? Come nearer, let me see."

Tradain obeyed, and the two inspected each other at close range. The wraith's skin was dry and insubstantial as a layer of dust. The hands were all but fleshless, their emaciation emphasizing extreme enlargement of the knuckles. Each joint was swollen to the size of a lorber. Remarkable.

The ancient, equally astonished, tweetled, "Why, you are only a child!"

"I'm no child."

"How old are you?"

"Thirteen."

"And a prisoner in this place?"

"Yes."

"Poor, miserable child!"

Tradain's eyes burned, on the verge of spilling tears. Anything would be better than that, and determined to forestall humiliation, he spoke quickly. "And how old are *you*?"

"How old?" Taken aback, the old man cogitated. "I could not say. I was born, I believe, in the year of the flood."

"Which flood?"

"The big one."

"How long have you been here?"

"Forever, I think."

Forever. Tradain had a sudden vision of himself, decades hence; shrunken, blanched, and senescent as the being before him, a prisoner in this place, forever.

No. It happened to others, but not to Ravnar liMarchborg's son. "Not to me," he muttered, unaware that he had spoken aloud.

"What's that?"

"Nothing. I'm sorry I struck you, sir. It was unintentional." Judging the profitless exchange concluded, Tradain turned back to the vegetable bins.

"One Fifty-Seven," the ancient announced.

"Sir?"

"Eh, but you have fine manners, child. I wonder where you learnt them. Nobody has called me 'sir' since—I don't remember when. Perhaps nobody has ever called me 'sir' before. Now that I think of it, I don't believe anyone ever has."

Maundering, doddering senility, but the poor old wreck couldn't be blamed. Best to humor him, without offering undue encouragement. Tradain essayed a faint smile, and a noncommittal nod, before redirecting his attention to the bins.

But the other, awakened to relentless sociability, was not to be put off.

"Here, I am One Fifty-Seven," the old man confided. "Officially, that is. Unofficially, I am sometimes known as 'One,' because I am first among surviving pols to take up residence in this place. Then again, ever since I lost the last of my teeth, the merrier of the guards have taken to calling me 'Fangs.' "

"Tell me," Tradain inquired, "are any of these jokesters so merry as Sergeant Gultz?"

"No. Nobody matches Gultz for jollity, unless it be the Governor himself."

"You call yourself a 'pol.' What is that?"

"A political prisoner, as opposed to a common felon, or 'fel.' The two groups are kept separated at all times—they do not even glimpse one another. This is meant to protect the fels from mental and moral contamination, but it works both ways, you see. Some of those fels, I am told, are strong and savage as maddened bears. Others, they say, are like poisonous snakes. Still others resemble giant insects armed with diabolical intelligence. I should not like to meet them! Believe me, my boy, you are lucky to be a pol."

"I'm overflowing with gratitude."

"Pols and fels," the ancient continued with verve, "are divided in every possible way, even down to the numbers they are assigned. Fels are even, pols odd, as in my own One Fifty-Seven. But you, child, may address me as Fangs. That is short, simple, and easily recalled to memory."

"If you wish."

"And you are called—?"

"Tradain."

"But have you not been given a number?"

"My name is Tradain liMarchborg."

"Ah, a touch of defiance, openly displayed. Garments of good qual-

ity, rumpled and soiled, but otherwise undamaged. A youthfully weedy figure, skinny, but showing no sign of chronic want. All things considered, it is
clear that you've not been here long."

Tradain's eyes widened a little. It seemed the old man wasn't quite
the dotard he'd initially appeared. The reference to "chronic want" recalled
his own extreme hunger. Returning to the vegetable bins, he made another
selection, this time a turnip of modest size and age. He devoured the thing
in a few gulps, then addressed a second at a more leisurely pace. The ache
in his belly began to subside.

"Tradain liMarchborg." Fangs mulled it over. "An old name, a noble
name. Your look, manner, and accent convince me that it might actually be
yours. Tell me, could not your father's influence secure your freedom? Or is
it perhaps your father who sent you here? Did you offend or disgrace him in
some way, perhaps disobeyed him, and now he teaches you a lesson, eh? Is
that it?"

"No."

"Well then, won't your own father speak up for his—"

"My father is dead," Tradain stated flatly.

"Ah, unlucky. But you've other kin, who may—"

"No."

"But how sad, my poor child. You are alone in the world, an orphan
with no protector, a prisoner, perhaps for life—"

"No. I'll get out somehow." The assertion slipped out of its own
accord, and instantly Tradain regretted it. The last thing he meant to do was
confide in this chatty, erratic stranger.

"Will you, now?" Fangs's expression of guileless interest was alarming. "And how do you plan to do it, lad?"

"I have no plan." *No tales for you to carry back to the guards, old
man.*

"Eh, but it's no easy thing to escape Fortress Nul. Should you hope
to do it, you must have a plan, and a good one. There's much to consider.
How, for example, would you get out of the building itself? The doors are
locked, the windows barred. If you did get out, you would find yourself in
one of the yards. How then would you scale the wall? It is very high, and
topped with broken glass, you know. And then, there are guards everywhere
about. How would you deal with them?"

"I don't know," Tradain mumbled, deliberately dull. *And if I did, I
wouldn't tell you.*

"But let us say that you managed to get over the wall," Fangs continued, with the air of a superannuated pedagogue. "Then you would find

yourself confronting the greatest obstacle of all—the true strength of the fortress. I mean, of course, the Lake Oblivion. Perhaps you think to steal a boat and row to shore?"

"I don't think anything." Tradain started in on another turnip.

"The boathouse is stoutly constructed, heavily locked, and well guarded. Perhaps you think of swimming the lake?"

Tradain shrugged vacantly.

"It is nearly three miles from this island to the nearest point of shore. Could you swim so far?"

"Don't know."

"Perhaps you think it no great feat, but you reckon without the water temperature. The lake water is frigid at all seasons of the year. Child, you can't begin to guess the paralyzing effect of very cold water."

Can't I?

"And even that is not the worst of it," Fangs tweetled on blithely. "The cold water sustains thickets of twining weeds, in which the unlucky are caught and fatally entangled. Worse yet—the thickets harbor eels. You've heard of the Oblivion eels?"

"Don't remember."

"Just so. 'Don't remember.' You have hit upon it. The bite of an Oblivion eel renders the victim senseless within seconds. Should he prove so fortunate as to awaken, his memory is blasted—an effect sometimes fleeting, sometimes permanent, always disconcerting. The lake swarms with Oblivion eels, and they are anything but timorous. Had you thought how you might deal with that problem?"

"No." Tradain set his teeth to work on a parsnip.

"It would seem, my poor child, that you've not granted this matter the attention that it deserves."

"Well. You've made it clear, sir. I see there's no way out," Tradain lied.

"You are giving up, then?"

"What else can I do?"

"Are you always so easily discouraged?"

"Isn't it best to accept what can't be changed?"

"Philosophical for your age, aren't you?"

"How else am I going to get on?" The weight of the other's regard had grown oppressive, and Tradain turned his back on it, deliberately terminating the conversation. He'd wasted enough time. One more parsnip, and then he'd better get to work stripping those lorbers—

Too late.

Corporal Woenich had reappeared at the head of the stairs.

"Let's see what you've got done, Thirteen," the corporal directed.

He had gobbled vegetables, and gabbed with the gaffer. Beyond that—nothing. Tradain was mute.

"Well, Thirteen? I'm waiting."

No possible excuse, no possible escape. His heart accelerated. He wondered which of his bones the corporal would break.

"He hasn't so much as touched a single lorber, Corporal Woenich, sir," Fangs's eager little voice piped up.

Two-faced, troublemaking, mealy-mouthed old ruin. Treacherous, an informer, just as he'd suspected. Tradain's bitter contempt momentarily eclipsed fear.

"And that is all on my account," Fangs announced. "It was one of my attacks, you see, sir."

"What are you blathering about now, One Fifty-Seven?" the corporal demanded.

"You remember my attacks, don't you, Corporal Woenich? You know, when I—"

"I know all about your attacks, you sorry old shit. They're disgusting, and *you're* disgusting."

"You're absolutely right, Corporal."

"I hate that wheezing and hacking of yours, and I can't stand those stupid choking noises. Makes me sick to listen. And I really want to puke when you start spewing that red froth out of your mouth. Revolting. Next time you do that, I swear I'll stuff that scraggly beard of yours right down your throat."

"Yes, Corporal."

"I can't understand why you don't just lay down and *die*."

"Well, that's what I might have done, Corporal, if it hadn't been for young Number Thirteen, here. He saved my life, indeed he did."

"Remind me to thank him."

"Stayed right with me, all through it," Fangs explained. "Breathed his own air down into my lungs when I needed it, kept me going."

"You don't *look* like you've just been sick, One Fifty-Seven. You don't seem no uglier than usual."

"Thanks to this lad here, Corporal. So naturally, he's had no time for stripping lorbers."

"Naturally." Corporal Woenich surveyed Tradain microscopically. "This true?"

Tradain inclined his head.

"All right. No disciplinary action this time, I guess, but don't let it happen again. And if that lamebrained, wheezing geezer over there gets taken with another of his fits, Thirteen, you just go ahead and let him croak. Understand?"

Tradain nodded.

"You'd better. Another slip, and you don't get off so easy. Now get to work." Corporal Woenich exited.

Tradain studied his fellow prisoner, and wondered how he could have missed the intelligence in the rheumy old eyes.

"Thank you," he said, almost grudgingly.

Fangs waved a deprecating hand.

Tradain turned back to the bins, picked out a cluster of lorbers, sat down on the floor, and began stripping the dry pods from their woody stems. The work was easily performed one-handed; a good thing, in view of his present state. His injured left hand, swollen and throbbing, was useless.

He has already managed to damage himself, and will no doubt lose his left hand when it festers . . .

The Ferret might be right about that.

He looked down at his hand; raw, oozing, and painfully inflamed. *Nothing, compared to Father's wounds.* But nasty enough, and possibly dangerous. His imagination lighted on the prospect of amputation, and stuck there.

"Skeeks, my boy."

Tradain looked back over his shoulder.

"Skeeks," Fangs repeated. "Take a couple of small, young ones. Chew them, and apply the resulting pulp to your hurts. This will reduce pain and promote clean healing. It is an old remedy, but still good." Correctly interpreting the other's expression of skepticism, he added, "What harm in trying?"

Tradain jerked a visibly distrustful nod and remembered to mutter, "Thanks." He turned back to his work, and did not look away from it again. His hand ached and burned atrociously.

What harm in trying?

Selecting a skeek of modest dimensions, he proceeded to follow the old man's directions, binding the bitter masticated mass to his hand with a relatively clean strip of linen torn from his shirt. Within minutes, the soothing properties of the tuber manifested themselves, and the pain perceptibly diminished. Impossible to judge whether the skeek actually promoted healing, but for the moment at least, there was relief.

Tradain resumed his work with renewed vigor. His fingers flew, and the pile of stripped lorbers grew swiftly. He never glanced behind him, or even raised his head, but was at all times acutely conscious of his companion's constant, appraising regard.

⋐ ⋑

Hours passed, the root cellar dimmed, and Corporal Woenich returned to check progress. Tradain's output of stripped lorbers was pronounced satisfactory.

Of the wheezing geezer, Number One Fifty-Seven, little or nothing substantive was expected.

That evening, Tradain was permitted to eat with the other pols. Dinted tin bowl and wooden spoon in hand, he took his place at the end of the long line snaking through the mess hall. His politically objectionable confreres, he noted, were uniformly scrawny, docile, broken-spirited, and morose—at least, in appearance; a far cry indeed from the fearsome fels of Fangs's description.

The line inched forward, its progress—closely monitored by the presiding guards—devoid of incident. Upon reaching the counter at the rear of the room, Tradain received a ladleful each of gruel and vegetable mash. This treasure he bore to one of the eight long trestle tables running the length of the room, took his seat upon one of the benches of raw planking, and addressed the meal.

Clouded water washed down the savorless food. Bits of unidentifiable grit or sand peppered the vegetable mash. The mess hall was silent save for the sullen shuffle of feet, and the muted slurp of collective dejected ingestion. Conversation was prohibited, as Tradain discovered upon inquiring of his nearest neighbor, "Are there second helpings?"

The pol thus interrogated hunched lower over his bowl. An instant later a long truncheon hit the tabletop with a startling bang, missing Tradain's bandaged hand by an inch or so. Shocked, he stared up into the red face of an irate guard.

"No chatter in mess." The guard knocked the table a second time for emphasis, leaving a fresh white gouge in the dingy wood. "Got it?"

Tradain nodded, and the other lounged off. For at least a minute thereafter he sat motionlessly regarding the grey slop in the bowl before him. The spell broke, and he resumed eating, mechanically spooning the glutinous matter without seeing or tasting, until it was gone. He did not attempt communication again.

The whistle shrilled, an officer bawled out a command, and the pols, closely guarded, marched from the room. As his own file moved, Tradain grew conscious of a quiet thunder filling the corridor behind him, a curiously ominous rhythmic thud of synchronized footsteps, and he didn't turn to look behind him, but heard someone mutter, "*Fels.*"

They marched him back to his own cell, locked him in, and after that there was nothing to do in the dark but lie down and try to sleep. He had expected the pain in his hand, together with the black recollections in his head and the misery in his heart, to keep him wakeful, but he sank into slumber almost at once.

The Ferret woke him at dawn, and he returned to the kitchen, and thence to the root cellar, where Fangs lay, huffing and snorting gently in his sleep. He wondered then if Fangs didn't live in the cellar. Perhaps the wheezing geezer, deemed unfit for labor, merited neither a cell nor a place at the table. Maybe the old man lurked all but forgotten in the shadows, subsisting as best he could on illicit gleanings from the vegetable bins. Hard to imagine such a pitiable creature as a criminal of any variety, and briefly Tradain wondered at the nature of Fangs's original offense.

Not that he meant to inquire.

He took a couple of minutes to replace the dressing on his hand, then set to work on the lorbers. The pile of pods grew quickly—today, Corporal Woenich would have no cause to complain—but the mindless mechanical labor furnished little distraction, and his thoughts drifted uncontrollably in all the wrong directions. He was back in the dungeons of the Heart of Light—looking down again upon Radiance Square—back in the Boneworks, clutching a severed human limb; no banishing those visions, it seemed.

Behind him, the stertorous breathing gave way to high-pitched honks and snorts, followed by fits of phlegmy coughing. Fangs was awake.

The old man sat up, caught sight of Tradain, and tweetled brightly, "And a very good morning to you, my boy!"

Tradain nodded, without turning around.

"How's the hand today? Better?"

"Ummm."

"I knew it would be. Those skeeks never fail. Mark my words."

"Ummhmm."

"Well, perhaps I shouldn't say *never*. In the case of certain wounds and serious maladies, the skeeks alone will not suffice. Then, it is necessary to drink rainwater, fortified with crushed dungwort, a quantity of rust, fermented parsnip mash, and chopped brain of cat."

"Ugh."

"Ah, yes, I know it sounds unappetizing, but the benefits are extraordinary!"

"Ummm."

If he noticed his companion's lack of enthusiasm, Fangs showed no sign. Undiscouraged, he prattled on, and presently Tradain excluded the piping voice from his consciousness. He had no desire to offend, but the old man's tongue wagged far too freely, and he was too inquisitive for comfort.

And he watched too closely, and his interest was far too pronounced.

Eventually Fangs subsided, the monologue blurring to groaning snores as he resumed his interrupted slumbers. Tradain worked on mechanically. His fingers flew, and his mind smoldered.

The hours crawled. Periodically, Fangs awoke to chatter uselessly at his unresponsive companion. In between bouts of attempted conversation, he sat, gnarled hands clasped about bent knees, wheezing and watching.

The root cellar dimmed. The kitchen menials marched off to join their fellow pols in mess. The meal—identical to the previous evening's— concluded, and the prisoners returned to their respective lightless cages. Sleep came to end the day, and there was rest, then dawn, and the Ferret, and more of the same.

So he passed a week, and then another. So he might reasonably expect to pass the rest of his life.

The oozing burns on his left hand dried, hardened, and peeled. The new red scars would eventually fade to white. There would be no amputation, thanks to the old man and his advice, or perhaps in spite of them. The hand, strong and dexterous as it had ever been, could now be used for work of any sort, but the recovery seemed to go unnoticed. Having once consigned his unpromising charge to the lower kitchen depths, the Ferret evidently meant to leave him there.

Fangs was becoming harder to ignore. As the days stretched into dreary weeks, devoid of human contact with anything other than guards and all-but-voiceless pols, Tradain found himself increasingly tolerant of the old man's indefatigable amiability. Fangs's covert surveillance never flagged, but at least his conversation was sometimes diverting. Gradually Tradain's monosyllabic response expanded, and although never quite abandoning all suspicion, he began to thaw.

Then there came a dawn whose first light failed to find the Ferret at his cell door. The light strengthened, the sun rose through the morning mists, and still nobody came to shepherd him to the kitchen. Around midafternoon, there was a ripple of distant human voices, uplifted in rage, or fear, or both, accompanied by the pyrotechnical pop of irregular gunfire. Tradain, all but glued to his barred door, peered up and down the corridor, but saw nothing. Equally unrewarding was the view from the window.

Voices and gunfire ceased. Silence reigned.

Afternoon stretched into evening, the cell darkened, and still nobody came. There was no meal and Tradain's empty stomach growled. He could only assume that his fellow captives shared his plight, which was presumably connected in some way to the afternoon's mysterious unrest.

Curiosity, uneasiness, and hunger kept him wakeful well into the night. Sleep came at last, and then a morning like any other, with the Ferret there at his door—a Ferret who steadfastly refused to answer any questions concerning the recent disturbance.

"No concern of yours, Thirteen. As a kitchen drudge, stuck down there with all those feeble rejects, you don't need to know," the Ferret loftily quashed unseemly curiosity. "Of course, if only you'd proved yourself fit for any kind of *man's* work, with the grinders, say, then you'd probably be in a position to *find out*, now wouldn't you? But you just didn't have what it takes. Well, never mind," he added, more kindly. "Maybe in another year or two, when you're bigger. Don't give up, Thirteen. If you try hard, you might make it to those Boneworks yet."

Down in the kitchen, there was no information to be had, but when he reached the root cellar, his luck changed, for there sat Number One Fifty-Seven, garrulous as ever.

"Eh, but it is good to see you again, my boy," Fangs declared, between puffs and wheezes. "I have missed your company!"

Some company, Tradain thought, with the beginning of shame. He smiled, a little uncertainly, for it dawned upon him that he was actually glad to see the chatty old remnant. He must, he supposed, be getting desperate. Helping himself to a couple of turnips from the bin, he inquired, "Any idea what was going on around here yesterday?"

"Do they tell you nothing, child?" Fangs appeared astonished. "Did you not know that the fels rioted? Upon receiving the remains of one of their own recently deceased comrades, along with instructions to chop the corpse in preparation for the Boneworks, their finer sensibilities were offended, and they made their displeasure known. I am told that one of the guards was hacked to pieces—"

"Small loss. Who told you?"

"Eh? Oh, but the word spreads," Fangs returned vaguely. "It spreads. And the word is, one guard dead and ten fels killed by gunfire, before the rioters were subdued. There are busy days ahead in the Boneworks, my child, depend on it."

"Will there be punishment?"

"For the offending fels, certainly. The leaders of the uprising may expect death, or perhaps a descent to the dungeons, which is worse than death, I am told."

"Dungeons?"

"Black holes, at the bottom of the fortress. Those who enter there never again emerge to behold the light. There they live out their lives in darkness and solitude."

"I'm sorry for them."

"Your sentiments are shared by a number of fels, several of whom have already vowed to avenge their fallen leaders." In response to the other's look of inquiry, Fangs added, "Word spreads."

"So that's what it was about." Tradain picked out a lorber cluster and began to strip it. "I could hear the shouting and gunfire from my cell."

"And I could hear them here—so clear, so strong and loud. Furious voices, from long ago."

"What?"

"Eh, forgive me, my boy, you can't hope to understand. You must think me wandering in the head. Don't bother to deny it."

Tradain, obedient, didn't bother to deny it.

"But it is all very simple and sensible, really," Fangs continued. "Easy to see, if only you knew anything of my past. No doubt, my child, you've sometimes wondered how such a creature as I ever came to the kitchens of Fortress Nul?"

Here, Tradain perceived, his road forked. An affirmative reply granted the geezer license to commence some endless, rambling, pointless reminiscence. A negative rebuffed the only friendly overture the fortress had to offer. It was Fangs, or total isolation.

He returned a guarded nod.

"I knew it. You could not succeed in concealing your curiosity." The old man appeared gratified. "Listen, then. As I have already told you, I was born at the time of the great flood, which preceded by some four years the death of the sorcerer Yurune the Bloodless. You have heard of great Yurune?"

This reference was one that Tradain could recognize. His mind winged to the ruined mansion, the haunted mansion, the malevolent mansion, ringed in iron trees. He had been there—an age ago.

"You must be wrong," he said.

"How so, lad?"

"Yurune the Bloodless died over a century ago. If you were truly born four years before his death, that would make you—" Tradain calculated rapidly. "One hundred ten years old!"

"Well?"

"Well, that's impossible."

"It is?"

"Yes. Well, not quite. But very unlikely. Anyway," Tradain concluded lamely, "it's not easy to believe."

"I am sorry to hear that. My father, whose name was Rhunstadt and whose face I barely recall," Fangs serenely resumed his story, "was steward to the sorcerer Yurune. My mother was one of the kitchen maids. It was a mark of the signal favor my father enjoyed that he, a servant, was not only permitted marriage, but even accorded the luxury of his own private living quarters. The family occupied a one-room wooden cabin, a stone's throw distant from the main house.

"It was not without reason that Yurune held his steward in such high regard," Fangs continued. "For it was said that my father Rhunstadt served his master both as steward and as sorcerer's assistant. My father it was, I heard much later, who scoured the countryside in search of the various raw materials required in performance of Yurune's nameless ceremonies. My father who brought back the herbs and seeds, the minerals and oils, the lizards, cats, rats, corpses, babies, and adolescent virgins. My father who ground seeds to powder, mixed solutions, kindled fires, anatomized cadavers, slit throats, collected blood in bowls and vials. Was it any wonder that Yurune valued such a servant?"

"And your mother had no qualms?" Tradain stripped lorbers automatically, his attention fixed upon the tale so unexpectedly absorbing.

"I cannot say, my boy. I was far too young to take note of such things, and the memories are dim. I recall, however, that I spent my early days in the kitchen of Yurune's house, where my mother peeled vegetables, turned the spit, and scrubbed pots. I remember it as a warm place, with a fireplace that seemed as big as a house. My father sometimes visited us there, when he had a spare moment or two in the afternoon, and I only recall a very large man with a curling beard, who would pick me up and swing me about until I felt that I flew high above the world. Rhunstadt, whom the local folk feared and loathed, was kind to *us*, I believe."

"And did you ever see Yurune the Bloodless himself?" asked Tradain.

"Once or twice, I glimpsed a face I remember to this day—narrow, elongated, bony, and pale as foam. Not past the prime of life, but framed in long white hair—longer and whiter than mine is now—with deep-set, slanting eyes that shone red in the firelight. My father bowed and scraped before that face, and I believe it belonged to Yurune. I have sometimes thought, since then, that he could not have been truly bloodless—not when his eyes gleamed so red.

"Those days I recall as peaceful and contented," Fangs continued. "But of course, I had no inkling of the anger seething all about me. Before I had attained the age of four years, that anger exploded, and the furious citizens of Lis Folaze marched upon Yurune's mansion.

"They came at dawn." The old man shut his eyes, the better to view mental images. "But I was awakened before that by the sound of my mother's sobs. Then came my father's voice, hurried and urgent. I don't know what he said, but a single oil lamp was burning, and by that small light, I saw him give her something. Then, all of a sudden, he was beside my cot. He knelt a moment to kiss my brow, then rose and left the cabin. I was never to see him again.

"My mother wept on, and I, easily affected by such things, soon joined her. Outside, the sky began to lighten, and then I heard the voices—a rumble of approaching thunder, a jumble of shouts, hoots, and howls—similar to those we both heard yesterday, but louder, deeper, and far stronger. It echoes through my memory, even now."

The old man paused, hearkening to remembered cacophony, then went on, "You are a well-taught child, and you have probably read accounts of all that followed. The mansion was gutted, its defenders slaughtered. Rhunstadt the steward, an object of popular detestation second only to his master, died alongside Yurune the Bloodless.

"During this time, my mother and I cowered weeping in our cabin, which, for a time, escaped the notice of the invading horde by reason of its sheltering greenery. But this could not continue indefinitely. At last, when the mansion was in flames, and the scope of interest had broadened, they broke in to discover a tearful, terrified young kitchen maid clasping a trembling tot. I remember sweaty, soot-blackened faces—loud voices—anger—fists and steel—and menace, a sense of the most extreme and immediate danger. Young as I was, I felt that keenly, and remember it very clearly.

"Probably, we were skirting death. But my mother possessed a few weapons—her youth, her sex, her clear complexion, her tears, her child, her quick mind—and I think she must have used them all to best advantage. Most important, nobody knew her for the wife of Rhunstadt the steward.

"There was an exchange, fraught with fury on the one side, tremulous terror on the other. I do not remember what was spoken, but I am certain my mother pleaded her absolute innocence and ignorance.

"Whatever she said, she said well, for nobody harmed us, robbed us, or burned the roof above our heads. One of the invaders even patted her shoulder in consolation, before departing.

"And so, my mother, having preserved both our lives, was now obliged to sustain them. Before the smoke had fairly cleared from the ruins of Yurune's mansion, she carried me into the city of Lis Folaze, and there found employment in the scullery of one of the comparatively respectable taverns—The Barrel Stave, it was, in Cooper Street. I wonder if it is still standing?"

"I don't know. Never heard of it," Tradain told him.

"Well, I can only hope that it is not, for my mother's lot in that place was an unhappy one, plagued with cold, hunger, and frequent beatings. Adversity failed to quell her spirit, however. She was a woman of enterprising disposition, and before another year had passed, she had persuaded Uncle to place her in comfortable lodgings."

"Uncle?"

"One of The Barrel Stave's regular patrons—a gentleman of some years, rank, and considerable wealth, I believe. I never knew his true name, but was instructed to address him as 'Uncle.' He moved us into fine rooms in Litanist Lane, and thereafter, life was agreeable and comfortable. Uncle, a frequent visitor, was generous and indulgent, even going so far as to hire a tutor for me. Thus I learned to read, write, compose, and compute—arts I should never otherwise have acquired. I loved to read. I devoured every book and manuscript, all that I could find, and their contents reside yet, whole and perfect, within my memory. Perhaps I should have produced writings of my own, if only—but there is no point in dwelling on that.

"So the pleasant years passed, and I, in my youthful heedlessness, never perceived the storm clouds darkening our horizon. I was aware, as anyone short of an idiot must have been, that a judicial body known as the White Tribunal had been established shortly prior to Yurune's death. I also knew that the Tribunal, relentless foe of sorcerers and all things remotely sorcerous, daily waxed in power and influence. And yet, I failed to recognize the threat. Well, I was only a lad.

"I do not know how they discovered Mother's identity, after so many years. I can only surmise that some infernally vigilant soul had somehow recognized her as the widow of Yurune's notorious steward, and denounced her.

"They came in the middle of the night," Fangs recalled. "Agents of the White Tribunal. They arrested Mother, and me, and grabbed our landlord for good measure. Uncle was not present at the time and, as far as I know, was never implicated. Mother and the landlord faced the Tribunal, and were ultimately Disinfected. I myself, too young to face a capital charge, was conveyed to this prison. At the time, I was thirteen years old."

Tradain's fingers stilled themselves, and his face was perfectly blank. There was a paralyzing coldness inside him. Like himself, this old man had come to Fortress Nul at the age of thirteen. Nearly a century had passed since then, and Fangs was still here, still a prisoner, grubbing in the root cellar. He had never managed to escape—nobody escaped Fortress Nul. And Tradain beheld the shape of his own future, empty and endless, futile, and utterly hopeless.

He'd do better to kill himself.

How? Stab yourself with a sharpened parsnip?

Starvation? Too protracted. Rope? Rope. Tear his own garments into strips, twist them together, and then at night, in the solitude of his own cell, with its barred window, set high in the wall—

Fangs appeared unaware of the other's reaction to his chance revelation. Still caught up in his own tale, he continued, "My mother, as I have already mentioned, was a woman of resourceful character. Though taken quite by surprise upon the night of our arrest, she nonetheless contrived to transfer her dead husband's final gift to my possession, with instructions to guard it well. I have obeyed, and I keep it yet."

Lost in silent desperation, Tradain neglected the requisite polite queries.

Following a moment's pause, Fangs announced, "Here it is." One fleshless hand rose to brush an ancient, faded rag of a neckerchief. The scarf, frayed and threadbare in spots, was folded into a limp triangle, the two crossed ends of which passed through a flimsy tin ring, so small and patently worthless that no one had ever troubled to steal it.

"Ummm," Tradain returned absently.

"We're back to grunts, my boy?"

The old man wanted some sort of acknowledgment, and surely deserved no less. Tradain produced one not insincere. "Must be good to have a family keepsake."

"Yes, but this is rather more than a keepsake. You recall its origin?"

"You said that your father gave it to your mother, the night before Yurune's mansion was attacked."

"Can you think why he did so?"

"He knew he was going to die, and wanted his wife to have a memento?"

"Partly, perhaps, but such a man as Rhunstadt was never motivated by tender sentiment alone. He gave the scarf and ring to his wife because they were by far the most valuable items in his possession, and stolen, to boot—purloined from his master's workroom. They were worth a fortune, he reckoned, to anyone who could figure out how to use them—a feat he might have accomplished on his own, had he been granted the time. All this my mother told me, years later. Now, my child, you must be wondering what might be so remarkable about an old rag and a gimcrack little ring?"

Tradain nodded.

"Come over here and take a look." Sliding the ring off, Fangs drew the scarf from his neck. Weak light filtering in through the recessed window greyly illumined a patch of dirty floor, on which he carefully spread out his neckerchief. Upon it, he laid the ring. "Come now, you must take a close look."

Tradain obeyed. Kneeling beside his companion's property, he surveyed each article in turn. Neither was quite what he had thought at first glance. The scarf wasn't actually plain, but covered with some busy pattern all but invisibly worked into its weave. The little ring wasn't a simple band of tin, but rather a braiding of minute filaments, too numerous to count. They were silvery beneath a film of discoloration, their substance not readily identifiable. Interesting, but uninformative. He wondered then if the old man's tale contained a single particle of truth.

"You are puzzled, I see," Fangs observed with satisfaction. "I do not blame you. I myself should never have recognized the worth of these treasures, had not my mother enlightened me."

Enlightened. Tradain kept his face blank.

"Take another look at my neckerchief," Fangs directed. "That pattern woven into the fabric is more than decoration. It is a form of writing."

Tradain complied. "Doesn't look like any writing I ever saw," he reported.

"That is because it is in code—the personal code of Yurune the Bloodless."

"You know, your mother *could* have been wrong."

"But she was not, my boy, she was not. I know this because I have broken the code—I have had, as you may well imagine, many years in which to do so. The task required endless application, but I succeeded at last, and now I am quite able to read the message woven into that scarf, provided the light is good, and my eyes are not blurring the way they sometimes do."

"What is the message, then?" Tradain was skeptical, but intrigued. The old man might be loony, or a liar, or both, but he was capable of spinning a good yarn.

"It is a set of instructions, detailing the procedure wherein the power of the supradimension may be accessed and channeled by means of an extraplanar object such as this ring of mine."

"Supradimension? Extraplanar? What do you mean?"

"The scarf fails to furnish much background information. Here is the best I can make of it. There exist, it seems, countless dimensions beyond the realm of human perception—endless creases, wrinkles, folds, and knots in the huge fabric of being. One such plane of existence, contiguous to our own yet largely unrecognized, comprises a realm of light, heat, and innate potency almost inconceivable. So charged with natural force is this upper plane, this supradimension, that even the smallest shred of its substance embodies a power that we humans are wont to call magical. And as for the inhabitants—"

"Inhabitants!"

"Certainly, the supradimension is peopled with sentient beings, intelligent but very unlike ourselves, whose occasional manifestations upon our inferior plane are perceived as the visitations of supernatural entities—gods, demons, malevolences—call them what you will."

"You'd better not let anyone hear you talking like that, Fangs!" exclaimed Tradain, startled for a moment out of his recently developed defensive detachment.

"You are alarmed for me, my boy? That is kind. But there is hardly anyone likely to note the indiscretions of so ancient a relic as myself. At this point, who would care?"

"I'm telling you, you're going to get in trouble. You're talking about magic, you've got a dead sorcerer's things on you, and that's more than enough to land you in the cauldron—"

"Eh, but I am already bound for the cauldron in the Boneworks, and how much longer can it be, in the natural course of events, before I arrive?"

"D'you have to *hurry?* Don't you know that you could be overheard by Woenich or somebody? How can you even be sure that I won't report you?"

"I am quite certain you will not. I have been observing you closely for some time, now—"

"I've noticed. Why do you do that? What are you looking for, what do you want?"

"I will explain all shortly, child. The greatest of the human so-called sorcerers," Fangs resumed his discourse with a toothless smile, "are those who succeed in communicating directly with the supradimensional entities, somehow persuading these beings to bestow a quantity of that indescribable power—"

"In return for a sum of human life-essence," Tradain concluded, as if by rote.

"I don't know anything about human life-essence, my boy. I don't even know what that is. Nor do I know how to contact a malevolence—Xyleel, Ogorious, Jypheel, or any of these great ones—because the scarf does not instruct me. The information woven into its fabric relates specifically to the use of an alien artifact such as the ring."

"You're telling me that this little ring of yours actually came from some other dimension?"

"It would be more accurate to say, I think, that the ring is wrought of some substance originating elsewhere. That is the source of its innate power."

"Power. Well. It doesn't look so powerful to me, Fangs. If you don't mind my saying so, it looks pretty ordinary."

"Yes it does."

"Does it glow in the dark, or anything?"

"Not that I'm aware of."

"Have you ever gotten any results at all?"

"None."

"So your instructions don't work. Doesn't that tell you anything? It seems to me—"

"I cannot tell if the instructions work or not," Fangs explained mildly, "because I have never yet attempted to follow them."

"I don't blame you. Even if it's all a hoax, it could be dangerous even to—"

"Fear has not hindered me. There is a more tangible obstacle. In order to follow the procedure as described, it is necessary to wear the ring. Look." Fangs displayed both his hands, fingers spread wide, swollen knuckles vastly conspicuous. "You see? Following two decades of labor in the Boneworks, this affliction came upon me. By the time I had finished deciphering Yurune's code, it was no longer possible for me to force the ring beyond the first joint of my smallest finger."

"I see." Tradain stared for a moment, and then, without prompting, picked up the ring and slid it effortlessly over the middle finger of his thirteen-year-old right hand. There was nothing at all out of the ordinary in the feel of the thin metal against his skin—it might have been any commonplace, cheap little ornament. Perhaps it was. "And that's why you're telling me all of this, and that's why you've been watching me from the first."

"You've a sharp, quick mind, my boy, but you are only partially correct. It's your youth, you see—your extreme youth, and your sad plight. It is as if I beheld myself long ago, when I first came to this place—but a self with a chance, as I had not, to live a very different life, beyond these walls."

"Beyond—?"

"And perhaps, with your help, I myself may draw my final breath in freedom."

"Nobody escapes Fortress Nul, they say."

"Quite right. It would take nothing less than a miracle, or magic."

"And a plan."

"There is already a plan. I have had ample time to refine it."

"What can be done with this magic ring of yours?"

"Nothing at all, until you have received some instruction. And there is the question. You know well the penalty of sorcery, or complicity in sorcery. As things stand now, your life is comparatively safe. Miserable, but secure. Should you be caught dabbling in magic, the situation would alter. Are you willing to undertake such a risk?"

Tradain met the ancient eyes, which were not senile in the least, but watchful and steady.

"When do we begin?" he asked.

❧ ❧

"The difficulty has been resolved, Premier Jurist," the Governor declared. "The leaders of the riot are dead, or else isolated, and order has been restored."

"Indeed." Gnaus liGurvohl surveyed his visitor minutely. The Governor of Fortress Nul sustained the scrutiny unmoved. The Governor's composure was commendable, but his competence was open to some question, and his character demonstrably bad. "You have held your current position some five years now, I believe."

"That is correct, Premier Jurist."

"Are you aware that the incidence of unrest in the prison has doubled during your term in office?"

"That is scarcely surprising, Premier Jurist. The prison population has more than tripled."

"That is your excuse?"

"My explanation."

"It is inadequate."

"I regret the Premier Jurist's dissatisfaction."

"It is the dissatisfaction of Autonn that you may the more justly regret." LiGurvohl permitted himself a majestic frown that failed to shake the other's apparent assurance. The Governor demonstrated no awareness of his own shortcomings, no real remorse, and no hint of appropriate humility. Such arrogance merited swift retribution. "I am informed that the insurrection took your supposedly competent staff unawares. Justify the failure of your intelligence apparatus."

"The riot broke out spontaneously, and quite suddenly. There was no question of advance warning. Understand, Premier Jurist. The influx of political prisoners these past few years has taxed our resources to the limit. In and of themselves, the pols represent little threat. Most of them are harmless."

LiGurvohl's frown deepened. The Governor seemed not to realize the critical, even subversive, implications of his own remarks. He was, quite clearly, one of those morally myopic of mortals susceptible by nature to the influence of malevolence.

"The true felons are another matter altogether." Unconscious of his blunder, the Governor continued his naively presumptuous analysis. "They are by definition impatient of rule and restraint. When subjected to intolerable abuse, they will inevitably resist."

"Abuse?" liGurvohl inquired. "So you term the justice of man and Autonn?"

"The fels are unlikely to grasp abstract concepts of justice, Premier Jurist." As if at last cognizant of his own error, the Governor colored perceptibly. "They are underfed, underclothed, overworked, overcrowded, and generally victimized, *as they see it.*"

"You pity them?" LiGurvohl saw the other's face change, and knew that his visitor yet possessed the capacity to profit by instruction.

"I observe them," the Governor returned, quite steadily.

"And your observations inform you—?"

"That violent men, goaded beyond endurance, prove consistent and essentially predictable. Have you not formed similar conclusions, Premier Jurist?"

LiGurvohl's eyes shifted to the office window. From his vantage point, two thirds up the Heart of Light's great Pitchfork Tower, he could gaze out over the city of Lis Folaze, quiescent beneath its mantle of mist, but secretly seething with unrest, treachery, and potential rebellion. *Violent men, goaded beyond endurance . . .* The enemies of Autonn walked abroad in the land, their dark intent hidden from commonplace regard, but manifest by means of a hundred subtle signs and signals clearly visible to the Premier Jurist, whose eyes were never deceived. Sometimes liGurvohl himself almost marveled at the power of his own vision, which was capable of penetrating the most perfect disguise. One glance alone sufficed to reveal the truth concealing itself behind the fairest mask. The briefest inspection served to confirm innocence or guilt.

And guilt was everywhere. He saw it all about him, every day, gleaming from the depths of countless eyes; a vast malignity overspreading the city, the nation, the world of humanity. Sometimes it seemed that he was the only one to see it clearly. The sheer magnitude of the threat might have overwhelmed a lesser man; but Autonn in His wisdom had chosen to bestow the gift of extraordinary sight upon a mortal fit to bear the responsibility. The Premier Jurist Gnaus liGurvohl was neither afraid nor confused. The Premier Jurist knew how to deal with evil.

His gaze returned to the face of the visitor. A small man, not malicious, but unintelligent and misguided. Autonn's charity embraced such a man, even while recognizing the recipient's unworthiness. The Premier Jurist would do likewise, within limits.

"I perceive hope for you," he observed. "For I believe you capable of growth. Were it otherwise, I should now consign you to the power of others less merciful than myself."

The Governor of Fortress Nul assumed an appropriately receptive expression, the falsity of which was quite apparent to the eyes of Gnaus liGurvohl.

"Tell me," the Premier Jurist commanded, "how I shall deal with you. Consider well, and then you may deliver judgment upon yourself." Such judgment, babbled by the contrite, often proved severe as the harshest critic might desire.

Not this time, however.

The Governor of Fortress Nul pondered a moment, weighing alternatives. Then he raised his eyes to those of his host, and replied, "I condemn myself to a substantial increase in funding, that will enable me to administer the prison in accordance with the highest standards of efficiency and security."

Gnaus liGurvohl did not stoop to anger. He had hoped for better things, but Autonn willed otherwise, and now nothing remained but the mechanics of conclusion.

"You disappoint me. Your impertinence and levity demonstrate your unworthiness," the Premier Jurist informed his visitor. "You are unfit to rule the Fortress Nul."

"Truly, Premier Jurist." The Governor inclined his head. "The same might well be said of any man."

"Take heed of insolence, unlovely in the sight of Autonn," liGurvohl advised. "Henceforth, you are relieved of authority."

"Very well. I shall depart the fortress within twenty-four hours."

"By no means. The late unpleasantness left several vacancies within the ranks of the prison guards. You will remain to fill one such vacancy."

"I decline the position."

"The matter is not open to discussion."

The former Governor fell silent. Perhaps the reformation of his character had already commenced.

"May your downfall serve to instruct your successor," liGurvohl intoned. "May your example teach him where his duty lies, may it inspire him to govern with firm resolution."

The sense of absolute certainty suffused the Premier Jurist. Deep in his heart he sensed Autonn's approval.

Six

Tradain felt as if he had been reborn. Following the endless interlude of terror and despair, there were at last other things— mental stimulation, a shared goal, hope. Internal icescapes melted.

He quickly established a routine. Early each morning, upon reaching the root cellar, he would attack the lorbers, stripping clusters as fast as his fingers could fly, and accomplishing an ordinary lackadaisical day's work within the space of two or three hours. When he had produced a heap of loose pods high enough to satisfy Corporal Woenich's expectations, he was free to wake Fangs, who always lay curled in the corner, sleeping soundly—so soundly, so deeply, with ancient face so still and greyish-pale that sometimes Tradain thought him dead. Such an old, frail creature might easily die during the night, and then—without Fangs, and all that he offered—existence would be insupportable.

His own heart always quickened at the thought, and at such moments, he could barely force himself to approach the still figure, for fear of what he might find.

But Fangs always woke at the first light touch upon his shoulder, opening dim, moist eyes to inquire bemusedly, "Eh, my boy, is that you? Ready for some more misery?"

But it wasn't misery, quite the contrary. It was fresh mental air, food and drink for the brain and heart—it was all the satisfaction in the world.

At first, Fangs simply translated the coded content of the neckerchief, interpreting arcane terms and directions as best he could. After that, Tradain was instructed to memorize the translation, word for word, forward and backward, until he was capable of taking up the recitation upon the smallest of cues, and continuing on to the end without so much as a pause for breath.

But that was the easy part. For once the instructions had been memorized, then it was time to follow them.

Initially, Fangs thought to train his young associate to perform the various mental and physical exercises unaided, but quickly discovered the impracticality of this scheme. Tradain was intelligent, willing, diligent, and invariably unsuccessful. The cause of failure was not apparent, and Fangs puzzled over it at length, eventually concluding that the sorcerous procedures demanded a level of mental discipline, control, and general maturity beyond the reach of even the best of adolescent minds. His own aged brain functioned perfectly, but there remained the matter of that indispensable, unwearable ring.

Eventually, they hit upon a workable method of collaboration. Right middle finger magically ringed, Tradain would perform the sorcerous rites to the best of his abilities. Gnarled hands lightly pressing his apprentice's temples, Fangs simultaneously did likewise, linking his own seasoned mental qualities to the other's youthful energy and fire. At the start, their efforts were clumsy and ill-synchronized; the results, disappointing. Gradually, with practice and repetition, they learned to sense the commingling of their respective forces; learned how to strengthen the mental bond and, ultimately, how to use it.

The first time Tradain felt the tiny alien current of nameless power singing through him, the sensation was so unfamiliar, so astonishing and alarming, that instinctively he shied away from it, ripping himself free of Fangs's light clasp and breaking the physical contact that supported the mental bond. The current vanished at once, and he, torn between relief and regret, spent the next quarter hour apologizing.

They tried again, but found themselves unable to duplicate that first success for another full three days, at which time, their minds again synchronized, and the ring encircling Tradain's middle finger impossibly incandesced, its cold light chilling the root cellar. And there was more than light, there was the alien force surging through them again, far stronger than before, too great to hold or control. Power was overflowing their unaccustomed bodies, spilling from their brains to flood the cellar with wild energy, certain to draw the hysterical attention of the guards—

Which somehow it did not. The silent hurricane in the root cellar escaped the notice of the bored guard in the kitchen beyond.

Eventually it subsided, leaving them both exhausted, awed, and triumphant. Thereafter, they proceeded with caution and science, often reviewing the message of the scarf, gradually learning to shape and direct that bewildering torrent of energy summoned from—wherever.

There came a day—perhaps eight weeks later, perhaps ten, it was hard to keep track of time in Fortress Nul—when their combined sorcerous efforts at last affected physical reality. A fist-sized turnip, subjected to unremitting invisible assault, gave way suddenly, softening and spreading into a puddle of moistly malodorous muck. A succession of parsnips, skeeks, and lorbers followed, each surrendering more easily than the last. Presently, a stinking brown lake covered half the cellar floor.

Fangs and Tradain regarded the lake, and then each other. No words were uttered. Their forces merged, the ring glowed, and the muck swiftly dried, reducing itself to a fine layer of inoffensive dust.

Tradain broke contact abruptly. He was gasping and giddy, unsteady on his feet, his blood all but boiling with excitement. Slowly he let himself sink to his knees. Beside him slumped Fangs, similarly depleted and elated. For a time, the two of them rested.

Fangs finally lifted his white head, to inquire between wheezing puffs, "Did I tell you once that I have got a plan?"

Tradain nodded.

"Well, my boy, would you not like to know what we are going to do next?"

"Let's melt Sergeant Gultz."

"That is a thought. First, however, we must practice, we must better ourselves, we must acquire technique. And after that, we shall see."

❧ ❧

They practiced faithfully, and the passing days brought steady improvement. Slowly they gained in knowledge and confidence; learned to merge their mental forces with speed and assurance, learned to govern the power flowing into them by way of the ring, learned control and precision.

Finally, upon the afternoon that the two discovered themselves capable of magically melting, desiccating, chilling, or heating virtually any small object, organic or inorganic, situated within some ten feet or so of their sorcerously conjoined selves, Fangs judged the time ripe at last to initiate the plan. By then, Tradain knew all the details of a scheme almost childishly simple, but quite possibly effective. All they needed was courage, coolness, Yurune's ring, and a fair measure of luck.

It was the bleak but hopeful time of winter's slow submission to an upstart spring; an excellent season, for at no other time of the year were land and lake so thickly shrouded in the heavy fogs designed to facilitate escape and concealment.

"Tomorrow, then," Fangs decreed, at the tired end of a successful day. "Tomorrow."

Why not today, why not right now? Tradain repressed the query, to which the response was obvious: *Too late in the day. The corporal will come within the next quarter hour to drag me off to mess, and our escape would be noticed right away.* Too risky. Fangs was right. Aloud, he simply declared, "I'm ready."

"I too, my boy. More than ready, although for what, I am not quite sure."

"What do you mean?"

"Stop a moment and think. Assuming that tomorrow's attempt proves successful, what exactly do you intend to do with your freedom?"

"Anything I please. That's what freedom means, isn't it?"

"Not exactly, but let it pass. Could you perhaps be a little more specific? Where will you go, what will you do, how will you live?"

Tradain was silent. He had not, he realized, given the slightest thought to such mundane practical matters. His imagination had only carried him so far as the actual moment of liberation, beyond which shone indistinctly glorious prospects, never before subjected to close scrutiny. Where *could* he go? He would be a fugitive, a juvenile, and penniless. No family left, no friends, no help, no home, no means of livelihood, with the possible exception of—

Temporizing, he inquired of his companion, "What will *you* do?"

"I have not the faintest idea," the old man confessed. "I scarcely recall the outside world. No doubt it will seem foreign, cold, and frightening. Very likely, I shall ache for the peace and familiarity of my root cellar. Perhaps, knowing hunger, I'll recall the vegetable bins with longing."

"Well, you don't have to go if you don't want to, you know."

"If I do not, then you cannot. I might give you Yurune's ring, but it would be useless to you."

"Useless for now. But someday, if I keep practicing—"

"That's the spirit. But you will not have to wait, my boy, for we shall proceed according to the plan. Your talk of practice interests me, however. You are a clever lad, and it has doubtless occurred to you that the ring, if properly exploited, might very much ease our path in the cold outer world?"

Tradain nodded.

"Eh, but I thought so. And the implication is clear, is it not?"

Again, Tradain nodded.

"You would not find the burden of an old man's company too galling to endure?"

"I'd be glad of your company, Fangs." Almost to his own surprise, Tradain realized that he spoke the truth. Suddenly the prospect of liberty regained the allure that it had briefly lost. He would not face the world alone and destitute. There would be a friend, and there would be Yurune's ring to play with. Given that combination, all things were possible.

He owed a very great deal to Fangs, he finally perceived, and a tide of unexpected affection welled within, threatening to swamp his composure. He would wax sentimental, if he said anything more.

Corporal Woenich's arrival saved him. That evening, in the nearly silent mess hall, he downed his customary portion of gritty mash without tasting it. *Last time.* Returning to his own cell, he reclined upon the thin pallet and hardly felt the cold, the damp, or the swarming insects. *Last time.*

Sleep was slow in coming. For several hours, excitement and anticipation kept him wakeful. For a while he lay staring through the window at the moon, ghosted with haze, and blackly striped with iron bars. *Last time.* After tonight, no more bars.

His fancies softened insensibly into dreams. The next thing he knew, it was dawn, and the Ferret was at his door. His cell swirled with dense, white mist; the classic White Beast rushing in off the sea.

Excellent. Nobody could hope to chase escapees through such a fog.

Down to the root cellar, *last time*, and there was Fangs, seemingly asleep in the corner.

But Fangs was wide awake, Tradain saw clearly. It was evident, from the high set of his shoulders, to the overly careless placement of his hands.

How could Corporal Woenich be taken in by so obvious a deception? How could he himself have been so often deceived?

Woenich departed, probably not to return for hours. Fangs opened his eyes. A significant lift of tufted white brows elicited a responsive nod. The old man sat up, and then, with Tradain's assistance, rose laboriously to his feet. A moment later the ring was upon the boy's finger, and the gnarled old hands were resting upon the youthful temples. Fangs and Tradain spoke at some length, in perfect unison. The younger partner's practiced gestures, impressive though they appeared, counted for much less than the invisible mental contortions of his elder.

The ring glowed, and icy light concentrated itself about the bars of the single window, set just beneath the low ceiling of the partially subterranean root cellar. The radiance intensified, the iron bars quivered, and presently crumbled away to dust. The light drained from the air, and the sorcerous partners fell silent. Exhausted, Fangs swayed on his feet. Tradain wheeled quickly, in time to catch the other as he collapsed.

His own breath came hard and fast as he lowered the perilously frail form to the ground. For several moments Fangs lay there, spent and laboring for air. Gradually, the desperate gasps gave way to easier wheezes and honks. Opening his eyes, the old man made as if to rise.

"Easy," Tradain advised in the lowest of whispers.

"No time to waste, my boy." Refusing assistance, Fangs dragged himself to his feet. A fierce paroxysm of coughing bent him double, and for a moment he seemed poised on the verge of one of his fabled attacks. The fit passed. The old man straightened and made for the window. His companion followed.

"Give me a leg up, my boy," Fangs requested. "I cannot do it alone."

Could he do it at all? Not the time to wonder. Tradain furnished the necessary assistance, and Fangs scrambled from the cellar.

"Come, hurry." The whisper filtered down.

Tradain hoisted himself through the window, out into a fog-blinded little yard that seemed full of wavering ghosts. All about him hovered pale, billowing forms, whose restless presence might have roused fear, had he not recognized their true nature. Frequent surveillance in clearer weather had long since taught him that the enclosed yard in which he stood was often used for drying the freshly laundered bed linen of the Governor and his officers. A collection of clean, damp sheets stirred disquietingly in the breeze.

With his white hair, colorless flesh, and greyish rags, Fangs blended almost invisibly into the fog. As his companion emerged from the cellar, the old man moved off, and the mists swallowed him alive.

Almost blindly, Tradain followed, beating his way through the ranks of flapping sheets, and then the wall was towering before him, and there stood Fangs, quietly waiting.

The granite barrier, tall and spiked, theoretically composed a section of Fortress Nul's outer wall. Assuming this assessment correct, the barren ground of Oblivion Rock lay immediately beyond; an inhospitable expanse, nearly devoid of vegetation, sloping sharply down to meet the frigid waters of the lake.

No words were exchanged. Once more their collective efforts set Yurune's ring aglow, once more the alien power filled them, and now, perhaps under the influence of hope and excitement, their mastery increased by the moment; fortunately so, for the task before them was demanding.

Together they strained their minds, and one of the great granite blocks at the bottom of the wall reluctantly began to crumble.

It seemed a horribly lengthy process. Tradain could somehow sense the resistance of the stone—the grim refusal to yield to external force, the innate pride and obstinacy—that was, however resolute, no match for the extraplanar power of sorcery. He could sense, too, the inexorable erosion, the fine layers of rock dust sloughing off one after another, each layer a whisper thicker than the last, as the will of the granite slowly buckled.

It was taking too long. They were bound to be spotted. Alarm gnawed at the edges of his consciousness, threatening to undermine mental focus. He blocked it out as best he could, for the loss of concentration spelled certain failure.

Disintegrating the window bars had been child's play by comparison, and the battle seemed endless, but at last the granite was conquered, its stubborn substance reduced to a heap of powder. Behind that heap stood another block, at least as large as the first, and the work continued; faster, this time, but still intolerably protracted.

By the time the second block had disintegrated, both fledgling sorcerers were tottering. Pain shot through Tradain's skull, while the ring upon his finger alternately burned and froze. He opened his eyes to behold a low, narrow tunnel piercing the thickness of the fortress wall. A cold current of damp air, wafting clouds of powdered stone, rushed in through the opening. Instantly his sweat-soaked face was caked with granite dust.

"Go, go!" Fangs urged in a whisper.

"Can you manage?"

"Go!"

Dropping to the ground, Tradain wriggled agilely through the hole.

Close behind, he heard asthmatic puffing. Once clear of the little passage, he turned to extend a hand, which was immediately grasped. He pulled, and out slid Fangs, on his stomach.

Sitting up slowly, the old man gazed about in wonder not unmixed with disbelief. Tradain did likewise, for he saw at once that they had succeeded in penetrating the outer wall. They sat upon a bare and chilly patch of rocky soil. Behind them rose the great granite barrier, and behind that, the full crushing bulk of Fortress Nul. Before them spread terrain silent and nearly naked, its unforgiving contours softly veiled in fog.

There was little to be heard, beyond the creak of Fangs's breath, the sigh of the breeze, the occasional thin, disembodied cry of a bird. No sound escaped the confines of the fortress. No voices, no footsteps, no scrape of saw on bone, no bubbling of cauldron, no grating of grinders. The odors carried on the wind, however, suggested much. There seemed to be no guards about. Beyond doubt, sentries stood watch within the towers placed at regular intervals about the ramparts, but the White Beast was all but certain to thwart their vigilance.

Out. Tradain's sensations were almost painful. What must they be for Fangs, who had spent a lifetime entombed in the fortress? He cast a sidelong glance at his companion.

The old man answered the glance with a nod.

"Go," he wheezed, almost inaudibly.

"Do you need to rest? Can you—"

"Go, go!"

Tradain required no persuasion. Already, his normal thirteen-year-old level of energy had all but restored itself, and he was burning to move. Jumping to his feet, he helped the other to stand.

Fangs had not yet recovered from sorcerous exercise. His limbs shook, and he leaned heavily upon his companion. Together they made their halting way down a steep, stony slope, and as they advanced, the lapping of water reached their ears. Another few steps, and they stood upon the verge of Lake Oblivion. At their feet, the leaden waters rippled away, to merge indistinguishably with the fog.

And now it was back to work again, but this time it was bound to be easier than demolishing blocks of granite—anything would be easier than that.

"Ready, my boy?" The whisper almost lost itself in the mists.

"Yes, but are you? Maybe you'd better—"

"Let us begin. We *will* be off. Begin!"

The frail old hands closed on his temples. He heard Fangs's voice, uttering the words that cleared and readied the brain, and he joined his own voice, his own intelligence and will, and now he could feel the whole of his partner's exhaustion, and the gigantic determination overriding it.

Fortunately, water proved comparatively manipulable. In the chill temperatures of winter's end, it was not so very difficult to induce limited freezing.

An experienced, accomplished practitioner—a Yurune the Blood-less—might have frozen all of Lake Oblivion solid, almost at a word.

A pair of amateurs were obliged to content themselves with less.

The joint effort concluded, and Tradain's inner tingling signaled success. His companion's suddenly slack weight sagged against his back. His own head briefly swam, but the physical reactions were already growing easier to control. A flush of pride momentarily warmed him; misplaced pride.

Fangs did it, not you.

He opened his eyes to behold a lustrous spur of ice, no wider than a footpath, thrusting out from the shore to pierce the belly of the White Beast. No telling how long the path of ice would continue to exist; whether it would melt naturally over the course of hours, or flash out of being in the space of an instant. The time might be measured in minutes, or less.

Seizing Fangs's arm, he half dragged, half propelled the tottering ancient out onto the frozen spur.

He had assumed that the bridge spanned the entire distance from island to shore. They had not traveled two hundred slippery yards, however, before the abrupt termination of the path forced them to a halt. The lake waters rippled at their feet, and the far shore was nowhere in sight. Extension of the bridge demanded additional sorcerous effort, and he wondered if Fangs was up to the job.

The old man applied himself, the ring glowed, and a second glistening strip solidified before them; this one separated from the spur on which they stood by a distance of some three feet. Having paused long enough to recover himself, Tradain easily hopped the gap, then turned and stretched forth a hand to his companion.

"I do not think I can do it, my boy." Breathless and limp, Fangs barely managed to squeeze the words out.

"Take my hand." Tradain was almost surprised at the calmness and steadiness of his own voice, as if he were the adult, speaking to a child. "I'll pull you across."

This reassurance produced the desired effect. Fangs did as he was told and, an instant later, stood beside his partner upon a free-floating strip of ice that wobbled dangerously beneath their combined weight. A few long strides carried them to the end of the strip.

"We must do better." Fangs eyed their work regretfully. "Far better than this."

Tradain nodded. "How much time d'you think we have?"

At that moment the deep voice of a bell rolled out over the waters of Lake Oblivion. Both fugitives started.

"It is the alarm," Fangs answered the unspoken question. "Our flight has been discovered."

"How? Woenich doesn't stick his nose down into that root cellar from one end of the day to the other!"

"He sticks it upon occasion, and this is evidently one such. It would seem that our luck has gone bad."

"Quick, then. More ice."

"My boy, I fear such efforts are useless. We are still miles from shore, and our time has all but run out. Our trail is clear, even in this weather, and the guards will soon be upon us. Through no fault of our own, we have failed."

"They haven't got us yet. Come on, Fangs, *try!*"

"Yes. Indeed I will *try*, my very best. Very well, let us begin with a neutralization."

"Neutralization? What—"

"As we have practiced. You remember."

Fangs bowed his head. He spoke softly but clearly, and Tradain recognized the verbal sequence readily enough. He joined, and found the restoration of sorcerously disrupted natural order quick and inevitable as the return of a compressed spring to its original shape. Success twinged through him, and he opened his eyes in time to see the last of the melting ice spur behind them resume its original watery state.

The guards would not be so quick to follow them now.

"Good!" Tradain exclaimed in a whisper.

"Eh, but do not be too quick to judge," Fangs advised.

They stood upon a narrow, unstable island of artificially created ice. Behind them rose the ramparts and towers of Fortress Nul, scarcely visible through the dense fog. Before them, nothing but the White Beast, and the hope of land somewhere behind it. Beneath and all around them, the inhospitable waters of Lake Oblivion. The clang of the alarm bell filled the air, a sound to strike like a hammer upon the mind.

Tradain strained his eyes, without reward. All the world had shrunk to this small patch of ice.

"And now," Fangs decreed, "for our very best. Let us take a moment to ready ourselves, and then strive as never before."

It wasn't easy to achieve mental detachment, not with the tocsin battering at his nerves, but Tradain managed it and, within an instant of commencement, knew that his partner had done the same. Perhaps desperation sharpened both their minds, despite extreme fatigue. Perhaps the endless hours of practice were paying off. Whatever the reason, their combined powers had noticeably strengthened.

Tradain felt it at once, and the sense of new potency fired his blood. Reinvigorated, he focused his thoughts, and knew to the depths of his being that Fangs simultaneously did likewise.

The ring glowed, and the White Beast flinched from the light. Nothing existed but water, volition, and an alien power flooding in to fill the carefully crafted inner vacuum.

This time it was different, the alteration indefinable but keenly felt. His mind, linked to his partner's, and wildly charged with the power rushing in by way of the ring, infused itself throughout his physical surroundings, permeating matter to create a medium susceptible to the merest flicker of the will.

This, then, was what it meant to be a sorcerer. No wonder men risked their lives and more for it. He didn't need to open his eyes to know what they had accomplished. He felt to his core the new existence of an ice bridge stretching from their present position to the shore of the lake, well over two miles distant. He clearly caught the precariousness of the path—its term of existence was limited—but for now, the way was open.

Tradain's lids lifted, and he beheld the reality of his psychic vision. A cold white path arrowed off into the fog. Excitement and exultation conquered weariness. He took a single step forward, breaking contact with his partner, and the old man tumbled full length.

"Fangs." Stooping, Tradain spoke urgently. There was no response, and he shook the other's shoulder. "Fangs!"

"Eh?" Gazing up with vague, clouded eyes, the old man answered in the faintest of wheezes. "What is that noise? An alarm? Are those fels rioting again?"

"It's not for the fels, it's for us. They're coming for us, the bridge won't last, we've got to move. Get up."

"But I could not possibly."

"I'll help. Lean on me."

"Impossible, lad. I am all done in. Just go ahead without me."

"Will you get up, or do I carry you?"

"You have not the strength for that."

"I'll drag you, if I must. The ice is slick, you'll slide nicely."

"My boy, this is madness, I would only hinder you. The way is clear. You can reach the shore in a matter of minutes. Take the ring and the scarf, and go." Lifting shaky hands to the kerchief at his neck, Fangs tugged feebly at the knot.

"I'm going to try slinging you over my shoulder. Let's have your arm. It'll be easier if you stand up."

"Lad, this loyalty of yours is suicidal. It is noble and idiotic. I implore you—eh, very well!" The old man broke off as his companion laid hands upon him. "Enough, I will come."

Fangs rose with the other's assistance, and the two advanced at a halting pace. Tradain's feet itched to run; he restrained them.

The breeze prodded the White Beast, and a yellow gleam of light winked through the fog. The light struck on the bridge of ice, and a shout arose: "Over there!"

The light waxed, and the prow of a boat appeared. The small vessel, manned by six guards, glided toward them, and the command rang out, "Halt! Down on your knees!"

"Run, lad!" Fangs commanded.

Tradain obeyed as best he could, dragging his companion with him.

For a moment the old man hung back, struggling in vain to free himself, then broke into a reluctant limping trot.

"Leave me!" he begged.

A spattering of gunfire forestalled reply. One of the musket balls barely creased Tradain's upper arm. Another took Fangs full in the back, flinging him face down on the ice. Kneeling, Tradain gently turned the still form. The old man's eyes were still open.

"Told you," Fangs wheezed. "Poor child!"

"There'll be a doctor at the fortress," Tradain promised.

"I do not want one. I have achieved my freedom. As for yours— someday, I am certain, there will be another chance. Believe this, my boy." A slight shudder shook him, and he died.

Tradain felt the other's death as a curious sort of inner quake, rocking the foundation of the unseen, unknowable structure supported by their joint efforts. There was little time to analyze the sensation. No sooner had the last breath departed the old man's lungs than the power sustaining the frozen bridge failed. The ice melted in an instant, and Tradain plunged down into the frigid water of Lake Oblivion.

The sudden shock of the cold momentarily dulled his wits, but his body responded with instinctive thrashings that quickly carried him to the surface. Shaking the water and streaming black hair out of his eyes, he glanced around. The boat, not far away, was swiftly bearing down upon him. Its occupants were shouting, their words unintelligible and irrelevant.

Without thought or hesitation, he swam away, making for the distant shore. The guards rowed bellowing in his wake.

Over two miles to land. He didn't let himself think about what he was trying to do. He knew only that he wouldn't let himself be dragged back to prison. He would escape now, or die trying.

But the water was really fearfully cold—cold as the drowning tank at the bottom of the Heart of Light. Perhaps he was actually still there, still trapped in the glass cylinder with his father watching his futile struggles; the last several months the delirious dream of a dying mind.

The hail of musket balls pelting the water assured him otherwise. He dove, deep as he could drive himself. The shouting cut off, and he was alone in a silent, clouded universe.

Alone?

He thought to glimpse a long form, lean and supple as a snake, and serpentine too in its movement, sliding along the edge of his vision. He turned his head quickly, but the thing was gone, if indeed it had been there at all. His lungs were already complaining. He looked up, spied the dark bulk of the boat indenting the luminous sheet of grey above, and altered direction accordingly.

Surfacing briefly, he gulped air, and dove again, but not before they'd spotted him. More shouts and shots, and then he was again solitary in silence. And cold—it was extraordinarily cold.

He could stay warm if he kept moving. *For how long?* Arms and legs pumping vigorously, he worked his way along underwater, and always winding along the periphery of his vision was that slim, sinuous form. Only now, there was more than one, there were at least two, or perhaps more—it was difficult to be certain.

Back to the surface, a quick unobserved gulp of air, then down again, into the dim cold, and the subtle snaky companions that *were* real, and numerous, and territorial.

He recalled then Fangs's description of the Oblivion eels, whose bite killed memory. He'd be safe from the eels in the boat of the guards, but death would be better than that. He swam on.

Moments later a sharp pain lanced his ankle—nothing resembling the huge smash of a musket ball, more like the prick of a needle—and he knew at once what it was. But that was about the last thing he knew.

He briefly glimpsed the Oblivion eel whipping away through the water. His ankle throbbed and burned, its heat almost welcome in the midst of that underwater chill. In fact, it felt rather pleasant. His mind darkened within his head, his memories died—another agreeable sensation—and his thoughts narrowed to nothingness, or nearly so. There still remained, upon a lower level of awareness, the knowledge that something his lungs desperately craved might be found above, on the other side of that rippled grey brightness. He headed for the light. His head broke surface, and he drank air.

A little way from him, the six occupants of a small boat sat yelling. Their frenzy meant nothing to Tradain, who trod water, watching in dull, puzzled interest.

They spotted him, and the outcry increased. Tradain experienced some mild uneasiness, a confused sense that all was not entirely right. He even thought of retreat, but such considerations quickly lost themselves in the great blackness swamping his mind. He no longer remembered to pump his arms and legs. The necessity of keeping his head above water escaped him.

He—distantly conscious of some discomfort—was going under for the third time when the boat reached him, and a guard leaned over the side to grasp his collar. Some irresistible force drew him from the water, hauling him up into the boat. There he collapsed to the bottom, lying limp and still as a dead fish. Even then, all consciousness did not immediately desert him, and for a time, he still heard voices.

"Did we all see what I think we saw?"

A gloomy assenting murmur, and the final grim summation: *Sorcery.*

"Next thing you know, official investigation."

"Questions. Snooping. And then, you can lay odds—the Tribunal."

"Old Boil-the-Blood himself, in the flesh, and on our necks."

"Wanting to know how it happened. Who was involved."

"Who's for the cauldron."

"The whole lot of us, most like."

There was silence, until some canny soul at length inquired, "Well, but where's the proof, though? I'll tell you, my eyes have been wide open all morning, and I haven't seen nothing so far out of the ordinary. Will any of you say different?"

Quiet, thoughtful muttering filled the boat. None of the guards, it appeared, was willing to say different, but one of them observed, "That's well enough, but what about this soggy little squeaker here?"

"Trouble. If there was doings, he was in on 'em."

"Pah, he's just a kid, what could he know?"

"Enough to land us all in the soup."

"Not since those eels got him. He's wiped clean as a boiled bone."

"You want to take a chance on that? I say, we throw 'im back, while we still can. Somebody give me a hand. Here, what's this he's got? Jewelry?"

A deft hand drew the ring from Tradain's finger.

"Oho, what a prize." Some anonymous wit scaled dizzying heights of sarcasm.

"Ratshit."

"A real treasure. You can give it to your girlie, and you're sure to have your way."

"Give it to the fishies, you mean. Like so." There was a small splash as Yurune's ring disappeared into Lake Oblivion. "Now, we send the squeaker after his property."

"Wait," a new voice advised. "Stop and think. We've already lost one prisoner—the old whitepoll's gone to the bottom of the lake. You want to explain how we went and lost *two*?"

"Besides," chimed in a cheery, helpful voice, "if we leave him alone in a cold cell, chances are he'll just up and die natural, what with the eel bites, and the dip in freezing water, and all. Then there's no questions, and everybody's happy."

"Sounds good to me."

"And *I* still say it's taking chances."

Thereafter, Tradain lost track of the debate, for the voices were blurring and fading. He caught only one final, clear fragment of a remark, before consciousness lapsed altogether.

". . . Nothing for it but to get rid of him."

❱❲

The pacific element among the guards must have triumphed, for he woke to find himself in a very small, very dank stone compartment. His uncomprehending gaze traveled slowly over weeping walls, scarred oaken door, granite floor. Weak light filtered in through an iron grille set into the ceiling. The still, stale quality of the cold air told him that the window above opened upon interior space. The place was bare, save for a pile of straw, on which he lay.

He sat up. His garments were wet. Vaguely, he wondered how they had got that way. It was very curious. Perhaps some explanation lay outside the chamber. Rising with care, for he found himself unsteady, he lurched to the door and discovered it locked. He had no idea why. Perhaps an oversight? Persistent knocking and calling, however, drew no assistance, and at length he subsided, more puzzled than ever, but generally acquiescent.

The questions wheeling sluggishly through his mind troubled him a little. A thorough ransacking of his memory, however, furnished no answers. Quite the contrary; in place of recollection, there was only emptiness. He discovered then, to his mild surprise, that he had no idea at all who he was, where he was, how he had come to this place, or why.

Seven

"The morning's dispatches include a full account of last night's disturbance at Fortress Nul," Gnaus liGurvohl informed his twelve fellow jurists of the White Tribunal. "It would appear that a number of felons, dissatisfied with the condition of their straw bedding in the wake of the recent flood, seized four guards and barricaded themselves in the mess hall, refusing to emerge without the present Governor's written guarantee of assorted concessions. It is hardly necessary to observe that these demands were rejected, whereupon the prisoners cut the throat of a hostage. Shortly thereafter, the officers of the fortress stormed the mess hall. In the ensuing melee, the remaining hostages died, together with one additional guard, and ten prisoners. Order was restored shortly before dawn."

LiGurvohl's eyes ranged the conference table. The faces before him revealed little, but here and there he glimpsed faint traces of perturbation, even doubt; the first small indications of moral decay. The influence of malevolence gained foothold even here, within the very bastion of the White Tribunal. The weaker vessels among his subordinates required careful handling, and close attention. Furnished adequate guidance, most of them were probably salvageable. In two or three cases, however, he found himself forced to consider the possibility of irremediable blight.

Jurist Fenj liRohbstat, for example. Transparently uneasy, uncertain, full of doubt and feeble apprehension.

As if eager to confirm his superior's judgment, liRohbstat spoke up: "These riots increase in frequency and violence. It looks very ill. Perhaps the former Governor should be reinstated."

"Impossible." LiGurvohl turned the full battery of his eyes upon his misguided associate. "The former Governor numbered among the slain hostages."

"Unfortunate." LiRohbstat's gaze fell.

"There are complaints among the citizens," dourly observed the Jurist Ertzl Goorskort, another colleague of questionable moral solidity. "They are calling for an investigation. They are calling for reform."

"They?" liGurvohl inquired.

"The citizens," Goorskort persisted. "We have received written exhortation from the City Council. There has even been unofficial inquiry from the Dhreve's palace. When news of this latest incident reaches the public—"

"No such intelligence will reach commonplace ears," Gnaus liGurvohl informed him. "The release of this information, potentially so inflammatory of ignorant minds, could only be viewed as an act of irresponsibility verging upon a betrayal of the public trust. The ordinary citizen requires instruction, improvement, and firm discipline to mold his character. Above all, he requires simplicity, clarity, perfectly comprehensible standards and rules. We of the Tribunal serve to furnish these commodities."

Some members of the Tribunal so served. Others, of inferior clay, demonstrated a reprehensible irresolution. LiRohbstat. Goorskort. And now the shallow, inconsequential Jurist Ziv liDeinler was flaunting his folly.

"Perhaps the matter warrants investigation," liDeinler suggested. "Certain small favors or concessions, though insignificant in themselves, might go far toward pacifying the prisoners, ensuring future tranquillity, and silencing potential criticism."

Gnaus liGurvohl did not give way to anger. Such distracting passions scarcely befit the emissary and servant of Autonn. He paused a moment, allowing profound contempt to supplant unseemly emotion. When he spoke again, his rich tones conveyed little beyond mild wonder.

"My colleague's suggestion grieves me," he confessed, and saw the faces circling the conference table wipe themselves clean of expression. LiDeinler himself sat very still in his chair. "I am at once saddened and surprised to discover an attitude of appeasement manifesting itself among the members of the White Tribunal. Such complaisance is worse than weak. It is an affront to Autonn, and a mockery of His justice. These felons consigned to the Fortress Nul—these thieves, cutthroats, roisterers, and common criminals of every description—owe too great a debt to repay within the space of a thousand lifetimes. And yet, Autonn in His compassion has offered even these human dregs the hope of redemption. By means of their toil and suffering, they are privileged to atone for their past deeds. By dint of sacrifice and prolonged mortification, it is possible for the select few to win forgiveness. The concession upon demand of favors, ease, comfort— all that the light-minded might unthinkingly describe as *mercy*—gravely subverts this process. The grand design of Autonn is not to be altered by mortal hands, nor His will thwarted by small intellects devoid of comprehension. In the matter of the recent disturbances, our duty is clear. The ringleaders must be identified and chastised, suitably punitive measures imposed upon the general prison population, while the current Governor of the fortress must be encouraged to assert firmer and more visible authority, lest he suffer the fate of his predecessor. Such seeming severity, though doubtless abhorrent to the felons, surely constitutes the truest mercy. I trust we are all in agreement upon this matter."

There was no reply. The jurists, imperfections notwithstanding, remained capable of recognizing great truth when they heard it. Gnaus liGurvohl set the dispatch from Fortress Nul aside, and the discussion moved on to other topics.

Unhappily, amnesia proved impermanent. Some protective instinct told Tradain that he didn't want his memories back, but inexorably, they returned. It was a long and slow recovery, perhaps protracted by the victim's resistance. Before six months had passed, however, his mind was whole again, recollections mercilessly intact.

For a while those memories had filled his head. One in particular:

Dungeons?

Black holes, at the bottom of the fortress. Those who enter there never again emerge to behold the light . . .

But Fangs, lacking firsthand experience, hadn't gotten it quite right. The dungeons weren't black, at least not all of them. Tradain's own particular hole was distinctly grey throughout the daylight hours. He could see well enough to study and learn by heart the contours of each individual stone in each of the four surrounding walls. He could see well enough to count the square stone blocks that composed the floor, to study the patterns of rust discoloring the iron bars of the grille overhead, to plait the straw that was his bed into knots, wreaths, chains, figures of birds and beasts, and then to unplait them again. But there wasn't much else to do.

Those incorrigibles among pols and fels consigned to the dungeons were not expected to toil in the Boneworks, the kitchen, the laundry, or anywhere else. They were not, in fact, expected to depart their respective cages for any destination other than the cauldron. Perhaps the more contemplative of prisoners welcomed the opportunity to cultivate inner resources, but Tradain liMarchborg owned no such philosophy.

It took him a while to understand that all commerce with the outer world, and its human population, had ended. For weeks, he persistently sought contact; with the unseen owner of the hand that daily thrust his food and water into the cell, with invisible prisoners in neighboring compartments, or with the guards that he sometimes glimpsed through the grille, as they passed to and fro along the corridor overhead. His queries, pleas, observations, demands, and complaints went unacknowledged. His accusations, insults, challenges, imprecations, and wordless screams were similarly ignored. At last, sore of throat and hoarse of voice, he grew silent.

He had been well off in the root cellar, he belatedly realized. That sojourn, with its camaraderie and its shared sorcerous endeavors, began in his mind to take on the golden aura of an idyll. He'd had a purpose then, a definite goal, mental exercise—

As the clouds cleared from his memory, he discovered the coded message of Yurune's stolen scarf, still firmly embedded there. He remembered every word, and he remembered how it had felt to use them. Without the ring, or something like it, however, those words didn't do him a particle of good. And the recollection of that tremendous power, echoing through his mind and along his nerves, so intense that he could still feel it, but lost forever, was hardly the least of his torments.

The bridge of ice, stretching all the way to the far shore. That moment, when it was all so real—

Gone.

And now? He would go mad if he dwelt on the contrast. Or else, he would go mad staring at the walls. Distraction of some sort was essential, and another remembered remark of Fangs's suggested a source.

I devoured every book and manuscript, all that I could find, and their contents reside yet, whole and perfect, within my memory.

There were books and manuscripts, though neither whole nor perfect, residing within his own memory. He had never been a true scholar like Rav, but his tutors had found him apt enough, and he had absorbed a good deal. Now, with great effort and greater patience, he might reconstruct those volumes in their entirety, or nearly so; an intellectual exercise likely to hold his attention for weeks or months to come.

Thus, his awareness turned itself inward, and he wandered imaginary landscapes that soon came to seem more substantial and immediate than his actual surroundings. It was colorful, that interior world; filled with life, movement, incident, variety—the very antithesis of his reality. Presently, he was spending nearly all of his waking hours in that other place.

There were, of necessity, periodic returns to his dungeon. Grudgingly, he allocated a measure of time to eating, and to such physical exercise as his cramped quarters allowed. These functions concluding, he withdrew.

So occupied, he scarcely noted the monotonous miseries of incarceration. When he had reconstructed and lingeringly pondered the contents of every book, manuscript, pamphlet, circular, or broadside that he had ever read—when he had analyzed, chewed, and digested every syllable—when he had, in fact, explored to the limits of his knowledge and memory, then he was obliged to venture beyond, into the unbounded realm of his own imagination.

When he did that, he discovered a kind of liberty he had never known, even in the days before he had come to Fortress Nul. Now, he could do anything, travel anywhere, with anyone—even resurrect the dead if he chose (as he often did). He could reshape the world as he willed, alter the laws of nature to suit his pleasure or convenience, hop the airless reaches from star to star, roam the existing universe, or invent a new one of his own.

Had he enjoyed possession of Yurune's extraplanar artifact, he might now have found himself particularly well qualified to use it.

The wretched intervals of dungeon reality informed him of time's passage. His shoes, grown far too small, had all but disintegrated. His garments had gone entirely to rags. His matted hair and filthy fingernails were long, while a luxuriant black beard covered half his face. He had no idea when the facial hair had sprouted, but it must, he indifferently supposed, have grown for a considerable period to attain its present length. Years, perhaps. But time meant little.

Probably, his gaolers thought him mad, if indeed they thought about him at all. But his mind wasn't truly diseased; only, for the most part, elsewhere, and intensely active.

ತಿ ನಿ

To: Premier Jurist Gnaus liGurvohl, at the Heart of Light, in Lis Folaze
From: Corridor Colonel Claar Kreschl, Acting Governor, Fortress Nul

Premier Jurist:
I find it necessary at this time to report a recent incident resulting in several fatalities. As you are aware, last month's initiation of the weekly Fasting Day has occasioned some predictable petulance, especially among those prisoners classified as felons. There have been numerous complaints, protests, petty disruptions, and assorted expressions of resentment hardly worthy of the Tribunal's attention. As of yesterday afternoon, however, inmate resistance flared into open rebellion. There is some confusion regarding the exact sequence of events immediately preceding the confrontation, but the most accurate reconstruction possible at this time suggests—

Acting Governor Kreschl, discreetly known to his associates as the Ferret, paused frowning in midsentence. *There is some confusion . . . most accurate reconstruction possible . . .* The words displeased him. They seemed so vague, so irresolute, so downright feeble. He couldn't afford to appear weak in the eyes of the Premier Jurist Gnaus liGurvohl, not if he wanted to retain his present position. And he did want. Someday, Kreschl was determined, the descriptive "Acting" would vanish from his title, leaving him Governor in full, in fact, and in perpetuity.

Striking out the offensive final lines, the Ferret amended:

The sequence of events preceding the confrontation occurred as follows. At the commencement of the afternoon's Second Shift in the Boneworks, a currently unidentified felon laid down his scraper, declaring himself unfit for labor, owing to extreme malnutrition. The shift commander—one Captain Neivay Gultz, a seasoned officer of proven excellence—ordered the malingerer back to work. The felon's insubordination persisted, and Captain Gultz accordingly administered a sound thrashing with a truncheon—

Acting Governor Kreschl paused again. The last sentence, he feared, might convey the wrong impression. Crossing it out, he wrote instead:

and Captain Gultz was obliged to impose corporal discipline, during the course of which the culprit—evidently unsound of constitution—suffered a fatal attack or seizure of unknown nature.

The spontaneous demise of their comrade enraged the prisoners, who rose up in a body, to dispatch Captain Gultz with clubs and blades of their own manufacture.

The Ferret hesitated, then rewrote:

to dispatch Captain Gultz with his own truncheon, which they snatched from his very grasp. At this juncture, the remaining officers opened fire upon the rebels, none of whom survived the volley.

The prison has been locked down for the past twenty-four hours, and order has been restored. Nevertheless, angry passions continue to run high among the felons, and it is clear that the rebellious impulse has incompletely spent itself. Hostilities are all but certain to resume within the near future, unless the prisoners receive at least token satisfaction. The abolishment of the Fasting Day might well go far toward mollifying the felons—

"No. No." Kreschl spoke aloud. It was all wrong, disastrously wrong. *Mollifying the felons.* How could he—a professional, a man of parts—how could he possibly have conceived such a namby-pamby, groveling phrase? And how could he ever have considered committing such words to a missive intended for the eyes of the Premier Jurist?

Acting Governor Kreschl visualized those judicial eyes—pale, penetrating, powerful—and a distinctly physical qualm assailed him. He considered the fate of his three incompetent predecessors, and his distress deepened. Those previous Governors had failed the Premier Jurist, they had bungled miserably. They had deserved all that came to them, and he had never pitied them before. But now, for the first time, he began to see how easily it might happen.

It wouldn't happen to him, however. The Acting Governor Kreschl, a master diplomat, knew how to deal with the big boys.

His tactics did not include self-condemnatory revelations to his superiors.

Internal difficulties at Fortress Nul would sort themselves out, soon enough. Indeed, the worst was already past, and the aftershocks of the up-heaval were sure to subside quickly. No need to panic.

No need to trouble the Premier Jurist.

Acting Governor Kreschl crumpled the unfinished document into a tight ball, which he flung straight into the heart of the fire.

He was off wandering the luminescent depths of those vast violet jungles overspreading the ocean floor of an imaginary world, half a cosmos and half a dimension removed from the human sphere, when something called him back. Tradain was reluctant to leave, for the jungle rulers—sentient Densities, their huge substance compressed to moderate size by the incalculable weight of the sea above—were engaged in an epic dynastic struggle, its progress marked by mutual wholesale slaughter as well as stealthy depressurization, and he wished to view the outcome. The summons, however, was not to be ignored, and gradually the stone walls solidified around him.

He knew at once what had dragged him back from the marine jungles. It was the novel intimation of discord—the clamor of human voices, the echo of footsteps, the crackle of gunfire. He had not heard such sounds in—he had no idea how long. Attention fully engaged, he listened closely. Voices and footsteps advanced like a rushing storm. There were shots, screams, curses, and it occurred to him that the tedium of prison life was less perfect than he had hitherto believed.

Some cautious impulse drew him back into the darkest corner of his cage. Moments later a small contingent of guards arrived at the grille overhead. They paused briefly, and gunfire blasted down through the bars, lead balls flattening themselves upon the granite floor. Then they were gone, their voices and footsteps receding, presumably as far as the next cell, where there were more shots.

He did not believe that this was the end of it, and he was correct. Moments later a roaring tide of humanity swept the corridor. Ragged, wildly unkempt figures were streaming over his head—he could see a host of hurrying legs—but nobody stopped to help or harm him, and he could only guess that the insurgent prisoners—for that was what they had to be—remained unaware of his existence.

The fels were rioting again, as they had rioted—how long ago had it been? Years? Decades? They had failed then, and they would surely fail now. Death or increased severity of captivity was all the reward that their efforts would win them, and it was just as well that he himself was locked safely away from the useless conflict. He might better have remained submerged in the violet jungles of his mind.

So he sensibly assured himself, and yet somehow the blood was rushing through his veins, and his heart was pounding with an excitement almost painful. Stepping to the center of his cell, he gazed up through the grille, but saw nothing beyond a section of the barrel-vaulted ceiling directly above. The quality of illumination told him that several hours of daylight remained. He listened, caught the uninformative echo of distant shouting, and the faint clang of a far-off bell.

That was all of it, all that he would ever hear or know. He would never learn the fate of the rioters, or the details of their futile revolt, although he could probably guess with fair accuracy. The bell tolled yet; presently it would cease, and that would be the end.

His attention was fixed on the space overhead. The sudden scuffling at his door took him by surprise, and he swiveled to face the sound. His rations for the day had arrived hours earlier, and there was no reason for his gaoler to return; unless, of course, the infuriated guards of the fortress were conducting a punitive massacre of prisoners.

He heard the scrape of a sliding bolt, the squealing protest of rusty hinges, and then, as he watched in disbelief, the oaken door that had never once opened since the day of his arrival slowly swung wide.

Tattered figures clustered on the threshold. Prisoners, beyond doubt. Judging by their brawn, their vitality, and their collective air of resolute ferocity, he faced the legendary fels. Tradain regarded them in mute wonder. The fels, equally astounded, stared back.

"Autonn's pizzle," one of them blasphemed softly, in evident awe.

"Is it alive?" another inquired.

It seemed that something in his appearance startled them, but they rallied quickly, and someone informed him, "We're busting the box."

His expression must have communicated incomprehension, for the speaker translated, "We're breaking out. Understand?"

Out? Tradain was silent.

"Deaf," someone opined.

"Witless," another corrected.

"Look, we've no time."

"Any more boxed down here?"

"This is the last."

"You want out," the first speaker told Tradain, "follow us. Up to you." With that, the fels departed.

Out?

Tradain stood staring after them. He might have thought the entire incident one of the more bizarre products of an always fertile imagination, had not the door to his cell stood wide open. After a moment he stepped through it.

His liberators were already disappearing up a stairway that rose at the end of a short gallery. He followed, gradually increasing his pace from walk to run. As he went, the clang of the alarm bell grew louder, musket fire crackled, and the clamor of furious voices swelled.

The hall at the top of the stairs was alive with disorganized humanity; with prisoners hurrying in all directions, prisoners dully immobile, prisoners dancing and cavorting, guards fleeing, guards and prisoners fighting hand-to-hand. The group that Tradain followed was halfway along the corridor, its five members forming a compact unit, capable of forcing efficient passage through the mob. He caught up quickly, and followed blindly. The passageways were unknown to him, and he had no idea where his new companions were going.

Out.

They seemed to know exactly what they were doing. Down the corridor they jogged purposefully, around a bend, and into a wide, high-ceilinged granite gallery, broadening at its terminus into a foyer, with a heavy door standing miraculously agape.

No guards at the exit. And beyond the exit—daylight, which he had never expected to behold again. There was even a little weak sunshine. He blinked incredulously at sight of it.

Across the foyer and through the door they sped, out into one of the large, enclosed yards of the fortress, *fresh air*, and now for the first time Tradain recognized the magnitude of the riot. It was in fact a full-blown rebellion, of a scope and violence perhaps unequaled throughout the grim centuries of the prison's history.

Vaguely, he wondered what had set it off. A colorfully abominable atrocity? Or, more likely, had some minor commonplace unpleasantness somehow touched flame to measureless stores of psychic gunpowder?

The fels had the advantages of numbers and passion, while their keepers possessed superior weaponry and discipline. In the end the guards would inevitably triumph, but for the moment, the two forces seemed almost evenly matched. Fiercest of conflict raged before the great gate in the iron-spiked granite wall defining the northern boundary of the yard. A double line of uniformed marksmen stood ranged in front of the exit. The chances of breaking through were virtually nil, but scores of prisoners were certain to die trying.

Tradain's liberators would not be among them. With an assurance
suggestive of preparation, the five fels ducked around a corner of the building, and he, uncomprehending, trailed close behind them.

They had reached a small, quiet extension of the main courtyard,
ordinarily overseen by a sentry posted in the watch tower rearing itself above
the nearest section of the wall. Today, however, the sentry assisted his colleagues at the gate, and the watch tower stood empty.

Now what? The high wall offered no foothold. To Tradain, rusty of
practical intellect, the obstacle seemed literally insurmountable.

He might have spared himself the worry. His companions were prepared.

Reaching beneath his yellow-grey smock, one of the fels brought
forth a coil of homemade rope, equipped at one end with a loop and a
running knot. He took a moment to shake the coil loose, and then, hardly
troubling to aim, twirled the rope and threw. The flying loop caught on one
of the iron spikes crowning the wall, and the knot tightened. The rope-artist
gave the loose end an experimental tug, grunted his satisfaction, then braced
his feet against the wall and expertly ascended.

One after another, the others followed. Tradain was last to go, and
now he blessed the instinct that had led him to exercise sporadically within
the confines of his dungeon. Although he retained some strength, the challenge of the climb almost defeated him. His breath was coming in gasps
before he was halfway up, and it wasn't difficult to see why. The rags fell
away from his forearms, and he beheld skin greyish-pale as the gruel he had
lived on, stretched over limbs whose emaciation revealed every bone and
sinew.

Scarecrow.

As he neared the summit of the wall, a trio of prisoners pursued by a
brace of guards rounded the corner of the fortress to enter the courtyard
extension. Taking the situation in at a glance, the prisoners whooped and
made for the dangling rope.

A sharp curse escaped the largest of the fels. Bending down from his
perch to seize the laggard's wrist, he hauled Tradain to the top of the wall in
one mighty pull.

The two guards halted and took aim.

Quickly someone gathered up the rope, and howls of frustration rose
from the prisoners stranded below.

The guards fired, winging one of their targets. Tumbling headlong
from his perch, the victim crashed to the ground, where he twitched once
and lay still. The rope, loosed from his hand in midair, now hung down the
outer face of the wall.

Without hesitation, the surviving fels commenced an agile descent. Tradain, again last, let himself slide almost freely, friction singeing his palms as he went. By the time his feet hit the ground, his companions were already yards distant, loping wolflike toward—?

The boathouse.

He stood in the open air, miraculously free of prison walls, but there was no time to marvel, for the others were fast retreating and he could not afford to lose them. He followed them down the bare stony slope to the shore of the lake, and then westward along the shore, with the unbelievable late afternoon sunlight thrusting through the thin mists to warm his face, and the amazing fish-vegetation-freshwater scent of the strand strong in his nostrils; west as far as the quay, beside which rose the boathouse.

Guarded, of course. Even now, in the midst of a riot, or particularly now, the boathouse could not be left unprotected. A couple of sentries stood before the door, statuelike aspect belied by nervously shifting eyes. Their uneasy attention was fixed upon the fortress, whence issued the incessant peal of the alarm, underscored by shouts, screams, and gunfire.

Two rowboats and one good-sized lakeflier were moored at the dock. Both boats were directly observed by the sentries; both sentries, armed with muskets. Tradain's companions never faltered. In silence they crept on, cannily exploiting all the cover of terrain and quay. When they crouched within yards of their preoccupied prey, two of the fels reached under their rags to bring forth heavy-bladed, crudely wrought knives. Rising, they threw in soundless unison.

How in the world had they managed to secure or manufacture weapons? No time to marvel at the ingenuity. The knives flew straight and true, burying themselves in the flesh of the targets. One of the guards, pierced through the throat, fell and died without a sound. The other—spouting blood from a chest wound—struggled to lift his musket.

The fels rushed him. The sentry managed to squeeze off a useless shot, and then they were upon him. A quick stroke of a homemade knife ended the contest. Pausing long enough to reclaim their weapons, together with the muskets of the dead sentries, the fels hurried to the dock, there to commandeer one of the rowboats. Tradain followed. Briefly he wondered at their choice of vessels—the lakeflier was by far the swifter craft. And by far the more conspicuous, he realized.

Almost to his surprise, they permitted him a place in the boat. His move to man an oar was roughly blocked. He was, quite obviously, of no use to them.

They loosed the mooring line, and embarked. Fortress Nul receded, and soon the mists softened the outline of the granite towers. The shore lay less than three miles distant. They would reach it in under an hour. There was no sign of pursuit, no sign that their escape had been noted at all; although a brace of guards had spotted them upon the wall. No matter. The attention of the entire garrison was otherwise occupied at the moment, and would remain so for some time to come. Before the riot ended, the fugitives would be long gone.

The synchronized strokes of the oars produced a sound oddly tranquil and soothing. Tradain allowed his eyes to drop from the fortress to the leaden waters of Lake Oblivion. Memories stirred. Somewhere far below lay the remains of Fangs, who had given him so much hope, and, with dying breath, urged him not to let it go.

. . . *someday, I am certain, there will be another chance.*

Fangs had been right, after all.

Not far from the old man's bones must lie the stolen magical ring; near at hand, but forever lost. He had not thought of that ring in years. But now he remembered the heat of it upon his hand, remembered the power surging through him, and the sudden rush of desire was unexpected as it was poignant. Beyond doubt, the clouded waters of the lake inspired strange fancies.

He looked up and, to his surprise, saw a light flashing through the fog. It came from Fortress Nul, probably from the highest tower. And an unusually powerful beam it must have been, augmented with lenses and reflectors, to cut the mists so incisively.

His companions cursed among themselves.

"What is it?" asked Tradain, and his voice, unused for so many years, emerged peculiarly harsh and hesitant.

One of the fels threw him a startled glance, but answered readily enough, "Signal to Lakeside Station. Watch. Over there."

Tradain's eyes followed the pointing finger. Moments later an answering light blinked from the shore. Collective cursing intensified.

"Lakeside guards alerted," his informant observed morosely. "They'll loose the hawks."

Hawks?

Further explanation was neither offered nor requested.

Not twenty minutes later, the boat bumped land, and its five occupants stepped ashore. They stood upon a narrow, pebbled strand. A few yards distant rose the trees of the great forest girdling Lake Oblivion. Beyond the trees rose the hills, and beyond the hills, invisible from their present vantage point, lay the city of Lis Folaze. The angle of the sun bespoke late afternoon. High overhead, a dark form wheeled upon motionless wings.

"Hawk," someone remarked, with hostility.

The great bird circled once and sped north.

"That's it. We're spotted," declared the largest of the fels, who might, by reason of his size, his lush tattoos, and his authoritative air, have regarded himself as the group's natural leader. "Go for cover. Scatter. Give those birdballs a good run. And remember, scum—if we bump eyes in Lis F'laze, I don't know you."

Appreciative grunts greeted this sally. Without further exchange, the four fels dashed for the shelter of the trees. An instant later, all of them were gone.

Tradain stood stupidly staring after them, and then his rusty mind resumed activity. He was alone, and on his own. For the moment he was free, as he had never expected to be. The terrain was not unknown to him, for he had roamed it as a boy. *How long ago was that?* The forest offered concealment, of which he had best avail himself at once, for swift forms circled above. A contingent of hawks, dispatched from Lakeside Station, scoured the area. Safe to assume that the guards of the station followed their progress.

One of the birds sped straight toward him, and Tradain ran for the woods. Seconds later, he stood in cool, mold-scented shadow. The odors were indefinably aged. The leaves overhead were warm-tinted, and a brittle brown carpet crackled underfoot. Autumn.

There was no sign of his erstwhile companions. They had gone their separate ways, but the inference was that all converged upon Lis Folaze. He himself would rather do otherwise.

The alternative?

No food, no shelter, no money. No friend, no magical ring. *I can hide out in the woods, and I'll build a shelter, and I'll be a mysterious hermit, living on berries and rainwater*—someone, he couldn't remember who, had spoken such words to him, long ago. Ridiculous then, and ridiculous now. Starvation loomed as a perfectly real possibility. For the immediate present, there was no real choice but to seek the city.

His illusory sense of invisibility shattered as a hawk burst through the canopy of leaves, diving so low that he caught the yellow flash of predatory eyes. A hoarse cry split the air, and then the bird was gone again; but not, he suspected, for long. Soon it would lead its masters to him. Should he suffer the misfortune of surviving recapture, he would receive the traditional punishment—amputation of a foot. The severed member would return to Fortress Nul, along with its former owner, who would then perform upon it the usual labors of scraping, boiling, and grinding; a penalty at once edifying and economical.

He began to walk north toward the city, ever deeper into the broad band of forest circling the lake. As he went, the trees grew denser, the mists thickened, and the light dwindled, until it seemed that early night was falling. On he marched, and the fresh breeze rustled the fiery leaves, and the reality of his liberty slowly warmed his consciousness. With that awakening came fear, a sensation he had all but forgotten. For the first time in untold years, he had something to lose.

Somewhere to the west, not far away, he heard the sound of shouting, followed by gunfire. Someone screamed shrilly, and the volume of shouting rose.

One of the fugitive fels, it seemed, had been taken.

Angling away from the noise, Tradain increased his pace to a jog. The voices faded, the forest deepened, and for a time he imagined himself as isolated as he had ever been in the depths of a fortress dungeon. But this apparent solitude was soon blasted by renewed outcry, this time directly ahead.

The woods teemed with guards, who seemed to have anticipated their quarry's probable course. Should he arrow straight for the city, he would trip over his own pursuers. Only a circuitous route could bring him to Lis Folaze.

Off to the south, he heard gunfire, and jubilant cries. Another fel must have died, or worse. The fear whose feel he had almost forgotten expanded like smoke to fill his awakening mind.

He would, he decided, describe a long, wide curve through the woods, emerging east of Ziehn's Tooth, and thereafter paralleling the tortuous course of the Black Bourn across miles of lightly populated countryside.

Another fifteen minutes of jogging, however, and he was growing short of breath. Years of close confinement had eroded stamina, and fatigue now slowed him to a walk. No sooner had his pace slackened than a hawk plunged down through the trees, circled so close that its pinions brushed his hair, and shot off screaming into the shadows.

Within minutes, the bird would guide its masters to him, and he could only hope that he wouldn't be taken alive. Had he but carried a homemade knife of the sort manufactured by the fels, he'd know himself safe from recapture. But he did not, and the fear inside him sharpened to a terror that renewed his strength to run.

He might, with luck, evade his human pursuers, but he couldn't outdistance that hawk. The bird's natural prey, the hunted mice and rabbits, were wont to go to ground in time of trouble, and Tradain would willingly have followed that example. As he fled, his eyes roamed everywhere in search of undergrowth thick enough to hide him. At this season of the year, there was none.

Kill the hawk? How, and with what?

He paused long enough to take up a big fallen branch. Moments later the raptor reappeared. As it swooped in low over his head, he swung the makeshift club with all his strength. A minute tilt of the wings effortlessly carried the hawk to safety, and then it was gone, its harsh cries receding through the dim forest reaches.

Now he could hear the buzz of human voices, still distant, but far too close. Tossing the branch aside, he strove to widen the gap, and failed. His lungs labored, and his pace slackened. The voices drew nearer.

He wanted to drop to the ground and lie there. Instead, he dropped from a trot to a walk, and the voices closed in on him. The hawk returned, triumphant shrieks resounding, and it glided barely above his head, insolent inches out of reach.

His heart hammered, and his lungs burned. His desperate thoughts darkened, and it seemed that the world did the same. The tree trunks rising about him and the branches arching overhead appeared to possess the somber solidity of wrought iron. There was something familiar in those iron trees.

Beyond them, just beyond—

Memories itched beneath the fear.

The trees thinned out of existence, and he found himself standing at the edge of a broad, bowl-shaped clearing. He knew the spot, now. On some unrecognized level, he must have been seeking it all along.

His sense of dimming light had been real enough. The weak sun was setting, and the hazy sky was flushed with faint color. Before him, the ground clothed in pallid vegetation sloped sharply downward. At the bottom of the hollow, where the vapors pooled, the trees resumed, their black branches plucking at four spiral towers. Out of the mists rose the ruined mansion of Yurune the Bloodless, its turrets darkly outlined against the warm-tinted clouds.

Exactly as he remembered.

The old mansion was haunted, beyond doubt. He told himself they'd never dare follow him in.

Eight

Down the slope he hurried, and behind him
heard the cry of the hawk, but never turned
to look back. Through the iron trees to the
basalt stairway, then up the stairs and
through the broken remnant of a door, into
the entrance hall, where he paused, panting.
He could run no farther, and didn't need to,
for Yurune's mansion offered sanctuary.

Didn't it?

Tradain looked out through a fissure
in the door to spy a quintet of armed guards
advancing upon the house, their approach
reluctant but resolute.

No sanctuary here.

He stumbled backward, defeat filling
his mind. They had him, unless by some
good chance Yurune's mansion furnished
the ultimate escape route; a knife left lying

in the empty kitchen this past century and more—an awl—a shard of broken glass—anything.

There had been broken glass strewn about underfoot the last time he had come, he was sure of it. Somewhere farther on, deep inside the house—

Through the ravaged chambers stole Tradain, and the reddish sunset light bleeding in through disintegrating window shutters fell upon piles of ruined furniture, charred hangings, broken ornaments—all exactly as he remembered from long ago. In all these years, nothing had changed.

Presently he came to a windowless corridor, thrusting into the heart of the mansion, and there the light failed completely. For a moment he hesitated, then behind him heard the voices of his hunters echoing under the vaulted ceiling of the entrance hall, and that decided him. Placing one hand flat to the damp wall, and stretching the other off into the darkness before him, he groped on blindly.

It wasn't as difficult as he might have expected, for the image in his mind was vivid, as if engraved there yesterday. He'd had a candle, last time. He remembered the yellow light jumping, the shaky beams snagging on countless cobwebs. Blackened stones, skittering roaches, pattering rats. He could still see them all. Presumably, his pursuers could not. With any luck, the darkness would discourage them, and they'd wait for dawn to resume the hunt.

He paused to listen, and caught the distant vocal gabble, steadily approaching.

The corridor ended, and he found himself in an antechamber illumined only by the faintest of reddish beams struggling in through a skylight four stories above. He glimpsed three great archways, beyond which lay deep shadow, probably cloaking galleries and stairways. At the far end of the room, a tattered hanging had been pushed aside to reveal a small door in the wall. The door stood wide open, as he himself had left it. Behind it— invisible at present, but well remembered—a flight of stairs descended.

He hadn't made it down those stairs, upon that last day of freedom. Young Glennian liTarngrav (*What became of the poor little brat, after her father's execution?*) had interrupted him.

But he had promised the house that he would return.

Crossing the antechamber, he stepped over the threshold, then turned to pull the tapestry into place behind him. A few grey spots were visible through rents in the heavy fabric, and he tweaked the hanging until the spots vanished. Once again, the darkness surrounding him was absolute.

He felt for the door, found it, and quietly closed it. Further manual exploration revealed the presence of a substantial bolt. As silently as possible, he slid it home. Motionless and blind, he stood straining his ears.

Voices. Footsteps. The guards from Lakeside Station had made it through the corridor. They stood in the antechamber, debating audibly. Soon the party split, and he heard the voices receding in two directions. Their willingness to continue the search suggested the presence of lanterns. Unfortunate. Obviously, they did not yet suspect the existence of the door behind the tapestry.

But they'll find it, eventually.

Take the opportunity to steal softly back along the stygian corridor, through the front door, out of the mansion, and back to the dubious shelter of the woods?

No good. Surely they'd have posted a sentry at the exit.

Rush the sentry? And get shot for his pains? Worse yet—the shot might not kill him.

In any case, he still wondered what lay at the bottom of those stairs. The place somehow exuded significance.

Down the stairs he cautiously felt his way, in hope of discovering— A *way out?* Unlikely. Otherwise, Yurune the Bloodless himself might have used it, a century ago.

A knife?

Down, down, into black nothingness, until he missed a step and stumbled at the bottom. A couple of sightless paces forward, and his outstretched hands encountered a stone wall. Another wall to the right of him. Only one direction to go.

He felt his way left, pushing every sense, to little avail. He heard nothing beyond the labored intake of his own breath, and that was good, for he dreaded above all else to catch the mutter of voices at the locked door above. He saw nothing, tasted nothing, smelled nothing beyond mildew. Felt nothing other than humid, chilly air upon his flesh, flat floor beneath his feet, and moist stone under his hands. Devoid of information, he inched along as far as another corner, where he was forced into another left turn, and then his outstretched hands were suddenly prickling with splinters.

A vertical wooden surface. *Door?* His fingers found the latch. He lifted, pushed, and the door gave way. He felt it swing open, and he stumbled through into a colder, deeper void.

Or so he thought for a moment, and then it changed.

His entrance must have triggered some device of Yurune's, for the air went subtly azure. At first he thought his deprived senses were taking their revenge upon his mind, then recognized his error, for the faint blue light radiating from floor, walls, and ceiling was eerie but unmistakably real. Shrinking back from that unnatural glow, he briefly contemplated flight.

Where?

He looked around him, and wonder eclipsed even terror.

That long-ago invading mob had never found its way down to Yurune's workroom. Here, everything remained intact, undisturbed, perfect as an undiscovered tomb; which, in a sense, it was.

All was as Yurune had left it. Shelves full of weirdly laden jars, bowls, sacks, bottles, devices of nameless function, forbidden books, burners, petrifactions, aetheric conflations, and artifacts—wagonloads full of illegality. What would the White Tribunal have made of all this? The crime exceeded ordinary expression. Words might have failed the Premier Jurist himself. It was almost amusing to consider.

Tradain's eyes swept the space before him, drinking perversion. His rudimentary comprehension of all that he viewed shocked him stupid for a moment or two, and then his mind came back to life. This, he saw at a glance, was all that the best imagination could conceive of magic, and more; this, in short, was the real thing.

A second glance informed him that the workroom was windowless, and furnished with but a single door.

The blue light didn't glow equally everywhere, but concentrated itself here and there. The significance, if any, of the favored sites was unclear. Instinctively he sought the brightest patch, and found himself hovering over a small iron cage containing a single, moldering folio volume.

The cage was secured with a heavy lock, but a single hand could slide between the bars to touch or turn the pages of the book. He did so, tentatively running one finger down a column of numbers and pictographs, still clear, sharp, and black as the day they were penned. The entries meant nothing to him, but something akin to a mild electric shock tingled his finger at touch of the paper and ink—a sensation not unpleasant. He turned a couple of pages to discover more numbers, more pictographs, all unintelligible, but reeking of arcane power.

A few pages later, the columns of figures gave way to lines of symbols, and comprehension dawned. He found that he could read the symbols easily—read them because they were identical to the figures woven into Fangs's scarf. He had learned that code years ago, and still remembered it well. Astonishing how Yurune's secret language had impressed itself upon his brain; it was all still there, perfectly intact.

He read attentively, and the nature of the folio's evident distinction soon disclosed itself. The passage he perused explained, in some detail, the various forms of communication possible between the mundane sphere of humanity and the radiant supradimension. The highest and most intense form of communication, it seemed, involved direct contact between human investigator and alien awareness.

Tradain found this comprehensible. He had absorbed the relevant concepts long ago.

The greatest of the human so-called sorcerers are those who succeed in communicating directly with the supradimensional entities, somehow persuading these beings to bestow a quantity of that indescribable power—

Fangs's words and voice, still with him. The old man hadn't known how to scale such heights, for his scarf hadn't instructed him. The folio, however, explained exactly how to do it.

Precision notwithstanding, the instructions would have meant nothing, had he not studied, practiced, and developed certain mental techniques years earlier. As it was, the procedure seemed in many respects familiar—a kind of elaboration of the method whereby he and Fangs together had channeled extradimensional power by way of an alien ring.

Now, no ring or similarly exotic appurtenance was required. According to Yurune's records, the sorcerer seeking the favor of a malevolence relied upon his trained intellect alone.

The feat demanded strength and flexibility of mind, combined with extraordinary powers of concentration. He had cultivated those qualities long ago, under Fangs's guidance. Years of solitary confinement had strengthened and refined them. Now, he fully believed, he would find himself capable of following Yurune's instructions, should he choose to try.

And really, he owed himself the opportunity. His connection to a supposed sorcerer had blasted his young life. At that price, he deserved compensation. He could scratch the itch of curiosity, and should his efforts prove successful, he might even elude his hunters.

Moreover, there was that memory. That long-ago moment of sorcerous mastery—a sensation like no other in the world. He would never forget.

His lips were already shaping silent arcane syllables. His mind almost automatically commenced self-preparation.

Yurune the Bloodless would probably have swallowed some sort of intellect-enhancing potion before commencing the rite. Tradain enjoyed no such artificial support; he would have to depend upon the natural stimulus of desperation to galvanize his mind. Eyes fixed on the pages before him, he began to speak.

The world receded, and time suspended itself. His awareness drew in upon itself, contracting to a single, white-hot point; so small, so powerfully agile, that it might succeed in threading a path through the maze of invisibly minute cracks riddling the barrier between dimensions.

An aspirant insufficiently strong and focused, or perhaps simply unlucky, might lose his way in that maze. His consciousness could roam the dimensional interstices forever, while his body remained inert and tenantless upon the mundane plane. Eventually, the physical body would die, and the marooned human intelligence, doomed to eternal isolation and madness, would turn its fury outward, preying murderously upon its fellow wanderers.

Yurune's posthumous warning might have daunted Tradain, had not the essential level of concentration automatically excluded all misgivings; excluded virtually everything, in fact, beyond distilled intention.

He knew upon some level that he passed through a shadowed boundary realm, but he scarcely noted, much less feared it, for all that he was had fixed itself upon the space beyond. The darkness slid away from him, metaphysical reality wrenched itself into a new shape, and he knew that he had reached another place, wherein a call might make itself heard. A call to— *Xyleel.* The name inscribed in Yurune's folio was with him yet.

Xyleel.

An entity, an intelligence, a great power. A malevolence. Perhaps the greatest of Them all.

His little human salutation and summons flew forth into the void, no doubt to lose itself there. Insofar as his intense preoccupation permitted expectation of any sort, he did not expect response; and there was none. Eternity ensued, and he called again, launching an insect buzz into infinity.

His unaccustomed mind could not long sustain total focus. The natural stirrings of his body called out to his straying consciousness, and the fear of permanent division rocked his concentration. The way back was filled with a thousand twists and turns. He couldn't hope to remember them all, he was sure to lose himself in the labyrinth—

Which, abruptly, ceased to exist. A great light was dawning, an insupportable radiance born of vacancy, and the interdimensional barrier gave way before it. Masses of shadowy substance seemed to vaporize, opening a broad, clear path back to humanity's plane. Alarmed, Tradain fled before the light, consciousness seeking the supposed refuge of his motionless body.

Home again. And whole again.

He opened his eyes. He stood in the workroom of Yurune the Bloodless, before the iron cage containing the most precious of folios. The subtle blue glow illuminating the chamber expired in the presence of the huge radiance crashing in from the other place. He had not escaped It. The— *what?*—the Entity had followed him back.

That was what he had sought, wasn't it?

He was trembling. Almost he ran for the exit, then remembered the Lakeside Station guardsmen hunting through the mansion, and restrained himself. There was nowhere to go.

The light waxed. Formless waves pouring into Yurune's workroom began to resolve themselves into a single, dazzling form—too brilliant for human eyes, too alien for human minds. Too vast for Yurune's workroom to contain, and yet, somehow, it did. The substance of the Other, transcending the limitations of natural law, seemed capable of altering worldly space, time, energy, and matter, as required. The resulting distortions all but confounded human perception.

It was coming straight at him, and he was trapped. Nothing to do but stand and confront the thing that he had called. Curiosity ripped through the fabric of fear. Narrowing his eyes against the light, he surveyed the visitor.

Impossible to take It in. The Entity was inconceivably foreign, and changeable as well, Its impossible contours shifting and reshaping themselves by the moment, each transformation more bewildering than the last. He might safely have described the malevolence Xyleel as vast, radiant, profoundly alien. Beyond that, there were no words.

Literally, no words. No sound of any sort, not so much as the hiss of terrified mundane atmosphere. Xyleel was uncannily silent, but not altogether uncommunicative.

Tradain felt extrinsic awareness impinging upon his own; a sensation almost intolerable to the uninitiated. Instinct urged him to slam shut the doors of his mind, guarding his essential self against invasion, but training suggested an altogether different course. Resisting every natural impulse, he closed his eyes, flung wide the doors, and invited the stranger in.

Icy brilliance filled him, laying bare each mental recess, sifting through his thoughts and memories, stabbing deep into the unmapped regions underlying sentience, and it took every iota of self-control at his command to endure the violation without struggle. Simultaneously, he experienced the workings of the other's intelligence; an intellect powerful and ancient beyond reckoning, but utterly unlike his own. Meaningless images—visual gibberish—flashed upon his consciousness. He thought he smelled the stars, and he thought he tasted time, and he thought he heard black lilies drinking midnight. Strong emotion shook him to the core, but he couldn't identify the feeling, which did not relate to any known human sensation. Numberless voices spoke in his head, swelling to a chorus, and their owners' identities merged with his own.

Beyond these lunatic fancies, born of a human brain's efforts to interpret data deriving from inhuman senses, he caught the intimation of gigantic light. This entity Xyleel, whatever He was, came from a place of light, was born of light, made of light, and sustained by light.

To Xyleel, humanity's inferior plane was a place of darkness, gross squalor, and filth.

Exile.

So much came through clearly, but it was not enough. He opened himself freely, and the images came flooding in; brilliant, disturbing, mystifying. He could make no sense of them. He and the malevolence shared the closest mental bond he had ever experienced, and yet communication was almost nil.

"Help me." Tradain spoke aloud, through force of habit. "Great Xyleel, I implore you."

No reply. A kind of ripple in the coldness occupying his center suggested that the words had been heard. No suggestion of comprehension, however.

"I am hunted. I am trapped here. Help me to escape."

Not so much as a ripple, this time.

"Hear me, Xyleel."

Nothing.

"Hear me!"

Another minute quiver of sentience from the malevolence, and still no indication of understanding, much less interest. But the images filling his mind altered, and he beheld illimitable lucent reaches, veiled in triple lambent atmospheres that pulsed and revolved in a never-ending dance. And sometimes, where the differing atmospheres met and contended, the luminosity intensified, and color unknown to human eyes distilled itself to tangible substance.

Another time, such visions might have roused Tradain's curiosity, but not now. The malevolence, lost in His own reveries, seemed inattentive to human importuning, even unaware.

"Xyleel!" His mounting desperation found voice in a shout. Drawing a deep breath, Tradain paused to compose himself. Yammering would not help him. What would Yurune the Bloodless have done?

The alien consciousness resided within him, for now. No telling how long it would remain. Inwardly, then, he must direct his thoughts and pleas.

His next attempted communication was silent. Focusing with all the intensity he had brought to bear upon his interdimensional assault, he plunged into his own mind. This time, eschewing words in favor of pictures, he painted his thoughts in colors whose glaring urgency finally drew notice.

?

A wordless inquiry. The malevolence's dispassionate curiosity twitched within.

It was, unmistakably, a direct if uncanny response to his own offering, and astonishment threatened for a moment to break his concentration. Collecting himself, he repeated his mute plea.

Xyleel understood him, but there was no reply.

He suffered through protracted silence, during which the alien consciousness, volunteering nothing of its own, leisurely surveyed his recollections of the flight from Fortress Nul.

A hint of intention radiated from the other, and it came to Tradain that Xyleel conformed to legend in one respect at least. He was willing, in some form or manner, to deal with humans.

There was nothing in the world He might not bestow—should He choose.

. . . somehow persuading these beings to bestow a quantity of that indescribable power—

Persuade how? Tradain considered. He had pleaded abjectly, for freedom or death, to little apparent effect. What beyond his own desperation had he to offer?

Yourself.

For the first time, the intellect of Xyleel communicated verbally. The deep silence shrouding Yurune's workroom remained unbroken, but the voice that echoed within Tradain liMarchborg's head might have issued from the unimaginable heart of a sun. All power and knowledge resided there, and yet the voice was almost halting, as if the constraint of discrete words burdened full expression.

Tradain's heart jumped, and his focus flagged, but it no longer mattered. Xyleel's attention was engaged, and contact would persist until He chose to end it. His confusion must have communicated itself, for the voice spoke again.

Proffer yourself unto Me, of your own free will. In exchange, I grant mastery of this plane's substance.

The hairs rose at the back of his neck, but Tradain inquired evenly and aloud, "What mastery?"

The powers belonging to those known as sorcerers.

The words ceased, and images resumed. Tradain beheld the nature of the force men called magical—witnessed the miraculous strength of it, recognized for the first time the manner in which extraordinary quantities of energy, originating upon another level of cosmic totality, might be used to rule physical reality upon mankind's plane; even to the extent of ordering the succession of tiny internal collisions that govern human perceptions, choices, and actions. A truly accomplished sorcerer might dance his fellow mortals like marionettes, provided his resolve remained unshaken by troublesome moral qualms.

But the sorcerous power was far from infinite. It was, in fact, not only limited in quantity, but inexorably reduced by expenditure. Each so-called magical act carried its own price in power, that price determined by the character of the act. With use, all magical power must eventually exhaust itself; a conclusion unavoidable by any means other than sorcerous abstinence, for the one feat that the power could never, under any circumstances, accomplish was self-renewal.

And when it was all used up? When repeated outlay at last reduced the magical capital to nothing?

Then you are Mine.

Once more, the words rang through his mind, the refulgent voice illumined the blackest interior corners, and he shuddered uncontrollably, but managed to ask the obvious.

"And if I never use all of the power?"

Your small span of existence upon this lower plane is doomed by its nature to brevity. When it concludes, you are Mine.

"And then?"

No reply.

"And then?" Tradain repeated. "What becomes of those who are Yours?"

It was his impression that Xyleel somehow excluded the question from His consciousness.

"You feed upon the life-force of humans, do You not?"

Emptiness.

"It is said that our vital energy strengthens and sustains You."

The implied query lost itself in vacancy.

"You are known as the great enemy of mankind," Tradain persisted. "It is believed that You seek the destruction of our race. How have we incurred Your hatred?"

This time, to his surprise, there was actually a response of sorts. No words, no images or tactile sensations, but only a measured trickle of emotional flavors, largely indecipherable, but encompassing neither hatred nor even pronounced antipathy. Clearly, the malevolence Xyleel harbored no particularly strong feelings toward humanity. If anything, His attitude smacked of a faint, infinitely remote pity. There was, however, a distinct sense of inimical purpose underscoring the communication.

"I do not understand. What purpose?" Tradain inquired, but his question was not permitted to touch the other's understanding.

There was a pause empty as oblivion, and then the silent words resumed.

Proffer yourself unto Me, of your own free will.

Confused, Tradain hesitated. He had thought himself prepared to face a malevolence. He had thought that despair armored him against fear and scruple alike, and now he found himself assailed by both. All well and good, if spectacularly illegal, to toy with the power of an extraplanar ring, but the bargain now offered by Xyleel was of another order of magnitude. Impossible to forget the teachings he had absorbed from earliest childhood. Impossible to ignore the doubts, the warning flares, the upheavals of conscience. He had not realized that he still possessed a conscience. Now, he discovered it alive and well.

    . . . *there are those among us so . . . twisted, and so vile . . . In exchange for the false and fleeting illusory power that men call sorcery, they have sold the life-force . . . They have abjured the ties and obligations of mankind, they have severed themselves from us . . . and, indeed, from all save the malevolences that they serve . . . We disown them, we cast them forth . . .*

Curious that his conscience should speak with the voice of Premier Jurist Gnaus liGurvohl.

Conscience, or superstitious fear?

Hardly superstition. The malevolence Xyleel was stupendously real.

The radiant soundless voice intruded upon his internal struggles.

I offer power to effect justice.

"Can You change the past? Can You give me back the years that I have lost?"

The past is currently nonexistent, and therefore materially inalterable. I offer you power to reshape your own recollections.

"Any madman, dreamer, or drunkard might do as much, without assistance. Can you bring my father and my brothers back to life?"

In the sense that your mind holds them, your father and brothers are currently nonexistent, and therefore irretrievable. I offer you power to create their perfect facsimiles.

"I'm not interested in cobbling mannequins."

I offer power to punish the guilty enemies of your House.

"Guilty enemies? I do not understand."

Behold the past.

Instinct pried his eyes open. This time, the vision was not internal, but glowing in midair before him. Tradain beheld two small, perfect figures, seemingly substantial—"cobbled mannequins," he might have called them—startlingly distinct and visible against a background shadowy and unfocused, but identifiable as a somberly furnished chamber. Not only were the human figures well delineated, but entirely recognizable. He saw before him the miniature simulacrum of Premier Jurist Gnaus liGurvohl, perfect down to the smallest detail of high-bridged nose and narrow jaw. Before liGurvohl stood a woman, angular and emaciated of figure, thin and tight-lipped of face, with twin blotches of passionate crimson staining her high cheekbones. Absolutely unmistakable. His erstwhile stepmother, the objectionable Lady Aestine. He hadn't thought of her in years.

The simulacra conversed, and their voices, traversing distance and time, were small and curiously metallic, yet he could hear them clearly.

The interview seemed well advanced in progress.

"Be advised, madam—your husband is indeed guilty of sorcery," Gnaus liGurvohl affirmed, with an air of relentless insistence.

Tradain stiffened, and the years slipped. For a moment he was back again in the Heart of Light, where that same voice addressed him in all-too-similar terms.

"My husband is guilty of many things, Premier Jurist—many things," Aestine replied. "But I do not know if he is guilty of *that*."

"In your heart, madam, you do know. Come, reflect. You have spent the better part of the morning verbally cataloguing the High Landguardian's almost innumerable offenses—"

"Oh, I've scarcely begun to name them all! You cannot know how cruelly he's treated me, how often he's wounded me! No one could know, because he's so clever, he contrives to keep his own reputation spotless. The world thinks him so high, so pure and noble, so perfect! The world thinks Ravnar liMarchborg can do no wrong! He's such an actor, and such a liar, he can make anybody believe anything! Well, let me tell you about the so exalted High Landguardian liMarchborg—"

"You have told me, madam, at some length. Now, let us isolate the essentials that will finally reveal all the truth. He is an actor, you say? And a liar?"

"The truth isn't in him, for all his virtuous front! He has *said*, time and again, that my happiness is important to him, but his *actions* show how little he really thinks of me! He doesn't treat me as he once did. He's distant, indifferent, when he knows perfectly well I'd do anything in the world for him. I've told him so. I've wept. I've pleaded upon my knees for his affection—yes, upon my very knees! I've even warned him that I'll kill myself—and I meant it, I swear I'll do it—but he cares nothing for that. He just mumbles a few easy, soothing, lying words, and then he gets away from me as quickly as he can. How it maddens me when he does that! I could kill him, or myself! I think he *wants* me to kill myself. He'd love to rid himself of me, so he could spend all of his time with those fish-eyed sons of his. As if I couldn't give him better sons! Tell me, Premier Jurist—in all honesty, do you think that a good husband slights his wife, and ignores her, and avoids her? Does he—"

"I am no judge of such things. You have characterized the High Landguardian as deceitful. Am I to assume that you question his fidelity?"

"I've often wondered—I've no proof, but it would certainly explain—yes, I *do* sometimes sense that he—"

"Your instinct is sharp and true. It has perceived the essential falsehood of liMarchborg's character. Now, madam, employ your intellect. Is it not logical, indeed inevitable, that an individual treacherous and disloyal in his personal dealings shall prove equally faithless to mankind in general?"

"I don't know anything about all that. I can only tell you that he treats *me* shamefully—yes, disgracefully. I *do* think about killing myself, you know—I think about it all the time!"

The simulacrum was weeping, tiny tears streaming down miniature red-splotched cheeks.

"It is necessary to consider larger issues." LiGurvohl serenely disregarded the other's extravagant misery. "The High Landguardian liMarchborg, a traitor to all humanity, is guilty of sorcerous abomination. This is an established fact. The criminal and his accomplices must be brought to justice, with all possible speed. In this matter, I expect your willing assistance. I demand it."

"Premier Jurist liGurvohl—" She sobered, and her sobs choked off. "I've already explained that I cannot help. Even if all you say is true, and I wouldn't be surprised if it *is*, there's still no evidence I can offer. Never once have I actually seen or heard my husband engage in any sort of forbidden practice."

"Perhaps in your innocence you failed to recognize the evil before you."

"Well. That may be. I don't know."

"You have stated that the High Landguardian, shunning your company, frequently seeks solitude."

"Very frequently. He mews himself up in his study. I've told him how insulting that is to me, and once I threatened to burn the door down unless he unlocked it. He must have heard me, but he didn't answer, and I *won't* be treated that way, I can't endure it, so I piled some oily rags against the door, and I took up a lighted candle, and—"

"During these periods of isolation, it is possible that sorcerous rites occur?"

"I suppose it's possible, but—"

"You will sign a statement, attesting that you have witnessed performance of such rites."

"But I haven't witnessed anything! I don't know what my husband does when he's alone."

"But you suspect, do you not? You suspect the worst, and not without reason. And you more than suspect—you know, beyond question—what manner of man is Ravnar liMarchborg."

"I am the *only* one who really knows. Oh, what I could tell you—"

"You will tell the entire world."

"I'd willingly reveal all that I know of his character—he deserves it! But I couldn't truthfully swear that I've ever seen anything remotely sorcerous."

"There exist truths of varying magnitude, madam. Allow me to instruct you. It is an inarguable fact that the greatest and highest degree of truth is that which reflects the most perfect image of objective reality. All truths strive toward this end. In this particular case, as you know, reality encompasses the guilt of the High Landguardian liMarchborg. In exposing his guilt, and confirming the reality that you intuitively apprehend, be assured you serve truth in its most rigorous aspect."

Aestine pondered, frowning.

"You serve justice, as well," liGurvohl continued. "You serve the humanity betrayed by Ravnar liMarchborg, and this act of philanthropy shall not go unrecognized. It is customary, as you know, to subject all household members of a known sorcerer to extensive questioning. Where suspicion falls, it is not uncommon to proceed to the Grand Interrogation."

Aestine shot a look into his face, and her expression altered, as if she suddenly recalled whom she dealt with.

"In demonstrating your allegiance to the principles defended and upheld by the White Tribunal," the Premier Jurist continued without pause, "you prove yourself free of the sorcerous taint, and therefore will be spared such inconvenience. Moreover, in appreciation of your service, the Tribunal will waive its right to confiscation of the convicted sorcerer's entire estate, contenting itself with limited indemnification."

"Something will remain?"

"A substantial portion."

"Then those three boys of his—"

"Doubtless share in their father's crime, and will surely share in his punishment."

Aestine stood motionless, staring up at him. The calculations clicking away behind her eyes were plain to see, even in miniature. Assuming elimination of the three loathsome liMarchborg sons, the property of Ravnar liMarchborg, whatever the White Tribunal left of it, must pass to the wronged widow, who surely deserved no less, in view of her many sufferings. Failure to cooperate with the Tribunal could draw consequences too dreadful to contemplate. And then, most compelling, existed the prospect of—

justice. The countless wrongs inflicted upon her by an indifferent, inconsiderate, unfeeling husband rankled in the depths of her heart. The courteous rebuffs, the polite exclusions, the disappointments, the silent humiliations, the pangs of unrequited love, the self-consuming blaze of impotent hatred— all that she had endured—all of it was with her yet, would always be with her, but now there was a possibility of retribution—repayment of sorts,— renewal of self-respect—

Some relief.

"He has done much evil," the Lady Aestine declared. Her listener was silent, and she added, uncomfortably, "I will do my duty, no matter what the cost. Conscience demands no less." Still no reply, and she added, almost defiantly, "I will do all I can to bring him to justice. If my testimony is not enough, then I am not to blame."

Gnaus liGurvohl answered at last, as if speaking from some mountaintop.

"As to that," he informed her, "you need not concern yourself."

Tradain was icy and empty inside, but fire licked the edges of the void. Before there was time to analyze the sensation, the scene before him softened and blurred. When it cleared, the Lady Aestine was gone. Premier Jurist Gnaus liGurvohl remained, in the same somber chamber, now glowing with candlelight. Before him stood a short, rotund, dapper male figure. A stranger.

No. Tradain frowned. The little man's plumply cherubic countenance, with its smooth pink cheeks, juvenile snub nose, and bright, apprehensive eyes, was vaguely familiar. Somewhere, he had seen it, more than once, a very long time ago. Puzzled, he studied the simulacrum's sober garb. Decent, plain, clean, and nondescript. Eminently respectable, but hardly the costume of a wealthy or significant personage. An unassuming carriage radiated humility.

"His guilt is plain, and his conviction, inevitable," liGurvohl stated.

Once again, the interview seemed well advanced.

"If it is inevitable, then why do you want my assistance? Can you not do without it?" The other licked dry lips. "Aren't there others you could ask?"

"When the trial concludes," the Premier Jurist continued imperturbably, "the lists of our allies and our foes must be compiled. In which will your name appear?"

"I am ready and eager to serve the White Tribunal." The little man's expression of fervent sincerity belied itself by a visible blanching of rosy cheeks. "But I do not quite grasp what is required of me. Am I mistaken in my understanding that the Premier Jurist has already secured the testimony of the High Landguardian liMarchborg's wife?"

"She is a foolish, prattling female, much given to absurd excesses of temper," liGurvohl returned indifferently. "The Tribunal does not choose to rely absolutely upon the evidence of so light-minded a witness. Moreover, the liMarchborg woman's statement contains no information relating to the activities of your own master, whose guilt, however obvious, must yet be established in court. For that, the testimony of a liTarngrav household member is desirable."

A *liTarngrav household member*. Of course. Tradain remembered now where he had seen that cherubic face. He was looking at a perfect simulacrum of Master Drempi Kwieseldt, household steward to the High Landguardian Jex liTarngrav. Former household steward. Former High Landguardian.

"I see." Drempi Kwieseldt swallowed.

"It is reasonable to assume," the Premier Jurist observed, "that a retainer so highly placed as yourself enjoys the confidence of his master."

"He does not actually *confide* in me, he—"

"And yet, you are in a position to observe closely. No doubt you possess information that must be regarded as privileged."

"Premier Jurist, please understand, my family has served the House of liTarngrav for generations. My father was household steward before me, and I hope that my son may follow in my footsteps. Always we have served faithfully, and—"

"Loyalty is a signal virtue, Master Kwieseldt," Gnaus liGurvohl intoned. "It may be misplaced, however. As you are an individual gifted with free will, it is your responsibility alone to select a worthy object of devotion. Should you fail in this, the moral fault is yours. You understand me?"

"Yes, Premier Jurist."

"It is hardly open to question," liGurvohl continued, "that the welfare of the human race in its entirety claims the first loyalty of the morally rational. It is precisely for this reason that the duty to assist in the suppression of the sorcerers among us supersedes every other obligation. The importance of this principle cannot be overstated."

"I understand, Premier Jurist."

"The validity of the lesser obligations, however, will be denied only by those small intellects devoid of compassion. A certain measure of loyalty to your own family, for example, is generally to be commended."

"So I have always been given to understand, Premier Jurist."

"The son you spoke of—I trust you regard him highly."

"My Pfissig is a clever, likely lad. He'll be a sharp steward, one day."

"Perhaps he may be more, for his father now enjoys the privilege of serving mankind and family, simultaneously. I will explain. Upon the conviction of the High Landguardian Jex liTarngrav as an accomplice in sorcery, your master's entire estate passes into legal guardianship of the White Tribunal. The liTarngrav holdings, as you know, are immense. The Tribunal is unstintingly appreciative of its friends as it is terrible in pursuit of its enemies."

This final observation brought a sickly smile to the face of the listener.

"It is time to demonstrate your loyalties, Master Kwieseldt." The simulacrum's miniaturized tones were surprisingly reverberant. In the reality of the past, Gnaus liGurvohl's splendid voice must have tolled like a passing bell. "It is time to prove yourself."

Drempi Kwieseldt puffed out his cheeks, twisted his fingers, and cogitated palely. Finally, he spoke.

"I have overheard them, together—my master Jex liTarngrav and his friend, Ravnar liMarchborg. I have heard what they said, when they thought they were alone, in the dead of night. Sometimes, I have secretly watched, and my mind has quaked with the horror of the sights I beheld. Now, at last, my conscience overcomes my fear, and I will relate the truth of all that passed between them."

Folding his arms, Gnaus liGurvohl gazed down from empyrean heights. "Omit no detail," he commanded.

The vision faded and vanished. Tradain stood staring at faintly blue vacancy. His mind seemed slow, almost unable to absorb the influx of information. In all the years of misery, he had blamed nothing beyond the impersonal cruelty of the White Tribunal. True, that fanaticism embodied itself in the Premier Jurist, and yet it was upon the court as a whole that he had fixed his enmity. The possibility of individual treachery had never occurred to him. Now that the facts had been revealed, however, he never doubted them, but sensed the truth to his core.

He dully supposed that he ought to be very excited, very emotional. In fact, he was neither. He was nothing much at all. There was only the frigid void, with the flames shivering along its edges, but he had an inkling that those flames would grow and spread, before long.

And now that uncanny voice was back in his frozen mind again.

Proffer yourself unto Me, of your own free will.

Impossible to deal with such an issue, at such an instant. Proffer? He could scarcely grasp the concept. His thoughts anchored upon miniature faces out of the past; upon miniature, metallic voices uttering the unspeakable. Still, a reply of some sort was required.

"I need more time," he said aloud.

The response, though immediate, did not emanate from Xyleel, in any obvious sense. He caught the staccato bursts of muffled shouting, not far away, and then came the rhythmic thud of heavy pounding. The paralysis gripping his mind loosened, and he understood that the guards from Lakeside Station had discovered the entrance at the head of the stairs, and now they were beating the locked door down.

There was no more time.

Once again, he spoke aloud.

"I proffer myself unto You, of my own free will."

The words were spoken, and a crazy exultation filled him. The intelligence touching his own stirred, and he sensed comprehension. An endless instant passed, and then reality altered. His body remained stationary, but his awareness was yanked out of mundane time and space, to confront Xyleel upon another plane.

There was darkness all around him, illumined only by the radiance that was the malevolence, and there were harmonic vibrations pulsing through him, but he hardly felt them, for his mind was at once occupied by and lost within Xyleel.

White-hot knowledge was burning into him, straight through accreted layers of living, to the very foundation of his memory, there to brand itself forever. There was nothing he had ever seen, or heard, or experienced in all his days, that he knew as intimately and vividly as he now knew the mind-gifts of Xyleel.

The process of transference was shocking, but not in the least painful, nor even truly fearsome, for his mind was swelling to contain the new understanding. He could feel the expansion, the burgeoning power, indescribable power, and the sensation was exhilarating beyond terror. Awareness of self lapsed altogether for a time, and there was only brilliance, the silent explosion of incorporeal growth, and a fleeting sense of unity with cosmic forces.

It ended, all too soon. Consciousness and body reunited. He was himself again, albeit a transformed self. He stood in the workroom of Yurune the Bloodless. His heart slammed, his pulses raced, and he was bathed in sweat. His head swam, but his mind was clear, clearer than it had ever been. A few feet above him, at the top of the stairs, his hunters pounded the locked door with a makeshift battering ram. The malevolence Xyleel was nowhere in evidence, although, he somehow knew, not far away.

He looked around him, and at once perceived a couple of alterations in Yurune's workroom. For one thing, several of the hitherto mysterious instruments occupying the various shelves were now recognizable and understandable. For another, there was a new light, glowing strongly blue in the corner.

The light beckoned, and he approached with caution. Alone upon a low, formerly unnoticed table stood an hourglass. The device, small enough to fit in a man's pocket, was simple and plain in design. Its fine granular contents were powerfully luminescent, source of an azure glow too assertive to overlook, and yet he had somehow managed to miss it, until now. Unconsciously, Tradain shook his head. He couldn't have missed it.

Bending low for a closer look, he saw that the hourglass was blocked, its bright grains trapped in the upper chamber. The bottom compartment was empty. The glass was meant for him; so much he recognized. Its use or import, however, remained a mystery, and there was no time to ponder the matter, for a crash overhead, followed by a yell of triumph, announced the destruction of the locked door.

Footsteps clattered down the stairs. Moments later a questing beam of orange lamplight muddied the sorcerous blue glow of Yurune's sanctum, and then four elated guards from Lakeside Station burst into the room.

Five of them had chased him to this house. The fifth must still be upstairs, standing sentry at the exit.

They stopped short at sight of him. They were staring. Evidently, something in his aspect startled them; perhaps his extreme stillness, or else his look of impenetrably remote tranquillity. Or perhaps some remnant of the glory that had lately filled him clothed him yet in a visible aura.

The paralysis broke in a moment, and the quartet advanced. Tradain watched, almost dreamily. All of them bore firearms, and one carried a pair of irons. He seemed somehow to view them from great heights; very small they appeared, anonymous as ants toiling under tiny burdens. One of them was speaking. The jaw wagged, and distorted syllables forced their slow way through gelatinous atmosphere.

He might have understood easily enough, had he chosen to listen, but the reward seemed unworthy of such effort. What reason to heed the discourse of insects?

One of the insects leveled its weapon, and the action arrested his attention. Some sort of defensive response was indicated, and the new knowledge boiling at the base of his brain suggested a method. Almost reflexively, so deep had the understanding been planted, he drew upon the new store of power to build a resilient, transparent atmospheric shield about himself.

The spoken words flew freely through the shield, straight to his ears, but he did not comprehend them at that moment. The insect fired, and such was the momentary state of his wildly enhanced mind that he was able to study the progress of the speeding ball, its collision with the invisible shield, and its unexpected rebound back upon its source.

Pierced through the heart, the luckless guard fell dead. A second promptly repeated his companion's error, with identical results. The remaining two turned and sprinted for the exit.

They had seen too much, and he couldn't let them carry their knowledge away. With effort, Tradain forced his winged thoughts into practical channels. He could silence these witnesses forever, but instinctively he shrank from murder. Swiftly he considered alternatives, and chose one.

They were already through the door and flying for the stairs, yet it was still quite easy to locate their panicky intellects, and to send the energy lancing into their brains. A controlled surge vaporized recent memory, leaving a gap that encompassed twenty-four hours or more. The loss stunned both victims, and for an instant Tradain experienced their shock and complete confusion, before the contact lapsed.

His sorcerous tension abated, and the surrounding shield ceased to exist. The events and sensations of the day overwhelmed him, and his strength gushed away like blood from a severed artery. He sank gasping to his knees. The room spun slowly about him, and he let himself slump to the floor. The cold stone floor pressed his wet cheek, his eyes closed, and he slept deeply.

⋘ ⋙

"My report, Premier Jurist." Major Fraynerl of the Soldiers of the Light saluted, and moved to retire.

"One moment." Gnaus liGurvohl halted his subordinate with a gesture. "Remain where you are, while I read."

Fraynerl obeyed with a visible reluctance that caught the Premier Jurist's attention briefly. The apparent blot upon the officer's conscience demanded investigation, but not now. LiGurvohl read, and his awareness of the other's presence faded.

The report, quite lengthy, confirmed the accuracy of the initial account of the great riot delivered by messenger from Fortress Nul precisely one week earlier, then went on to describe the aftermath in some detail. The Fasting Day Rebellion—by far the greatest insurrection ever to explode

within the prison confines—had started in the prison yard, below the locked
mess hall; thereafter swiftly spreading to the West Corridors and West
Tower, then out into the central courtyard, the East Corridors, and the
various sublevels. Combat had raged throughout the afternoon, with considerable loss of life on both sides, and the intervention of a squad from Lakeside Station had failed to restore perfect order. A gang of fanatical inmates,
ensconced in West Tower, had held their position throughout the night. At
dawn, the arrival of a relief column under Fraynerl's command had effectively crushed all remaining resistance. The West Tower rebels—trapped in
their stronghold, and confronting the choice between surrender and starvation—had opted for self-immolation. Somewhere or other, they had managed to obtain a barrel of powder, which they'd touched off around noon.
The resulting explosion had destroyed West Tower, its occupants, and a
half-dozen disadvantageously situated Soldiers of the Light, thus bringing
the Fasting Day Rebellion to its spectacular conclusion.

Since that afternoon, the debris had been cleared away, the bodies
collected, identified whenever possible, interred, or, as circumstances warranted, consigned to the Boneworks. Unfortunately, a number of the corpses
recovered from the wreckage of West Tower had been burned beyond recognition. Surviving prisoners known as active participants had been suitably
chastised, along with those caught attempting flight during the riot. Of those
seeking escape, all were accounted for—either recaptured or dead—with
one exception, currently unidentified. A general suspension of all privileges,
together with a disciplinary reduction in rations, educated the entire inmate
population. Fortress Nul was once again tranquil, and would no doubt
promptly resume its usual efficiency of operation. A number of procedural
alterations, initiated by Major Fraynerl prior to his departure, would greatly
improve prison security, thereby eliminating all possibility of recurring disturbances.

Gnaus liGurvohl scanned the list of Fraynerl's alterations, which
were intelligently engineered and mercilessly severe. He nodded his grudg-
ing approval. His eyes scanned the subsequent pages of the document,
which contained an assortment of individual statements, inventories, and
inspection reports, including a list of those individual prisoners indefinitely
accounted for, and presumed to rest among the charred dead. A single
notation caught his eye:

FNID#13. liMarchborg, Tradain. Pol. Sublevel 4, Corridor D, Compartment 5. Remains recovered from West Tower, tentatively identified,
.00012;6709. Confirmation pending. Viable osseous material salvaged,
.00012;6711. File closed, .00012;6711.

The Premier Jurist sat quite still. The name reverberated through his mind, and he glimpsed an adolescent face from long ago, but it was gone in an instant, replaced by the adult face that was its prototype, by the father's face, *Ravnar's* face . . .

The memories came flooding back then, and for once he was powerless to exclude them. It all returned in an instant—the names, faces, and recollections dating back to boyhood, the details he had thought forgotten, the memories of Ravnar—all the intolerable sensations of the past, immediate and intense as ever.

They flashed behind his eyes in the space of a heartbeat. He could feel them along his every nerve, and there was no escape as the horrific, triumphant closing sequence rushed upon him: Ravnar in the Heart of Light, Ravnar subjected to the Grand Interrogation, Ravnar at the moment of Enlightenment, Ravnar gone—finished as he deserved, utterly expunged at last . . .

Wasn't he?

An internal spasm shook the Premier Jurist. Revulsion, guilt, and an inexpressible ecstasy blended indistinguishably, and for a moment he was nothing more than a commonplace mortal, prey to degrading mundane emotion. So he had been in the early days, before he had learned to lose and find himself in the glory that was Autonn; before he had discovered the direct and personal link with the Benefactor that set him so much apart from ordinary men. Once he had been weak, filled with uncertainty, unsure of his own worthiness, questioning even the validity of his own convictions. Once, he had been feeble, indecisive, and afraid. But then infinity had touched him, lifting him above himself, above others. All doubt had vanished like foggy vapor burned off by the rising sun, and since that time, he had known beyond doubt that he worked Autonn's will in the world.

He knew it still.

The Premier Jurist drew a deep breath, and was himself again. The liMarchborg-tainted recollections fled his consciousness, and anger rushed in to fill the resulting void. He looked up to find Major Fraynerl regarding him attentively. Annihilating syllables rose to his lips, but he repressed them. Fraynerl, after all, had performed his task ably. Autonn's justice demanded an alternate victim.

Dipping a quill, liGurvohl wrote out a few lines, affixed his signature and seal, then handed the document across the desk.

Major Fraynerl scanned his orders, and his brows rose.

"To be effected without delay," the Premier Jurist commanded. "That will be all."

Fraynerl saluted and departed.

No doubt the major would dispatch his commission efficiently.

Within the space of hours, Fortress Nul's criminally negligent Acting Governor would find himself en route to the Heart of Light, under armed guard. Before another week had passed, Kreschl would answer for his blunders to the White Tribunal, a prospect so pleasing that the Premier Jurist's anger vanished as if by divine intervention.

There were no dreams to trouble his slumber, no recollection of past, or consciousness of present. When next he opened his eyes upon the workroom of Yurune the Bloodless, he knew where he was, and remembered all that had happened, remembered most vividly, but questioned the truth of those lurid visions. The malevolence Xyleel. The purchased power. Real, or would he wake to find himself breathing dungeon air at the bottom of Fortress Nul?

Real.

Two dead guards to prove it.

Prolonged sleep had steadied his mind, and now he could take stock of mental contents. A swift inventory confirmed the presence of new power and knowledge, along with something else. The recollection of self-sale had imprinted itself upon his memory with the implacable permanency of a written contract. His acceptance of Xyleel's nebulous terms was undeniable and irrevocable.

Rising slowly, he cast wondering eyes about the room. The glow in the corner drew him, and he approached to gaze once more upon the enigmatic hourglass. Somehow, while he slept, the thing had unblocked itself, and a quantity of luminous matter had sifted down into the lower chamber, where it lay lightless as any ordinary sand. Nothing sifted now, however. Cautiously he bent to take a closer look. He had no idea why such a detail should claim his interest, but it did.

He brushed the glass with a careful fingertip, and his sense of connection deepened. At that moment, vast light chilled his interior, and an effulgent voice shone within.

To rule the— There was a pause, as the speaker sought the appropriate word to convey a concept imperfectly expressed in human language. *The—intelligence—of others is—costly.*

Tradain stiffened, and his startled gaze swept the workroom. The malevolence Xyleel was nowhere to be seen. The impossible voice spoke inside his head, and there was no place to hide from it. But the words themselves meant nothing.

His incomprehension must have announced itself, for he felt alien volition press his memory, and then he recalled that the store of power granted him was a limited quantity reduced by expenditure, with each sorcerous act carrying its own particular price.

Costly, Xyleel had called his new recruit's premier effort. To rule the intelligence of others was costly. He had ruled the awareness of two human guards by obliterating twenty-four hours worth of their recollections, but he had done so at fairly substantial personal expense. Far cheaper, in a real sense, simply to kill both men, a feat requiring almost negligible arcane power.

The traditional ruthlessness of sorcerers was suddenly quite understandable.

Similarly obvious—the import of the hourglass, *his* hourglass. The lucent matter in the upper chamber, he now perceived, represented his remaining portion of sorcerous power. The lightless granules in the lower compartment told him how much he had spent. He wondered if Yurune the Bloodless had used this same device; had watched his own power sift away, grain by grain. Ultimately, Yurune had died, no doubt passing into possession of the malevolence Xyleel, or another of His ilk. A ripple of voiceless confirmation stirred his brain, and Tradain shivered.

"What becomes of those who are Yours?" he inquired aloud, and this time, almost to his surprise, there was an answer, of sorts.

Again the alien images filled his inner vision, and he beheld the brilliance that he now recognized as Xyleel's natural habitat, the dazzling supradimension of Fangs's description. Fangs had spoken too of the inhabitants, sentient beings calling themselves—

The Aware.

The Aware. Now he could see them, unbearably brilliant, overwhelming in their sheer impossibility of form, and the sight might have blinded him had he viewed it through physical eyes. Their voices—or what might have been likened to their voices—reached him, wordlessly and soundlessly, through the medium of his mind. The Aware, he realized, communed intellect to intellect, their thoughts rising and blending in a great concert of disturbing beauty. At first he believed the harmony flawless, but gradually, as he listened, began to pick out small discords, minor imperfections that soon became impossible to ignore. Some among the Aware, it seemed, possessed intellects inherently out of tune; minds unable or unwilling to conform. There was a name for such deviates, he dimly sensed. They were known as—

Anomalies.

Anomalies, dotted here and there throughout the radiant throng. One of them, his voice outstandingly strong and dissonant, recognizable as the malevolence—

The Presence.

The Presence Xyleel. Others, milder in light, subtler in disharmony, but nonetheless offensive to their compatriots. As Tradain looked on, the bright tide of the Aware ebbed away, leaving a group of Anomalies stranded in perpetual isolation. The erratic pulsations of the rejected conveyed intense feeling, most of it unknowable. Two distinctly recognizable emotions, however, came through clearly: a collectively profound sadness and, in the case of Xyleel alone, an overwhelming anger.

The scene changed. Xyleel, harboring vast rage, had somehow entered the inferior dimension of mankind's existence, wherein His natural radiant energy lent Him the power of a god or demon—

An exile.

An exile, but effortless master of all He surveyed. Thus, His purpose in trafficking with a succession of human sorcerers and sorceresses was by no means apparent. The faces of those selling themselves to the Presence Xyleel in exchange for power flashed by, too numerous to count. One after another, they lived, tasted dominance, died, and vanished.

"What do You want of them—of us?" Tradain asked almost unwillingly.

There followed so long a silence that he thought the question had been excluded, but then the unexpected answer came:

Contamination. Poison of the Nether plane. Filth.

"What?"

Contamination, which your race calls—intelligence.

"I do not understand."

Consciousness, and its effluvia. This form of polluted Netherly—energy—I collect and store.

"Why?"

Again, the length of silence suggested inattention, and again, a startling reply eventually arrived: *Behold the future.*

Once more the burning vision of the Radiant Level filled his mind. He gazed upon the endless glowing reaches, the three lambent atmospheres, the luminous inhabitants. As he watched, a tremendous flood of toxic force poured in through a rent in dimensional barriers. Corrosive tides washed Radiance, dimming the light, dirtying and diminishing the Aware; disrupting their pulsations, smothering their mental voices, and dulling their brilliance, until they seemed little more than squalid mud-creatures of Netherness.

"You will foul and ruin Your own plane?" asked Tradain.

He caught a wordless affirmation, and then a couple of distinct syllables, hazed in what he could only interpret as fathomless bitterness:

Exile.

"You store human minds until You've enough to accomplish Your
aim?"

Another wordless affirmative.

"How long will it take?" The queries followed swiftly upon one another, for there was no telling how long the other's communicative humor
would last. This particular question, however, drew no reply, and he sensed
that the human concept of time was meaningless to Xyleel.

"Where are those minds now?"

Inwardly, he glimpsed a forgotten little sub-pocket of existence, outside the plane of men, its perpetual dimness brightened by the intermittent
small glimmerings of disembodied intellects.

Like fireflies in a cave, he thought. Are they still conscious? Do they
remember? Do they retain identity?

The unspoken questions drew an unequivocally positive response.

"And when You loose them at last upon Your own dimension," he
dared to probe, "the intensity of the atmosphere will quickly destroy them?"

Negative.

"They—we—will continue to exist, upon the Radiant Level?" he
inquired, astonished.

Experience the future.

White chaos engulfed Tradain, permeated and owned him. He had
no body, yet his senses persisted, and the surrounding brilliance scourged
his vision, the roar of a fiery avalanche overwhelmed his intellect, while the
heat of countless suns consumed but did not annihilate him. There was no
room for thought, for defense or resistance, for anything beyond agony too
great for his mind to encompass. No escape into unconsciousness. No relief
and, presumably, no terminus, for time described perpetual ellipses upon
the Radiant Level.

He was screaming, but didn't know it until the preview concluded,
and he found himself standing unharmed in Yurune's chilly workroom, still
screaming. He ceased. He was shaking. His throat ached. Nothing else hurt.

We shall meet again.

The alien light within faded, and the Presence Xyleel withdrew.

Nine

He stood alone in the workroom. The trembling of his limbs gradually subsided, and he looked about him. Two dead guards on the floor. Countless shelves loaded with arcana, property of a slaughtered sorcerer. Books, artifacts—perhaps he'd want them for himself, one day—but not now. Little table in the corner, supporting an hourglass filled with luminous matter. *His* hourglass, counting out the finite span of his power. He realized then that his ruined rags possessed no pockets fit to contain the new acquisition.

His eyes strayed to the nearest corpse, its waist encircled with a wide belt, from which depended a small leather pouch. Kneeling beside the fallen guard, he fumbled briefly with the buckle, then slid the belt from its owner's body. For a moment, he seemed to see himself as if from above—a filthy, wretched figure, down on its knees, despoiling the dead. Hardly recognizable as Ravnar liMarchborg's youngest son.

Just as well. Recognition was the last thing he wanted.

He clasped the belt about himself. Much too big, likely to slide right off his miserably emaciated frame. Tying the leather ends in a bulky knot, he turned his attention to the pouch, discovering therein a pair of dice, a greasy deck of cards, and, to his surprise, a sizable sum of money. He counted quickly. Sixty-six auslins, in coins and notes, sure to prove useful. Rising, he stepped to the table, slid the hourglass carefully into the pouch, and exited the workroom.

The open door at the head of the stairs admitted a wash of anemic grey light. Daylight. Tradain ascended, emerging into the antechamber. Back along the windowless corridor he felt his way, back through the ravaged chambers, alert at all times to the presence of surviving guards. He encountered nobody until he reached the entrance hall, where two of his erstwhile pursuers loitered, dazed and dull-eyed. They offered no hindrance as he walked straight past them, out the front door, and down the basalt steps, to pause at the bottom in the shade of the iron trees.

No sign of the fifth Lakeside guard. The fellow must have fled during the night. Did others of his ilk still comb the woods? No matter. He was more than capable of dealing with all of them, now.

He walked away, and Yurune's house soon disappeared behind him. The heavy morning mists closed about him, almost blotting the world from view, but his pace never faltered, for these woods of his boyhood were deep-rooted in his memory, and his feet still knew the way.

Through the ghostly forest he hiked, over the hills, to the top of Ziehn's Tooth, from which the city of Lis Folaze was visible on a clear day. Today was not clear, and in any case, he wasn't looking. His sight turned itself inward, there to dwell at obsessive length upon the visions vouchsafed him in the depths of the ruined mansion. Again and again he viewed them, lingering over every word and gesture.

The faces, acid-etched. Aestine, at once hysterical and calculating, aflame with hatred. Drempi Kwieseldt—fearful, greedy, sly. And Premier Jurist Gnaus liGurvohl. LiGurvohl the Incorruptible. Glacial, merciless, relentlessly righteous. Moral model to the masses. Fanatic, criminal, liar, murderer. LiGurvohl.

And there were other faces there in his thoughts, as well. Ravnar liMarchborg, in the Heart of Light's torture chamber. Rav and Zendin, in Radiance Square. Jex liTarngrav, calmly confronting annihilation. The

Ferret. Sergeant Gultz. Corporal Woenich. Fangs, dying. And then, no more faces, none for years.

The pictures danced behind his eyes. Behind the pictures, deep at his center, yawned that void edged in flame, and the flames were spreading to engulf him. He'd been cold for years, and now he was burning alive. *As if prematurely consigned to the Radiant Level.*

The mental images changed. The white chaos howled through his mind, the heat and brilliance devoured him. The Radiant Level. Fear concentrated his anger. *Proffer yourself unto Me, of your own free will.* Would he have obeyed, had he comprehended the price of Xyleel's assistance? Impossible to judge and, in any case, academic. He had struck his bargain, and the malevolence had made good His promise. The thing was done. There had been little choice, after all.

Because of them.

Aestine. Kwieseldt. *LiGurvohl.* They had sent him to Fortress Nul, and thence to the perpetual agony of the Radiant Level. And they hadn't even regarded him as an enemy. To them, his existence had simply offered minor inconvenience.

The internal heat intensified. He'd do anything in the world, he realized, to quench those fires. Anything at all.

He was drenched with sweat, despite the coolness of the morning. Deep gulps of the damp, pine-scented air brought no relief. Inwardly, he burned on.

Down from Ziehn's Tooth he made his way, through the woods to the Dhreve's Highway, and on along the road toward the city, now visible through the mists. The whitewashed brick and stone dwellings rose about him, sooner than he expected; evidently, Lis Folaze had expanded outward since he had last traveled this route. Traffic appeared on the highway, and he advanced alongside the carts and wagons, neither courting attention nor particularly seeking to evade it.

The Conquered Malevolence inn appeared, every one of its hundred fanciful lanterns blazing in defiance of the fog. On he went through the wilderness of merchants' booths and stalls, more numerous now than in the past, with the singsong chants of the professional litanists louder and more insistent than he recalled. He lingered a moment to listen, and the voices beat at him. Surely, they had not seemed so intrusive long ago, nor had the surrounding displays of protective charms and amulets offered such huge and gaudy variety.

On he went through the old city gate, now graced with no fewer than a dozen warding talismans. Now he walked upon cobbled streets, crowded with creaking conveyances and pushing pedestrians, surroundings exotic and almost shocking to senses accustomed for years to dungeon monotony.

How many years, exactly? For the first time, he wondered, and that initial question was followed by a host of others, all of them overwhelmed by simple physical need. He hadn't tasted food since yesterday morning, hadn't even thought of it, but now found himself famished to the verge of sickness.

A problem easily solved. Sixty-six auslins reposed within the dead guard's purloined pouch.

A decent-looking cookshop stood just across the street. Astounding odors wafted from the wide-open door. Beef in red wine, his nose registered, recalling nearly forgotten scents from long ago. Onions, spices, and plenty of garlic. A pang knifed him, so sharp that he almost mistook it for grief.

Crossing the street, he stepped through the cookshop door, only to find his path blocked by a burly youth shielded in an apron and armed with a broom.

"Out," the youth commanded.

Wordlessly opening the pouch at his belt, Tradain dipped within for the cash sure to validate his social worthiness, but never got the chance to display it.

"Out!" The youth swung his broom.

The blow, aimed randomly, caught the side of his head. Tradain staggered, but stayed on his feet. The youth, he decided, was the raw material of which the guards at Fortress Nul were made. A Sergeant Gultz in embryo. The thought was extraordinarily potent. The rage flared in his head, the sorcerous knowledge boiled at the base of his brain, and his mind came within a hairbreadth of spinning the sequence that would result in the other's prompt reduction to components.

It would be so very easy. So satisfying. So relaxing.

He refrained, with effort. The youth was fortunate beyond expression.

"*Out*, streetcrap! Now!" The broom swung.

The blow clipped his jaw, and Tradain fell sprawling on a dirty plank floor. The broom hovered about his ears.

"Get up and get out. Before I lose my patience," the youth advised.

Dizzy and confused, he hauled himself to his feet and lurched from the cookshop. The voice of its guardian spirit echoed in his ears.

"Slimeguts, you better be glad you got off so easy!"

Outside again, with the coins still jingling plentifully in the dead guard's pouch. Surely, someone would be willing to take his money.

But the next cookshop refused him, and so did the one after that. He tried a down-at-heels tavern next, with identical results.

Inexplicable. But then he wandered into a quiet plaza, where the still water puddling beneath a public pump offered a clear reflection, and he saw himself for the first time since the night he had been plucked from his father's house.

He scarcely looked human. His thick black hair, uncut for years, hung in lank, dirty tangles, nearly down to his waist. A long, heavy beard obscured most of a face gaunt and haggard, at once youthful and aged. Above the beard glittered eyes of peculiar brilliance, and disquieting, almost alien expression. A lunatic's eyes, or perhaps a changeling's.

He looked down at himself to behold a painfully scrawny, repulsively dirty frame, barely covered in verminous rags. No wonder they hadn't let him into the cookshops.

Through the streets he wandered, instinctively seeking the bowels of the city, where a miserable appearance offered no particular disadvantage. The lanes twisted and constricted about him as he went, the buildings aged and deteriorated, and the garbage heaps proliferated. The stench of filth and poverty poisoned the air, while a thousand uglinesses assailed his eyes and ears, but he scarcely minded; by comparison to Fortress Nul, it was all magnificent.

Presently he came to shabby little Cooper Street, lined with tumble-down tenements dating back a century and more. At the bottom of the street stood a seen-better-days tavern calling itself The Barrel Stave, and something about the name teased his memory, but he couldn't have said why. He saw at a glance all he needed to see—that The Barrel Stave was squalid, mean, and dingy enough to tolerate his presence.

He walked in, and found the place empty save for the proprietress, a gimlet-eyed harridan of some fifty years, armed with an ax-blade nose, prominent brownish teeth, and pert pink bows in her suspiciously plentiful yellow hair. Her eyes narrowed at sight of him, and instantly he displayed a handful of small coins. She nodded, and he seated himself at a rickety table beside the door.

"Ale-wine-whitespirits?" the woman demanded.

"Food," he told her.

"Too early. Supper at five."

"You must have something," he returned, and saw her frown at the sound of his voice, with its educated accent and its metallic, curiously unused quality.

"Bread. Butter. Cheese. Pickled lorbers. Cold sausage, if you want to pay extra."

He nodded, gave her money, and she brought him the food, together with a bottle of cheap red wine. Thereafter she retired to her refuge behind the bar, where she sat chin in hand, watching him unwinkingly.

He soon forgot about her. For a time, the alleviation of acute hunger occupied his full attention. The meal, plain and poor though it was, seemed to him royally lavish. The wine, despite its vinegar edge, surprised him with its intensity of flavor; and then he remembered that all he'd drunk years earlier, as a boy at his father's table, had been served to him well watered. Never before in his life had he tasted wine undiluted.

Hunger subsided, and the thoughts temporarily excluded crowded in to take its place. The inevitable question arose: *What now?*

Where to go, what to do? In the most immediate sense, easily answered; restore his own appearance to some semblance of normality, enabling him to move freely and inconspicuously among men. Find shelter.

And then?

He found that the faces had worked their way back to the front of his mind. There they were, again—liGurvohl, Aestine, Kwieseldt, and the others—and the hate rose up to choke and burn him. Automatically he took a gulp of wine. No relief there. If anything, alcohol fueled the fires. Setting the bottle aside, he asked the proprietress for water.

"Pump's out back," she informed him, without stirring.

He wasn't ready to move yet. In any case, the coolest of water would hardly quench the internal flames—only action could do that. Action. He thought about it. The possibilities were many, and intensely colorful. With his newly purchased powers, there was almost nothing he might not accomplish.

I offer power to punish the guilty enemies of your House.

The effulgent voice of the Presence Xyleel illumined his memory.

Justice. Not such a bad offer, although the price was very high. Justice upon the three of them, particularly liGurvohl. A goal, a purpose, something to live for.

He would have it. He would extract fair value, or some value, for the price he had paid.

Remarkable how encouraging that thought was. The fever abated, for an instant. Precarious peace descended. Justice.

The red fancies sizzled yet at the edges of his mind. His eyes, roaming in search of distraction, fastened upon a sheet of yellowish paper, left crumpled on the seat of a neighboring chair. He picked up the paper, unfolded it, and discovered a woodcut illustration reproduced in black ink, with printing below the picture, and a surrounding decorative border. He held a mass-produced notice or circular of some sort. He studied the woodcut, and his interest quickened.

It was a cartoon—a caricature, actually—depicting thirteen men seated about a dinner table. Each of the men was clad in voluminous white robes of office. Each jurist thus depicted was monstrously obese. Each face possessed considerable porcine individuality, but only one was known to Tradain. Despite the grotesque fleshy exaggeration, he recognized the long jaw, high-bridged nose, and hooded eyes of Premier Jurist Gnaus liGurvohl. The banquet table was loaded with platters, each piled high with miniature mansions, townhouses, warehouses, tenements, taverns, and shops. He spied liTarngrav House on one of the plates. LiZauber Mansion—the Red Rook Inn—and others that he knew. The buildings all bore forked pennants marked with the insignia of the White Tribunal, indicative of judicial confiscation. At the center of the table stood a large tureen shaped like a cauldron, filled with soup wherein tiny human figures bobbed and splashed. One of the diners, sporting an unabashed leer, was ladling the soup into serving bowls. Another was carving neat slices of masonry off the ornate facade of Frissheim's Pavilion. The Premier Jurist liGurvohl was at work with knife and fork upon a domed edifice recognizable as the Dhreve's palace. The caption below the picture read: **We extend our compliments to the famous trenchermen of the White Tribunal, whose appetite for justice is never sated.**

There followed a date, and Tradain stared at it. Thirteen years, he calculated. Thirteen years since the night that the Soldiers of the Light had come to his father's house. He was twenty-six years old. He had spent half of his life in prison.

He would give way to rage, if he stopped to think about it. He needed something else to think about. That cartoon. Certainly worthy of attention. He looked at it again. Well conceived, well executed, even amusing, in a mordant sort of way—and dangerous as lightning. Easily sufficient to land the artist in the cauldron, unless things had changed considerably in the last thirteen years. Enough to compromise beyond salvation the owner of the establishment in which such a piece of sedition was discovered. He shot a glance at the hostess. She was still watching him, and although she saw him scanning the circular, displayed no sign of uneasiness. Perhaps she didn't know what he held. The caption, after all, was a little oblique—and the average citizen was illiterate. But then, the picture spoke clearly for itself, in language comprehensible to all.

Quite likely, the woman had no idea at all what he held.

She caught his eye, and remarked nonchalantly, "Really something, eh?"

For a moment he considered bolting from The Barrel Stave, but then collected himself so far as to inquire in his rusty voice, "You've looked at this?"

"Sure." She grated a cackle. "That one's pretty good, I'd say, but I've seen better. Did you catch the one with the whole band of thirteen, all holding hands and floating in the air, raised aloft by the power of their own farts, with the people down in the city streets below holding their noses and running for cover? That one really made me laugh, it was great. Did you see it?"

He shook his head.

"Too bad. But you know the one they called 'The Black Tribunal,' with the jurists done up as crows, with beaks and black feathers, and all?"

"No."

"Everyone's seen that one." She looked as if she didn't believe him.

"I've been away." Her expression didn't alter, and he added, "A picture like this could get you in trouble."

She shrugged.

"Here—" He offered her the cartoon. "You'd better burn it."

"I'm not worried."

You should be.

She must have glimpsed something in his eyes, for she added, "Look, if they went after everybody caught with a Blowflies broadside or funny in hand, they'd have to round up the whole population."

"Blowflies?" he inquired.

"Have you been living in some other *world*?"

"Yes."

"Well, I guess that might account for the hair. Take another look at that sheet. The edging."

He obeyed, noting for the first time that the decorative border was in fact composed of the recurring motif of a black fly, with gauzy crosshatched wings.

"Anyway," his hostess continued, "for the past two years and more, the Blowflies have been flooding the city with these pictures and writings, all of it red-hot stuff, just thumbing their nose at the Tribunal. They've even got their own monthly journal. *The Buzz*, they call it. Pretty funny, eh?"

"Ummm."

"So they're yammering for an end to the Disinfections—an end to the Grand Interrogation—an end to the Tribunal itself—oh, there's nothing they won't dare. And these sheets of theirs turn up everywhere, all over town. You could paper the Dhreve's palace over with 'em, there are that many. There's nobody to be found, hasn't seen these things, plenty of times. Except you, that is."

"These Blowflies—I suppose no one knows who they really are."

"Right. They're so anonymous, they probably don't even remember their own names."

"And what do people make of their message?"

"Message?" Her loquacity evaporated. She folded her arms. "Couldn't say. I just like to laugh at the cartoons."

He had overshot his mark, and further conversational endeavors fell flat. Presently he departed The Barrel Stave, with the owner's eyes boring holes in his back as he walked out.

Out on the street again, and for a time he walked aimlessly, preoccupied with recent discoveries. Thirteen years in prison. Thirteen years, with never a trial, never even a criminal charge. And now, he had come back to a city crushed in the grip of the White Tribunal, but manifesting some small stirrings of discontent. These Blowflies. (And why in the world had they chosen such an unappetizing title?) Literate, energetic, prolific, and remarkably audacious. Risking their lives, in the service of a cause to which they must be deeply devoted. Who were these Blowflies, and how much influence did they actually wield?

Despite his abstraction, he noticed that eyes were sticking to him as he walked, and heads turning as he passed. Even here, in the scruffiest of slums, his appearance was outlandish. Best to do something about that, and soon. A minor effort of will—little more than a mental hiccup—would suffice to transform him. But his fingers moved of their own accord to the pouch at his waist, tracing the contour of the hourglass within, and he hesitated. Very clearly, he could visualize the granular contents of the glass—the dull quantity expended, and the luminous quantity remaining. Xyleel had furnished a generous measure of power, but hardly unlimited. He would do well to conserve where possible, and recourse to sorcery, where simple mundane methods would serve, represented unconscionable waste.

Not far away, a peeling painted sign bearing the image of a razor proclaimed the presence of a barber. Entering, he was obliged to offer at least double the going rate before the barber could be persuaded to touch his locks. At length, shaven and shorn, he received a hand mirror in which to inspect the results. The reflection he beheld resembled a youthful Ravnar liMarchborg run through a mangle. The likeness between Tradain and his father had always been marked, and time had emphasized the similarities. There was the familiar bony structure of Ravnar's face—same chiseled jaw and nose, same prominent cheekbones. Same intensely blue eyes under very black brows. But Ravnar's complexion, albeit fair, had displayed a healthy color, while the mirrored face was cadaverously grey-pale. Ravnar's eyes had been filled with a thoughtful tranquillity, but his son's were fever-bright, and turbulent with nightmares. And Ravnar's countenance, even at the end, had never appeared so haggard, so shadowed and prematurely aged, so set in bitterly melancholy lines.

Even as he watched, the bitterness deepened upon the face in the glass. Returning the mirror to its owner, he exited the barbershop, proceeding next to a vendor of secondhand clothing, where the pickings proved meager. Rags, for the most part; the sorry unwashed remnants of intrinsically shoddy goods. Everything too big or small, filled with holes and evil odors, stained with wine and worse. Sleazy finery, glistening with fake gold lace. Ancient, yellowing linen. Threadbare dressing gowns and nightcaps. Nothing remotely usable, with the possible absurd exception of a full set of charcoal-grey robes, brightly blazoned with the embroidered badges and emblems of a Strellian physician. The robes were clean, sound, of excellent quality, and cut to fit nearly anyone. Briefly, he wondered at their presence. To what wretched straits had their former owner descended?

He wasn't minded to spend the day searching from shop to shop. The physician's possessions included a square-brimmed hat, a pair of low grey boots, and a leather valise fitted out with scores of small glass bottles. He bought the lot, together with one more item—a pair of spectacles with lenses of smoked glass, dark enough to conceal eyes all too readily recognizable to anyone recalling the late High Landguardian Ravnar liMarchborg.

New purchases bundled under his arm, he made his way to a public bathhouse, where the accumulated dirt of years was soaked and scoured from him. Thereafter donning the Strellian physician's robes, in all their spurious respectability, he felt himself free for the first time that day to walk abroad without shame. His prison rags he discarded, retaining only the dead guard's leather pouch, which he stowed in a pocket of the grey gown.

There were no shadows to judge by, but the clock chimes ringing through the mists proclaimed the lateness of the hour. He needed to find shelter before nightfall, and he did not intend to lodge himself in the slums. Striding swiftly east, he soon came to a decent bourgeois neighborhood, where all lingering doubts regarding his own appearance soon allayed themselves. The pedestrians he encountered—soberly worthy personages, by the look of them—were nodding to him with more than mere civility. The pronounced inclination of assorted heads, the frequent tipping of various hats, conveyed distinct esteem, even deference. He remembered then that Strellian physicians were accounted the finest in the world. The rich, titled, and great of all nations sought the skills of such men, and the community harboring a doctor armed with a degree from the University of Eschelleria might consider itself privileged.

Presently he came to the bank of the silver Folaze, and followed the river north to Singlespan Bridge, where he crossed over into Eastcity, solidly comfortable realm of physicians, lawyers, and merchants of substance.

Physicians. Excellent.

He stood in a quiet, handsome plaza, with a pretty little fenced park green at the center and immaculate dwellings edging the perimeter. Several of the buildings bore the forked pennants of the White Tribunal. The pedestrians about him were well fed and well groomed, the carriages and sedan chairs well maintained. The street sign before him read SOLEMNITY SQUARE, an apt title.

At the south side of the square rose an imposing slate-roofed edifice, with walls of white stone, decorative patterns of matte black porcelain, brass lamps polished to a glitter, and a tastefully discreet sign in the window: ROOMS TO LET.

At some astronomical rate, no doubt, but what of that? Money no longer concerned him.

Presenting himself at the front door, braced to confront hostile suspicion, he encountered only geniality. The landlord—one ruddy and bouncy individual, calling himself Master Einzlaur—greeted the prospective tenant with enthusiasm, and once again, Tradain marveled at the power of the Strellian physician's garb.

Einzlaur led him through the available suite, which proved spacious, clean, attractively furnished, and abominably expensive. A palace, in his eyes. He agreed to the price without haggling, promptly producing a security deposit that left but a single auslin lying at the bottom of the leather pouch.

No cause for worry. A happy Master Einzlaur bowed his way from the glossy marble foyer. Tradain was alone, and a certain subtle uneasiness drained from him. He had grown unaccustomed, he realized, to anything other than profound solitude.

There was a practical matter demanding immediate attention. He set the dark spectacles aside. Drawing the last silver coin from his pouch, he initiated upon it an endless self-replicating sequence; a minor feat of sorcery, accomplished at little expense. Bemused, he looked on as the silver stacks piled themselves atop each bare horizontal surface, expanding from table, to mantel, to chair seat, to footstool. When they were starting to march across the floor, he called a halt, for his rooms, although large, scarcely offered unlimited storage space. As things stood, he would need a substantial coffer to contain the sheer bulk of silver.

Picking one of the synthetic auslins from the mantel, he looked closely. Tarnish in the crevices, sharp nick in the edge, a dent in the cheek of the sculpted Dhreve—in all respects, a perfect replica of the original coin.

How much power had this feat demanded? Drawing the hourglass from his pouch, he stood watching the fugitive granules drop into lightless death. The sight induced unbearable tension. Experimentally, he upended the hourglass, only to watch the luminous matter ascending impossibly and unstoppably from lower to upper chamber.

Not a pleasing spectacle.

He set the hourglass aside. Arcane power bled from the room, and he stood alone in the midst of his new silver hoard. He was a rich man, but hardly contented. Money in and of itself meant nothing. The silver screamed for use.

He was deeply tired. It seemed that the use of sorcery always exerted that effect. Dragging himself from the sitting room to the bedchamber, he fell facedown upon the silken counterpane, and the fragmented plans and memories whirling about his mind dissolved into dreams.

Hours later, he awoke to darkness and deep silence. It was the dead of night. His wildly colored dreams vanished, instantly and utterly. He could not recall a single vivid scrap. But somehow, as he slept, all confusion had resolved itself, his thoughts had ordered themselves, and he knew what he was going to do.

For a while he lay there, drinking the silence, his eyes wide open and blind. Then, rising slowly, he felt his way from the bed to the door, out into the hallway, and thence to the sitting room, brightened with the cold blue glow of the hourglass he had left on a table amidst piles of silver coins. He'd best take care of that hourglass, he reflected. It wouldn't do to let the blatantly unnatural article be seen. He didn't particularly want to see it himself, but undeniably the thing had its uses.

He took up the hourglass, and blue light guided him to the marble foyer, out into the corridor beyond, then through the front door, to which he now possessed a latchkey. He emerged into a blind, chilly world of nocturnal mist. He heard no voices, no footsteps, no clatter of wheels on pavement. Lis Folaze slept beneath its heavy blanket of fog, or so it seemed.

Passing from Solemnity Square, he crossed Singlespan Bridge, then continued on along the river as far as Brilliant Bridge, whose distinctive lights beamed powerfully through the fog. The lanes clustering at the foot of the bridge were dim, with only the occasional glow of lantern or street-light to illuminate the white marble walls and columns of grand town-houses. He could see little, even with the aid of sorcerous luminescence, but his pace never slackened. He could easily have found his way in total darkness.

Soon he came to the house he sought—the home of his boyhood, the former property of the High Landguardian Ravnar liMarchborg.

Tradain stopped dead, staring as if stunned. For an instant, his mind emptied itself of thought, and he was sensible only of a painful sort of inner constriction, powerful enough to stop his heart. The moment passed. Mind and heart resumed functioning.

Deliberately, he surveyed the house, straining his eyes to pierce fog and darkness. He glimpsed no emblem of the White Tribunal, no sign of judicial confiscation. No sign of habitation, either. The ground-floor win-dows were boarded, and debris littered the front steps. Despite its beauty, worth, and desirable location, the place was obviously vacant.

Quite possibly, the property had passed into the hands of the Lady Aestine, upon the execution of her husband. If so, it seemed that she had chosen neither to inhabit nor to sell it. What might account for such waste of a valuable asset? Conscience, perhaps? Did she have one?

He would certainly find out. Assuming, of course, that Aestine was still alive. For the first time, the possibility of her death entered his mind, and he instantly rejected it. Apart from various hysterical nervous disorders, her health hadn't been bad, and she wasn't so very old.

She must still live.

Tradain cast a quick look left and right. Still no sign of human pres-ence, and he slid quietly into the shadows of the narrow alley separating his father's house from its nearest neighbor. As he passed between the two buildings, automatically he tapped the successive smooth marble blocks of the nearest wall, as he had done a thousand times in the past.

Emerging from the alley at the rear of the house, he hurried straight to the back door and rattled the latch. Locked, as he had expected, but a tiny exercise of sorcerous power resolved all difficulty. A certain morbid interest constrained him to observe the hourglass, and he watched a single, luminous granule fall.

He entered, shutting the door behind him. The atmosphere in the back mud closet seemed colder than the outer air. Drawing a deep breath, he listened closely, and heard nothing—not so much as the tick of a clock. In all likelihood, no clock had ticked upon the premises for years.

The mud closet opened on the kitchen, which he viewed by faint, cold light. Always, in the past, this room had vibrated with activity. Always, there had been a fire, warmth, voices, life. And now—nothing. The room was dead—the house was dead.

There was something infinitely disturbing in the sight of the lightless hearth. The musty air seemed colder than ever. It had been a mistake to come here, he should have known better. For a moment he contemplated retreat, then pushed the notion aside. He had come to this place with a purpose, after all.

Out of the kitchen, through quiet, well-remembered chambers whose furnishings were swathed in ghostly, once-white dust covers, to the front foyer, where the formerly gleaming floor was deep in dust, and the fragile intricacy of the crystal chandelier was smothered in canvas. He paused there, and the memories flared like fireworks. Booted feet thudding, imperative alien voices, the bite of iron fetters. The High Landguardian Ravnar liMarchborg, and his sons, in chains. Confusion. Incredulity. Terror.

The stairway rose before him, its dark, lustrous wood dimmed with dust. His fingers sought the underside of the banister, to encounter deep gouges, mementos of his childhood experiments with his first penknife. Ownership of a genuinely keen little steel blade had gone straight to his head, he recalled. He had exuberantly plied that blade everywhere, and the marks upon the house remained to this day. His depredations had gone apparently unremarked, and as a boy, he had simply imagined himself fortunate to elude detection and retribution. Strange that it had never occurred to him before now that the servants would inevitably have discovered and reported the damage to his father, and that Ravnar had chosen to ignore it.

His eyes traveled halfway up the staircase. In his mind, he beheld a thin, pale figure poised quivering there, white hands clenched on the dark banister. Lady Aestine, watching as the Soldiers of the Light took her husband and stepsons away. She had known the charges against them to be false, she could have disclaimed her own lying testimony, she could have said something, even then. Even later. But she had chosen to maintain lethal silence.

She must still be alive.

Up the stairs he hurried, and Lady Aestine's tremulous ghost wavered before him, then vanished. Along the second-story hallway he strode, but couldn't resist pausing outside his own former bedchamber. After a moment he pushed open the door, and looked in.

The blue glow of the hourglass revealed bed, clothespress, washstand, desk, and a couple of chairs, all canvas-covered. Probably they were the same furniture pieces that he had once lived with, but he couldn't be certain—their shrouds robbed them of identity. As for his old personal belongings, nothing appeared to remain. Clothing, books, games, and gear—all of it was gone. There were no ghosts inhabiting this chamber. There was nothing at all.

On he went, past Zendin's old room, then Rav's, until he reached his father's suite, at the end of the corridor. The door gaped wide, a voiceless insult to the former tenant, for Ravnar liMarchborg had never left the door open. Happenstance, or some tiny, vengeful malice of Aestine's?

He walked in, and his eyes automatically roamed in search of a curio cabinet's glass wreckage. Nothing left of it, of course. Like his own former bedchamber, this room had been purged of personal belongings.

To his right, the door to Ravnar's study yawned symbolically. Should the room beyond prove empty, then he had undertaken this furtive, dismal quest in vain. His pulses quickened a little, and he went in.

The study was not empty. The big old desk and chair still remained, their contours recognizable beneath their canvas wrappings. The four walls were lined floor to ceiling with shelves, and the shelves were still filled with volumes, some of them nearly priceless. Ravnar liMarchborg's collection had been accounted one of the finest in Upper Hetzia. Aestine had not presumed to tamper with it.

His slow gaze roamed the shelves. A wealth of knowledge reposed there, the accumulated wisdom of countless dedicated lifetimes. His own formal education had terminated abruptly at age thirteen, and now his plans demanded that he present himself to the world as a learned man. There was no time to read and absorb a hundred well-chosen volumes, or even a dozen. Fortunately, he didn't need to.

The titles jumped out at him. One caught his attention and held it. *Wroqula's Encyclopedia of Natural and Unnatural History*. Not a bad starting point.

He was, he realized, about to expend a considerable quantity of sorcerous force. However, both need and reward were great. Pressing his fingers to the leather spine of the chosen volume, he took a deep breath, relaxed his muscles, and tensed his mind, then recited the syllables and performed the gestures facilitating focus. His consciousness traced the appropriate path, opening conduits in itself, and the alien power flowed into him. He bent that power upon *Wroqula's Encyclopedia*, and the contents of the book were his.

The assimilation of information resembled a miniaturized version of the process whereby sorcerous knowledge had first branded itself upon his intellect. Now, as then, he sensed the expansion of his mind, the swelling to accommodate new comprehension; but this time, the upheaval was relatively slight and brief.

Animals, vegetables, minerals. Stars and clouds, auras and emanations, wind and rain, ghosts and Visitations, oceans and deserts—a mental gulp, and he had all of them, perfectly intact unto death, and perhaps beyond.

Next? His gaze wandered. Another title caught his eye: *Explorations: The Sea of Ice.* He stretched forth one hand. A moment later, and the northern lands—their topography, geology, climate, flora and fauna, contending human cultures, history, legends—all were his.

History. Geography. Biography. Mathematics. The sciences. Physics and metaphysics. The arts. Philosophy. Literature and languages. Logic and rhetoric. All present, all available, and he helped himself freely, taking particular care to familiarize himself with the language, history, habits, and customs of the land of Strell.

He scarcely kept track of his acquisitions. One book followed another, speeding into his mind with the force of benevolent missiles, until he felt his memory quaking under the strain. Exhausted, he sank into the swaddled chair, let his head and eyelids droop, and rested there.

Slowly, the heat in his brain subsided. Raising his head, he glanced about him. His father's study appeared unchanged, which almost came as a surprise; he had half expected to see the volumes glowing with their own internal light. His eyes ranged the shelves, and so many of the works he beheld were now familiar, their contents lodged firmly in his memory. He didn't know the actual number, but the total must have run well into the hundreds. In the space of an hour or two, he had become an impressively learned man.

At a price, of course.

He didn't want to look at the hourglass, but his eyes strayed of their own accord. The glass rested on the desk before him, its lucent contents streaming from the upper chamber. Despite his extreme fatigue, alarm stirred. The flow was so swift, so relentless, it looked as if it would never stop. A malfunction, surely. He could not have expended such quantities of power so quickly. He resisted the impulse to upend the hourglass. He had tried that once, and it didn't work. Was the granular stream slowing? No. *Yes.*

It was.

The miniature flood dwindled to a halt, and he let himself breathe again. Still a great deal left to use, still *plenty* left. Enough for his purposes, at least. His hand closed hard upon the glass, but the light streamed uncontrollably through his fingers.

Rising, he exited the study without regret, made his way down the stairs, through the kitchen, and out the back door into the rear court, where he gulped deep draughts of the chill, foggy air. His new lodgings lay miles distant, and he was much too tired to walk all that way. No other means of transportation available at such an hour, however, and it occurred to him that a small mental twitch would serve to recharge his flagging vitality. A tiny sorcerous feat, so easily accomplished—

He thought then of the lucent granules sifting down through the hourglass, and he began to walk, feet dragging. As he went, his awareness turned inward, to dwell in wonder upon newly acquired treasures, and soon he forgot all else, including his own weariness. He hardly noticed which way his feet carried him, but some vigilant corner of his mind must have mapped the route, for presently he found himself back in handsome Solemnity Square, where the plentiful, polished lanterns lit the way to his new lodging house.

He mounted the spotless marble steps, and spied a foreign object lying there. A small stack of pamphlets—coarse yellowish paper—black ink—some sort of ornamentation—

Frowning, he stooped and picked up a pamphlet, noting at once the presence of a familiar insectile emblem. The Blowflies, again. While he had wandered the night, fondly imagining himself alone upon the silent streets, others had been out, and hard at work. Probably these pamphlets lay scattered all over the city. He thumbed quickly through a couple of pages. No cartoons this time, only printing. An essay of some sort. He would read it, when he found the time. Not tonight.

The thoughtful frown remained fixed in place as he let himself into the foyer, and then into his own rooms. They were ingenious and methodical as they were audacious, these anonymous Blowflies. Their system of mass production and discreet delivery ensured thorough distribution of imaginative sedition throughout the city of Lis Folaze and, probably, beyond. Very effective. Perhaps he might profit by the Blowflies' example. In fact, he certainly could.

Dropping the pamphlet onto a tabletop all but buried in silver coin, Tradain betook himself to bed.

Two days later a modest but very legible sign appeared in the front window of a ground-floor apartment in a fine lodging house in Solemnity Square:

Dr. Flambeska
Physician of Strell
Now Accepting Patients
Systemic Imbalances Corrected

Before the sun had finished burning a hole through the morning mists, the callers were starting to arrive.

TEN

"Yes, but surely you can spare me half an hour," the Lady Aestine insisted.

"The sun is up. It is time for me to be on my way," her husband told her.

"But you need to eat before you leave. I've had the servants set out a meal in the morning room. There's smoked eel, a braided caraway seed loaf, fresh apple cider, preserved cherries—all your favorites. I gave careful instructions, because I wanted everything to be *perfect* for you, and it seems to me that the least you could do—" Her voice was rising and Aestine paused to compose herself. Kreinz didn't approve of shrill, strident women. He regarded a soft, well-modulated voice as a mark of true femininity. He was correct, of course. He always was. "Just fifteen minutes," she coaxed gently.

"Fifteen minutes," Kreinz indulged her.

She meant to use them well. Her husband must carry away such lovely recollections of their last moments together that he would yearn for reunion throughout the term of their separation. Arm in arm, they proceeded to the morning room, where the lush breakfast laid out on the damask-draped table was every bit as alluring as she'd intended. There were no servants in evidence. This morning, the Lady Aestine wanted her husband all to herself.

They sat, and she served him, then filled her own plate.

Kreinz sipped his apple cider, and frowned. "I wonder if it is starting to ferment," he said.

"Oh, no!" Alarmed, Aestine took a swallow. "No, no, it's still sweet."

"Are you quite certain?"

"Absolutely. Believe me!" She was most anxious to reassure him, for teetotaler Kreinz regarded alcohol as a toxic threat to body, mind, and morals. He had never actually forbidden her wine or ale, but she had given them up of her own accord to please him, accounting the sacrifice a negligible price to pay for his approval.

"Well, I shall trust your judgment, madam," he declared, to her delight. Draining off his cider, he applied himself to the food.

For a time there was silence, while she sat watching him eat. His every move, she noted for the ten-thousandth time, was beautifully economical, almost surgically precise. He moved as if incapable of error. So far as she knew, he *was* incapable of error. Throughout the ten years of their marriage, she had never known him to be wrong about anything.

Even his outer appearance, she mused, reflected his inner perfection. His traveling garments, for example—so well tailored, so meticulously ordered, so immaculate. *Fussily neat,* his detractors might have caviled, but that would be jealousy speaking. His facial features—classically regular, with nary a blemish to mark them. His brown hair—freshly trimmed, faultlessly groomed, showing not a trace of grey, despite his forty years. Whereas she, a year his junior, had been secretly plucking the grey hairs from her own head for longer than she cared to admit, even to herself. This was a small vanity of which she was rather ashamed. There was no need to conceal the marks of advancing age from her husband. The Honorable Landsman Kreinz liHofbrunn was too profound and noble of mind to concern himself with trivial externals. *Wasn't he?*

Anyway, he hadn't married her for her beauty, or even for her fortune, but rather for her character. This she never doubted.

The minutes were flying. It was her job to fill them.

"How is the omelet?" Aestine inquired.

"Correctly cooked," Kreinz decided, after a moment's consideration.

"I'm glad," she replied, with feeling, for his standards were high, and he would rather go hungry than tolerate inadequacy. He chewed on contentedly enough, and it came to her that he didn't seem particularly perturbed at the prospect of leaving her. Carefully excluding any note of accusation, she murmured, "I'll miss you terribly, you know."

"I shall only be away for a month."

"*Only?* How can you say *only?* To me, it will seem like a century!"

"It will pass quickly enough," he assured her equably.

"Not for me—" she began, and cut herself off. Assuming a tenderly melancholy air, she remarked, "Jursler and little Wiltzi will miss you, too."

"My sons must learn that wealth and rank impose certain moral obligations. As Landsman of Arnzolf, it is my duty to address the needs of the estate and the tenantry, before winter's onset. Jursler will inherit Arnzolf, one day. It is not too early for him to acquire some sense of his future responsibilities."

Lady Aestine nodded. Her husband's logic was as unassailable as his principles were lofty. Sometimes she almost resented both, but this morning, they seemed to offer an opening, of sorts.

"Certainly, Jursler must learn how to manage an estate," she agreed. "And how better to learn than at his father's side? Take him with you to Arnzolf." Moistening her lips, she leaned forward in her seat. "Take *all* of us with you. Jursler, Wiltzi—and me." Heart beating fast, she awaited his reply.

For a moment he stared at her as if astonished, then smiled kindly and replied, "That is out of the question."

"But why? *Why?* Tell me why it should be out of the question! It would be good for Jursler—you just said so yourself!"

"Yes, but not this year. Next year, perhaps."

"Why *not* this year?"

"Because the existing plans do not allow for it."

"Then change the existing plans!"

"They have been formed with some care, madam. It strikes me as frivolous, even somewhat irresponsible, to talk of changing good plans upon no better basis than a sudden, casual whim."

"How can you speak to me that way? Is it some little casual *whim* that I want to be with my own husband? And is it a *whim* that I believe that my husband should want to be with *me*, and with our children? Does our entire marriage, and all of our life together, amount to nothing more than some small *whim* of mine? Don't you even *care* to be with your wife and your sons?"

"Assuredly," Kreinz informed her serenely, "at the appropriate time. Approximately one month from today. Perhaps a day or two less, if we are fortunate."

"Fortunate—*oh!*" Aestine's hand tightened on her goblet, and she came within a nerve of throwing it. Then she caught her husband's eye upon her, and controlled herself. Kreinz would be disgusted and deeply offended by such a display. He expected far better of his wife. She mustn't scream, she mustn't scold, she mustn't beg, or quarrel, or nag. None of those things helped—quite the contrary, in fact. They would only drive him away, just as they had once driven—

But she didn't allow herself to finish the thought.

She took a deep breath. "I am sorry. I didn't mean to lose my temper. It's just that it's very difficult for me, a weak woman, to face the prospect of spending so long a time alone, deprived of my husband's wisdom, support, and guidance."

"Ah." Kreinz nodded his understanding and compassion. "I know it is difficult for you. But I must counsel you to resist fear and doubt, the two great portals whereby the influence of malevolences habitually gains entry. In your husband's absence, you must rely upon the benevolent power of the Defender Autonn. Call upon Him, wife. Submit yourself to His rule, place yourself entirely in His hands, and He will teach you to find strength."

"Yes." She nodded respectfully, but inner turmoil refused to abate. Her husband's reply, while irreproachable, was somehow less than satisfying.

Kreinz folded his napkin into a neat rectangle and placed it carefully upon the table.

"You aren't leaving yet?" Aestine appealed. "You haven't even touched the almond pastry, and I gave Cook special instructions—"

"The quarter hour has elapsed, madam. In fact—" Kreinz consulted his pocket watch. "It has been exactly nineteen minutes."

"Oh, surely not! Your watch must be wrong!"

Without troubling to reply, he rose from his seat and walked from the room. Aestine scurried in his wake, catching up with him in the front hallway. He pulled the door open, and the sharp autumn air swept in. The liHofbrunn carriage, its roof laden with baggage, awaited him in the street before the townhouse, but he didn't walk out to it. Stooping, he picked up something that lay touching the threshold.

"What is that?"

"Printed matter," Kreinz informed her. "Two separate sheets. A profligate use of paper and ink, in my opinion."

"I'm sure you are right. What sort of printed matter?"

"Let us see." He read swiftly, then told her, "Here is a broadside, advertising the services of one Dr. Flambeska, calling himself a physician of Strell. He is capable, he informs us, of suppressing internal rebellions, correcting systemic imbalances, eliminating pathological inequities, redistributing errant humors, exorcising the Invisible Poacher, cleansing the blood, fortifying the bowels, interpreting dreams, replacing lost teeth, restoring lost beauty, resolving cardiac confusion, repairing lesion and contusion, promoting glandular collusion, repelling verminous intrusion—these are foolish, idle claims," Kreinz concluded.

"Perhaps so." Aestine couldn't disguise her interest. "But I've heard great things of this Dr. Flambeska. He has set up in Solemnity Square, these past few weeks—he is young, but astonishingly learned—he has popped up suddenly, like an actor entering through a trapdoor. They say he performs marvels and miracles."

" 'They' say? To whom do you allude?"

"Oh, friends—servants—merchants—"

"I see."

His tone and expression were forbearing. Aestine felt the blood heat her cheeks. She said nothing.

"No doubt these informants of yours are well intentioned," Kreinz conceded. "I do not believe them guilty of deliberate falsehood, in most cases. They are, however, misguided in their belief that mortal intervention greatly influences the state of human health or vitality. Do men own such power or knowledge that they are capable of comprehending, much less governing these matters?"

A response was expected. Aestine shook her head.

"Correct, madam. We know nothing. We are all but powerless. It is by the will and suffering of Autonn alone that mankind is shielded against the malevolent influence that is the source of all disease. Look at me. Throughout my life, I have placed my entire trust in the Defender Autonn. Have you ever known me to be ill?"

"Never." She spoke with conviction. His health was perfect.

"Then what is your conclusion?"

"That my husband is a wonderfully wise man." Aestine knew she had been foolish, and she wanted to change the subject. "What's the other one you've got there?"

"This?" Kreinz's handsome face hardened. He stuffed both circulars into his pocket. "It is a piece of filth, with which I would not offend the eyes of my wife."

She was intensely curious, but knew the futility of open argument.

"Then tell me a little about it," Aestine suggested, eyes downcast. "Enough to arm me against all danger confronting our sons in their father's absence."

For a moment he weighed the request, then chose to grant it. "We have received yet another seditious communication from those miscreants calling themselves the Blowflies. I will not trouble you with a description of the contents, which are vile, obscene, and contemptible. It is enough for you to know that the legions of malevolence yet assail the virtue of Autonn's servants."

She would have loved to know exactly how they assailed it, but Kreinz deemed such information unfit for her eyes and ears, and he was undoubtedly right. There was no point in quizzing him, especially now. She imagined the subject closed, and was surprised when he spoke again.

"What incredible folly, that they should presume to leave their droppings here, upon the very threshold of an Ally." Kreinz permitted himself a slight curl of the lips.

For the second time within the space of minutes, Lady Aestine felt the intractable blood rush to her cheeks, and this time, in response to a compliment. Her official status, attained years earlier, of Ally to the White Tribunal was a source of sincere pride to her present husband, to her sons, to friends and kin—to everyone except herself. There could be no question in any mind that she deserved her title and honors. A woman driven by principle alone to denounce her first, erring husband and stepsons to the White Tribunal had demonstrated the quality of her moral character beyond all possible doubt. Certainly, she qualified to serve as a model of stern integrity to all Hetzian matrons, and as such she was widely regarded. The reluctance with which she accepted such public acclaim was generally mistaken for modesty, thus enhancing her virtuous fame.

"What impertinence, what an affront to me, to every member of my household—but above all, what an unforgivable insult to my noble wife," Kreinz complained.

"It's no insult to us in particular," Aestine demurred uncomfortably. "These Blowflies simply blanket the city with paper."

"It is unacceptable. It is outrageous. Are there no limits to their insolence? Will they smear their excrement across Radiance Square itself?"

"Very likely."

"I only hope that I may live to see these criminals unmasked and brought in chains to the Heart of Light." Kreinz displayed an uncharacteristic note of emotion. "The Premier Jurist liGurvohl is just the man to deal with them."

"Yes."

"A superbly dedicated and energetic public defender, Gnaus liGurvohl. Peerless, in fact. We are privileged to enjoy his services."

"Indeed."

"You have received the Premier Jurist's invitation to the Winter Commendation?"

"Yes." Aestine's discomfort intensified. The Winter Commendation to which her husband referred was a huge and leadenly formal banquet, annually honoring noted Allies and benefactors of the White Tribunal. Once a year, the favored guests assembled in the Hall of Ceremonies at the Heart of Light for an interminable evening of indigestible fare, and equally indigestible speeches. Aestine liHofbrunn's name was never left off the list of invitees. Much as she detested the affair, there was no escape. She sighed. "It will be same time as always, at the end of next month."

"Ah." Kreinz appeared gratified. "I shall return in ample time to escort you, madam. As always, I shall be immensely proud to do so."

"Husband." The compliment brought tears of painful pleasure to her eyes. "That's something to look forward to, being there with *you*. In the meantime, though, you're going away, and—oh, I can't bear it!" Unable to contain her emotion, she flung both arms around her husband and pressed her lips to his.

He stood perfectly still. There was no flicker of response, which could hardly have surprised her, for she knew full well that Kreinz disapproved of affectionate demonstrations without the confines of the bedchamber. And even there, morning was not the appropriate time.

He suffered her embrace for a few moments, then gently disengaged her arms and set her from him.

"No time left for nonsense," he observed, with a smile tolerant of her puerility. Once again, he consulted his pocket watch. "See, it is already three minutes past the hour."

"Then why hasn't the clock atop the tower sounded?"

"What?"

Just then, the clear chimes tolled through the morning mists.

"See?" Aestine triumphed. "The great clock never lies. I told you that watch of yours must be off."

"It is." Kreinz was thunderstruck. "You are right. I did not think it possible, but it is true. My watch is inaccurate. Unreliable. Imperfect. Here—you take it." He thrust the timepiece in her direction. "Take this thing. I do not want it about me."

Lady Aestine obeyed. "But what shall I do with it?" she inquired.

"Have it set to rights," he commanded. "If that is not possible, then discard it, without delay."

"Kreinz, you cannot mean that."

"Madam?"

"This watch belonged to your father, and before that to your grandfather."

"Well?"

"You wouldn't just throw it away, would you?" An inexplicable dread chilled her heart.

"The sole function of a watch is to keep the hour," Kreinz told her, a little surprised that an explanation of the obvious should prove necessary. "If this one does not do so properly, then what possible reason have I to keep it?"

&ª &³

Following her husband's departure, Lady Aestine filled the empty day as best she could. For a while she busied herself with issuing orders to the various servants—a time-consuming task, for administration of the liHofbrunn household according to Kreinz's exacting specifications was a complex undertaking.

Thereafter, she applied herself to her correspondence, and this kept her occupied for hours. The missives to friends and kin required little exertion, merely consisting of a well-ordered catalogue of triumphs, accomplishments, and recent acquisitions. This list transferred almost effortlessly from letter to letter. Even less demanding proved communication with the lawyers, bankers, tradesmen, and craftsmen, all of whom drooled for liHofbrunn patronage. Far more challenging, however, was the latest petition from the League of Allies, that prestigious association of local philanthropists basking in the warmth of the White Tribunal's favor.

She didn't care much for the Allies, herself. But membership meant everything to Kreinz. The power of her name to gain entree, as she well knew, constituted one of her greatest personal attractions. She couldn't very well afford to throw it away.

This month, the Allies called for an investigation into the background and possibly sorcerous activities of the sexagenarian majordomo in the Honorable Landsman liGrembeldk's household. Such a petition, signed by a majority of the membership, and discreetly deposited in the Hungry Man's mouth, would draw the Soldiers of the Light to the liGrembeldk doorstep within the span of a week or less. Of course, little real harm was apt

to come of it. The Honorable Landsman, partially accountable for the mis-
deeds of his retainer, would find himself obliged, in proof of his own good
faith, to pay substantial damages to the victims and to the Tribunal. He
would also suffer the inconvenience of locating, engaging, and training a
suitable replacement for the inevitably Disinfected majordomo.

Aestine was genuinely sorry to subject the Honorable Landsman
liGrimbeldk, with whom she had no quarrel at all, to so much trouble and
indignity. She would rather have avoided the entire unfortunate affair.
Membership in the League of Allies, however, imposed certain obligations,
as Kreinz might have put it. She had a position to maintain, responsibilities
to the League as a whole, and thus, no real choice in the matter. The
Honorable Landsman liGrimbeldk would just have to accept the necessity
of personal sacrifice.

Sadly, the Lady Aestine affixed her signature to the petition.

This done, she allowed herself the pleasure of writing to her husband—a long, intimate, passionate letter, the first of the many dozens she
would pen during his absence. He was unlikely to respond, of course—
Kreinz would be much too busy at Arnzolf to find time for correspondence—but at least he would see them, he would think of her, and she
would be in his mind.

She ate lunch with her two young sons, then spent a couple of hours
playing with them. As always, she made an effort, when she remembered, to
disguise her pronounced preference for the older boy. Not that little Wiltzi
wasn't adorable. But Jursler was a sturdy, square-jawed miniature of his
sire—how could she help loving him the best?

In the late afternoon her lonely labor over an embroidery hoop was
interrupted by the entrance of a servant, bearing two items discovered lying
before the front door. One was another of those ubiquitous printed flyers
advertising the services of Dr. Flambeska. The other was a small package
wrapped in rose-colored satin, ribboned in gold. The flyer she set aside. The
package she examined with keen interest. No tag, no writing, nothing to
reveal the nature of the contents, the identity of either the sender or even
the intended recipient. Presumably, the offering was meant for Kreinz or
else for herself. Or perhaps—the thought quickened her heartbeat—this was
a gift to her *from* Kreinz. He was thinking of her, he was missing her—

Unfortunately improbable. Her husband, although the very best of
men, was scarcely given to sentimental gestures.

If only—

Dismissing the visibly interested servant, Lady Aestine unwrapped
the package, which yielded a tiny porcelain jar, very plain, filled with a
cream-white, waxy substance. Sealing wax? Tiny candle? Candy or condi-

ment? Cosmetic? She sniffed, and her puzzled frown vanished. Perfume it
was, and a fine, expensive one, at that. Beautiful, in fact. Smiling, she
dabbed the scent behind her ears, along her throat, upon her wrists. The
fragrance, at once flowery and spicy, with an underlying, unidentifiable
tang, filled her nostrils delightfully. For a moment her head almost swam.

If only Kreinz could smell it.

He hadn't sent it to her, that was certain. In which case, who had?
Was it possible that the Lady Aestine liHofbrunn had a secret admirer? Her
delight expanded. Not that she would seriously consider the possibility of
actual indiscretion—never, never ever—and yet—

Here she was, aged thirty-nine, but still capable of arousing mascu-
line admiration. It was like a draught of the wine that she hadn't tasted in
years. Still smiling, she turned to the nearest mirror. Late afternoon sun,
slanting in low through the window, sidelighted her face, cruelly emphasizing every line and shadow. Her happy expression faded, to the further
detriment of the image. Was her face really so thin, so pinched and sharp-
featured? One hand rose to touch the faintly wrinkled skin beside her eyes.
The lines were all but invisible, she decided, so long as she didn't smile. But
there, there in her hair—

Taking a step nearer the mirror, she peered closely. Yes, definitely, a
grey thread glinting there. Right in front. She yanked the offending hair
from her head. Too late. There was no way Kreinz could possibly have
missed it.

He had said nothing, but what must he have thought of her? Did he
find her repulsive, now that she was growing old? Did he wish that she
would conveniently disappear? The bitter tears burned her eyes. The mirrored face contorted unattractively, and the tears streamed down her cheeks.
Then her eyes dropped to the little porcelain jar, the gorgeous fragrance
soothed her, and the tears dried themselves.

Greying, thirty-nine years old—but somebody still thought her worthy of tribute.

She kept the jar with her for the rest of the day. When her nose grew
lazy and ignored the odor, fresh applications to her skin offered reminder.
The scent worked its way deep into her waking mind, and when she betook
herself to her wide but solitary bed, the fragrance followed her into sleep.

Such fortification, however, did not exclude the most dreadful of
dreams. The source of her nightmares, she did not know. Her turn of mind
was not analytical. If obliged to guess, she would have cited the pain of
separation from her husband.

Whatever the cause, the visions were ghastly. She dreamed that she
lay in her own bed, in her own chamber—a particularly deceptive piece of

solid fact that lent fantasy a confusing air of reality. The chamber itself—
although undoubtedly the one she shared with her husband—seemed curiously changeable in appearance, its windows apt to shift in size and position,
its furnishings oddly mutable and frisky. Sometimes, the room seemed to
belong to herself and Kreinz, and sometimes, it seemed to spring full-blown
from a past that she rarely allowed herself to remember, much less consider.

Aestine flipped from one side to the other. Her search for comfort
proved fruitless. Eventually, she realized that she did not lie alone.

Kreinz back home, so soon? Had he changed his mind about taking
her with him?

She opened her eyes. It was nearly midnight, of a foggy autumn
night. No night-light burned in the bedchamber, for Kreinz could never be
persuaded to countenance so pointless and unnecessary a waste of good fuel.
And yet, somehow, she could see clearly.

Aestine gazed into the face of the man lying beside her to encounter
eyes of a crystalline blue that was unforgettable, glinting beneath brows
whose shape and blackness were unmistakable. It was the man whom she
referred to in her own mind as The Other, upon the infrequent occasions
that she found herself obliged to recall his past existence. His name she
never thought of, for the very syllables were freighted with recollections far
too disagreeable to confront voluntarily. Just now, however, both past existence and name were impossible to ignore.

The High Landguardian Ravnar liMarchborg. With her again.

He had changed little in the thirteen years since they had taken him
away, but there were some small alterations. The face that once had ruled
her thoughts to the point of obsession was dark with bruises and dried blood.
The lips were puffed and split, the eyes ringed with swollen, purple flesh.
Improbably, the battered features retained a measure of their beauty.

He lay on his side, propped up on one elbow. His bare body, she
noted unwillingly, was blotched with great, raw, oozing sores. Wet matter
from his wounds dampened the bedclothes. He must have been suffering
considerable pain, yet his expression was serene, his manner characteristically courteous, as he observed, "I told you to expect me home by early
morning. It seems I am a little late. Pray forgive me, madam."

His voice hadn't changed in the least. She would have known it
anywhere.

He gazed at her expectantly, as if awaiting reply. She tried to swallow,
and failed. She strove once or twice to speak. Nothing came out. She tried
to move. Her limbs refused to stir.

"You seem taken aback," Ravnar observed with a whimsical smile.

"A bit." This time, she managed to answer. Her voice was small, thin, and quavery, but audible enough.

"But not displeased, I trust?"

"Displeased? I—am—I am—"

"Yes?"

"Surprised," Aestine told him. "Quite surprised. Extremely unprepared, and, er—surprised. Yes."

"And why is that?"

"Well, Ravnar—you've been away a goodish while, now haven't you?"

"And you, imagining yourself abandoned, were alarmed? Foolish little poppet. Are we not man and wife, one flesh, wedded forever?"

"Unto death," she suggested.

"And beyond, madam."

"I don't remember anything like that in our vows."

"Consider them rewritten."

"You never used to talk that way."

"I like to believe I've acquired some insight."

"You never used to call me a little poppet, either."

"I was niggardly in my expressions of affection. Happily, it is not too late to rectify the error."

"It isn't?"

"What do you think?"

"You've—you've certainly changed, Ravnar."

"More than you can possibly imagine. Shall I tell you how, and why?"

"You probably have better things to do. You were always so busy."

"I have rearranged my priorities."

"Not on my account."

"Isn't that what you wanted and demanded?"

"I don't remember."

"I do. Quite clearly."

"Well—you don't need to be worrying about it now, Ravnar, really you don't."

"Your great desire is granted at last. Aren't you happy?"

"That's good of you, very good indeed. But, really, I wouldn't want to impose."

"I assure you, wife, it is my very great pleasure."

"Wife?"

"Forever. You once doubted my fidelity. Are you reassured?"

"Oh, yes, but—but things change, you know. After all, you've been gone an awfully long time, Ravnar. Years and years. I mean, be reasonable."

"Is husbandly devotion to be governed by reason? Is it not consuming, overwhelming, impatient of paltry constraint? Is it not just such passionate devotion that you have always longed for? Rejoice, madam. It is yours at last."

He stretched a hand toward her. The fingernails had been torn out. The bones were smashed to a pulp. She shrank away from it, but found herself inexplicably unable to quit the bed.

"*I am yours.*" The groping hand closed on the back of her neck. Its touch was cold as indifference.

He drew her to him, and she perceived that his damaged flesh radiated a faint greenish light. She fought hysterically then, and succeeded, almost to her own surprise, in tearing herself free of his clasp.

"*I'm married!*" Instinct prompted her to blurt the one truth that might banish him, once and for all. "I have another husband, now! A live one!"

"Life perhaps imparts a certain superficial advantage. But can his constancy equal mine?" Ravnar inquired. "When you denounce him to the Tribunal, will his affection endure?"

"I don't know what you're talking about!"

"Stretch your memory."

"I'd never denounce Kreinz! He is blameless!"

"So was I."

"You weren't, you weren't! You treated me badly—you made me wretched—"

"Thereby meriting torture and death?"

"That wasn't any fault of mine! You can't blame me for what happened! I'm sorry they hurt you, but I had nothing to do with it!"

"Aestine, Aestine." Ravnar shook his head. "Do you think you can lie to me? Foolish little poppet."

"Don't call me that!"

"Dear wife—"

"Don't call me that, either!"

"Madam, calm yourself. Your faults are forgiven. As for my own, I am here to make amends. Rest assured, you'll never more lack for husbandly tenderness and attention. From this moment on, I will always be with you."

Once again, he caught her in an icy embrace; and this time there was no fighting free. His greenish flesh, she discovered, wafted a stench of putrefaction that merged sickeningly with the fragrance of her own perfume. She gagged, struggled, and her terror heightened to blind panic as he caught her jaw in one cold hand, turned her face to his, and kissed her lingeringly.

For a moment reason all but lapsed, and she hardly knew where she was or what she did. Somehow, she managed to wrench her head aside, gulp air, and voice her horror in a shattering scream, a scream that woke her.

Aestine sat bolt upright in bed. She was shaking all over and drenched in sweat. The room was lightless, and she was utterly blind. She wasn't certain where she was, and she couldn't be sure that Ravnar liMarchborg did not lie beside her in the dark. She didn't dare investigate the featherbed. She didn't dare move. The screams blasted from her.

The door swung wide, and light spilled into the chamber. In came her concerned maid Bettken, bearing a candle and comfort. There was no sign of dead Ravnar. It had been nothing but a dream, albeit remarkably real.

Aestine's shrieks gave way to convulsive sobs. Her maid clucked, petted, soothed. Gradually, her racing heart slowed, and her trembling ceased. She was still alarmed, but a little ashamed of her own fear. She had made something of a fool of herself. Just as well that Kreinz hadn't been present to see it. He would have chided her childishness, and rightly so.

Aestine dismissed her servant. The bedchamber was dark again, and the darkness seemed to press with a tangible weight. She was still perspiring, despite the coolness of the night, and sleep refused to come. At last, she decided to permit herself an illicit luxury. Rising from the bed, she groped her way to the fireplace, where she knelt to apply the poker to the embers of the banked fire. An orange glow lightened the darkness, furnishing wherewithal to light a tiny oil lamp.

In defiance of Kreinz liHofbrunn's dictates, the oil lamp burned through the night.

The dawn brought peace and sanity. She had passed through the worst night of her life, but it was over.

Aestine rose and dressed, with Bettken's assistance. The maid's round face reflected nothing beyond respectful concern. No contempt, no suspicion, no comprehension. She had not, after all, learned the dangerously revealing content of her mistress's nightmare. Really, the girl knew nothing.

Her maid, Aestine reflected with some satisfaction, was a good, quiet, devoted, and industrious creature, competent to mend the finest lace, but not at all pretty. Sadly blemished of large-pored complexion, sparse of dull hair, and crooked of yellow teeth, with little native wit, and less education, Bettken possessed no attraction likely to catch the eye or imagination of a man.

Except for youth, of course.

She was not more than seventeen years of age. Her body, though shapeless, was fresh and flexible. Her eyes, though small, were capable of languishing. Quite possibly, she retained her virginity. Kreinz lauded perfect innocence in women. His standards were so very high.

Aestine thought about it. Around midmorning, she summoned the household steward to her, issuing commands that would ensure constant, discreet surveillance of Bettken's activities. Should the girl prove loose-tongued, or otherwise loose, her mistress would know, within hours. If necessary, it wouldn't be hard to send an erring servant packing, off to the country or off to the streets.

Thereafter, Lady Aestine felt better and safer. She could afford the time to consult a dressmaker, a milliner, a new hairdresser. She could work on herself, and know that she was making progress, or at least that she was staving off deterioration. She could enjoy a leisurely lunch with her sons, during the course of which, little Wiltzi paid her a compliment.

"Mama, you smell good."

She glowed briefly, then realized that some remnant of yesterday's perfume probably clung. That fragrance, its beauty notwithstanding, was tied by association to the ghastliest of nightmares. She would certainly never wear it again. As for the porcelain jar, she would throw it away, or give it away. To Bettken, perhaps.

She wrote three long letters to Kreinz that afternoon, without mentioning the nightmare. Kreinz placed no credence at all in dreams and visions, quite correctly dismissing them all as worthless trivial excreta of undisciplined minds. Moreover, the contents of this particular dream really didn't bear close scrutiny. Those accusations of Ravnar's—the terrible things he'd said—

All true.

Were Kreinz to demand explanation—

Aestine shuddered. Should her husband learn the truth of all that happened, thirteen years ago—should he discover her great perjury—then her life as she knew it would end. He would sever his connection with her, she would no longer be his wife. He would keep the children, and to guard against contamination, he would permit them no contact with their soiled mother.

Even though it hadn't been her fault. Even though she'd really had no choice. Even though Ravnar liMarchborg had certainly deserved punishment.

They tortured him.

He'd probably been guilty. He must have been. The Premier Jurist had been certain of it. LiGurvohl had assured her that she was doing the right thing, absolutely the right thing, and it was his business to know.

Only Kreinz wouldn't see it that way. Kreinz, with his uncompromising probity, sometimes seemed almost too perfect for the real world.

He'd never forgive her.

On the other hand, should his happy ignorance continue undisturbed, then there was simply nothing to forgive. And why should it not be so? There was no reason at all for anyone ever to discover unpleasant realities, provided she herself cultivated discretion—which she fully intended to do.

No cause for concern.

By nightfall, she had all but succeeded in excluding the unsettling incident from her mind. Only one concession to fluttery nerves she allowed herself. Although it was not the proper night of the week for it, she ordered the servants to draw her a hot bath. Immersing herself in the great copper tub, she vigorously scrubbed her body, face, scalp, and hair, working hard to expunge every last lingering trace of the perfume that instinct told her linked itself to psychic upheaval.

She rubbed herself almost raw with cloth, sponge, and pumice. She soaped, lathered, and rinsed three separate times. She applied a different perfume, of assertive formula. All trace of yesterday's suspect fragrance was either eradicated or overwhelmed.

So reason assured her.

But somehow, the scent clung through repeated washings. Somehow it seemed to permeate her being, sinking through layers of skin and flesh to meld with the substance of her bones.

Imagination? Of course. She was perfectly clean, with a new perfume liberally applied to her purified skin.

The Lady Aestine betook herself to bed. Soon she slumbered, and shortly thereafter, she dreamed.

She found her disembodied self floating beneath the high ceiling of a windowless stone chamber, redly lit, and filled with instruments better left unexamined. She hardly noticed her surroundings, for her attention anchored upon the naked figure of her first husband.

The High Landguardian Ravnar liMarchborg occupied a great oaken armchair, to which he was attached by leather straps at wrists, ankles, and neck. His flesh was spotted with wet sores. A couple of faceless figures, devoid of identity, were busy ripping patches of skin from the prisoner's limbs.

Ravnar writhed in his bonds, but no sound escaped him. His courage was all but superhuman. How very like Ravnar.

Prey to horror, remorse, and a certain resentment, Lady Aestine hovered over the scene. She imagined herself invisible, until the moment that Ravnar glanced up to behold her. A look of dreadful hope transformed his face. He was going to speak, and she didn't want to listen. Her dreaming consciousness darted this way and that in search of exit, of which there was none.

"Tell them," Ravnar urged her, "that you lied."

The concept possessed a certain lunatic appeal. Confess the truth. Save Ravnar's life. She'd never actually wanted him to die anyway, only to suffer a bit. Save him, and he'd be indebted to her forever—

"Tell them."

At what cost? She'd sworn falsely, and perjury was a crime. To deceive no less august a body than the White Tribunal itself was triply a crime. That the victim was her own husband further compounded her error. Her confession probably wouldn't save Ravnar; she would only succeed in incriminating herself. She could be imprisoned, or worse. Impossible.

"I'm sorry," she whispered.

"Tell them—" Ravnar began, and broke off with a half-stifled cry as a bloody strip of flesh was torn from his chest.

Her own involuntary cry was far louder than his, but somehow nobody heard it, except Ravnar himself, who gazed up at her with blue eyes full of unendurable entreaty. She didn't want to look at him, she didn't want to see any of it, but her disembodied self possessed no eyes to shut, and the torture chamber possessed no exit that she could locate.

Now they were smashing his hands with iron mallets, and Ravnar was screaming, and she was screaming too—

She awoke, shivering and tearful, to discover Bettken at her side in a lamplit bedchamber. Blazing relief filled her as she sat up to clutch at the servant's proffered hand.

"There, there," Bettken intoned. "There, there."

"Oh, I had such a dream!"

"I know, ma'am. I know. I could hear you yelling, and talking, and carrying on."

"Talking?" Aestine went cold all over. "Talking?"

"Chatty like a litanist, you were."

"Really." Aestine released the other's hand. "And what, precisely, did I say?"

"Oh, I don't know, ma'am."

"What do you mean, you don't know?"

"Well, the words weren't so clear."

"You must have understood some of them. Well, didn't you?"

"Some. I guess." Bettken's eyes slid away.

"What were they? Look at me when I speak to you. I said, look at me. That's better. Now, what were the words?"

"Nothing that made much sense, ma'am."

"*Don't lie to me!* Don't you dare! Now you look me in the eye, and tell me exactly what you heard!"

"I don't know!" The frightened tears were streaming down Bettken's face. "It was all jumbled! Please, ma'am, I really don't know!"

"*Liar!*" Aestine slapped the maid's face with all her strength. Overpowering fear and rage fired her nerves, and she repeated the blow. Bettken, terrified and whimpering, stumbled backward from the bed, one hand pressed to her cheek. Somehow, the sight fueled Aestine's fury. Her voice rose to a shout. "Whatever game you're trying to play with me, you're going to lose! Now get out of my sight, you sneaking, prying, two-faced little trollop! Get out before I kill you!"

Bettken fled. Aestine flung herself back upon her pillows. She was panting for breath, and her heart hammered. Nausea rolled over her in waves. Closing her eyes, she lay still, and the sickness passed.

Further sleep was out of the question. Her brain burned with a hundred fears. Throwing the covers aside, she rose from her bed to pace the room. Back and forth, again and again, until she grew weary, but even then, she didn't dare seek sleep.

Dawn broke greyly, and Aestine's internal blaze reduced itself to smoldering embers. The hideous night was over at last, and she wanted nothing more than to forget the entire episode. She was even willing, she decided by the sane light of morning, to grant that snooping maid the benefit of the doubt. The girl was probably innocent and stupid as she appeared.

That day, she pursued her accustomed activities, despite her pronounced fatigue. Her hands were ceaselessly busy, and her mind continually occupied, to the exclusion of all dark fancies. She managed to acquit herself creditably, successfully concealing all external signs of perturbation—or so she believed, until the late afternoon, when she happened to catch sight of herself in one of the mirrors.

She looked tired, haggard, and pale. Not surprising, in view of last night's miseries, and nothing that a good night's sleep wouldn't cure. But she was beginning to fear sleep, almost as much as she desired it.

Fear notwithstanding, she nodded off over her embroidery in the early evening. She sat in an upholstered chair, beside a lively fire. The comfort, warmth, and jumping flames lulled her. Her lids dropped, the dreams filled her head, and then Ravnar was there with her in the sitting room, standing beside her chair, with the wetness from his many wounds dripping down onto the rug. Ravnar, with his greenish decaying flesh, his blue eyes full of knowledge, his intolerable pseudo-endearments. Ravnar, seemingly solid, and appallingly amorous.

She shrieked herself awake, dismissed the solicitous servants drawn by her cries, and then sat waiting for the strength to return to her shaking limbs. When she could move again, she dropped to her knees beside the chair and pressed both palms to the floor. The rug there was damp and distinctly sticky.

Aestine recoiled violently. Her embroidery work lay nearby, where it had fallen unheeded from her lap. Tearing the ornate handkerchief from the hoop, she wiped her hands dry, then balled the fabric and hurled it into the fire. For a moment she watched her work burn, then turned her face away. A gleam of gold caught her eye. Her dread deepened. Slowly she reached under the chair, to bring forth a small, bright object.

A gold button, embossed with the liMarchborg arms. An expensive little vanity, very distinctive, which she recognized readily. She had given Ravnar liMarchborg a set of a dozen such buttons, upon the occasion of their second wedding anniversary. He'd had them applied to his best coat, and worn them upon the grandest occasions.

The button followed the handkerchief into the fire. Aestine buried her face in her hands. For a few moments she tried to convince herself that she was still asleep, and horridly dreaming.

The attempt failed. Lifting her head, she stared into the heart of the flames, where the button still lay, plainly visible. She turned her back on the sight. A sob shook her.

Thereafter, her haunted life degenerated. She couldn't begin to account for her first husband's ghastly reappearance. She hadn't the least idea why Ravnar should choose to return exactly now, after so many years of considerate quiescence. And she wasn't inclined to request an explanation, despite the dreadful frequency of opportunity.

For she couldn't fall asleep without encountering him. Not for an hour, not for a minute. She had only to close her eyes, let consciousness drift, and he was there with her. Sleep was now her enemy, a realm of horror to be avoided at any cost to body and mind.

The days marched. She had never before realized how long she could go without rest. Far beyond the point of natural collapse, she continued to function—directing servants and tradesmen, planning menus, writing letters, communing with her children, yanking grey hairs, and oiling cuticles. These tasks she performed conscientiously, and justice demanded recompense in the form of at least transitory tranquillity.

Such reward, however, was not forthcoming, for Ravnar insisted upon following her into the waking world. The evidences of his uncanny presence were turning up all over the house. Gold button in the sitting room. Monogrammed ivory letter opener in the bedroom. Whiff of unusual pipeweed in the morning room—and no member of the liHofbrunn ménage was permitted to smoke. Even, horribly, a thread of black hair clinging to the washbasin in the master bedroom. She disposed of them all, secretly and fearfully. After a week, she disposed of Bettken, as well. No telling what the nubile little slut had seen or overheard.

Ravnar's resentful spirit had returned, so much was undeniable. Or else, the possibility suggested itself unexpectedly, these dreadful visitations, and these offerings perceived by no one other than herself, were nothing more than overripe fruits of a tropically heated imagination.

Delusions? Guilty fancies? When she had no cause whatever for guilt?

It was all so monstrously unjust. She had done nothing in the world to warrant such punishment.

Unfair that she, unable to sleep, should wax tired, droopy, yellow of skin, hollow of eye, and—the adjective intruded itself uncontrollably—*ugly*. Unfair that her nervous stomach should rebel, routinely ejecting its contents each evening, as darkness drew nigh. Unfair that her hands should shake, her muscles twitch, her heart palpitate. Terribly unfair that her temper should suffer to such an extent that servants trembled in her presence, and even her two sons had lately taken to avoiding her. And unendurably unfair that a communication from Kreinz should arrive at such a supremely inopportune moment.

In the midafternoon, a footman brought her the letter, together with another of Dr. Flambeska's advertisements. Ordinarily, Aestine would have been delighted. Today, uneasiness excluded every trace of pleasure. With some reluctance, she broke the seal and scanned the missive.

As she feared, Kreinz had written to announce the imminence of his homecoming. Affairs at Arnzolf had concluded some days earlier than expected, and he would return to Lis Folaze in one week's time. She checked the letter's date. Her husband would be back the day after tomorrow.

He was bound to notice her nervous, sickly, melancholy state. He would be repelled; worse, he would be inquisitive. She would face one of his calmly relentless interrogations. He would methodically demolish all resistance, and she would end by telling him everything.

And then?

Aestine let the paper flutter to the floor. She stared blindly at the fog pressing the windowpanes, and the panicky tears streamed down her face.

Eleven

"You thought I would forsake you? Foolish little poppet," Ravnar reproved, and reached for her.

Aestine shot upright. Her eyes were wide open, and blind in the dark. She was fully awake, but consciousness did not free her, for she was not alone. Ravnar still lay beside her, his weight depressing the mattress, and it was vile beyond endurance that his ghost should possess power to pursue her beyond the realm of dreams. Torn between horror and rage, she clenched her fist and struck out fiercely.

To her surprise, the blow connected. She felt her knuckles strike bone, and there followed a grunt of pain. Aestine shrank away from the sound. The featherbed quaked as unseen but tangible weight shifted violently. An invisible hand tore the bed curtains open, admitting a stream of winter moonlight.

"*What is the matter with you?*" Kreinz liHofbrunn demanded.

She could see him, now—angry white face, one hand cradling his newly injured jaw. For a moment she stared, dumbfounded, and he repeated the query. Aestine found her voice.

"I'm sorry!" she cried. "Forgive me!"

"And how often am I to forgive you, madam?" Kreinz inquired frostily. "During the week that I have been home, this episode has repeated itself nightly."

"I know. I'm sorry."

"My rest suffers, and I am visibly bruised."

"I'd rather tear my own heart out than hurt you! You know that, don't you?"

"I am beginning to wonder."

"Please don't say that! What can I do to prove that I'm sorry?"

"Spare me your apologies. Rather, I would desire an explanation."

"I've already told you." She could hear her own voice rising to a guilty squeak. Carefully, she lowered the pitch. "I've had bad dreams. It could happen to anyone, couldn't it?"

"I must wonder if such frequency of happenstance does not suggest significance."

"It probably suggests indigestion." Aestine's attempted laugh emerged a feeble titter. "Or perhaps female trouble. You know the weakness of our sex, husband."

"It is a weakness easily supported by the huge strength of Autonn. Will you not call upon Him?"

"Oh, but I have, really I have, many times. But the dreams keep coming."

"There must be a reason for that. What do you think that it is?"

Aestine was silent. It was happening, exactly as she had feared. The moonlit bedchamber was cold, but she could feel the sweat tingling her armpits.

"Does the topic fail to engage your interest, madam?" Kreinz inquired.

"I don't know anything about *reasons*," she returned, unable to suppress every note of resentment. "You make it sound as if it were all my fault!"

"Perhaps the content reveals the origin," Kreinz persisted. "Describe the latest dream."

"I can't, I don't remember!"

"What, none of it?"

"None!"

"That is curious. Almost extraordinary, in fact."

"Well, I can't help it, Kreinz! But I don't want to bother you with all of this. Can't we just go back to sleep?"

"And awaken to another of your transports? In any case, I am your husband, and it is my duty to provide guidance, particularly inasmuch as the issue commences to press. Remember, the Winter Commendation approaches. You cannot very well appear in your present condition—you are scarcely fit to be seen."

"If I'm so *ugly* that my husband is shamed to be seen with me, then I'll just have to stay home."

"You will do nothing of the sort. I am resolved to overcome this difficulty, but cannot succeed without adequate information. Therefore, I insist that you relate the content of your latest dream, without further delay."

"I don't want to talk about it!" The words burst spontaneously from Lady Aestine. "Would you just *leave me alone?*"

For endless moments Kreinz surveyed her expressionlessly, before answering, "Very well. So be it."

Radiating hostile dignity, he rose from the bed.

"What are you doing?" cried Aestine.

"Complying with your request."

"Where are you going?"

"To another chamber, where I may hope to lie undisturbed."

"No, don't go! I didn't mean what I said!"

"Did you not? So long as you persist in flouting your husband's wishes, I must assume that your professed desire for solitude is sincere. Far be it from me to deny you the spiritual and physical isolation that you crave."

"Kreinz, don't leave me here all alone, I can't bear it! I love you, I want to be with you!"

"The evidence suggests otherwise. Will you furnish the information I require?"

"I can't—I don't remember anything!"

"I do not believe you," he informed her dispassionately. "There would seem little point in disputing the matter, and so, madam, I bid you good night."

"Don't go, Kreinz, *please!*" Sobbing, Aestine stretched forth her arms in appeal, a gesture that spent itself uselessly upon his retreating back. He stalked out in silence, and the door closed behind him.

Aestine struggled for breath. Her despairing gaze traveled the moonlit chamber in search of help or inspiration. Through the burning blur of tears, she discerned a white sheet lying atop the little bedside table, and recognized Dr. Flambeska's circular. She seized it desperately. She could not distinguish the individual words at that moment, but there was no need— she'd read them many times, and they were engraved upon her memory:

   . . . *suppressing internal rebellions* . . . *redistributing errant humors* . . . *interpreting dreams* . . .

And more, much more. People called this Strellian physician a miracle worker.

Her situation demanded no less.

The miserable night ended at last. The winter morning dawned, unwontedly clear and bright. A few stray beams of pale sunshine actually gilded the streets through which the liHofbrunn carriage made its way to the Eastcity, and Number Sixteen Solemnity Square.

Lady Aestine gazed about her with approval. The neighborhood, though less elegantly fashionable than her own, was immaculate, dignified, and prosperous. The house wherein Dr. Flambeska resided was handsome and reassuringly solid. Even more reassuring was the sight of the blazoned vehicles grouped before the entrance. The Strellian physician, it might be inferred, had within a short period established a very impressive practice indeed, suggesting abilities of the highest order. All very promising. Now, if only the fellow's discretion equaled his popularity—

Bidding her coachman await her return, the Lady Aestine marched to the front door and forcefully plied the brass knocker. The door opened at once, and she confronted a plump, ruddy individual, whose status was not immediately apparent.

"Admit me to Dr. Flambeska," Aestine commanded.

"Appointment, ma'am?" the stranger inquired.

"No."

"Well, I'm sorry, but the doctor's full up today. If you like, I'd be happy to set up an appointment for you. Two days from now, there's a vacancy—"

"That is not satisfactory. Not at all. No."

"Best I can do, ma'am."

"I said *no*." There was no response, and Aestine demanded with a hint of menace, "You are this physician's servant, I presume?"

"That I am not, ma'am. I'm Einzlaur, owner of this property. During the day, I'm engaged to receive the doctor's callers."

"You are his employee, hence his servant. Conduct yourself accordingly, fellow."

"I—"

"You will admit me to the doctor, at once. Don't *argue* with me—just obey your orders."

"Ma'am, I would if I could, but you don't understand. There's a string of patients, with appointments, all here before you. They have their rights, don't they? Now, if you could just come back, day after tomorrow, you'll—"

"*I said, don't argue with me!*" Aestine could feel her temper slipping. Understandable, in view of the other's infuriating stupidity, but she couldn't afford to give way to emotion now. She took a deep breath and spoke carefully. "Listen. It is imperative that I see Dr. Flambeska today. This instant. I don't know anything at all about these other patients you speak of, but they'll simply have to understand that my case is urgent." The other's red, dubious face didn't change, and she added, "Do you recognize me? Do you know who I am, who my *husband* is, and who our very good *friends* are? Well, do you?"

"Can't say that I do."

"Then listen." She whispered her name in his ear. Annoyingly, his face didn't change at the sound of it. "Carry *that* to your master."

"If you want, but it's not going to make any difference, everybody waits their turn."

"*You imbecile, I can't wait!*"

"Emergency. If you say so." Einzlaur shook his head bemusedly. "You'd better step inside, ma'am." He let her into a gleaming marble vestibule. "I'll just be gone a moment, and then, if you like, we can set up an appointment for you." He was gone before she could answer.

Then he was back again, transparently astonished, to announce, "Dr. Flambeska will see you right away."

"Ah." Success mollified the Lady Aestine. A burst of bitter complaint died unspoken upon her lips. Really, the impertinence of an incompetent servant deserved no such notice. "Show me to him."

"This way, ma'am."

He led her into the doctor's apartment, through a little antechamber, where the less favored patients glared at her as she swept by them, her head held high. Beyond the antechamber lay a larger, much dimmer chamber. Einzlaur ushered her in, and there left her.

It took a few seconds for her eyes to adjust to the gloom. Then she looked around her, taking quick note of heavy draperies excluding most of the morning light, thick rugs deadening sound, motionless cool air devoid of revealing odors. She took a tentative step forward, and her skirts brushed an obstacle of some sort; hassock, footstool, stray cushion—she could hardly have said what it was.

"Oh, intolerable!" Aestine muttered.

"I implore your patience, Landswoman." A singular voice spoke from the chamber's deepest concentration of shadow.

The sound stirred the hairs at the back of her neck. "Who's there?" she whispered. "Who is it?"

"I am afflicted with a morbid sensitivity of the eyes," the voice continued, "and cannot endure strong illumination. It is the price that I pay for abnormal acuity of vision, both physical and psychic."

"Dr. Flambeska?"

"Your servant, Landswoman."

She could see him better, now—a still figure, seated behind a large desk in the darkest corner of the room. The loose robes of his vocation masked the outline of his form. The wide, square brim of the traditional Strellian headgear shaded his face. She could discern little of his features. She didn't believe that he was very old, but could hardly have explained the basis of that impression. His voice—low, even, slightly foreign—suggested education, rigid self-command, and an indefinable eccentricity. This last seemed less a function of the musical Strellian inflection than of a certain peculiar quality that she could only have described as somehow rusty, or unused. Something in those faintly metallic tones struck her as familiar. The sensation was distinctly unnerving. Formless apprehension stirred at the pit of her stomach.

Ridiculous. "Your servant," he had called himself, and rightly so. As a physician, the man might legitimately regard himself as superior to tradesmen. For all of that, he was a hireling, his services for sale.

Aestine lifted her head and spoke with a hint of gracious condescension. "You are highly recommended, Doctor. I can but hope to encounter abilities justifying the effulgent reputation."

She thought she saw him smile.

"Put them to the test," Dr. Flambeska suggested dryly. "Be seated, Landswoman, and tell me how I may serve you."

An armchair faced his desk. Aestine cautiously lowered herself into it. "I am troubled with—with unquiet slumbers. I require a strong and reliable sleeping draught."

"So much you might purchase of any ordinary apothecary," the doctor observed. "Why do you come to me?"

"I do not care to place my health and safety in the hands of random little streetside mountebanks. Besides—" She looked away, suddenly unable to endure the pressure of his invisible gaze. "It must be a particularly powerful potion, one that will infallibly eliminate all—all possible—all disturbances."

"Disturbances of what nature?"

"Bad dreams." She had to force the words out. "I mean—that is to say—bad dreams."

"Ah."

She waited, but he said nothing more. What sort of a doctor was this? The silence stretched beyond Aestine's endurance, and she found herself chattering to fill it. "I've been having these dreadful dreams for the last several weeks, you see. They destroy my rest, and I'm so terribly *tired* all the time. I'm afraid to sleep, I can scarcely eat, my nerves are quite unstrung, and I'm completely wretched. My two boys, they're finding their mother a bore these days, but children are like that, selfish you know, and they just won't understand how I feel. And my husband—he, he's losing his patience, he doesn't like to be around me, he doesn't understand, or really care, he doesn't, and it's all so awfully *unfair*. I deserve better, and I can't go on like this, I swear I can't! Sometimes I think about killing myself, you know. I mean it. I'm so unhappy, so miserable and desperate, so—so—"

"Tell me about the dreams," Dr. Flambeska instructed quietly.

"Why?" Aestine fired a frightened glare into the shadows. "They're nasty, what else do you need to know?"

"The content of dreams, particularly of recurrent dreams, is apt to prove revealing as it is significant. Trust me, such information may well furnish the insight required to treat your complaint most effectively. Describe the dreams."

"I don't want to—I don't feel right speaking of them, they're not very nice, or proper. Can't you just give me the sleeping potion that I want?"

He said nothing. Silence expanded to fill the chamber, and Lady Aestine couldn't bear it. The words, overflowing the vessel of restraint, began to slop out of her mouth. She had a brief, vivid image of herself as a stone gargoyle crouched atop some public edifice, with the swift stream spouting unstoppably through her widespread jaws.

"I was married to a monster, when I was young," she confided in a taut whisper. "I was a girl, innocent, utterly enamored. Great love clouded my judgment. I did not recognize my husband—a famous High Landguardian, of ancient lineage—for the libertine, liar, and criminal that he was. More important, I did not recognize him as a sorcerer. How could I do so, childlike and ignorant as I was? How was I to know evil when I encountered it, in my husband and his three sons? I did not see it, for a long time. I was blind, and childishly foolish. I must confess this."

"Speak freely," the doctor urged mellifluously.

"Eventually," Aestine continued, "through the agency of those wiser than myself, my eyes were opened. I saw the truth, and I spoke the truth."

"The truth, Landswoman?"

"The higher truth, the *larger* truth, toward which all realities strive. All this was explained to me."

"To your satisfaction?"

"Who am I to judge such things?"

"Who indeed?"

"I served justice," Aestine continued, "and for this, I have received some public praise, of which I am perhaps unworthy."

"Perhaps."

"Doctor?"

"How does this relate to the dreams you have mentioned?" Dr. Flambeska's interest was unmistakably genuine.

"My first husband, the monster, has returned," Aestine heard herself reveal. "Returned to haunt my dreams. Listen, Doctor, he takes the attitude that I betrayed him, when everyone knows he was guilty! It's ridiculous, it's unfair—I did the right thing, the best thing for everyone, and now I'm being made to suffer for it, when I should be lauded! Where is the justice in that?"

"Tell me what you dreamed."

"Must I?"

"Your choice, Landswoman." The doctor relapsed into inscrutability.

Her eyes roamed the chamber. Nothing there to see. She slanted a glance back toward the shadowy doctor, and caught the glitter of his hidden eyes. He was watching her, and she felt the intense concentration of his attention. She knew then beyond doubt that she claimed his special regard, and the realization flashed along her veins. She had caught his eye. He was almost certainly younger than she, but not immune to her charms. How heady, how delightful. Her spirits leapt. She still possessed value. And somehow, she would find a way of letting Kreinz know it. Invite the doctor to dinner, perhaps?

"What can I tell you?" she murmured, tilting her chin at him.

"Your dreams."

"Will they reveal all you wish to discover, Doctor?"

"It is not a bad beginning."

"And the ending?"

"For you to determine. Come now, Landswoman. Tell me your dreams, else I must assess our interview as empty."

"What—" She smiled secretly. "Would you cast me forth into the street?"

"I would plumb the very depth of your distress." His strange voice was oddly gentle and cold. "Permit me to assist you."

His dark presence drew the heart and soul out of her. She heard a woman's voice babbling, and knew that it was her own.

The dreams gushed out of her in a torrent of words. All levity and flirtation left her as she spoke, all recollection of anything beyond the nocturnal visions, and the horror of them. She told Dr. Flambeska of Ravnar liMarchborg's uncanny return, of his unjust accusations, his veiled vindictiveness, even of his unspeakable, punitive caresses. She told of the gruesome mementos strewn throughout the house—the dead man's personal possessions, the hair, the awful damp spot on the rug. She told of her broken sleep and shattered nerves. She told of Kreinz liHofbrunn's reactions to her plight—his understandable impatience, his relentless and alarming curiosity. She told everything, and when she was done, she burst into a storm of weeping.

Dr. Flambeska said nothing. For a time the moist hammering of her sobs filled the room. Eventually, her despairing energy flagged, her outcry diminished to snuffling gasps, and it dawned on her that Dr. Flambeska offered neither comfort nor encouragement. No advice or diagnosis, no sympathy of any sort. He was watching her, quietly and very steadily. Shouldn't he at least say something? Wasn't that his job?

She fell silent. The seconds crawled. He said nothing at all.

At last she prodded, timidly. "Doctor?"

"Landswoman?"

"Well?" No answer, and she prodded harder. "What do you think it all means?"

"That is a question you must answer for yourself, Landswoman, if it is to be answered at all."

Ordinarily, such evasiveness on the part of a social inferior would have annoyed her. Just now, she found herself oddly abashed.

"Will you not help me?" she heard herself beg. "I think I must die, if you don't."

"What do you want?"

"Relief—peace—a cure. What else would any of your patients desire?"

"It varies greatly. The term 'cure' is very much open to interpretation. What is it that you really seek, Landswoman? What would make you truly well?"

"Sleep," she answered at once. "Oh, sleep! And—even more—"

"Yes?"

"I don't know quite how to put it—" Aestine cast about for the right word. "I suppose I mean assurance. Security. Yes, that's it. Certainty."

"Certainty of what?"

"I've never really thought about it."

"Think about it now. It is important."

She didn't really need to think. The truth popped out, and she could hardly have stifled it if she had tried.

"I want to know, beyond all question, that Kreinz loves me. I want to stop worrying about it, day and night. I want to be *sure*."

"Good. Now, I think, we make some progress. And what would make you sure, Landswoman?"

"I don't know. Isn't that for you to say? You're supposed to be the doctor."

"A good doctor is always guided by his patients' instincts."

"Well—" Aestine frowned. The interview, though hardly conforming to expectation, was anything but uninteresting. An odd blend of trepidation and excitement filled her. "I think—some sort of medicine, or—or special elixir. Something to *make* him love me forever, whether he wants to or not. Something—"

"You describe," Dr. Flambeska interrupted, "a love philtre."

"Oh." She hadn't thought of it in such terms. The word "philtre" smacked less of science than of sorcery. "I don't know—"

She paused, as the idea took hold. A love philtre. Some harmless but potent little draught, guaranteed to fix Kreinz's affections in their proper orbit, for all time to come. In short, reliability. Yes, she was beginning to realize. Unsavory though its connotations, a love philtre was just exactly what she really wanted. How clever of the doctor to help her to realize it.

She signaled her acquiescence with a wary if hopeful nod. To her surprise, the doctor shook his head.

"I do not deal in love philtres," he told her.

"Oh. I see. Well. In that case—" Resentment kindled. "In that case, why did you lead me on to tell you that I wanted one? Why did you do that to me?"

"Landswoman, you hardly require artificial assistance to ensure your husband's affections. Your own personal attractions are more than equal to that task," Dr. Flambeska assured her imperturbably.

"Oh." Aestine's irritation ebbed. Still, she was not satisfied. "I wish I could be sure of that, I need to be *sure*."

"It is as I surmised," the doctor informed her. "Your greatest ills and terrors are rooted in simple insomnia. Uninterrupted rest will restore vigor, tranquillity, and confidence."

"I already told you I want a sleeping draught."

"Your conclusion is correct, as far as it goes, but more is required. Your ravaged nerves demand psychic support, throughout your waking hours."

"My husband's devotion—"

"Has never truly been lost to you, as you will shortly discover. I am capable, Landswoman, of furnishing you the means whereby your troubled serenity shall be restored."

So saying, Dr. Flambeska reached into a drawer to bring forth a pair of tightly corked glass bottles, both of which he placed on the desk before him.

Aestine leaned forward in her seat for a closer look.

"Here"—the doctor's finger tapped the larger bottle—"is a sleeping potion of uncommon efficacy. Two drops of this substance added to a cup of milk, or any such similarly innocuous beverage imbibed before retiring, will ensure a deep and dreamless slumber, unaccompanied by physical or mental disturbance."

"Sleep! But—is it dangerous?" Aestine inquired. "Could I become slave to this substance, if I take it for too long?"

"No. It is a sedative devoid of addictive properties."

"Good. But what if I mistakenly drink too much? Might I then sleep, and never waken?"

"Impossible, Landswoman. Rest assured, I would not entrust a patient with any substance possessing potency to terminate her existence. That is a burden I do not care to assume."

"Oh." She had the general sense that he had just said something meaningful, but the words did not seem to relate specifically to herself, and she was not much inclined to seek explanation. "And what's in the other bottle?"

"There is the additional fortification that your particular case demands." Dr. Flambeska's forefinger tapped the second vessel. "It is a soothery of my own invention."

"Soothery?"

"A single spoonful of this liquid will infallibly calm the heart and mind, upon occasions of greatest trepidation. A difficult interview, a crucial public appearance, a disturbing confrontation, or the like. It is, I must emphasize, precisely for such occasional use that the soothery should be reserved. It is a very reliable but somewhat extreme measure. You understand me?"

"Certainly, Doctor." Aestine waited, but he said nothing more. Very soon the silence grew oppressive, and she cast about in her mind for some means of filling it, but found none. Evidently, the interview was concluded. A nervous giggle escaped her.

"Well. You have been of great assistance, and I thank you, Doctor." Rising, she extended an open palm, upon which lay a gold twenty-auslin piece. "This should more than cover your fee, I think."

To her surprise, Dr. Flambeska made no move, and again, she thought she caught the muted glint of a smile.

"I will accept no payment," the doctor informed her, "until I am assured of your complete satisfaction. Make use of the draught and the soothery, Landswoman. Experience the results, and then if you are fully contented—at that time only, we shall speak of payment."

"Well." Aestine found herself at a loss. She supposed his attitude to be very noble, but didn't quite know what to make of it. Unless—the thought dawned like a spring morning—he granted special dispensation because she herself was special. His interest was unmistakable, even to such modesty as her own. The close-lipped, complicitous little smile made its reappearance. "You are very generous, Doctor. Really, I don't know what to say."

There was no reply, and her smile contracted a little in the cold. "Well." Still no answer, and she heard herself jabber, "I shall return shortly, no doubt the bearer of good news."

Silence. Plucking both bottles from the desk, she gave herself leave to sidle from the room.

Past the resentful patients in the antechamber Aestine strolled, murmuring for their benefit and her own, "He is surely a genius." Out into the street, where her own carriage awaited, and then, away.

She had what she needed, and she would now be well. The Lady Aestine leaned back in her seat, with a sigh. She could afford to relax, to let her thoughts dwell at length upon the intriguing Dr. Flambeska, and all that had passed between the two of them.

She thought about him all the way home. And yet it never entered her thoughts that the doctor sat alone in the dim chamber long after she had left, his eyes fixed upon an hourglass, through which the luminous granules sifted inexorably.

Tradain liMarchborg set the glass aside. Strange, almost unreal, to see her again, after so many years. The encounter had affected him less than he had expected. She was smaller than he remembered. Older, of course. Nervously loquacious; had she always talked so much? Vain, deluded, narrow . . . a silly little woman.

Unconsciously, he shook his head. Unintelligent she might be, but all the more dangerous for it, and not to be underestimated. She possessed great destructive capacity, now as always. And terminating her career was a deed no less philanthropic than deeply and personally satisfying.

It would be. It had to be.

TWELVE

The soporific was every bit as effective as its inventor had promised. Yes, the Lady Aestine reflected for the thousandth time, Dr. Flambeska was indeed a genius. A benefactor to humanity, and her own particular savior, for he had given her back her repose and her life.

She slept peacefully, these days. Ravnar liMarchborg had retreated back into the dark swamps of memory, and his importunate ghost no longer haunted her dreams. The house was free of uncanny mementos. Aestine's own health, temper, and appearance had greatly improved. And Kreinz had consented to return to the conjugal bed.

Thanks to the Strellian physician, life was good again. Almost perfect, in fact.

But not quite.

The Winter Commendation loomed alarmingly imminent. She would have given half her jewelry collection to avoid attendance, but escape was impractical. Moreover, her own reluctance, as Kreinz frequently reminded her, was senseless as it was childish.

"I do not comprehend your attitude, madam," he had observed upon numerous occasions. "Do you fail to recognize the honor such recognition confers upon you?"

"No."

"Then why do you not wish to accept your just due?"

She couldn't very well tell him. She couldn't exactly describe the profound discomfort engendered by the annual ceremonial celebration of past deeds better left unexamined. He wasn't apt to prove the most sympathetic or lenient of judges.

"I suppose I am shy." She shrugged girlishly.

"Ah. I should have realized. Such modesty is appropriate and becoming in a woman. It is possible, however, to emphasize even the loveliest of virtues to the verge of absurdity, and you stand in some danger of doing so. Come, madam—you will receive your just deserts."

The prospect failed to please. She didn't allow herself to wonder why. Some things weren't worth thinking about, and yet, she was obliged to answer.

"Oh, but there will be so many people about," she essayed.

"The very best people," returned Kreinz, with satisfaction.

"And the occasion is so very—formal." Leaden, lifeless, tedious, and interminable was what she really meant, but her husband would hardly appreciate such candor.

"The dignity and propriety of the proceedings never fail to delight me," Kreinz rejoined. "In our current age of pervasive laxity, it is gratifying beyond measure to encounter men of gravity and consequence, upholding the strictest standards of decorum. I am, as always, very much looking forward to the ceremony. I should like to assure myself that my wife shares my sentiments."

"I'll try, Kreinz."

The conversation, or variations thereon, repeated itself frequently throughout the days preceding the Winter Commendation—the sole blight upon an otherwise happy time.

In accordance with her promise, Aestine tried hard to achieve the requisite optimism, and failed. Kreinz, of course, had no idea what he asked of her. He could never fathom her inward cringing, and actually expected her to enjoy the public acclaim.

Enjoy. Had she possessed a sense of humor, she could have appreciated the irony.

The ritual commendations were bad enough in and of themselves, but dismal experience had taught her that greater ordeals invariably followed. The recipients of public honor were expected to render thanks. She would stand alone upon the dais at the front of the Hall of Ceremonies, in the Heart of Light. She would face a battery of critical eyes, and she would have to *speak* to them, to all of them at once. Her mouth would go dry as last year's leaves. Her hands would shake, and her belly would churn. The carefully prepared words would fly straight out of her head, and she would stand there, red-faced and wretched, stammering nonsense in a ridiculously high-pitched voice.

So it had been upon the occasion of her first Winter Commendation, some dozen years earlier, and so it had been every year since. The passage of time never mended matters—a reality that her husband refused to acknowledge. Kreinz rarely condemned her fears and follies; for the most part, he simply ignored them. No doubt he was right to do so.

And now, the inescapable horrors were all but upon her, and Dr. Flambeska's soporific no longer guaranteed unbroken sleep, and Kreinz was growing irritable again. Stronger measures were required.

Fortunately, the doctor had provided her with such.

He had advised her to reserve the "soothery" for emergency use alone, and she had obeyed. The potion remained untouched in its tightly corked bottle, but the time to taste it had surely arrived.

Winter's evening, and Lis Folaze lay swaddled in fog. The liHofbrunn carriage—liberally equipped with large lanterns, preceded and flanked by runners bearing links—rattled over the cobbles at a good pace. To its two passengers, the world beyond the confines of the four silk-padded walls was invisible.

The Lady Aestine leaned back in her seat with a sigh of contentment. The feeling of isolation—the illusion that she and her husband were alone, sole survivors in an otherwise uninhabited city—was anything but unpleasant. Fondly, she squeezed his hand. To her delight, she felt the pressure returned. Kreinz was pleased with her. And indeed, why should he not be, now that she had recovered her courage and her spirits?

What a dreary, tiresome fool she had made of herself. Was it any wonder that Kreinz's temper had shown signs of fraying? Who could blame him?

Fortunately, Dr. Flambeska's soothery had proved effective beyond all reasonable hope. A double spoonful, swallowed late in the afternoon, had warmed her blood, stiffened her backbone, restored all her confidence, and more. In short, she felt wonderful.

Now, as the carriage hastened toward the Heart of Light, and the evening's ponderous festivities, nothing short of pleasurable anticipation filled her. She was about to immerse herself in a warm bath of collective admiration. Kreinz had been right all along. But then, he always was.

The creaking rumble of the wheels altered, and she knew they must be crossing Immemorial Bridge. Aestine peeked out the window, but caught no glimpse of the river below. All the universe lost itself in the dense, torch-tinted fog.

The bridge lay behind. They had reached Lisse Island. Fifteen minutes later the carriage passed under a massive archway into the main courtyard of the Heart of Light. The two passengers alighted, and the Lady Aestine blinked, almost dazzled by the glare of numberless lanterns. The great sandstone edifice, extravagantly illuminated in honor of the occasion, for once lived up to its own name. This brilliance, however, did not extend to the guests. The visitors streaming in through the open front portal were uniformly clothed in rich but sober garments, of old-fashioned, distinctly conservative cut—the men in padded doublets and loose knee breeches devoid of decorative slashes; the women in ample skirts draped over farthingales.

Aestine herself was gowned in velvet of the deepest garnet, with jet beadwork sedately embellishing the wrists and high neckline. The dress was becoming to her complexion—the color nipped six or seven years off her age—and suitable to the event. Beyond doubt, it was exactly the right dress. Kreinz was proud to be seen with her; she could read his pleasure in his eyes. Her own victorious smile flashed in response, and for a moment she had to fight a highly inappropriate urge to giggle. She took her husband's arm, and together they marched into the Heart of Light.

In the lofty vestibule, they joined the slow human tide flowing toward the Hall of Ceremonies. The pace was stately, in accordance with the dignity of the company. The hum of conversation was continual, but suitably hushed.

Aestine discreetly scanned her fellow guests. Most of the faces she recognized, at least by sight. Virtually the entire League of Allies was present, together with an assortment of favored nonmembers, culled from the best and wealthiest of households. Notably absent, however, was any representative of the LiGrembeldk clan; an understandable omission, in view of the recent Disinfection of the Honorable Landsman liGrembeldk's elderly majordomo.

Aestine marked but scarcely considered this clear evidence of the liGrembeldk fall from grace, for her attention fixed primarily upon the women in the throng. None of them, she decided, was as attractive as she. None represented any sort of threat to the stability of her marriage. She might not be the youngest, or the shapeliest, but she had a certain special quality, an indefinable magnetism transcending ordinary beauty. And she possessed style, as well. There wasn't a woman in sight so tastefully dressed as she. Many of them were positive frumps. The unseemly giggles rose again to her lips, and she managed to suppress them.

"Look!" Aestine exclaimed in an undertone. Jogging her husband's arm, she pointed. "Look over there at liZauzinz's platter-faced wife, all done up in that excremental brown brocade! Have you ever seen anything so ridiculous? She resembles a midden in motion, does she not?"

"A rather superfluous observation, madam," Kreinz reproved.

"I think it's pretty good, actually. Midden in motion. I like the alliteration, don't you? Or do I mean assonance? Or maybe I'm thinking of euphony. Or—"

"Are you quite well, madam?" Kreinz was looking at her strangely.

"Certainly, my darling. I feel marvelous, in fact. So free. So light, and liberated, and unafraid, like a bird released from a cage."

"Beware heedless flight, wife. Liberty must not be taken for license."

"That's true. You're absolutely right. But then, you always are. I'm not just saying that, it's a fact. You're always right. You're really quite wonderful, Kreinz. Have you any idea how much I love you?"

"It is hardly the time or place."

"I dote on you, I worship you, I can't live without you. Give me a kiss."

"Is this some misguided attempt at humor, madam? Remember where we are."

"Why don't we just shave off into one of these empty rooms? We can shut the door, and no one will miss us."

"Have you taken leave of your senses?"

"But I only want to show you how much I love you." This time, the impulse to giggle could not be totally suppressed, and a small titter fought its way free.

Kreinz stopped dead in the middle of the corridor and swung her around to face him. "Are you drunk?" he demanded in a furious whisper.

She shook her head, momentarily abashed by his expression.

"Then what is the matter with you?"

"Nothing at all, Kreinz. I'm very well indeed."

"You hardly seem so. Have you no dignity, no sense of fitness? Compose yourself at once, and conduct yourself properly. Otherwise, I must send you home."

"Oh, please don't do that! I'll behave, Kreinz. Really."

He surveyed her narrowly, then jerked a reluctant nod. Their progress along the corridor resumed.

For a little while, the Lady Aestine walked in silence, but her eyes continued to roam the throng, and presently the urge to express herself waxed irresistible. "Look over there, at liWenzlorf's wife, with all that huge mass of black hair, obviously unnatural, and that demure little costume, fit for a maid of fifteen. She thinks herself very fine, no doubt. She imagines, because her shape is still fairly good, that every man will take her for a young beauty, but it is perfectly plain that she's forty, if she's a day. She resembles nothing so much as some deluded delinquent dotard tricked out in a pinafore. Deluded delinquent dotard. That's another good one, isn't it? Really, the woman makes me laugh."

She giggled. Kreinz darted a sharp glance at her, but said nothing.

They entered the Hall of Ceremonies, a cavernous, echoing chamber, mercilessly bright. Ordinarily, the place was filled with chairs. Tonight, an immense, damask-draped table stretched all the way from the back of the room to the foot of the dais at the front. The great board allowed space for hundreds of diners, each of whom had been positioned with a careful eye to relative status, as measured in terms of rank, wealth, and judicial favor. Meticulously lettered cards marked each place, with the lesser guests relegated to the social wastes at the foot of the table, rising aspirants ranged along the middle, and privileged friends of the Tribunal grouped near the front. The chairs at the forefront were occupied by the twelve lesser jurists of the White Tribunal. The place of honor at the head of the table, reserved for the Premier Jurist Gnaus liGurvohl himself, was invariably left empty throughout the course of the annual banquet; for the Premier Jurist could hardly allow himself to be viewed indulging in commonplace ingestion.

The Lady Aestine liHofbrunn and her consort had been seated at the top of the table, actually alongside one of the jurists. Near at hand sat their almost equally favored compatriots. She herself was neighbor to the Regarded Drempi Kwieseldt, a notable whose honor and fortunes, though currently high, dated back no further than the occasion of his former master Jex liTarngrav's destruction. The downfall of the High Landguardian liTarngrav accompanied the exposure and execution of the sorcerer Ravnar liMarchborg. Thus, by association, the Lady Aestine found herself unbreakably linked to the Regarded Kwieseldt; always placed near him at public events and private gatherings, forever connected, no matter how she might despise him.

And despise him she did. Despised his pink and pudgy little face, with its too frequent, too effusive smile. Hated his rotund little figure, his soft little manicured hands, his beautifully shod little feet. Abhorred his piping little voice, his prim little gestures. Couldn't stand his uneasy presumption of equality with his well-born betters, such as herself; or his excessively careful manners, reflecting the social uneasiness of a jumped-up little menial inwardly aware of his own inferiority. Above all, she loathed the simple fact of his existence, which served as a perpetual reminder of past events better forgotten.

At least he hadn't dragged his mousy bourgeois wife along. But the son was present, the paste-faced weasel with the drippy red nose. He had been seated down near the bottom of the table, which meant that he was here as a friend of the Tribunal in his own right, and his status accordingly weighed; otherwise, he would have remained near his father. What was the young lout's name, again? Pfissig. That was it. She had trouble remembering that, for in her own mind, the Regarded Drempi Kwieseldt's son and heir was always Weasel Kwieseldt, a title both appropriate and aurally pleasing. Although, it occurred to her for the first time, Queasy Kwieseldt might be almost as good. A loud giggle escaped her.

The sound caught Drempi Kwieseldt's attention. He turned in his seat to face her, and the plump pink smile that she hated beamed upon her.

"Landswoman liHofbrunn!" Kwieseldt exclaimed, with his usual objectionable cordiality. "How delightful to encounter you. You are looking radiant, as always. Splendid occasion, is it not?"

"It was," she heard her own oddly unfamiliar voice answering, "until you arrived."

"Landswoman?" His smile wavered, but held. Evidently, he expected a joke.

"Your mere presence, Master Kwieseldt, suffices to transform all occasions." Before he'd had time to analyze, she inquired in a voice that seemed to arise somewhere outside herself, "And how is your precious lad Queasy—I mean, Pfissig?" She giggled quietly. "Well, I trust?"

"Er—yes, thank you, very well. Healthy and hopeful."

"Hopeful. But how delightful. It is fitting that a young man of such golden prospects as those belonging to your little Weasel should enjoy the very brightest of hopes. And whereon do these hopes center, might one ask? But no, don't tell me. Let me guess. What should any healthy, red-nosed young man hope for, beyond love, true love? And marriage, perhaps?"

"Er—you are very merry, Landswoman." Kwieseldt was clearly non-plussed, but his smile soldiered on. "It is indeed the case, as you have correctly noted, that my son Pfissig has attained the marriageable age."

"My, how careful you are, Master Kwieseldt! How very circumspect, how cautious and proper. Now that you've confessed so much, however, I shan't rest until I discover the name of the fortunate maiden upon whom your Weasel has fixed his drippy-nosed hopes. No, don't tell me. Let me see, can it be—" Aestine applied a thoughtful forefinger to her chin. "Can it possibly be your little ward, the liTarngrav girl? A rather odd sort of creature, I'm told, and daughter to a proscribed House, but—and here is the essential point—a *noble* proscribed House. Her father, after all, was a High Landguardian, of the oldest lineage. Your very own former master, as I recall. The possibility of bagging an authentic, blue-blooded liTarngrav must surely tempt Queasy-Weasel, whose own recently acquired gentility can only be described as precarious. Wouldn't you say?"

The Regarded Drempi Kwieseldt was staring at her, literally open-mouthed. After a few seconds, he so far collected himself as to inquire, "Landswoman liHofbrunn, are you quite well?"

"Why do people keep *asking* me that, when I've never been better in my life?"

"If you will permit me to say so, Landswoman, your manner this evening is rather—er—singular, and as your friend, I feel it incumbent upon me to—"

"Friend?" Aestine interrupted melodiously. "Friend? Do you actually flatter your pathetic, vulgar little self with the delusion that we are *friends*? Master Kwieseldt, has it truly escaped your notice all these years that I can't stand you?" He was still gaping at her, and the sight was so comical that she found herself unable to stifle a shrill giggle. She had a vague sense that she really ought to curb her tongue, but the truth was spilling out of her, and it felt glorious. "Don't you realize that I detest everything about you, from your repulsive little affectations right down to your squalid little aspirations, and that I always have? Your society disgusts me, as it no doubt disgusts any person of quality, and when I am forced to shake your common little hand, I must wash a dozen times before I feel clean again."

Kwieseldt had gone purple-red as he listened, but at the final remark, the color drained from his visage.

"Oh, Master Kwieseldt, I wish you could see your own face." Aestine smiled charmingly. "With those round, popping eyes, and those round cheeks, and that rosebud mouth set in a round O of astonishment—you look exactly like some chubby little cherub, transfixed with an arrow. You must tell me, when you feel up to it, whether it stings much—the arrow, I mean."

She turned away, with an exhilarated little giggle, which died as her glance fell upon her husband, sitting directly across the table from her. Kreinz, she suspected, would scarcely approve of her performance. He could be a little repressive, at times. Fortunately, he had noticed nothing, for he was deeply engrossed in conversation with that sickening simpleton, the Regarded Madam liWenzlorf, and it was quite disgusting the way she was simpering up at him, batting her long black lashes for all they were worth. Really, the woman was so crude, so *obvious*. Perhaps, before the evening ended, there would be an opportunity to tell her so.

Not now, however. Scowling, Aestine turned to her neighbor on the left, the hatchet-faced Jurist Fenj liRohbstat of the White Tribunal, and began to ply him with questions. The exchange, every bit as tedious as she had anticipated, was blessedly interrupted by the arrival of the soup course.

Aestine swallowed a spoonful. Stone cold, of course, having traveled hundreds of yards from the kitchens. Opaque, almost thick as porridge, unappetizingly dark brown in color. Flavor—commonplace beef-barley, and woefully underseasoned, at that. Absolutely typical of the annual Winter Commendation, where the fare was heavy and bland as the conversation.

The dishes followed in leaden succession; root vegetables boiled to mushiness, boiled meats, fowls roasted to near total juicelessness, tough-fibered game, gummy sauces, once-fresh fruit slices sunk in sticky dark honey, like sad prehistoric beasts trapped in a tar pit. No wine, of course. At least the bread was good; fresh, crusty, and obviously baked elsewhere.

Aestine nibbled bread, and chatted with Jurist liRohbstat. The cockroach Drempi Kwieseldt did not presume to address her again. The hum of conversation filling the Hall of Ceremonies was muted, but no other sound intruded upon it. The walls of the building were thick. The screams and moans arising from the torture vaults below, or the cells around and above, remained inaudible. While she entertained liRohbstat, the Lady Aestine kept a watchful eye trained upon her husband and his dining companion. The liWenzlorf idiot was still fluttering at Kreinz. She meant to have a word with that woman, by and by.

The meal concluded, and the dishes were cleared away. An expectant hush enveloped the Hall of Ceremonies. Seconds later the Premier Jurist Gnaus liGurvohl appeared upon the dais at the front of the room. Aestine caught her breath. Throughout her life, the sight of liGurvohl never ceased to produce that effect on her. There was something indescribably arresting and impressive in the presence of that upright, white-robed figure.

Despite his age and silver hair, he seemed to radiate a power almost super-human. His voice, when he spoke, reinforced the visual effect; always a splendid instrument, it had, if anything, waxed in resonance with the passing years.

"Citizens and guests, in the name of the White Tribunal, I bid you welcome," liGurvohl proclaimed. "We have gathered here this evening to honor those individuals whose devotion and efforts throughout the course of the past year have signally advanced the cause that unites all morally sentient Hetzians—the eradication of the sorcerous blight infecting our nation. It is right and fitting that the many quiet heroes and heroines among us receive the public recognition that their extraordinary services merit. For it is only by grace of the energy and loyalty of the courageous and the concerned that the White Tribunal continues to function in its protective capacity. We jurists of the Tribunal depend upon the support of the citizens to assist us in our great task. Alone, we are feeble as children. Sustained by the favor of Autonn, and the strength of our compatriots, there is nothing we may not hope to accomplish. In the end, it is the conjoined strength of multitudes that will achieve the ultimate triumph."

The Premier Jurist spoke on, but the Lady Aestine lost the thread of his discourse, allowing her mind simply to drift on the ebb and flow of that remarkable voice. For a time she even forgot the interaction between her husband and Madam liWenzlorf. Presently, however, she became aware that liGurvohl's introductory remarks had concluded, and that the real, mind-numbing activity of the evening was actually under way. One by one, the recipients of judicial commendation were being called to the dais, to accept the symbolic white cockade, and to express becomingly humble gratitude.

The High Landguardian Runki liJunzkoldt was first to be summoned. LiJunzkoldt, a hirsute and bandy-legged hero, had distinguished himself simply by virtue of his frequent, munificent contributions to judicial coffers. The drain upon his own resources must have been severe, but a worthwhile investment, in view of the resulting domestic security. So long as the golden flow continued, no member of the liJunzkoldt household need ever fear an accusation of sorcery.

The High Landguardian Runki stepped up to the dais, amidst dutiful applause, to accept his token from the hand of Gnaus liGurvohl. He blathered out his thanks at fervent length, then returned to his seat.

The High Landguardian Lartzl liZauzinz was next, and his speech of acceptance was a fair replica of his predecessor's. Then came the Honorable Landswoman Nylvie liOrmsler, who adorned her performance with prettily sentimental tears. Then the Regarded Biedr liWenzlorf, and more of the same. And so they came and went, one after another, in a never-endingly grateful parade.

The Lady Aestine found it impossible to keep track of them all, or indeed, to mark the contents of their virtually indistinguishable paeans. Up and down, back and forth, boring, boring, boring. She let her mind wander far away. The parade continued. Presently, the sound of her own name being called broke the glaze of indifference.

Her turn at last. Heart beating fast, she rose to her feet. Her eyes flew to her husband's face, and she saw him smiling at her. She beamed back at him. A giggle rose to her lips, but she managed to hold it in.

Chin up, modestly ecstatic smile in place, she swept to the front of the hall. Maneuvering her long garnet skirts with skill and deliberate grace, she mounted the dais. A few more paces brought her face-to-face with Premier Jurist Gnaus liGurvohl. She'd almost forgotten how tall he was, and how penetrating his pale eyes. But tonight, she was not afraid of him. Tonight, she feared nothing. The amazing voice washed over her. Even now, she wasn't quite picking up every word.

". . . *Honorable Landswoman Aestine liHofbrunn . . . member of the League of Allies . . . civic benefactress . . . admirable accomplishments . . . loyalty, generosity, and service . . . in appreciation whereof . . .*"

He was handing her the white cockade—another, to add to her ever-expanding collection. She took it, with a broad, brilliant smile that for some reason deepened the vertical crease between the Premier Jurist's brows. Time to render thanks. Aestine turned to confront the audience. She saw hundreds of faces, hundreds of eyes watching her, and she wasn't afraid of them at all. She wasn't even mildly uneasy. She had never felt better. A high-pitched giggle bubbled out of her. The audience, mistaking it for nervousness, laughed sympathetically.

"Well. I hardly know what to say." That was entirely true, for the prepared speech had fled her mind. But Aestine was not worried, for her voice seemed to have taken on an active life of its own, and somehow her voice didn't find itself at all at a loss. She tossed her head coquettishly. "I suppose I *ought* to say that I'm unworthy of such an honor. That would be the *proper* thing for a modest woman to say, and I know my husband would approve. Because my husband, you see, regards modesty as an essential quality of the virtuous woman, along with obedience and propriety, and my husband is always right. Always. Aren't you, Kreinz?"

Again, her audience laughed. Kreinz smiled stiffly.

"But honesty is a tremendous virtue as well," Aestine resumed when the laughter died. "And honesty compels me to admit that I *am* worthy of this honor—entirely worthy. I deserve it, more than anyone. I really don't think that anybody here deserves it *half* as much as I do. You want to know why?"

She surveyed her audience, to encounter amazement writ large upon every countenance.

"Because nobody here has suffered, as I have," Aestine confided. "Nobody else has been horribly persecuted, as I have. Listen, if you people had the least idea what I've been through lately, you wouldn't just be handing me some piddling little white cockade, you'd be setting up my statue in Radiance Square! You'd be writing tributes to me, and naming *buildings*, and *ships*, and *children*, and things, after me! You see, my own courage and generosity have cost me dearly. I've been dreadfully and unjustly tormented. Worse—I've been haunted.

"You people don't know what I'm talking about, so I'll explain. You probably all remember—well, the young ones like Weasel-Queasy down there at the bottom of the table might not remember—but most of you know that I was once married to the Enlightened sorcerer, the High Land-guardian Ravnar liMarchborg. It was my testimony before the White Tribunal that was largely instrumental in bringing the criminal to justice thirteen years ago, and for that, I was justly lauded.

"But have I been left in peace to rest upon my well-earned laurels? No, I have not—for Ravnar has lately returned, to torture me! Would you believe that he dares assume the role of the injured party? He complains that I perjured myself in swearing that I'd witnessed him engage in sorcerous rites. Well, it's true that I never actually *saw* it with my own eyes, but isn't that a silly little technicality? I mean, everybody knew that he was guilty! Everybody knew it, even though he pretended to be so perfect! He was a cruel, cold-hearted monster—nobody knew that better than I. He never cared anything at all about *my* feelings. He was guilty! And when I stood up before the White Tribunal, thirteen years ago, and swore that he was guilty, I was serving the larger truth! LiGurvohl told me so, and he should certainly know! Anyway, when it was so clear that Ravnar was going to fall, no matter what, who can blame me for saving myself? Who among you wouldn't have done the same?

"As for the rest of it, I take no responsibility. I'm sorry he was put to the Grand Interrogation, really I am, but it wasn't my fault, was it? And as for those three boys of his, they weren't my concern. Anyway, they were very cruel to me, and probably in league with their father. They were just like him!

"So you see," Aestine summed up, "my afflictions have been

undeserved as they are unbearable. But for the skills of an exceptional physician, I don't think I should have survived to be here with you this evening. I've suffered terribly for the sake of my country, I've sacrificed and sorrowed more than anyone, and therefore know myself justified in my assurance that I fully *deserve* tonight's commendation, and more."

Aestine paused, breathing heavily. For several seconds there was no sound to be heard—not a whisper, not a cough, not so much as the hiss of an indrawn breath. Really, the silence was extraordinary. Why weren't they applauding? Her eyes ranged the length of the table, sliding over many a set and stony face, to light at last upon her husband's visage. What she saw there chilled her.

Kreinz's expression was peculiar, even alarming. Why in the world was he staring at her that way, as if he gazed for the first time upon some exotic, repulsive wonder in a freak show? Why was his mouth all twisted up into that ugly sneer of disgust, and why were his eyes burning with such— what? Loathing? Horror? Both? What could he have seen, or heard?

In her mind, she listened to her own voice, temporarily imbued with a will of its own, hurrying on and on along its own inconceivable course, and it seemed then, for the first time, that she actually heard the words she had just spoken. With recognition came comprehension, and she knew then exactly what she had done.

Aestine's mouth worked, but no sound emerged. Her voice, so appallingly audible moments earlier, seemed to have trapped itself in her constricted throat. And she needed that voice, to take back those lunatic words.

I didn't know what I was saying, she wanted to shout. *None of it was true. I was mad. I was drunk. I was ensorcelled.*

Again she strove to speak, again failed, and the panic boiled up inside her, for she was doomed, unless she could somehow make them understand.

But they do understand. A remarkably sane, subtly familiar voice spoke, somewhere deep in her mind. *They understand perfectly.*

Nightmare. She was having another of her nightmares. At any moment Ravnar liMarchborg would appear, to label her a foolish little poppet. Dreadful, but only imaginary. Aestine squeezed her eyes shut. When she opened them, a moment later, it was to discover the scene unchanged, and absolutely real. Correction. There were some slight changes, visible upon the faces of various spectators, whose initial astonishment was giving way to hostility. And Kreinz—his expression—his eyes—worse than outraged, worse even than contemptuous, his eyes were so—

Removed. That calm, truthful, indefinably familiar voice spoke again, deep inside her mind. *Uninvolved.*

She knew then, beyond the slightest tremor of a doubt, that Kreinz was finished with her. He would never forgive her, never again be her husband. The connection between the two of them was broken forever. All that was plain in his eyes, but she couldn't let herself see it.

Instinctively she turned away, only to confront the implacable gaze of the Premier Jurist. Even thus, she imagined, he must appear as he presided over the Grand Interrogation. Of this, she might shortly be granted opportunity to judge for herself.

She had, after all, publicly confessed to felonious perjury, resulting in the execution of a High Landguardian and his sons. She had even gone so far as to implicate the Premier Jurist of the White Tribunal himself. *LiGurvohl told me so* . . . a slip of the tongue that made him her mortal enemy, and an error she was unlikely to survive for long. A terrified sob broke from the Lady Aestine.

LiGurvohl's face did not alter. Presumably his profession had inured him to the various expressions of human misery. She could not endure the pressure of his remorseless scrutiny. They were all staring at her as if they watched some sort of loathsome monster, all of them, all hating her, and she couldn't bear it.

Weeping bitterly, the Lady Aestine backed away from the Premier Jurist, as far as the edge of the dais, where she turned and stumbled down the stairs. At the bottom, she picked up her skirts and fled for the exit at the back of the Hall of Ceremonies. Past the multitude of silent spectators she sprinted, half expecting to be forcibly halted, but nobody made a move to arrest her flight. She hurtled through the open door, out into the mercifully deserted corridor.

The corridor enclosed her, and then she was in the vestibule, and then she was out in the glaringly lit courtyard, where she halted to gaze about her in confusion. The place was full of carriages, scores of them, hundreds of them, and she could spend hours trying to locate her own, and she didn't have hours, she had to get out *now*, this instant.

"LiHofbrunn!" She hardly recognized the voice that sped from her lips as her own, so shrill, and discordant, and wild it was; so utterly lacking in the soft restraint that Kreinz considered pleasing in a woman. *"LiHofbrunn!"*

"Here, madam."

She wheeled to confront one of the household footmen, and saw the fellow's eyes widen at sight of her flushed and tear-stained face.

"Take me home!" Aestine commanded. He didn't move, but stood staring at her stupidly, and her voice rose to a shriek. *"Home!"*

"At once, madam."

She followed him to the liHofbrunn carriage, and as she went, she became aware that she was muttering over and over, as if to invoke a charm, "Home. Home. Home."

She climbed in, and the door closed behind her. The coachman snapped his whip, and the carriage rattled to life, swiftly bearing her from the courtyard, under the sandstone archway, and out into the foggy regions beyond.

"Home. Home. Home." She could hear her own voice, still muttering.

She knew when the carriage passed over Immemorial Bridge, but thereafter lost all track of time and place. Fog blotted out the city. She had no idea where she was, or where her refuge lay.

"Home. Home. Home."

You no longer have a home. It was that inexorable inner voice again, and this time, she recognized it. She wondered somewhat at the absence of Strellian inflection, but the distinctive metallic timbre was unmistakable.

Aestine stuck her head out the open window, filled her lungs with chill winter mist, and shrilled a command at the invisible driver.

"Coachman! Solemnity Square!"

The carriage halted, and the Lady Aestine jumped out. The house she sought arose before her, its lanterns alight, its curtained windows glowing. Good. The inhabitants were at home and still awake. Approaching the front door, she plied the knocker violently. She was fully prepared, should circumstances warrant, to summon her driver, with a crowbar. Such measures proved unnecessary, for the door opened almost at once. The Einzlaur person stood before her, his ruddy face crinkled with surprise.

She pushed past him without a word. Rushing straight across the marble foyer to Dr. Flambeska's apartment, she kicked the unlocked door open and strode on in.

The little antechamber was empty. The room beyond was not.

Lady Aestine paused on the threshold. The place was not quite as she remembered, and it took a moment to identify the difference. Last time, the shadowy dimness had swallowed all color. Tonight, the warmth of lamplight heightened the rich hues of the window hangings and the thick rugs underfoot. Dr. Flambeska sat at his desk, with a ledger spread before him, and a quill in one hand. Her initial impression of his youth was reinforced by the sight of that hand, but she could see little else. His face, though turned toward her, lost itself in the shade of his wide hat.

"What have you done to me?" The words exploded from her. There

was no immediate reply, and she answered her own question, "*You have destroyed me!*"

"What is the precise nature of your complaint, Landswoman?" the doctor inquired.

"Hypocrite, you already know! You did it on purpose, don't deny it. Those potions you gave me—that soothery—I think it's poisonous, and sorcerous! Yes, I'm sure it must be sorcerous, and I'm going to say so! Do you hear me, you charlatan? You're going to be sorry you ever—"

"The soothery failed to perform as promised, madam? You found no ease, no happy assurance?"

"Too much of both! I swallowed it, and felt free to blurt out secret truths certain to destroy me."

"Had you an ear for archaism, you might have expected as much."

"I don't know what you're talking about! But I do know that you planned this, you *wanted* it to happen! You took advantage, you deceived and *plotted* against me—"

"Why should I do so, Landswoman?"

"Yes, why? That's what I've come to find out! I trusted you, I relied on you! How could you do this to me? I've never harmed you, I don't even know you. I've never harmed anybody at all—"

"The effect of the soothery has worn off, I see. But let us try to correct a couple of misstatements. You do know me, Landswoman, and you've harmed many. Your lying testimony sent Ravnar liMarchborg and two of his sons to execution, and condemned the third son to a living death. Your motives were varied, but not the least of your incentives was the personal promise of Gnaus liGurvohl that the bulk of Ravnar liMarchborg's estate would pass to you."

"That's a lie!"

"It is no lie, nor is it a lie to recall that you once attempted to burn Ravnar liMarchborg alive in his study."

"No! He was in no real danger, I was only trying to make a point! How did you—"

"Following the death of your husband," Dr. Flambeska continued, his voice gradually ridding itself of Strellian inflection, "you deemed it politic to demonstrate conspicuous loyalty to judicial interests. Such demonstrations frequently took the form of cooperative denunciation. Since Ravnar's death, scarcely a year has passed that your name has not attached itself to accusations resulting in some unfortunate's execution. The most profitable of such coups ended in the Disinfection of the High Landguardian Hins liStrohlhurn, thus diverting the Landsman's wealth to the coffers of the White Tribunal. The most pathetic and reprehensible plunged the

Honorable Landswoman Klaro liBreisenbane and her three young daughters into the cauldron."

"They weren't all *that* young, it wasn't as if they were children! And I wasn't the only one to sign that denunciation! Anyway, it all happened over ten years ago. How did you—"

"It must not be supposed," Dr. Flambeska spoke on, "that your victims sprang from the ranks of the wealthy and titled alone. In all likelihood, no one has ever troubled to keep count of the various servants, retainers, tradesmen, and similarly insignificant wretches falling prey to your malice."

"Malice?" She was genuinely shocked. "I?"

"They are not all entirely anonymous and forgotten, however. No doubt his kin still recall the face of the recently murdered Irsto Groyst—"

"Who?"

"The old majordomo at liGrembeldk House, Disinfected a couple of weeks ago. Perhaps the incident has slipped your mind."

"That wasn't *my* doing. Anyway, he—"

"Then there is the matter of Bettken, your own innocent maidservant, turned out of doors to starve, or worse."

"Innocent? She was a harlot and a prying slattern! She—"

"The girl has been decently provided for, by the way. I have seen to that."

"You have seen! What has any of this to do with you? How did you even know about what's 'er name—Bettken?"

"I've excellent means of observation."

"You've been spying on me! You've paid someone in my house to inform—some sneaking, mercenary traitor. Well, I can afford to laugh at slander, it won't touch me! The world knows what kind of woman I am. I have friends—position—influence—"

"Do you? After tonight?" the doctor inquired.

"What could you know about tonight? You weren't even there!"

"And yet I know that tonight you stood before that small assemblage whose membership constitutes your world, to confess your blackest crime. Hereafter, your life alters."

"Don't say that to me! Don't say it! How can you know these things? How can you treat me this way? And why? Are you some sort of malevolence, sent to torment the innocent?"

"I am no more a malevolence, Landswoman, than you are an innocent. I have already said that you know me."

"For the past few weeks—"

"Far longer. Search your memory. When you recognize me, you will comprehend all."

"What became of your Strellian accent?"

"I am Hetzian, and I have never set foot outside this country."

"I don't understand, and I can't play this horrible game of yours! If we know each other, then just tell me who you are!"

"I will do better than that." So saying, Dr. Flambeska drew the desk lamp nearer himself, removed his wide hat, and turned his face to the light.

"*Ravnar*," the Lady Aestine whispered.

"Ravnar liMarchborg is dead, Landswoman. In the sense that your mind holds him, he is currently nonexistent, and therefore irretrievable." Somehow the doctor sounded as if he were reciting something learned by rote.

"Of course you are dead, Ravnar. D'you think I don't know that?"

"I am not Ravnar." The doctor's distinctive and perfectly unmistakable blue eyes sought hers. "He had three sons. You remember?"

"Yes, certainly. They all resented me, they were rude and cruel. No matter how they behaved, though, you always sided with *them*."

"Look at me, Aestine. Come to your senses, and see clearly, for once in your life. I am Ravnar's youngest son, consigned by your doing to the Fortress Nul, these thirteen years. Now I am back, and it is time for the truth between us. You know what you did, and you know who I am."

"Those three boys. I always had trouble keeping their names straight. And it was all so long ago."

"Speak my name. You have not forgotten it."

"Must you torture me, Ravnar? Have I not suffered enough?"

"*Tradain liMarchborg*," the doctor exclaimed with startling vehemence. "I am Ravnar's son, Tradain liMarchborg. *Look at me, Aestine.*"

"Ravnar's son?"

"Do you understand?"

"No. Ravnar's son? His son? What could you want of me now, after all these years?"

He was silent. It almost seemed that the question confounded him.

"You shouldn't have come back," Aestine observed dully. "It isn't right. You really shouldn't be here."

"You've a debt, Landswoman."

"You've persecuted, betrayed, and ruined an unhappy woman. Isn't that enough? What more could you want of your victim?"

"Victim?"

"Do you wish to whip me, perhaps to drink my blood? Would that make you happy, Ravnar's son? For I see you live to vent your cruelty upon the harmless and helpless."

"Look at me, Aestine. *See me.* I am Tradain liMarchborg, whom you buried alive, and whose family you destroyed. Will you look at me, and acknowledge the truth?"

"Gladly! The truth is that none of it was my fault! The White Tribunal passed judgment—I didn't do it! I wasn't responsible! It was the Tribunal! It isn't fair to blame *me!*"

For a time there was silence so profound that the tap of anonymous footsteps in the street outside was clearly audible. Dr. Flambeska spoke at last.

"I thought, when you recognized me, that you would comprehend all." He was staring at her, almost in disbelief. "I was wrong."

"What is there to comprehend? I—"

"You are unassailable. Your world may shatter, but your mind remains impervious. It is a kind of strength, I suppose."

"What do you mean?"

"That it is time for you to go."

"Oh. Yes. I want to go." She took a couple of slow steps toward the door, and paused to look back at him. "You must understand that I never meant any harm. What happened was none of my choosing. Events took their own course, and I simply couldn't control them. I was as much a victim as anyone, you know. I'm really sorry things turned out so unpleasantly."

"You are sorry?" His look of incredulity deepened. "You've wrecked human lives by the dozen, and you are merely—sorry?"

"Well—" She shrugged, with the faintest suggestion of petulance. "Really, what else can I say?"

Head adroop, and feet dragging, the Lady Aestine departed.

Her carriage awaited in the street before the doctor's lodgings, but the thought of its silk-lined confines, padded and tufted like an expensive coffin, repelled her. She wandered off blindly into the fog, and for an indeterminate period, trudged the unfamiliar streets of Eastcity. Eventually, it dawned upon her that she was quite lost. Hopelessly lost, in fact. She might never find her way home.

You have no home.

It was quite possible that Kreinz would refuse her admittance. Almost certainly, he'd keep her away from the boys. As their father, he had the legal right, but it wasn't fair, she wasn't really to blame for all that happened, she'd had no choice. *Unfair.*

The tears rose to her eyes, brimmed over, and spilled down her cheeks. Dr. Flambeska's face, *Ravnar's face*, filled her mind, and she remembered how dreadful she'd felt, the night they'd taken him away. Her conscience had troubled her terribly, but it hadn't really been her fault, because she'd meant to warn him. She'd even gone to his study that afternoon, fully prepared to tell him everything, but he'd proved so clearly reluctant to admit her to his precious sanctum that she'd lost her temper, broken a glass curio cabinet, and withdrawn, the message unspoken. Things might have been very different, if only he'd been nicer to her, and so, in a very real sense, Ravnar had brought his misfortunes upon himself. It wasn't right to blame *her*.

She had come to the bank of the Folaze. Miserably, she plodded on along the water's edge, until she spied the lights of Singlespan Bridge, beckoning through the blur of fog and tears. Instinct led her out onto the deserted bridge, where she paused, leaning heavily upon the guardrail, to listen to the invisible water lapping at the pilings below. She heard nothing else. So far as she knew, she was utterly alone.

But not for long.

They would be coming for her, as soon as it was light, she realized. Soldiers of the Light, or Dhrevian Guards, or perhaps simply the officers of the Watch, she didn't know which, and it hardly mattered. One way or another, the arrest of the self-confessed felonious perjurer was inevitable. And after that? Criminal charges, a trial of some ghastly sort, disgrace and imprisonment, or worse. She might even face the White Tribunal itself. And she was a famous *friend* of the Tribunal—she had furnished support and assistance, time and again!

No matter. She could expect no loyalty, and no mercy. She could expect nothing beyond cruelty, treachery, and betrayal, for that was the way of humanity; a truth that she, in her innocence, had never fully recognized, until now.

Nowhere to hide. No help from those who *should* have cared about her.

Bitter sobs racked the Lady Aestine. The salt tears fell from her eyes, to mingle with the fresh water of the Folaze. She could still hear the wavelets plashing, and it seemed to her then that the river spoke, in tones inexpressibly lovely and comforting; spoke of escape, of safety, of rest, and of peace.

Aestine listened, and her sobs subsided. She clambered up onto the guardrail, and sat there for a little while, contemplating her past life, and the various selfish, unappreciative, abusive ingrates who had filled it.

When they discover what they've driven me to, they'll be sorry they treated me the way they did!

With this consoling thought in mind, she launched herself from Singlespan Bridge, plummeting through the mists toward the sole safe haven to be found in a cruel and unjust world.

Thirteen

The small stream of falling granules thinned to a halt. Tradain felt the icy prickling of his flesh, the chilling of his mind, and knew that he was not alone. Several seconds elapsed before he could bring himself to lift his eyes from the hourglass and look upon the Presence Xyleel.

The malevolence was transparent and ghostly, His brilliance comparatively muted. Evidently, He had seen fit to project but a small fraction of His totality across the dimensional barriers. Even thus diminished, the spectacle was all but unendurable. Within moments Tradain averted his gaze. His eyes closed of their own accord, and this exclusion of the outer world heightened the unwilling receptivity of his mind. For a ghastly unmeasured span, he felt the invasive alien presence sifting coldly through his recent memories, and there was nowhere to hide from the scrutiny. Then it ended, and he heard the soundless radiant voice of Xyleel.

She is gone. She has terminated her own sentience.

"The woman?" Tradain inquired aloud, as if the spoken word might serve to stave off impending doom. The news failed to surprise him. Neither did it please nor grieve him. He had expected fierce triumph, but he felt nothing at all.

Her substance remains nearly intact, its alteration as yet almost negligible. In the sense that your mind holds her, she is retrievable.

"Why do You tell me this?" There was no reply, nor indication that the query had reached the other's awareness, and Tradain essayed, "Do You wish me to restore her?"

No quiver of responsive intelligence.

"Do You reproach me?"

Nothing. Tradain became aware that he was pouring words into unbearable emptiness, much as the Lady Aestine had once chattered under analogous circumstances. He fell silent, allowing the pause to stretch, and in that comfortless quiet, felt the intelligence of Xyleel again surveying the contents of his mind. When he could stand it no longer, he opened his eyes and demanded, "What do You seek?"

The wordless reply conveyed a sense of emotion wholly indecipherable.

"I do not understand." Rising from his chair, Tradain paced the room in an unconscious, futile effort to dislodge the mental intruder.

You have punished the guilty. You have achieved a measure of justice.

"Yes." *What is that to You?* he wanted to shout, but didn't dare. *Why do You haunt me? The hourglass is far from empty, it's not yet time.* Too late, he recalled that his thoughts were perfectly intelligible to the visitor.

Xyleel comprehended, but there was no answer.

Tradain's uneasy paces lengthened. For some reason he found himself thinking of a nightmare he had visited upon the Lady Aestine, the one in which Ravnar liMarchborg had said, "Your great desire is granted at last. Aren't you happy?"

The pressure of the alien presence in his mind waxed intolerable. He considered flight, but pride paralyzed him. The silence was torturous, and desperation squeezed words out of him.

"Great Xyleel, I am puzzled." He sounded surprisingly composed. "You are powerful beyond reckoning. Here upon the plane of humanity, Your potency is unopposable. Why then must the Netherly minds You collect proffer themselves willingly unto You? Why trouble to obtain human consent? Why not simply take all that You desire? Does the power of Autonn prevent You?"

His own agitation subsided as he spoke. The questions he voiced were of such elemental interest that curiosity all but excluded dread.

It seemed, however, that human curiosity would go unsatisfied, for there was no response; no indication, in fact, that the queries had been noted. Had inquisitive impertinence offended the malevolence? The emotions of Xyleel were incalculable, but He had surely proved Himself capable of vast anger.

Eternity revolved, and then the alien images exploded in his mind; blazing visions, colored with feeling, and studded with a few distinct words.

Autonn. The name came through clearly as if spoken aloud. There was a universe of meaning in that silent inflection, none of it translatable into human terms. *Autonn.*

The visions were incomprehensible, filled with killing light and illimitable darkness. Tradain beheld a protean brilliance, a Presence of the Radiant Level, similar to Xyleel in type, but visibly the less in intensity. He caught intimations of sadness, and—?

His mind groped. *Fear.*

Fear, or something like it. Before there was time to consider this intelligence, new information reached him.

She is elsewhere.

The words were distinct, but their meaning was not.

"*She?* Autonn—she? That is impossible. I have misunderstood You."
It came to him, wordlessly, that he had misunderstood nothing, and yet he resisted. "At the ceremony of Enlightenment, thousands of spectators behold the miraculous likeness of Autonn, who manifests Himself in male form."

Unreality.

"I do not understand. The likeness possesses temporary reality, experienced by a multitude. Do we not perceive an aspect of Autonn?"

Unequivocal negative.

"Then what is the image?"

The knowledge vouchsafed by Xyleel blossomed in his brain. His mind winged back through the years, a century and more, finding its way at last to the Heart of Light, where he discovered a dark-draped chamber occupied by two men. One of them was white-haired, fungus pale, with oblique pomegranate-seed eyes deep-set in a narrow, ageless face, and Tradain realized that he looked upon the sorcerer Yurune the Bloodless. The other man—greying, balding, spreading, and sagging—owned a nondescript countenance well designed to mask a remarkable character; for he, recognizable from a vast array of surviving portraits, was none other than the first

Premier Jurist of them all—the legendary Celz Ruegler, founding father of the White Tribunal, which forever bore the imprint of his mind and his will.

The exchange was perfectly audible. The first Premier Jurist Ruegler, pragmatically devoid of shame or conscience, solicited the notorious sorcerer's services, in consideration whereof, he offered permanent immunity from judicial interference, augmented by unlimited access to the Tribunal's archives.

Yurune the Bloodless, pallidly amused, acquiesced.

The scene shifted to moonlit Radiance Square, where the Bloodless labored alone in the close, dark space beneath the raised platform abutting the Heart of Light. The task he performed—installation of a sorcerous black-lens—was relatively undemanding, requiring only a minimal expenditure of arcane power. It was accomplished within minutes. Afterward, Yurune lingered there, allowing himself the luxury of solitary relaxation, for all the world like an ordinary human being. And while he rested in the cramped dimness beneath the platform, he reached into his robe to bring forth an hourglass, through which a couple of luminous granules sifted.

Tradain stiffened. He knew that hourglass. He also knew just how its owner had used the power that it measured, to create a persistent visual Receptivity, sensitive to the collective expectations of its beholders, and sustained upon periodic offerings of human fuel. Very simple, and very effective.

The vision altered. Yurune the Bloodless taught the Premier Jurist Ruegler the secret of conjuring the Receptivity. Yurune flashed violently out of existence. The Receptivity continued.

Autonn's image—a long-lived illusion, a fraud, and a cheap one, at that. That was all it was, all it had ever been.

For the first time in more years than he could count, Tradain laughed aloud, so jarringly that he startled himself.

"Do the present jurists know?" he inquired.

Negative.

"LiGurvohl?"

Negative.

Dupes, all of them. Probably there was nobody else in the world who shared his knowledge. Perhaps, despite the pointless, pathetic outcome of his assault upon Aestine liHofbrunn, his bargain with the Presence Xyleel might yet prove rewarding.

At the very least, there was information to be had.

"Autonn permits this public travesty?" Tradain essayed.

Xyleel's consciousness excluded the question.

"Where is Autonn now?"

The small confines of your universe do not presently contain Her.

"Does another universe contain—Her?"

No reply in words, but he caught the intimation of an alternate reality, one of the countless dimensions external to mankind's plane. There, the Anomalous Presence Autonn, exiled from Her native Radiant Level, resided in the company of misfits similar to Herself. Only occasionally did She deign to favor murky Netherness with Her presence.

"She is drawn here by Her compassion for humanity?"

The creatures of this plane do not impinge upon Her awareness.

"You mean, Autonn the Defender hasn't noticed human existence?"

A wordless affirmative reached him.

"That is impossible." Tradain spoke aloud, apparently to himself. "She has overlooked our lives, our cities, our wars and explorations, inventions, discoveries, and all our great works!"

No acknowledgment, despite Xyleel's unmistakable proximity. The weak, mocking echo of his own voice rang through the psychic void: *Great works?*

Tradain considered. This latest revelation blasted both human pride and fundamental human belief. The urge to argue and deny was natural but futile; there was no reason to doubt Xyleel's veracity. It was his definite impression, in fact, that the very concept of mendacity was alien to the malevolence. Still, certain questions tickled his mind, and another such opportunity to satisfy curiosity might never present itself.

"If Autonn is unconscious of humanity as You claim, then what draws—Her—to our world?"

The question flew off into nothingness, or so it seemed, and then the delayed answer boomed like a silent gong.

I.

The expression of selfhood came through very strongly, but the images, sensations, and occasional words that followed were far less comprehensible. He caught a sense of ancient conflict, sporadic, sometimes intense, devoid of personal animosity, yet charged with emotion. Xyleel's characteristic anger burned on, but none of it seemed directed against Autonn, an Anomaly and exile like Himself. Visions of a ruined Radiant Level, forever fouled with Netherly filth, fed and warmed His mind. Autonn, it might be inferred, opposed Her compatriot's dire purpose, but seemed to possess no concrete means of resisting His superior strength. The term "Sentient Symbiosis," wafted upon clouds of appeal, reached Tradain's consciousness.

He requested clarification. None was forthcoming.

The alien passions boiled in his head, some of them more or less comparable to human responses, others forever unknowable. One truth, however, manifested itself clearly. Autonn, the so-called Defender, cared nothing for mankind. She sought Netherness from time to time for one purpose alone—persuasive communion with the Presence Xyleel.

Autonn's brilliance faded from mental view. Vivid, violent images of the Radiant Level's destruction glared from the intellect of Xyleel. Toxic floods darkened the lambent atmospheres, drowning the great collective music in darkness, again and again, the repetition increasingly unendurable.

Tradain's battered consciousness sought uselessly to shield itself. At last, a feeble question, earlier proposed and still unanswered, furnished a flimsy barricade.

"Why not seize the human minds that You require?"

The psychic hammering suspended itself. Merciful internal stillness reigned for a time, during which the attention of Xyleel focused elsewhere.

And then returned.

The malevolence was present, immediate, and willing to answer His protégé's question. The response arrived in a silent burst of powerful sensation, most of it mystifying, but one element quite identifiable—profound revulsion.

Its object?

"The forcible coercion of intelligence offends You?" Tradain hazarded.

Intense affirmation, and then soundless words.

UnAware. Beyond Anomalous.

The syllables were crystalline, but his confusion scarcely diminished. Before he could request clarification, the effulgent voice resumed.

You have punished the guilty. You have achieved a measure of justice.

Again? For a moment it seemed as if time had slipped gears.

A reply of some sort seemed expected. He had none. The silence lengthened, and then abruptly emptied. As soundlessly and inexplicably as He had arrived, the Presence Xyleel departed.

Tradain found himself alone, his innermost thoughts once again solely his own. He was a little light-headed, a little shaky, and numb with cold. A good fire burned on the grate, the atmosphere was comfortable, but he was chilled to the marrow. Stiffly, he knelt before the fire, extending his hands to the blaze. The flames jumped and writhed, their shifting forms recalling the luminous mutability of the Presence Xyleel.

He did not wish to think of Xyleel, or of the pact he had made, or of the price he would ultimately pay in exchange for—?

You have punished the guilty. You have achieved a measure of justice.

Justice. A bargain at any price, wasn't it?

He had punished the guilty, no doubt about it. Aestine liHofbrunn's face took shape in the flames. Her parting words echoed: *I'm really sorry things turned out so unpleasantly . . . Really, what else can I say?*

Literally her parting words, probably the last she had ever spoken, and she had died uncomprehending, unchanged, essentially untouched. Small satisfaction to be found in punishing such an enemy as that.

But the others would be different, he assured himself. The Regarded Drempi Kwieseldt. The Premier Jurist Gnaus liGurvohl. They would surely be very different, especially liGurvohl. They were his true targets.

Aestine's fiery image flickered out of being, as if symbolically, and Tradain realized that he did not know the means of her death, or the location of her body. Probably the malevolence would have told him, had he but thought to ask. The smallest flutter of sorcery would furnish all the information he desired, and his lips automatically began to shape the syllables fashioned to prepare his mind. Then he thought of the granules sifting through the hourglass, so many of them falling so swiftly, and his lips stilled themselves. There was no need to squander precious resources. Aestine liHofbrunn had been a citizen of some prominence. Within a matter of hours, the printed accounts of her interesting demise would find their way to the streets. With any luck, one or two of those accounts might even prove more or less accurate.

∂∞ ∞∂

"The account is absolutely accurate," the man who chose to call himself "the Tocsin" insisted. His real name was Meustri Vurtz, but only one present knew it. His thirteen listeners appeared unconvinced, and he added, aggressively, "My source is perfectly reliable."

There was a dubious stirring among the others, and finally one of them inquired, "Was your source an eyewitness, present at the banquet?"

"I am not at liberty to say."

"Oh, come on, Tocs," urged one of the members, an assertive stout matron improbably styling herself the White Gardenia. "Be reasonable. We'll lose all credibility with our runners and readers alike, if it turns out we're feeding 'em tripe."

"Are you calling me a liar?" The Tocsin's normally pale face darkened.

"No, no, of course not," an indefinably androgynous member known as Brimstone soothed. "The Gardenia only meant—"

"That I am inept, perhaps?"

"No, no—"

"I beg to differ. That is exactly what she meant. And when exactly, might one inquire, can it be that I lost all ability to distinguish truth from falsehood? It seems to have happened while my attention was otherwise engaged. Instruct me, if you will. When did I become a blithering idiot, whose word and judgment are not to be trusted?"

A halfhearted chorus of denial arose. The Tocsin ignored it. His skinny figure tensed, the color in his face deepened, and his perpetually feverish eyes heated.

"I am the founder of this group. I've more experience than anyone here, more ability, and far more knowledge. How dare you whippersnapper amateurs question my competence? I said, how DARE you?"

Tocsin was shouting, and a ripple of unease stirred his colleagues, but there was little real cause for concern—the chance that his voice would be heard outside the locked and shuttered house was minimal. Here at the northern edge of the city, almost within roasting range, as the popular expression went, of the Melt itself, the occupied dwellings were few and far between, the population was low, and the traffic was sparse. The vast, shapeless heap of stone still glowed as brightly as it had upon the night its component warehouses and tenements had been sorcerously dissolved, over a century earlier. The icy white light was thought to induce madness, cancer, sterility, impotence, lycanthropy, and a thousand other ills. Not that anything of the sort had ever been proved, but the mere suggestion of arcane peril had stopped the heart of the once-bustling neighborhood. The majority of deserted buildings had fallen to ruin. Those few sorry shells still occupied housed a motley collection of paupers, squatters, transients, and misfits, to which latter category Meustri Vurtz—alias the Tocsin, former professor of natural history, widowed father to a Disinfected son, embittered founder of the illicit Blowflies group—undoubtedly belonged. The streets were silent, dirty, and pocked with deep holes, but never dark; for the eerie white light illuminated every recess and cranny, even upon the foggiest of nights. Virtually every citizen of sound mind shunned the influence of the Melt. For that reason, the ramshackle house of Meustri Vurtz offered the ideal haven to those desirous of privacy.

The house was almost perfectly suited to its present purpose, but not quite. A drawback existed.

"D'you really doubt the truth of this account, or are you just afraid to touch it? Eh?" The Tocsin surveyed his fellow Blowflies with contempt. "Too hot for you to handle, with your tender white hands? A little too risky? Well, if you coddled darlings can't take it, then there's no reason at all for you to stay. I don't need any of you, I can go it alone if I have to. If you've no stomach to fight, then maybe the lot of you'd better just clear off. You can find your own way to the door."

Typical of the Tocsin, or Toxin, as he was surreptitiously dubbed by his followers. At times, his spleen seemed to border on lunacy. Devoid of patience and prudence, but gifted with huge courage and dedication, he was an admirable comrade and a deplorable leader. His rule could hardly be dispensed with, however, for several reasons, not the least of which involved the honor naturally due the founder of the organization. Beyond that, the Tocsin was owner of this very convenient, discreet old house, so well suited to the needs of the group. Beyond even that, the house contained an ancient but fully functional printing press; not a readily available commodity. All things considered, Master Tocsin's preeminence was hardly open to question.

"I don't know why I bother with you people! You're like children, most of you. You have no understanding. You don't know the White Tribunal, you have no idea! You think you do, but you're ignorant!"

He was about to launch once more into the story of his brilliant, gifted, handsome, noble son, Disinfected victim to the vicious tyranny of the White Tribunal. He was about to speak of his peerless wife, dead of grief. He was going to start yelling about his own ruined career, his shattered hopes, his blasted life. Old Toxin had many a legitimate grievance, no doubt about it, but everybody present had already heard the tale, more than once. Many a weary eye rolled.

Fortunately, another voice intruded itself.

"I was present at the meeting early this morning between Tocs and his informant," announced the Tocsin's titular second-in-command, known to all as "the Chair"; rational of intellect, daring but cool of judgment, and true if unacknowledged leader of the group. "The source, whose safety, like our own, demands anonymity, was not present at the Winter Commendation yesterday night, but received information from one of the guests. It is not the first time that we have dealt with this individual, who has in the past proved consistently reliable. Thus I perceive no reason to doubt the truth of the latest report, which contains information capable of compromising the Tribunal's integrity, perhaps beyond recovery. The Landswoman Aestine liHofbrunn, a prominent member of the League of Allies, has publicly confessed to felonious perjury, resulting in the wrongful Enlightenment, thirteen years ago, of her first husband, the High Landguardian Ravnar liMarchborg. I do not know how many of you may recall the case—"

"I recall it," the Tocsin interrupted. "An abominable outrage."

A mutter of concurrence arose.

"The Landswoman's statement is invaluable," the Chair continued

dispassionately, "for in it she has voluntarily revealed herself as a liar, indi-
rectly a murderess, and, above all, as a willing tool in the hands of a corrupt
judiciary. Never before has so highly placed an individual confessed to so
much. This in itself is remarkable, but Landswoman liHofbrunn has gone
further yet, even so far as to implicate the Premier Jurist liGurvohl himself.
How many witnesses, we must now wonder, has Gnaus liGurvohl or his
fellow jurists suborned throughout the years? How many innocents have
died as a result? In view of these issues, I'd regard Aestine liHofbrunn's
disclosure as potentially the most devastating weapon ever to fall into our
hands—but only effective to the extent that the information is made public.
Are we agreed upon that point?"

Confirmation was prompt and all but unanimous, for a few well-
organized words from the mouth of the Chair carried far more weight with
the Blowflies than the most passionate ranting of their ostensible leader.
There remained but a single voice of lingering skepticism.

"Just why should this liHofbrunn frou-frou suddenly elect to spill her
guts all over the dinner table?" demanded the diminutive bulldog of a Blowfly known as the Pickax; a font of relentless energy, whose lack of formal
education in no wise detracted from his intelligence. "Makes no sense."

"Conscience," the Tocsin informed him.

"Took a while to break her down, didn't it? Like thirteen years? Tell
me another."

"I will tell you only that this report is an accurate record of the
woman's statements," the Tocsin countered, glaring. "That is all you need
to know."

"She might've said what she's said, but who's to know if a word of it's
true?" the Pickax persisted.

"And why should a rich Landswoman incriminate herself falsely?
Ruin herself for good?" the Tocsin demanded. "Eh?"

"Could be she's loony." The Pickax shrugged. "Or maybe just drunk.
Or mad for attention, any which way she can get it."

"If so," the Chair suggested, "then a famous friend of the White
Tribunal stands revealed as a lunatic or inebriate, given to freakish flights of
fancy. If, on the other hand, her disclosures are accurate, then she's lied
under oath, in court. Either way, her word is obviously unreliable—and it is
upon the strength of this woman's word that the White Tribunal has condemned a wide variety of victims. It's my intention to begin an investigation
of the Landswoman's past, to discover the names of those destroyed by her
agency, and to learn what I can of their circumstances. Any pertinent facts
that any of you can furnish will be welcome. When I've collected sufficient

material, I'll prepare an article for publication. Needless to say, I'll also expect to report on the Landswoman's immediate situation, as such information becomes available. In the meantime, the account of last night's events is printed up and ready for distribution." A flick of the Chair's gloved hand encompassed the dozen bundles heaped in one corner of the room.

"I'll need extras," the White Gardenia declared. "I've recruited two new runners, likely lads, both apprentices in—"

"Take what you need," the Tocsin cut her off.

This time his rudeness was justifiable, for the Gardenia verged upon indiscretion, and anonymity of membership was to be guarded at any cost. The identities of the individual runners composing each of the dozen Blow-fly Gangs were known to each Gang's superintendent alone. The twelve superintendents in turn were known to one another only by their various aliases. The true names of the individuals presently seated at his kitchen table belonged only to Meustri Vurtz, the Tocsin. This information, committed to coded writing, reposed in safe seclusion; the secret of its location entrusted to the Chair, thus ensuring the cohesion of the organization, in the event of the Tocsin's death or capture.

The White Gardenia's face flushed, belying her cognomen. She subsided, without another word. The Tocsin gloweringly surveyed his followers.

"I take it we are all agreed," he opined. "That is, unless anybody else has any complaints, veiled slurs, or objections to offer?"

Nobody did. The superintendents of the twelve Gangs collected their bundled issues of *The Buzz*, then thankfully departed their leader's presence, exiting the house in discreet small groups, despite the unlikelihood of observation. The Chair moved to follow.

"Stop," the Tocsin commanded, and his subordinate politely obeyed. "Stay here awhile. I want to talk."

The other sat, without visible reluctance.

For several moments the Tocsin stoked his own internal fires, and then the words started to pour out of him.

"They are tepid." He frowned after his vanished associates. "They lack fire, resolve, and true commitment."

"No." Perhaps no one other than the Chair might have contradicted the Tocsin with impunity. "They are deeply dedicated. Each would willingly die under torture for his or her convictions. Each has proved it, a hundred times over."

"You believe this?" For a moment the Tocsin seemed encouraged, then relapsed into pessimism. "Ah, but what do you know? You are only a youngster yourself. Clever and courageous enough—I'll grant you that—but lacking experience. What have you actually seen, with your own young eyes, of judicial tyranny? *I* have witnessed much, you know—including the destruction of my own world. You might not think it, to look at me now, but once upon a time I was a man of some success and consequence. I was a professor of natural history, well regarded, blessed with a fine home, a devoted wife, and a son, an extraordinary son . . . Did I ever tell you about my son . . . ?"

As the familiar complaints poured forth, the Chair strove hard to achieve the requisite expression of sympathetic interest. The Tocsin's undoubtedly genuine sufferings deserved as much, at the very least, and yet it wasn't easy to listen to the same sad story, repeated time and time again, year after year. Sooner or later, patience and tolerance were bound to fail.

The Chair focused upon consolatory thoughts. Even as the Tocsin rambled on, the twelve superintendents were hurrying toward their various home territories. Within the space of the next couple of hours, the printed matter would reach the runners. Surreptitious distribution would begin even before sunset, for the more reckless among them made it a point of honor never to wait. The majority of runners, however, desirous of survival, displayed a modicum of prudence. The bulk of circulation always proceeded under cover of darkness. By tomorrow morning at the latest, all of Lis Folaze would know what had happened at the Winter Commendation.

". . . Judicial murderers. Bloodsuckers. Cannibals. Hypocrites. Tyrants . . ." The Tocsin was still fulminating.

The Chair nodded absently. The diverging cogitations of each Blowfly were cut short by the sound of a sharp rapping at the kitchen door; the quick two-three-two beat that was a standard signal of the group. The Tocsin rose and opened the door, to confront a breathless Brimstone.

"What?" demanded the Tocsin.

"News," the other announced. "Picked it up before I was out of sight of the Melt. They're saying that the Landswoman liHofbrunn's corpse was fished out of the Folaze, downstream from Singlespan Bridge, early this morning. Suicide, by the look of it."

"Before she could be compelled to recant her confession," the Chair observed at once.

The three colleagues regarded one another for a moment. A poisonous smile curled one set of lips.

"So much the better," observed the Tocsin.

❧ ❧

"One of these tablets, dissolved in a cup of distilled water, following each meal," the doctor instructed.

"*Water?* Flambeska, I never touch *water*," the Regarded Jitz liKronzborg objected. "Will these things dissolve in wine?"

"No. You must reduce your consumption of wine, and give up spirits altogether—"

"*What?*"

"And try to stay away from the deep-fried cream pastries, the pâté in puff paste, the chili-oil eels, and especially the lard-smackers."

"*Why?*"

"Trust me."

"Oh, I know you physician fellows. You're only trying to scare me." There was no reply, and liKronzborg inquired, a trifle uncomfortably, "Anything else?"

"A little exercise wouldn't hurt."

"That's a matter of opinion. Shouldn't I hire a litanist to chant for me?"

"By all means, should you relish such entertainment. Be certain you don't neglect my instructions, however. Otherwise, your intestines, already fractious, may well rise in open revolt. That is a rebellion you do not wish to confront."

"I suspect you exaggerate." The Regarded liKronzborg spoke without conviction. Again, there was no reply, and he stretched forth a plump-fingered hand to take up a tiny glass jar, filled with mauve tablets. "One after each meal? In water?"

The doctor nodded.

"Does it really have to be distilled?"

"Boiled, at the very least."

"I have my doubts. But I'll try, I suppose."

"Come back in a month, and let me look at you again."

"Umf. Maybe. No spirits? At all? I don't see the necessity of that. Well. We'll see." Rising from his chair, Jitz liKronzborg slid the jar into his pocket and waddled manfully from the room.

Tradain sat watching his last visitor of the day depart. His hopes for liKronzborg were not high, but sometimes patients surprised him with unexpected displays of good sense.

The door closed behind the Regarded Jitz. Tradain sighed. He was alone again, and solitude no longer offered its former comforts. These days, in the absence of the distraction offered by a steady stream of patients, his mind was apt to occupy itself unpleasantly. Far too often, he found himself thinking of the Presence Xyleel; of the luminous granules pouring through the hourglass; of the horrifying future he had chosen for himself; and, most recently, of the Lady Aestine, and the hollowness of his victory over her.

Justice.

Tradain shook his head. No point dwelling on it. He was stale, that was all his trouble. He hadn't stirred from his lodgings all day long. He needed to get out, to change his surroundings, to keep busy. It was late afternoon of a winter's day, and already dark outside. At the Fogchaser, that handsome and pricey tavern just off handsome and pricey Solemnity Square, the tables would be filling. People. Faces. Conversation. Wine and food. In all probability, he would find the Regarded Jitz liKronzborg there, filling up on brandy and lard-smackers.

Rising, he exited his rooms. Before he'd made it from the building, however, his excited landlord waylaid him.

"Have you seen these yet, Doctor?" Master Einzlaur flapped a couple of paper sheets. "No, of course you haven't, you've been cooped up with your imaginary invalids all day. The first of these things was lying on the doorstep early this morning. The other turned up around noon. When I read 'em over, I could barely stop myself from rushing right into your office, I was so bowled over. That Landswoman liHofbrunn the Blowflies have taken after—she was here! She came to see you, a few weeks back. I remember the name. How could I forget it, when she kicked up such a row? '*Do you know who I AM?*' she kept going on, and I didn't then, but I certainly do now. I tell you, Doctor, it's definitely the same one! Just take a look!"

Accepting the printed circulars, each bordered with the distinctive Blowfly motif, Tradain read swiftly. One of them contained an account of the events at the Winter Commendation that he himself had sorcerously observed. All that took place within the Hall of Ceremonies had been faithfully reported. Descriptions and quotations were accurate, up to and including the moment that Aestine liHofbrunn had fled the room. Beyond question, the Blowflies' informant had attended the ceremony. In all probability, the report had been written within hours of the banquet's conclusion, prior to the discovery of Aestine's suicide, perhaps even prior to the drowning. Interesting.

The anonymous essayist had scarcely confined himself to a disinterested narration of events. The Blowflies never published without purpose, and the sensational revelation of Aestine liHofbrunn's past perjuries furnished the richest of raw materials. The writer did not fail to draw the appropriate inferences, proceeding by logical steps to inevitable conclusions of judicial corruption, rapacity, cruelty, and general redundancy.

. . . *The White Tribunal,* Tradain read, *originally designed to protect the inhabitants of Upper Hetzia, now performs the very opposite function. The power of the sorcery supposedly threatening the lives and welfare of all citizens can scarcely match the genuine menace of the court dedicated to the eradication of sorcery. Conceived as a means to a beneficial end, the ascendancy of the White Tribunal has become an end unto itself, in furtherance whereof, the jurists manifest their readiness to sacrifice every principle of justice, decency, and humanity. It must not be forgotten, however, that the collective will, though long slumberous, retains the power to end the White Tribunal's existence, within the space of a single day, an hour, or a glorious instant . . .*

Not bad. Although, of course, a cartoon would have possessed much greater popular appeal.

"Those Blowflies ever get nailed, they'll *yearn* for the cauldron, before they're done," Einzlaur observed.

Nodding mutely, Tradain proceeded to the second circular, this one obviously composed some hours subsequent to the first, and containing a report of the Landswoman Aestine liHofbrunn's watery death.

So she'd drowned herself. Following her interview with the false Dr. Flambeska, she'd wandered off alone into the fog. Impossible to know if the desperate intentions had taken concrete shape in her mind as she had walked. Eventually, by accident or design, she'd reached Singlespan Bridge. Perhaps she'd hesitated there for a while, or maybe she'd acted swiftly, with resolution. One way or another, she'd ended by flinging herself through cold and darkness. So much for Aestine.

Pointless. Pathetic. He pushed the counterproductive thoughts from him. His landlord's voice prodded.

"Doctor, did you have any idea—?"

"The Landswoman came to me with complaints of a sleeping disorder, which I was able to treat successfully," Tradain replied, in deliberately pompous Strellian persona. "She did not fully confide in me, however. Lacking complete knowledge of her true situation, I failed to anticipate her self-destruction. This I greatly regret."

"Well, you can't blame yourself. You're not a mind reader, after all."

"Ah, but perhaps a physician must be, at times." He judged it advisable to change the subject. "This piece of sedition, here—has it been seen by many others, do you think?"

"No doubt about it," Einzlaur asserted, with the gusto of the born gossip. "I was over at the Schnutzi Stalls early this morning, and there were copies lying around all over the place. People were taking 'em up by the handful, and some show-off was even reading one aloud to the unwashed.

Same thing going on at Green Arch, around noon. Right now, I just came from the Fogchaser, and the place is boiling."

"And what do people make of it all?"

"A lot of noise is mostly what they make of it all. There's a swarm of different opinions buzzing around. Plenty of talk, loads of vaporing. The odd fistfight, here and there. If you trot on over to the Fogchaser, you're likely to find yourself sucked into some endless, boozy debate."

"Ah, you Hetzians. I shall never accustom myself to your ways. These journalists, for example—these Blowflies. They risk their lives, they are dedicated people, and no doubt wish to be taken seriously. And yet, always they manifest a certain childish levity—they publish such foolish little cartoons, and they adopt the name of a noxious insect. Why should they so undermine their own dignity?"

"Well, I can't speak for them, but it's my guess they're taken seriously enough, childish levity or no. If they're caught, the Tribunal will take them seriously, you may be certain. As for the name, that's another joke of theirs. Right after the first few leaflets appeared, a couple of years ago, the Premier Jurist issued a public denunciation, in which he called the scribblers—let me make sure I get this right—" Einzlaur frowned. "He called them 'vile blowflies, spawning in putrid filth, spreading corruption and moral disease throughout the community.' Now, there's high language for you, the real thing."

"Admirable."

"The next publication to turn up after that was titled *The Buzz*, and the writers were calling themselves the Blowflies. Everybody thought that was a nice touch."

"You Hetzians." Smiling, the doctor shook his head. "So amusing."

"Well, if you want even more amusement, just take yourself over to the Fogchaser. You'll come away with your head spinning."

"My friend, always I prefer to maintain perfect equilibrium."

"You Strellians. So literal."

"Nevertheless, I shall follow your advice."

So saying, Tradain walked out into the foggy winter darkness and, without benefit of linkboy, found his way to the Fogchaser, which was every bit as crowded and charged of atmosphere as his landlord had promised. Seating himself in the darkest corner of the well-appointed taproom, he ordered a plate of chili-oil eels, a bowl of lard-smackers, and a stein of potent winter punch.

The food and drink arrived. The cook at the Fogchaser knew his business, and the eels were properly infernal. Tradain addressed his meal with appreciative caution. While he ate, he listened, and soon the vocal hum filling the room began to resolve itself, and he was able to distinguish individual scraps of conversation.

Allusions to the Blowflies circular were surprisingly frequent. It was, in fact, remarkable how many patrons had read the latest essay, and how fearlessly they spoke of it in a public place. Presumably, the sheer volume of journalistic distribution furnished reassurance. He could only infer that the proprietress of The Barrel Stave had voiced the prevailing public perception, weeks earlier:

Look, if they went after everybody caught with a Blowflies broadside or funny in hand, they'd have to round up the whole population.

The voices chattered and clattered. Tradain sat motionless, straining to sort them out. He soon perceived that Einzlaur had been right. Opinions varied, differences abounded, debate crackled, and speculation was intense.

. . . Perjured witnesses . . . false accusation . . . wrongful Disinfection . . . corruption . . . deliberate misrepresentation . . . imaginary sorcery . . .

Astonishing, some of the phrases that were flying around so freely. All but impossible, in earlier years, for the complaints and criticisms revealed a widespread disillusionment, deep discontent, a pervasive suspicion of judicial motives and methods, formerly unthinkable; or at least inadmissible in mixed company.

Presumably, scenes of a similar sort were repeating themselves all over the city. The Blowflies, whoever they were, must surely be pleased with the popular response to their latest offering. Very likely, they were out and about the town, wallowing in secret success. One or more of them might even presently inhabit the Fogchaser taproom.

Tradain's covert gaze slid from face to face. He noted an endless variety of type, age, and expression; but nothing in any countenance to suggest the reality of underground illicit journalist, underlying the mundane mask. He could penetrate such a mask at will, of course, but never intended to bend his sorcerous powers to such an unprofitable end.

Whoever they were, he wished them well. And he had served them well, he realized, for the latest ripe journalistic pickings had materialized by his agency alone. And there would be more to come, assuming the success of his plans. The Blowflies had every reason to thank their nameless benefactor, whose sorcerous powers were helping them to dispel the myth of a widespread sorcerous threat. Not that he desired their thanks, as the assistance he rendered was purely incidental. For the present, his own aims and those of the Blowflies fortuitously coincided; beyond that, their activities scarcely touched him. In all likelihood, the whole gang of secret scribblers would end in the cauldron; the common fate of the immoderately idealistic.

Regrettable, but no concern of his. Their efforts to dislodge the well-nigh unassailable White Tribunal were almost certainly futile and, in any case, irrelevant—for the fate of only one of the jurists held the slightest significance.

►◄

"Number Sixteen Solemnity Square," declared the liHofbrunn coachman.

"You are certain?" Premier Jurist Gnaus liGurvohl subjected his hapless visitor to a prolonged, penetrating gaze. Despite advancing years, the power of his remorseless rainwater eyes remained unimpaired.

"Absolutely certain, Premier Jurist." The coachman nodded fervently. "No halts, no detours. That night, I took her straight from the Heart of Light to Number Sixteen Solemnity Square."

"And this is the residence of—?"

"Her doctor. That foreigner who's made such a splash. Flambeska."

"Her first visit?"

"By no means, Premier Jurist."

"Her husband, the Honorable Landsman liHofbrunn, has accompanied her in the past?"

"Never, Premier Jurist."

"I see. State the duration of her visit."

"I didn't mark the time, Premier Jurist. I couldn't be sure, I wouldn't want to give you the wrong information, I'm—"

"An hour?"

"Not nearly so long as that."

"A half hour?"

"Less. Else I'd've felt the chill, sitting there waiting, like that. Maybe about a quarter of an hour, and then she came out, looking like a mountain had just fallen on her."

"There were signs of a physical altercation?"

"No, nothing like that. It was the look on her face, and the way she moved."

"I see. And then?"

"And then, instead of getting back into the carriage where she belonged, she just dragged on off down the street by herself. 'Madam,' I called after her, 'madam, won't you let me take you home?' But she just wandered away like she didn't hear me, like I wasn't there."

"You made no attempt to follow?"

"That wasn't my place, Premier Jurist."

"She said nothing?"

"Nary a word. I'd tell you if she had. Believe me, I'd tell you every-thing."

"I do believe you, for I am capable of detecting the subtlest untruth. It is impossible to lie to me."

"I wouldn't ever try it, Premier Jurist. Besides, I got nothing to lie about."

"I hope, for your own sake, that you do not. Following the Lands-woman liHofbrunn's departure, what did you do?"

"Came back here to the Heart of Light, to collect the master. Told him where I'd last seen his wife, and asked if he wanted to look for her. He said no, she was no concern of his, so I just took him on home."

"I see. Shall I assume you have related all you recall of that eve-ning?"

"Yes, Premier Jurist. All." The coachman found himself subjected to another microscopic scrutiny, which he managed to sustain with negligible fidgeting.

"You have recorded this man's statement in its entirety?" liGurvohl demanded of his scribe.

The scribe inclined his head.

"Your signature is required," liGurvohl informed the coachman. "Do you know how to write?"

"My name, yes."

The document was placed before him. Accepting a quill from the scribe, the coachman laboriously printed out his own name in block letters. When he had done, he looked up with an air of virtuous accomplishment.

"That will suffice, for now. If your testimony is desired by the White Tribunal—"

"I'll do my duty gladly, Premier Jurist."

"I daresay. The deportment of his servants speaks well of your master. You may go."

❧ ☙

The coachman thankfully departed. For some moments Gnaus liGurvohl sat reviewing the contents of the servant's statement, which proved unex-pectedly suggestive. Aestine liHofbrunn's connection to the foreign physi-cian, and the strength of his influence over her, were surely worthy of investigation. The nature of their final interview, in particular, demanded clarification. LiGurvohl twitched the tapestry bellpull that hung beside his desk. Moments later a burly officer clad in the uniform of a Soldier of the Light entered the office.

"Premier Jurist." The officer saluted.

"Captain." The Premier Jurist regarded his minion in silence, for a moment or two. He had verged upon ordering the immediate arrest and interrogation of Dr. Flambeska, but the most cursory reflection revealed the disadvantages of this move. Although a newcomer to the city, the Strellian doctor had already achieved a certain measure of renown. His patients numbered among the wealthy and blue-blooded, and his arrest would hardly go unnoticed. The disclosure of the fashionable physician's tie to the deceased Landswoman liHofbrunn could only heat public interest in a wretchedly embarrassing incident best forgotten as quickly as possible. Those detestable servants of malevolence calling themselves the Blowflies were already flooding Lis Folaze with their scurrilous reports. Somehow they had learned exactly what had happened at the Winter Commendation—their informant had obviously been an eyewitness—and the inferences they had drawn from a deranged female's babbling were dangerous, and vicious in the extreme. The arrest of the dead woman's doctor, an undeniable manifestation of judicial concern, would only furnish fresh ammunition to the scandalmongers.

There were times when a certain measure of discretion best served Autonn's interests.

"You will dispatch a pair of your best agents to Number Sixteen Solemnity Square," liGurvohl commanded. "They are to observe the actions of the foreign lodger calling himself Dr. Flambeska. They will note this physician's comings and goings, his habits, and his conversations. They will take particular care to secure the names of Flambeska's visitors, patients, acquaintances, and associates of every description. The subject is to remain unaware of observation, but I want him watched day and night."

Fourteen

Sergeant Orschl of the Select Squadron ordinarily enjoyed his work. He liked his exemption from the restrictions of the military uniform worn by his fellow Soldiers of the Light. He liked the assorted disguises his job in surveillance obliged him to assume, particularly when he got to pass himself off as a rich man, with fine clothes and lordly airs. He liked the independence, the variety, and the freedom from daily routine. Above all, he liked watching other people, discovering the intimate secrets of their lives, thereby achieving a certain intangible power over them, while they remained ignorant of his very existence. Yes, there was much satisfaction to be found in such work.

The current assignment, however, was a dead bore.

His disguise, as a groundskeeper at the little park in the middle of Solemnity Square, offered little diversion, and the object of surveillance offered even less. He'd been watching the lodger at Number Sixteen for three days now and, in all that time, had witnessed nothing of interest. It seemed that the foreigner, Dr. Flambeska, led a remarkably quiet life, with work occupying nearly every wakeful hour. The doctor's habits were quiet and orderly. He rose early, ventured forth to breakfast at a nearby cookshop, then returned to his own lodgings around midmorning. Thereafter, his patients began to arrive, one after another, in an endless succession of handsome carriages and blazoned sedan chairs; rich, highborn patients, many of them overdressed, overfed, and probably prey to no ill beyond boredom.

The stream of patients rarely slackened before the late afternoon, or sometimes early evening. When his work for the day was finished, the doctor walked abroad in the winter darkness, wandering the city alone, without destination, and seemingly without any purpose beyond beneficial exercise. He was easy to shadow at such times, for he walked at a moderately brisk pace, without the slightest effort at concealment, and his figure, clad in the Strellian robes and topped with the square-brimmed hat, was distinguishable even at some distance. Never did he stop to speak with anyone.

His daily perambulation concluding, the doctor invariably took his evening meal at the Fogchaser, where he always sat alone. If some neighboring diner chanced to address him, he answered courteously and briefly. Otherwise, he ate in solitary silence. He seemed to have no friends, no women, no social recreation of any description; which was odd, in view of his youth, apparent vigor, and affluence, but not particularly incriminating.

After dinner, Flambeska always walked straight home to Sixteen Solemnity Square. Sergeant Reschbek of the Select Squadron, who, disguised as an itinerant litanist, drunkard, or both, manned the nocturnal shift, reported that the doctor neither emerged from his lodgings, nor received visitors, throughout the night. Sometimes the lights in his rooms burned late, but the shutters were always tightly closed, and there was no guessing what went on behind them. Probably, nothing of interest.

Dr. Flambeska, the Sergeants Orschl and Reschbek agreed, was without doubt one of the quietest, most sedate, and generally tedious individuals they had ever yawned to observe. Poor fellow had no life to speak of. He was thoroughly predictable, unimaginative, obviously innocuous, and inexpressibly dull. In short, not much more than a physician-automaton. Between the two of them, the sergeants took to calling their dreary subject "the Clockwork."

Thus, it came as a surprise to Sergeant Orschl, one raw winter's day,

when the Clockwork actually varied his routine. It was only a small departure from the norm, and probably insignificant, but at least it made a
change.

The Clockwork, according to his custom, emerged from his lodgings
in the late afternoon. It had already been dark for an hour or more, and the
big, polished lamps of Solemnity Square were beaming tremulously through
the restless fog. The Clockwork hiked north, along the Folaze. Dutifully,
Orschl followed. As always, the subject displayed no awareness whatever of
observation. In any case, there was never anything much to observe.

Then, quite unexpectedly, the Clockwork paused in the pool of light
cast by the great lantern topping the street sign at Luculent Circle. He
clapped his hands once, and a covey of eager linkboys answered the summons at once. This in itself was singular, as the Clockwork habitually displayed an impressive ability to find his way unaided through the deepest
shadows. Singularity intensified, as the Clockwork selected a fortunate linkboy; handed money and a small, darkly wrapped package to the chosen
courier; issued instructions, inaudible to the watching Orschl; then stood
watching as the linkboy sped off like a shooting star, the light of his torch
disappearing into darkness and distance.

Sergeant Orschl cursed silently. He hadn't been close enough to
catch the verbal exchange. He had no idea what the package contained, or
for whom it was intended. He could shadow the linkboy, abandoning the
primary subject of surveillance, in violation of one of the most elementary
precepts of the Select Squadron. Or else he could follow the rules, stick
with the subject, and probably learn nothing.

If only he could split himself in two. If only Reschbek were present.

There was no time for cogitation. In accordance with his training, if
not his instincts, Orschl stayed where he was. The linkboy, and all he knew
or carried, vanished. The Clockwork continued his random stroll for a time,
then circled back toward the Fogchaser and dinner.

Orschl followed; watched his subject consume an expensive stew of
shellfish braced with wine, serpent fungi, and blue tavril; then trailed the
other back to Solemnity Square.

The door shut behind Dr. Flambeska, who would almost certainly
not emerge again before morning. There was nothing more to be seen.
Sergeant Orschl relaxed, with a sigh. He had done the right thing, and there
was no reason for self-recrimination. He'd complied with regulations.

For all of that, he couldn't stifle every doubt and question. He might
never mention it to another living soul, not even Reschbek, but he couldn't
stop wondering about the contents and destination of that package.

"Package for you, sir," the majordomo announced. "Delivered not five minutes ago."

"Really. How curious. I have bespoken nothing." Pleasurably intrigued, the Regarded Drempi Kwieseldt accepted a small parcel wrapped in black velvet. The majordomo hovered inquisitively. Kwieseldt's brow creased, and his voice sharpened. "That will be all."

The servant withdrew, wafting subtle reproach. Kwieseldt's frown deepened. He had not meant to deal harshly with an old and valued employee of proven loyalty.

But then, what constituted real proof, in such a case? For the most trusted of servants, as the Regarded Drempi Kwieseldt knew only too well, were capable of turning upon their masters. There wasn't a one of them that could be relied upon absolutely, especially by a rich man, as he now was; a man whose wealth was bound to excite envy, greed, and malice . . . One couldn't be too careful.

Kwieseldt shook his head, banishing gloomy speculations. He seemed cursed, in recent years, with a tendency to brood. Just now, however, the unexpected delivery furnished welcome distraction. Carefully, he examined the package. Very elegantly wrapped, but no tag, no label, no identifying mark of any kind. Deliberately prolonging the enjoyable suspense, he slowly stripped away the velvet covering, to reveal a gilded airtight tin, containing a generous quantity of pipeweed. Kwieseldt sniffed, and his pinkish brows rose in surprised appreciation. Golden Trueleaf, its rich fragrance unmistakable. Very scarce, very expensive, lately all but unobtainable. A fine gift indeed.

From whom? Once again he examined the tin, the discarded velvet wrapping, even the ribbon. No card, no inscription, no clue. It seemed the donor meant to preserve anonymity, which was odd; for he might ordinarily have expected such an offering to accompany a flowery written request for a loan, a charitable contribution, a substantial favor of some kind or other. As a rich man, he was bombarded with such pleas . . . But not this time. Or at least, he cautioned himself, not yet.

No matter. The prospect of future wearisome importunings would not mar his pleasure in the gift. Filling his pipe with Golden Trueleaf, the Regarded Kwieseldt lit up. The first puff soothed and relaxed him; the second warmed his spirits. Indeed, the power of the Trueleaf was magical, yet by some blessed miracle, not illegal.

Kwieseldt inwardly expanded as he smoked, and he gazed at his surroundings with unusual satisfaction. He occupied the private sitting room that was part of the vast master suite, and it really was marvelously beautiful, with its hangings of gold-embroidered emerald silk, its masterfully carved ceiling, its spectacular floor, patterned in six subtly contrasting shades of green tile, its priceless furnishings, porcelains, and ancient bronzes. Sometimes he forgot how splendid it was, or rather he forgot to look. But he looked now, and soon his roving eye lighted upon a pair of lofty marquetry window shutters, closed against the winter darkness, but not locked.

At once, Kwieseldt was on his feet. A couple of quick little paces carried him to the window, and then his nervous short fingers were sliding the gold-plated steel bolt into place.

Done. He drew a relieved breath, then smiled, a little ashamed of his own alarm. The probability of an intruder breaking in by way of a second-story window overlooking a well-lighted, well-peopled city thoroughfare was low indeed.

But not impossible, he couldn't avoid admitting to himself. There was no limit to the hideous ingenuity of the criminal mind. There was no predicting the stratagems whereby the thieves, cutthroats, and swindlers might contrive to penetrate the home of a wealthy man. The house, equipped with heavy doors and strong shutters, was armed with the newest and trickiest of locks. Sentries patrolled the corridors day and night, while fiercely vociferous mastiffs roamed the grounds. But a wealthy man was always a target, and the world abounded in predators lured by the famous treasures of liTarngrav House.

Kwieseldt Mansion. Thirteen years, and he was still committing that same mental error. Absurd, but understandable. For centuries, the place had been known as liTarngrav House. Never, in all that time, had the descendants of the original builder allowed the property to slip from their grasp. But now, this incredible palace wherein he and his forebears had toiled for generations in the service of noble liTarngrav masters—now at last, it all belonged to Drempi Kwieseldt. Someday, he would pass the great legacy on to his own son Pfissig, and always, for as long as stone rested upon stone, this house would bear the name of *Kwieseldt Mansion.*

So much had his loyalty and service to the White Tribunal earned him. *Loyalty?* An odd internal qualm chilled him. He filled his lungs with the richest smoke, and the feeling passed. His chin came up. *Kwieseldt Mansion.* His own, his private kingdom. Unappreciated, of late, for a rich man was beset with so many cares and obligations. He really owed himself some pleasure in his own domain, and he hadn't enjoyed a good gloat in years.

Exiting the sitting room, the Regarded Kwieseldt wandered slowly through the master suite, his eyes devouring marvels and magnificence, but always touching conscientiously upon each and every window. All shuttered, all properly locked. Excellent. One couldn't be too careful.

Trailing clouds of Golden Trueleaf fragrance, he issued forth into the endless second-story corridor, notable for its immensity, its double row of spiraling marble pillars, and its fifty evenly spaced, identical chandeliers, each linked to the next with long ropes of faceted crystals. Yes, the chandeliers were certainly extraordinary. There was not another such matched set to be found in all of Upper Hetzia, perhaps in all the world. Kwieseldt eyed the stupendous overhead glitter with approval for a moment, then his gaze dropped to the juncture of the great central passage and one of its countless tributaries, and his satisfaction deepened, for there stood the armed sentry at his appointed post, sharp and alert as he was supposed to be.

The sentry saluted smartly as his master passed. All was well, everything secure.

On along the corridor Kwieseldt made his way, and his heart lightened as he went, for all of the household guards were properly deployed, and all the window shutters were firmly bolted.

Great liTarngrav House—*Kwieseldt Mansion!*—was tranquil and silent, its massive stone walls excluding the clamor of the outer world.

But not all clamor originated outside. As Kwieseldt neared the broad stairway that descended in double curves beneath the mansion's towering dome, the squawk of angry voices halted him in his tracks. He stood outside his young ward's chamber. He could hear her in there, berating someone— and it wasn't at all like Glennian liTarngrav to verbally castigate erring servants. After a moment there came a sullen reply, and he recognized the nasal tones of his son Pfissig.

"Your imagination is running away with you," Pfissig informed her.

"There's no point in denying it," Glennian returned. "You were caught red-handed. It's not the first time, but it had better be the last."

"Are you *threatening* me?"

"Sounds that way, doesn't it?"

"This is absurd."

"I agree. Absurd and distasteful. Haven't you a shred of honor?"

"I will not listen to this foolish female carping. I really haven't the time."

"Before you slink off, understand this. You are to keep your hands off my belongings. And you are never again to set foot in my room."

"Your room? Perhaps you'd better think again. You have no room, Mistress Mendicant. In case the tiny detail has slipped your mind, I'd best remind you that this house and everything in it belongs to my father. Someday, it will all belong to me. You'd do well to remember that."

"Oh, you little *toad*—!"

"That's no way to speak to me. Mind your manners, or it will be the worse for you. As for your insulting suspicions and accusations, you'd best keep them to yourself, or people might just suspect that precious mind of yours is turning rancid. Sometimes, you know, I fear for the state of your mental health. Indeed I do. And now, if you'll excuse me, I will withdraw, for there is little point in continuing so tiresome a conversation."

The door opened, and Pfissig emerged, ostentatiously weary. His lips were frozen in an unwavering little smile of languid amusement. His round face, however, was revealingly flushed, and his chronically inflamed nose was even redder than usual. Behind him stood Glennian liTarngrav, scowling, her arms folded.

"Don't come back," she advised.

"What is this?" demanded the Regarded Drempi Kwieseldt.

Pfissig stopped short at sight of his father. "Nothing, sir," he replied. "A small misunderstanding. Our Glennian has worked herself into a pretty little tizzy over nothing, that is all."

"Tizzy. Such a colorful expression." Drawing a deep breath, Glennian stepped forth from her chamber to confront her guardian. "Re'Drempi, I didn't want to bother you with this, but now that you've overheard, I must ask your help. Please, I implore you, command your son to stay out of my room. Not ten minutes ago, I came back here to find him searching through the drawers of my desk."

The Regarded Kwieseldt felt the color heat his cheeks. He knew he was every bit as red-faced as his own son, and he knew that it was ridiculous, but couldn't help himself. Glennian liTarngrav, though only a young woman, and under his legal guardianship at that, somehow possessed the ability to disconcert him; and she'd always had it, even in childhood. It was not something that she did deliberately. In fact, she seemed unaware of her own power. Kwieseldt couldn't fully explain it to himself, but supposed it had something to do with her family resemblance to her father, his own former master, the High Landguardian Jex liTarngrav. Not that she really looked very like him, for in Glennian, Jex's muscular stockiness diminished itself to girlish slenderness; his ruddy boldness of facial feature refined to pale delicacy; his carrot-colored hair muted to deep chestnut; his galaxies of freckles dwindled to a restrained sprinkling across the bridge of the nose. Above all, her intelligent eyes were entirely her own—clear grey-green, speckled with brown, thickly lashed, and uptilted at the outer corners. "Witch eyes," Kwieseldt called them in his mind, and he'd had ample opportunity to judge, for those eyes were exactly on a level with his own, although she was not above middling feminine stature. For all of her individuality, she recalled her father in a thousand unconscious tricks of face, voice, stance, and gesture.

"Re'Drempi—" Glennian prodded.

Kwieseldt found his wits. "You've an explanation?" he inquired hopefully of his son.

"Certainly," Pfissig answered without hesitation. The little smile remained fixed in place. "I searched for a lost book, nothing more. We all know Glennian's fondness for books. Her room is crammed with them. I wondered if the volume I sought might by chance have found its way to her chamber, and so I meant to ask her to check her shelves. I knocked on her door, drew no response, and decided to step inside and take a look around. I am very sorry if I presumed, but truly, I intended no offense."

"There, you see, he meant no harm—" Kwieseldt commenced.

"Then why was he rummaging through my drawers?" Glennian demanded. "And the clothespress as well?"

"I did nothing of the sort." Pfissig's fixed smile and unblinking blue eyes gave him the look of a plump-faced mannequin. "You misinterpreted. You are confused. Perhaps you had a glass too much wine at dinner."

"I saw him, and tonight wasn't the first time." Ignoring Pfissig, Glennian addressed herself directly to her guardian. "Re'Drempi, the problem is easily resolved. Only consent to install a lock upon my chamber door, a lock to which I alone possess the key—"

"Really, I think my foster sister indulges her sense of humor, at our expense," Pfissig opined. "Surely she cannot be in earnest, when she speaks of altering the house to suit herself."

"A single lock is a very small alteration, but it would mean a great deal to me." While responding to Pfissig's complaint, Glennian still contrived to appear unaware of the young man's existence.

"Our Glennian means well, but she is excitable, and sometimes she forgets certain realities," Pfissig observed, with an air of patience. "She forgets that Kwieseldt Mansion is not *her* house."

"By no means. I am constantly reminded," Glennian returned, and the grim line of her jaw was pure Jex liTarngrav. "Re'Drempi—"

"Enough." Kwieseldt's head was spinning. "Enough. Children, do not quarrel. Glennian, I will consider your request, and inform you of my decision." It was an intoxicating sensation to know that a member of the noble liTarngrav family waited upon his will, but Kwieseldt let no sign of satisfaction touch his face. "Pfissig, I want you to stay out of her room. And you might tell her you're sorry."

"Certainly, Father." Pfissig's little smile remained nailed in place. "I am eager to do all in my power to restore household harmony, and therefore will not hesitate to say that I am sorry, very sorry indeed, that Glennian should think so ill of me. I am sorry, too, that she so grieves herself with unjust suspicions. I am truly sorry, for *her* sake, that she must bear the burden of a heart so sadly troubled, so devoid of peace and *trust—*"

"That will do." The Regarded Kwieseldt jogged his son's arm. "Come away from here."

The two of them strolled off down the corridor. Behind them, the door to Glennian liTarngrav's room closed with more than necessary firmness.

"Why must you always plague her?" Kwieseldt demanded.

"But, Father—" Pfissig had finally allowed his smile to expire. His wide blue eyes beamed injured innocence. "I have done nothing. She's the one who quarrels with *me*."

"She could not, if you did not allow it. You are a man, it is up to you to take the lead. Try to make yourself more agreeable to her."

"What for? She's a sharp-tongued, high-nosed, ill-tempered vixen. Why should I exert myself to please her?"

"My boy, try to understand that Glennian liTarngrav has suffered immense losses in her lifetime—"

"Well, she has her criminal father to thank for that."

Among others. "She is an orphan, and penniless—"

"All the more reason she should appreciate your generosity in allowing her to stay here—your charity."

"Not so. Her position as the dependent of a former retainer, here in this great house that once belonged to her family, must be intensely galling—" *But how much the worse, should she ever learn the truth?*

"It could be much worse. She should be properly grateful."

The records are sealed. She will never know. "You might try to make things easier for her, my boy. You might try to get on with her." Kwieseldt met his son's eyes. "For I will confess to you, it's been my fondest hope, these thirteen years, that you might one day choose to ennoble the Kwieseldt line by marriage."

"What, you mean to Glennian?"

Kwieseldt nodded.

"No, thank you very much. I expect, when I marry, to look higher than the beggarly daughter of an Enlightened sorcerer. I want a wife of respectable family. After all, we are gentlefolk, now."

"Just barely." . . . *recently acquired gentility can only be described as precarious.* The malicious words of Aestine liHofbrunn cut across Kwieseldt's memory. "And you speak of respectable family? Son, the blood of liTarngrav is the oldest, purest, and highest to be found anywhere. That

House has frequently furnished wives to royalty. The line of Kwieseldt would benefit immensely by such an infusion, while the fortunes of the liTarngravs stand to improve. Everyone concerned might expect to profit greatly by such a match."

"But I don't like her, Father. I don't want her."

"You cannot say she's not pretty."

"Perhaps, if you admire that skinny, too clever, sharp-edged type. Myself, I prefer a shorter, rounder, softer sort of female, with golden hair, and all the attractive womanly attributes. She will be meek, gentle, quiet, properly admiring of her husband's intelligence, and willing to accept his guidance. That is not Glennian liTarngrav."

"No," the Regarded Kwieseldt conceded, "I suppose it isn't. Nevertheless, there is at least one more point I would desire you to consider. In the event of a reversal of an earlier conviction, the property confiscated by the White Tribunal could conceivably return to its original owner, or that party's heirs. Should such a reversal occur in the case of the High Landguardian Jex liTarngrav, then Jex's sole offspring, his daughter, Glennian, would—"

"What are you saying?" Pfissig demanded. "Reversal of conviction? That's impossible."

"Perhaps. Perhaps." Kwieseldt gnawed the stem of his pipe. "Only— you have heard the whole story of Aestine liHofbrunn's public confession of perjury. By her own admission, the testimony she offered at the trial of her husband was false. Of course, the three sons of Ravnar liMarchborg died years ago, so there is nobody left to claim that property. Should Jex liTarngrav ever achieve similar posthumous exoneration, however, his heiress yet survives. Do you follow me, son? If you were safely married to Glennian liTarngrav, then, no matter what might happen—"

"I understand you." Frowning, Pfissig studied his father minutely. "But I must say, it all seems very far-fetched. What possible flaw could weaken the case against Jex liTarngrav? Surely there is none? Is there?"

"Probably not, but it would not be prudent to overlook even the remotest of possibilities. Ponder my advice at your own leisure, if you will, but for now, let's speak of this no more. I seem to be developing a terrible headache."

His headache worsened throughout the ensuing hours, and presently the Regarded Kwieseldt took himself to his solitary bed. The sedate presence of his wife might have proved comforting at such a time, but she reposed in her own apartment at the far end of that gigantic central corridor. It was an arrangement less than agreeable to either of the two parties concerned, but obligatory, in Kwieseldt's opinion; for a wealthy man, master of liTarngrav

House—*Kwieseldt Mansion!*—was bound to uphold certain fashionable conventions of his elevated status, one of which involved the divided living arrangements of a married couple. Still, he missed her, at times.

His head ached fiercely. Sleep was impossible. Presently, pain expanded to encompass nausea. Cold sweat bathed his face, and his stomach heaved. Dragging himself from his bed, he staggered across the room to the commode. There was only just time to lift the lid, before the Regarded Kwieseldt vomited violently. Dropping to his knees before the ornate chair discreetly housing the pot, he rested panting there for a moment, then vomited again. Nausea receded a little, but his headache was worse than ever, and now the room was wheeling dizzily about him. The bellpull that might have summoned a servant's assistance hung beside the bed, centuries distant, and, in any case, what help could any servant offer?

The Regarded Kwieseldt stayed where he was, prone before the pot, until the nausea hit again, and he retched repeatedly, but there was little left in his stomach to lose. By now he must have cleaned himself out, but the headache was killing. He wished it *would* kill him, and quickly.

What in the world had he eaten at dinner that so violently disagreed with him? Kwieseldt mentally reviewed his last meal. Nothing there that he hadn't tasted a thousand times in the past. Nothing but the finest, freshest ingredients, prepared by the best of cooks, shared by family members and guests. Nothing there to poison him. And then he thought of the mysterious offering of expensive Golden Trueleaf pipeweed, whose rich smoke he had so eagerly inhaled—the offering whose sender chose to remain anonymous. A great terror smote him then, and he cried out for his servants, but there were none within earshot, and he couldn't reach the bellpull, couldn't even crawl to it.

The tears of helplessness and fear streamed down Kwieseldt's chubby cheeks. Miserably, he wondered who his enemy could be. Some random anarchist, resenting the plenty and privilege enjoyed by a wealthy man? A malicious prankster? Some vengeful wretch smarting under the sting of a fancied injury? *Or a real one?* He tried to push the thought away, for it wasn't the moment for self-reproach, and yet his mind insisted upon recalling the names and faces of the various unfortunates that he, as a staunch member of the League of Allies, had assisted to destruction. First and chief among them, of course, was the High Landguardian Jex liTarngrav. The memory of liTarngrav's public Enlightenment was still shockingly fresh, despite all his efforts to expunge it, and it struck him then that Jex's daughter, young Glennian, might have poisoned him. Certainly she had motive and opportunity.

But no, that was absurd, she knew nothing at all of the part he'd played in her father's downfall. He'd always been kind to her, given her a home, given her anything she wanted, and she was fond of him, he was sure of it. No, it couldn't possibly be Glennian.

Such ghastly speculations were intensifying his headache. It was truly torturous now, quite the equal of anything to be found in the cellars of the Heart of Light. Kwieseldt moaned freely, without fear of compromised dignity. There was nobody to see or hear.

He had no idea how long he remained there, facedown on the floor. He was aware of no suspension of agony, yet at some point must have drifted into slumber or delirium, for he found himself dreaming of the Winter Commendation, and there again was the Landswoman Aestine liHofbrunn, standing before her assembled peers, with the unbelievable confessions spilling blithely from her lips. And there beside her on the dais stood the Premier Jurist Gnaus liGurvohl, stilly watching.

I was serving the larger truth! LiGurvohl told me so, and he should certainly know!

What a look the Premier Jurist had given her then! Chilling, really. She'd been wise to finish herself off, after that . . .

Fear kicked Drempi Kwieseldt wide awake. The dream was extraordinarily vivid and clear in his mind, for the moment superseding even physical pain. Implacable rainwater eyes haunted his memory.

Nothing could be worse than the enmity of Gnaus liGurvohl. Kwieseldt couldn't imagine what had possessed Aestine liHofbrunn to publicly goad the Premier Jurist with perilous disclosures, but in doing so, she had doomed herself beyond hope . . . *a foolish, prattling female, much given to absurd excesses of temper* . . . liGurvohl had once dismissed Aestine, and yet, the Landswoman had possessed explosive information, potentially threatening to the entire White Tribunal. Though outwardly cordial as his majestic persona allowed, the Premier Jurist had very likely wished her safely buried.

And he himself, the Regarded Kwieseldt realized, possessed exactly such threatening knowledge. Like Aestine, he had perjured himself, at liGurvohl's command.

Something to think about. Probably irrelevant, for he had held his tongue these thirteen years, thereby demonstrating his complete trustworthiness. Surely the Premier Jurist recognized a friend and ally. Still—something to think about.

The Regarded Kwieseldt carefully raised his head to gaze about the room. Dawn light was pushing in through the chinks of the securely locked shutters. The horrendous night was ending, and he was still alive. The poison, if such there was, had failed to finish its work. His headache, though very much in evidence, was clearly subsiding, for now he found himself capable of rising to his feet and lurching back to the bed. He yanked the bellpull twice, before allowing himself to collapse.

He had to spend the entire day in bed, but the long rest helped, and he was able to rise the next morning, drained and a little wobbly, but essentially well.

He meant to stay that way. When a second anonymously offered parcel arrived in the afternoon, this one containing a quantity of costly Zief's Unguent, he ordered the package and its wrappings immediately burned. He also commanded that all future couriers bearing such gifts be detained for questioning; but this was a prospect he dreaded, for in it lay the possibility of a discovery too awful to contemplate. Should the packages in fact issue from the Heart of Light, he really didn't want to know.

But the days passed, no more mystery parcels reached the mansion, and the Regarded Kwieseldt's terrors began to abate. His nerves had been stretched to the breaking, but now, he was certain, he could afford to relax. The obscure assault had failed, he had survived, and now it was all over.

His mood was positively cheerful upon the day that he finally ventured out into the raw dankness of a winter's afternoon. His custom of strolling the wide, tree-lined boulevards of his own wealthy neighborhood had suspended itself of late, but now he deemed it safe to resume the pleasantly mild exercise.

Down the street marched the Regarded Kwieseldt, chin firmly set, and head held high. The breeze in his face was cold but bracing, and he gazed about him with satisfaction. The striking black and white marble mansions of the wealthiest Hetzians arose around him. Ornate lanterns decked the bare winter branches overhead, and the flagged walkway beneath his feet was immaculate. Straight ahead and near at hand, its overwhelming dome impossible to ignore, towered the Dhreve's palace.

He was a lucky man indeed, Kwieseldt reflected, to inhabit such a neighborhood. When he thought back on the servile obscurity from which he had risen to his present heights, he could hardly forbear marveling at his own good fortune.

Regarded Drempi Kwieseldt, gentleman of consequence and substance, close neighbor to no less than the Dhreve Lissildt himself.

Near the bottom of the avenue stood a tall old redtooth tree, and beside it Kwieseldt paused to contemplate the royal palace. As he stood there, motionless in plain sight of all the world, he felt a very brief stirring in the foggy air just above him, and then heard the solid thunk of something striking the tree trunk upon which he nonchalantly leaned. Puzzled, he looked up to discover a heavy, broad-bladed knife, its point sunk deep in the wood, quivering no more than an inch or two above his head.

A strangled yelp escaped Kwieseldt, and he stumbled backward from the tree, staring wildly in all directions. He thought to catch a flash of movement in the shadowy mouth of a small alley a few yards distant, but it was too brief for certainty, and he had no desire to investigate. All around him, the normal bustle of the thoroughfare continued uninterrupted. Carriages, sedan chairs, and delivery wagons navigated the street, while the well-heeled pedestrians sauntered along the walkway. Nobody heeded the Regarded Drempi Kwieseldt, nearly transfixed by an assassin's flying knife. It had all happened so quickly, and so unobtrusively, that the incident had gone unnoticed.

He might have *died*, right there in the street. He might die yet, Kwieseldt realized, should the assassin intend a second attempt. He should never have risked such public exposure, he must have been mad.

His feet began to move, almost of their own accord; slowly at first, but soon he broke into a pell-mell gallop, making for Kwieseldt Mansion, and safety. And now he did attract attention, for many a pedestrian stopped to observe the interesting spectacle of a well-dressed, cherub-faced gentleman, arms pumping and short legs churning, as he fled up the avenue as if chased by malevolences.

He didn't dare glance back over his shoulder as he ran. Should he find himself pursued, then his legs would turn to jelly, and he would collapse. His breath was coming in gasps, there was a painful stitch in his side, and his footsteps were starting to falter, but he never let himself pause. And then liTarngrav House was rising before him, and he stumbled up the broad marble steps, into the shade of the massive colonnade, and through the great gilt front doors, which he slammed behind him.

Eyes squeezed shut, and back pressed to the door, the Regarded Kwieseldt gulped air desperately. Presently his frenzied heartbeat slowed, and he opened his eyes to discover a knot of servants, studying their shaky, sweaty, disheveled master in undisguised wonder. He was beyond caring. Ignoring the battery of inquisitive eyes, Kwieseldt made his quivering way to the second story, and the sanctuary of his own bedchamber. There he immured himself alone for the rest of the afternoon.

Slowly, his intense terror subsided to manageable levels. In the early evening he summoned the majordomo to him, and issued a set of orders providing for the immediate, extensive improvement of Kwieseldt Mansion's interior and exterior defenses. He would now be safe, the Regarded Kwieseldt assured himself; safe as any rich man could be in an envious world. Of course, he would never again dare set foot outside his own house, unless accompanied by at least a pair of armed bodyguards. But that inconvenience was a small price to pay for safety, peace of mind, and protection from knife-wielding assassins sent by—whom?

The fortification of the mansion was swiftly completed, and the Regarded Kwieseldt felt himself secure, so long as he remained within doors. The gloomy winter days dragged on, no further incidents occurred, and he told himself that the danger, whatever it had been, was truly past. He thought he actually believed this; and yet his appetite was poor, his nights often sleepless, and his nerves consistently ragged. But that was understandable, he reminded himself; even inevitable, for he couldn't spend all of his time at home. A wealthy man, a prominent man, bore many responsibilities.

There were the semimonthly meetings of the League of Allies, for example. He couldn't miss a meeting, it would look very ill. Even more important, his presence was expected from time to time at the Dhreve's court.

Expected—required—obligatory; so much was certain, if unspoken. For the Regarded Drempi Kwieseldt served as a devoted defender of judicial prestige and interests at the various courtly functions and ceremonies; as a spokesperson, almost as an unofficial representative of the White Tribunal. It had never been formally specified that his willingness to act in such a capacity was a condition attached to the great gift of liTarngrav House. It had never been necessary to do so, for the terms were perfectly understood by all parties concerned.

No shirking such responsibilities, which too often forced him out into public. But he never went forth undefended, and certainly he was safe in his own home. Kwieseldt Mansion was impregnable.

On a monochromatic winter's afternoon, some three weeks following the delivery of the Golden Trueleaf, the Regarded Kwieseldt stepped from his private sitting room out onto a balcony overlooking the great central courtyard of his house. From that balcony, he could survey a splendid expanse of gardens, filled with fountains and sculpture, all invisible from the street. At this time of year, of course, the plants were largely dormant, and the fountains were dry, but this scarcely mattered. The point, and source of true satisfaction, lay less in the contents of the enclosure than in its remarkable urban seclusion. The vulgar throngs, out there upon the street beyond the wall, knew nothing of this place, whose hidden beauty had been created to please noble liTarngrav eyes alone.

And now it all belonged to Drempi Kwieseldt.

Advancing to the balustrade, Kwieseldt rested his elbows upon the black marble coping and leaned forward to survey his domain. Masterfully planned pleasure grounds down there, with graceful flagstone paths, whose lovely curving design was quite visible from his high vantage point. Handsome statues dotted the gardens, to excellent effect, and it occurred to Kwieseldt for the first time that a likeness of himself, the current master, might with perfect propriety grace the collection. Drempi Kwieseldt's marble image, watching over the secret garden, forever.

Excited by the idea, he leaned forward, straining his vision to pierce the winter mists.

He heard a slight grating of stone, and felt the marble shift beneath his weight. An instant later a great slab of coping slid from position and crashed down into the gardens below. Kwieseldt tottered giddily. He clutched at a baluster, caught hold of it, and so managed to save himself from following the stone.

He sank to his knees and rested there, gasping and shuddering. His desperate grip upon the baluster did not relax for several minutes. When at last he so far collected himself as to survey his surroundings, he realized that the danger had not, after all, been so very great. The balusters were closely spaced, and thigh high. He was unlikely to tumble over that barrier.

But he *could* have. It wasn't impossible.

As Kwieseldt's fear abated, anger rose to take its place. His servants—his lazy, good-for-nothing, overpaid, useless *servants*—should have noticed that a block of coping was loose. That was their job, to look after the master's safety. He would identify and dismiss the careless culprit. He would dismiss the lot of them.

Abandoning his death grip on the baluster, he rose to his feet, stamped back into the house, and tugged the nearest bellpull. A servant answered the summons within seconds. Vituperation sprayed from the master's lips. The servant hastened out onto the balcony.

A close examination of the guardrail revealed the separation along its entire length of the coping and its supports. All traces of mortar had been chipped away, and the marble blocks balanced precariously atop the balusters, held in place by nothing more than their own weight. The work would have taken one man many hours. More likely, a team had performed it.

When? How? Who?

His enemies had penetrated Kwieseldt Mansion. Or else, even more appalling, resided within the mansion, among the countless servants. Either possibility was insupportable. The Regarded Kwieseldt issued hysterical orders. A thorough search of the house revealed an inexplicably unlocked downstairs window. An equally painstaking investigation of the grounds discovered nothing more than a single, small object trodden into the mud below the wall at the quiet east end of the garden; a bedraggled, forgotten white cockade.

⁂ ⁃

After that, there was no peace. They were in his house. They were everywhere. Among his friends, his servants, possibly even his own family members. The kindly, solicitous faces that surrounded him day and night were masks, nothing but masks.

Kwieseldt mewed himself up in his own apartment, with armed guards stationed at the entrance. Only his wife, his son, and a couple of demonstrably devoted retainers were allowed in. *But the High Landguardian Jex liTarngrav must have regarded Drempi Kwieseldt as demonstrably devoted.* The League of Allies meetings and assorted courtly functions could and would go on without him. He didn't care how it looked.

His world had shrunk, but at least he would be safe.

Or so he thought, until the morning that he woke to discover a yellow spider with blue markings motionless on the pillow beside him. A Topaz Executioner, beyond question. Aggressive, notoriously venomous, and quite unmistakable, with those azure blotches. Its victims lingered in torment for days, with bodily putrefaction preceding death.

Kwieseldt shrieked and bounded from the bed. Still screaming, he stumbled backward, tripped, and sprawled full length, striking his head painfully upon the corner of a footstool as he fell. Slow, wet warmth began to course down his forehead. He hardly noticed. Dragging himself to his feet with some difficulty, for he was dizzy and his vision in one eye was redly clouded, he lurched to the door, threw it wide, and howled for help.

One of the demonstrably devoted retainers was there in an instant. Pointing a shaking finger at the pillow, Kwieseldt gasped faintly, "Topaz— Topaz—"

Nothing could better have demonstrated devotion than the careful alacrity with which the servant approached the bed. For some moments, he studied the arachnid from a distance of several feet; scooped up a tankard of worked silver, and advanced another few cautious paces; observed minutely for a while, then smiled, turned to face his master, and said, "Liar."

"*What?*"

"It's only a Yellow Liar, sir. Harmless little spider, even beneficial. Helps to keep the grounds free of flying pests—beetles, blowflies, and the like. Easy to mistake for a Topaz Executioner, they're very much alike. But you can always tell the difference if you just look at the blue marking right behind the head. You see, on the Executioner, it's always shaped like a ring, but the Liar's got a— You can't see it from where you are, sir, wouldn't you like to come a little closer?"

"No! Get rid of that thing! And summon a physician! Can you not see that I am wounded?"

"Got a little cut across your forehead, sir. Doesn't look like much. I'm sure the barber can fix you fine in a wink—"

"I don't want the barber! And I don't want a horse doctor, either, if that was to be your next suggestion! Get me a proper physician, one who knows his business! You understand me?"

"Yes, Regarded. Er—if I may ask—which physician?"

"Oh." The question took Drempi Kwieseldt by surprise, but he couldn't let himself appear indecisive. He thought rapidly, and a name came to mind. "The one whose circulars keep turning up on our doorstep. That foreign fellow in the Eastcity. Yes. Summon Dr. Flambeska."

Fifteen

They told him that Flambeska would never come. They told him that the uppity Strellian physician never stooped to house calls. But the Regarded Drempi Kwieseldt insisted, and his judgment proved sound. Dr. Flambeska answered the summons at once, which came as no surprise to the summoner, who knew that no physician in his right mind would refuse the master of liTarngrav House. *Kwieseldt Mansion.*

The doctor arrived in the midmorning. He was expected, and the guards admitted him at once. A footman led the way up to the second story, along the great corridor to the master's apartment, where the visitor submitted without complaint to a brief search. No weapons were discovered upon his person or within the bag he carried, and he was permitted into the bedchamber.

The Regarded Drempi Kwieseldt lay in bed, propped up on pillows purged of multilegged visitants. His head was clumsily bound in blood-stained linen. He started nervously as the door opened, then recognized the distinctive garb of a Strellian physician, and let himself relax a little.

The doctor seemed young, but it was hard to be certain, for his form concealed itself beneath a loose grey robe, and his face hid in the shadow of a square, wide-brimmed hat. A pair of dark spectacles furnished additional camouflage.

"Regarded." Flambeska bowed easily, then straightened and approached the bed.

An inexplicable qualm assailed Drempi Kwieseldt. He could hardly account for his own dread, as there was nothing particularly intimidating about this unarmed doctor, who had come upon the kindliest of missions. Perhaps it had something to do with the other's economy of movement, his quality of stillness that had nothing to do with repose. Or perhaps it was simply the fellow's exoticism, his odd dress and foreign accent. In any case, there was no cause for such absurd uneasiness in the presence of a social inferior, and the master of Kwieseldt Mansion took refuge behind negligence.

"Ah, there you are at last, Flambeska," he murmured with a palely patronizing smile. "I trust I have not too greatly inconvenienced you."

The doctor answered neither the smile nor the implied question. "You have suffered a misfortune," he observed. "I will examine the injury."

Beyond the Strellian inflection, there was something a bit unusual in the timbre of that voice; a certain metallic, unused quality.

The doctor extended a long-fingered white hand, and Kwieseldt instinctively shied away from it. The hand withdrew at once.

"If I may," Flambeska requested dryly.

Kwieseldt felt the blood rush to his cheeks. He was making a fool of himself before the doctor fellow. Frowning, he nodded, and the hand was back about his head, its touch light and very sure, but he had to exert every ounce of willpower to prevent himself from flinching.

The Strellian knew what he was doing, so much had to be granted. Stripping the clumsy amateur bandage away, he proceeded to bathe the cut, then apply salve, and never once did Kwieseldt suffer the slightest twinge of pain.

"It is a shallow gash," the doctor declared. "The bleeding has already ceased. It is not necessary to stitch the wound."

Kwieseldt nodded, without trusting himself to speak. He felt himself on the verge of tears, so intense was his relief. No stitches. No hideous needles violating his Regarded flesh. For the life of him, he couldn't control the trembling of his hands. He hid them at once beneath the bedclothes, but it was too late. The doctor had certainly seen.

Expertly, Flambeska bandaged the wound, and still there was no pain. This task accomplished, the doctor drew back a little to survey his patient.

Kwieseldt fidgeted under the prolonged, wordless scrutiny. He felt foolish, and curiously naked, lying there on his back in bed, with his bandaged head and his trembling hands. He felt as if the visitor's eyes, invisible behind their smoked lenses, could see straight into his head, to read all the fearful, guilty, avaricious thoughts residing there. He decided then and there that he didn't like Dr. Flambeska, and the recognition of his own hostility gave him courage to lift his chin and meet the other's gaze squarely.

The silence lengthened. Unlike the Lady Aestine, the Regarded Kwieseldt resisted the impulse to fill it, and it was the doctor who spoke first.

"The wound upon your head is superficial, Regarded. Have you sustained no other injury?"

"A few bruises."

"I will examine them."

"That won't be necessary."

"I see." Another long silence crawled by, and then at last the doctor suggested, "Be so good as to describe the circumstances of your mishap."

"What for?"

"The minor injuries of the moment frequently serve as the visible manifestation of underlying ills. The close perusal of apparently irrelevant or insignificant facts often furnishes insight to the alert physician."

"Not this time. I simply tripped over a footstool, fell down, and hit my head. That's all."

"Do you often trip over footstools? Have you trouble with your vision?"

"My eyes are excellent!"

"And your coordination?"

"Just fine, thank you very much."

"Would you regard yourself as unusually prone to accident?"

"Not unusually. Listen, Doctor, I'll tell you what it was. I woke to find myself lying beside a spider—"

"A very common complaint."

"I mistook it for a poisonous Topaz Executioner—it really was remarkably like—leaped out of bed, and tripped. So you see, it was only—"

"Are you afflicted with a particularly pronounced detestation of spi-ders, insects, snakes, scorpions, or the like?"

"Not particularly. Only in this case—"

"Your reaction was extreme. Perhaps your general state of mind is to blame?"

"I *have* been troubled in thought, lately. My slumbers and digestion both suffer. I am burdened with a thousand cares and fears."

"Of what nature?"

"Does it matter?"

"Regarded, in order to effect a cure, it is necessary to determine the cause. All information must be viewed as potentially useful."

"I see." Kwieseldt waited a moment or two, but the doctor said noth-ing more. "Oh, very well. If you think it might do some good."

He began to speak, reluctantly at first, of recent, horrid events. He told of the attempts upon his life, of the illness that was not natural, the accidents that were not accidents. He spoke of the infiltration of Kwieseldt Mansion, the untrustworthiness of his servants, the incompetence and venal-ity of his hired guards, the diabolical brilliance of his powerful foes. He spoke of his sleepless nights, his wretched days, his fears and his miseries.

As the accumulated terrors poured out of him, the Regarded Kwieseldt experienced a certain pleasant release of tension. Forgetting his initial dislike of the Strellian physician, he confided all, holding back no detail, and his sense of relief intensified. The rush of words halted at last. The Regarded Kwieseldt looked down at his hands, and saw that they had ceased trembling.

"I feel better." He surveyed his doctor, almost with gratitude.

"You have begun to heal yourself," Flambeska explained. "But the process is far from complete. The respite you find here and now is tempo-rary in nature. The root of your problem remains whole, and the vile weed will surely rise again."

"Oh." Kwieseldt folded his hands tightly. "Can you not give me some sort of soothing draught, or powder, or essence, designed to steady and quiet my nerves? Would that not address the problem?"

"It might eliminate the symptoms, but only for a little while, and at considerable cost to body and mind. No, Regarded. For the sake of your own health, your very life, you must confront the true source of distress."

"That is impossible. I've already told you that my enemies are secret, and anonymous, and—"

"You've no idea who might wish you ill? You know of no specific individual, or individuals?"

Kwieseldt looked away. He thought of the white cockade discovered in his garden. He thought of Gnaus liGurvohl's rainwater eyes, fixed upon the Lady Aestine, who had killed herself shortly thereafter.

"I suspect," he admitted. "But I do not know."

"The uncertainty—that is hard to bear, I imagine."

"Terrible. Oh, terrible!"

"To know, beyond doubt—even if it is to know the worst—that would be better, would it not?"

"Much better! But impossible."

"To a gentleman of your resources, Regarded—master of Kwieseldt Mansion, a voice at the Dhreve's court, famous friend of the White Tribunal—"

"You do not understand, Doctor. My enemy—or rather my premier suspect—is vastly powerful, eminent, and unassailable. He is far beyond the reach of my poor powers."

"Perhaps not."

"What do you mean?" Kwieseldt glanced up quickly to meet the other's opaque glass gaze.

"Only that your enemy, whoever he may be, cannot hope to evade all observation."

"Oh, but he can. You don't know. This is a personage so high, so great—well, there's no opposing him. It's useless even to try. I had best accept my fate."

"If that is truly your wish, far be it from me to interfere. But what if it should happen that this being whom you fear is not your enemy at all? What if you should find him entirely uninvolved, in no way responsible for your recent misfortunes?"

"Then, I would be whole again. My life would be renewed." Drempi Kwieseldt couldn't suppress the tears that rose to his eyes.

"Excellent. That is the attitude I hope to inspire in my patients."

"Ah, but what's the use of dwelling on golden dreams? They only render reality the worse by comparison."

"We do not speak of dreams, Regarded. We discuss a course of treatment engineered to relieve your mind of the uncertainty that preys upon your spirits. To that end, it is necessary to observe the actions of a certain great man whose name you dare not utter. I do not need or care to know his identity. Whoever he may be, however high and inaccessible, be assured it is possible to watch him. Day or night, wherever he might lodge, you may view him at your own convenience, and he will remain unaware of surveillance."

"Flambeska, what are you talking about?"

"I will show you." The physician's leather bag yielded a fist-sized sphere of black iron, which Dr. Flambeska presented to his patient. "Take it. Look at it."

Puzzled, Kwieseldt accepted the sphere and examined it closely. The thing was lighter in weight than its size suggested. Obviously it was hollow, probably quite thin-walled. He turned it around in his hand. Dull black cast iron, smooth, and quite featureless save for a single, coin-sized hole. He applied his eye to the opening, and peered into unrelieved darkness. Gingerly he inserted one finger to grope the interior, and discovered emptiness. He raised it to his ear, and heard nothing. As a last resort, he even held the opening to his nose and inhaled deeply, but caught no odor.

Kwieseldt placed the sphere on the coverlet beside him. His questioning eyes rose to the visitor's black lenses.

"You see nothing, Regarded?" Without awaiting reply, the doctor continued, "That is as it should be, for the safety of all concerned. This means of treatment must not announce itself to the ignorant. It is not intended for the commonplace patient, any more than a visit from Flambeska of Strell is bestowed upon the vulgar or the unworthy. But the master of Kwieseldt Mansion deserves special consideration."

"Well. That is most gratifying." The Regarded Kwieseldt found his initial dislike of the Strellian physician fading. The fellow was a little odd in manner, perhaps, but really quite discerning. He knew how to bathe and bandage a wound to perfection, but his preoccupation with a dull ball of iron was difficult to fathom.

"The Iron Vigilance is ready to receive its imprint," Dr. Flambeska announced. "Once the impression of the subject's physical reality has registered, you may observe that individual at will, and you may continue to do so until such time as the Vigilance is cleansed and readied to receive a fresh imprint."

The Regarded Kwieseldt stared. "I haven't the least idea what any of that means," he said. "Did you just make it up?"

"By no means. Fortunately, the patient needn't understand the principle of the sphere's operation in order to enjoy the benefits. Take up the Vigilance, Regarded. Apply your eye to the opening, and then, in your own mind, visualize the face of your suspect. Try to see it in its entirety, omitting no detail of feature or complexion. Concentrate until you see him clearly, as if he stood before you in the flesh."

"Why? What will happen?"

There was no reply. Kwieseldt shrugged and obeyed.

It was easier than he might have expected; all too easy, in a way. He stared into the blackness of the sphere's interior, and Gnaus liGurvohl's countenance seemed to take shape before his eyes. He thought of the high

forehead, the thin, high-bridged nose, the long, narrow jaw, and the beautifully drawn, merciless lips. Above all, he thought of the great, pale eyes,
their brilliance framed in shadow. Kwieseldt strained his mental vision, and
other details sharpened into focus; grey hairs sprinkling the dark brows, deep
vertical crease marking the brow, the contemptuous curve of the nostrils.

The Premier Jurist's face seemed to glow in the darkness before him,
immediate and disturbingly real.

Kwieseldt's breath quickened. His palms were starting to sweat. The
face was a bit too real for comfort. Almost he could have fancied that it
possessed a life of its own, the eyes reflecting expressions that he himself had
never imagined. Moreover, the image seemed to possess a remarkable solidity that he could hardly account for. Almost it might have existed in three
dimensions.

Gnaus liGurvohl tightened his lips and turned his head away.

Kwieseldt gasped, and dropped the Iron Vigilance. For a moment he
stared at the sphere where it lay among the bedclothes, then raised his eyes
to the shadowed visage of Dr. Flambeska.

"My nerves are unstrung," Kwieseldt heard himself apologizing. "My
imagination is playing me false."

"Not at all, Regarded," the doctor contradicted serenely. "The Iron
Vigilance has received its imprint, that is all. Henceforth, you may survey
the subject at your own discretion."

"I don't believe it."

The doctor did not deign to reply. Hesitantly, Kwieseldt picked up
the sphere again, and gingerly approached his eye to the opening. The
glowing image within was small, but remorselessly clear and sharp.

Gnaus liGurvohl sat at a desk, its surface covered with orderly stacks
of documents. He was reading one of the papers, and as he read, the crease
between his brows deepened. Dipping a quill, he jotted a brief notation, set
the written matter aside, picked up a small bell, and shook it impatiently.

If the bell rang, no sound of it reached Drempi Kwieseldt.

A servant or clerk of some sort approached the desk, halted, and
bowed low. Gnaus liGurvohl spoke at length, and with some evidence of
anger.

Not a word was audible to Drempi Kwieseldt.

Tearing his gaze from the Iron Vigilance, Kwieseldt turned to ask his
visitor, "Is it real?"

"The images appearing within the Vigilance reflect current reality,"
returned Dr. Flambeska. "You see the subject as he truly appears at this
moment."

"How can that be?"

"A technical explanation serves little purpose. Suffice it to say, the device offers potential relief."

"Indeed." Heart beating fast, the Regarded Kwieseldt squinted into the Iron Vigilance.

Gnaus liGurvohl sat at his desk. Before him trembled the hapless underling. Silent torrents gushed from the Premier Jurist's lips.

Kwieseldt watched until he could stand no more, then turned back to his doctor and inquired, "Is there any way that I can hear what he's saying?"

"I regret I cannot offer miracles, Regarded." Dr. Flambeska permitted himself a wintry smile.

"No, of course not. I did not mean to suggest—certainly, I appreciate—" Kwieseldt returned his attention to the Iron Vigilance, within whose confines the Premier Jurist liGurvohl, alone again, labored over his innumerable documents. LiGurvohl no doubt pursued his great vocation—the destruction of the sorcerous menace threatening all of Upper Hetzia. And it occurred to Kwieseldt then, for the first time, that the device he now held in his very own hand—the device that he was actually using, *enjoying*—that such a spectacularly weird contraption could never have been created without recourse to—

Sorcery. In the direst degree.

He didn't like to think about it. He was the Regarded Drempi Kwieseldt, friend of the White Tribunal, sworn enemy of sorcery and all things sorcerous. It didn't pay to be anything else. He knew that well, and yet, somehow, here he now lay, intimately connected with an object of dubious legitimacy. *Stupendous illegality.* He could hardly have said how it came about, but here he was.

With the Iron Vigilance in his hand.

What was this foreigner who had brought it? Kwieseldt slanted a quick glance up at his physician. The doctor's face was all but invisible and, in any case, unreadable.

He ought to relinquish the sorcerous object at once, and denounce the donor. That would certainly be the right course, by far the safest course. And yet—and yet—

Driven by an impulse too strong to resist, Kwieseldt peered again into the sphere, to behold the Premier Jurist bent industriously over correspondence. Probably correspondence. Nothing so alarming there, assuming that the paperwork included no warrant authorizing the arrest of Kwieseldt Mansion's master.

But why should it? The suspicion was absurd.

Absurd?

The Premier Jurist liGurvohl toiled harmlessly, or so it appeared.

But the Iron Vigilance itself was far from harmless. The thing reeked of sorcery, and its user invited Disinfection, a fate avoidable by means of a letter of denunciation, discreetly deposited in the Hungry Man's mouth. Such a letter, accusing Dr. Flambeska of sorcery, or of traffic with sorcery, would cleanse the Regarded Kwieseldt of all possible complicitous taint.

Kwieseldt chanced another covert glance at his doctor. He learned nothing beyond the other's inscrutability, which was beginning to wear on his patience. Flambeska's silent omniscience was impressive, but abrasive. He'd had enough of intimidation in his lifetime. He didn't need more now, from random foreign physician fellows.

Where did you get this thing? Kwieseldt managed to suppress the question. His visitor would almost certainly refuse to answer. In any case, he really didn't want to know. The less he knew, the better off he was. His own safety demanded immediate disengagement; at cost, without saying, of the Iron Vigilance.

Kwieseldt studied the sphere. He couldn't resist peeking into its dark recesses, one last time. Applying his eye to the opening, he saw Gnaus liGurvohl, poised beside a tall window, gazing down upon the city of Lis Folaze from the heights of the Heart of Light.

It was a rare and exquisite thing to hold such an advantage over the Premier Jurist.

A perilous advantage.

Tearing his eyes from the sphere, he forced himself to begin, "I hardly think—"

"Do not be too swift to decide, one way or another," the doctor cut him off neatly. "I advise you to retain the Vigilance, for now. Make much use of it, over the course of the next several days. If, at the end of that period, you discover no improvement in your own condition, then we shall devise a new method of treatment."

"But, this thing, it's obviously—"

"Intended for the use of the select, alone. I do not often resort to such measures, but will make an exception in favor of Kwieseldt Mansion's master. If I do not hear from you within the coming week, I shall assume successful results."

"But—"

"For the moment, our business is concluded, and I wish you good morning."

"Flambeska, your payment—"

"We will speak of it another time." Dr. Flambeska bowed low and departed. The bedroom door closed behind him.

The Regarded Kwieseldt lay motionless, the Iron Vigilance clasped loosely in one hand. He hadn't meant to let the doctor leave without the device, but it had happened so quickly that he'd had no time to act, and perhaps no real inclination. It wasn't too late to protect himself, however. There was still time to call Flambeska back.

But the moments passed, and Kwieseldt lay silent, brow furrowed. Presently, he lifted the Vigilance to his eye.

Tradain walked the corridor alone. No footman or guard hovered at his elbow, for it was tacitly assumed that the visiting physician fellow could find his own way to the door. That assumption was correct, for he had visited liTarngrav House often as a boy, and the recollection of its chambers and galleries was still surprisingly fresh in his mind. His eyes roamed as he went, and everywhere beheld familiar sights; the endless array of matched chandeliers overhead, the twisted columns, the gigantic mirrors—he remembered them all. He and his two brothers had run footraces along this very passageway. Their boots had darkly scuffed the polished floor, and a liTarngrav servant had complained, and there had been an official reprimand from their father . . . It might have been yesterday.

The memories offered welcome distraction from thoughts of the interview just concluded. He did not wish to dwell on the image of the Regarded Drempi Kwieseldt, his enemy and target, lying in bed looking so—

Small. Ineffectual. Insignificant.

Kwieseldt, of course, was considerably more dangerous than he appeared. The cherub concealed poison fangs, and it wouldn't do to forget it.

Farther along the corridor, down the curving staircase to the cavernous, glittering entrance hall, and as he descended, the memories intensified almost magically. He couldn't have said why.

He reached the bottom of the stairs, and the immediacy of the past was overwhelming. Almost he might have been a boy again, the events of the last thirteen years the stuff of nightmares. The very atmosphere seemed charged with bittersweet nostalgia.

He became aware of the music, then—delicate, supple notes teasing his ears. Involuntarily he paused to listen. Someone nearby was playing a harpsichord, and playing it very skillfully. The melody was engaging, and somehow familiar. He had heard it in the distant past, but couldn't identify the tune or composer, and certainly couldn't explain his own sense of cold dread. The music was all sunlight and fresh air—bright, youthful, and innocent. He couldn't imagine why such a wholesomely charming confection should rouse so dark a sense of impending doom.

His eyes raked the hall. Not far away, a gilded door stood ajar, and he remembered that the music room lay beyond. His recollections of that chamber were dim, for its contents had never strongly claimed his interest. But he was interested now.

Approaching almost stealthily, he looked in. He remembered the place, now. High ceiling, frescoed with clouds, winged horses, flying chariots; huge arched windows, warmly glowing parquet floor, and a staggering collection of instruments, both antique and modern. There were several he couldn't identify, despite all his learning, but the big, elaborate harpsichord was easy to recognize. A young woman sat playing it. He glimpsed a straight, slim back, clothed in russet velvet; a long, white neck; and a heavy, burnished mass of chestnut hair, defying the restraint of tortoiseshell combs.

The color of that hair scratched at his memory. It was an unusual shade, he ought to know it; just as he ought to know why that young birdsong music chilled him to the bone.

She must have felt his presence, for the music ceased, and she swiveled to face him. Her face was pretty rather than beautiful, with clear, even features, lent distinction by a pair of remarkable greenish eyes—wide, intelligent, subtly tilted at the outer corners, and set beneath arching brows, several shades darker than her hair.

There was no mistaking those eyes. They had altered in expression over the course of thirteen years, and yet, in some ways, they hadn't changed at all. Little Glennian liTarngrav, all grown up. An adult, but ward of her father's betrayer. His investigations had taught him long ago that he might find her here; they had not taught him whether she knew the role her guardian had played in Jex liTarngrav's destruction. He had given the question no great consideration, for the answer held no importance to him, but now he wondered.

He need wonder no longer, however, at the unsettling nature of the melody, for now he recognized the tune that the child Glennian had dreamed up and hummed aloud years ago, during that long hike from the mansion of Yurune the Bloodless, back to the city of Lis Folaze. "Just one of my things," she had called it, with self-conscious carelessness, but the notes possessed an unexpected power. For an instant time shivered, and he was a boy again, hurrying home through the autumn woods, with that tune in his ears and no inkling whatever of the catastrophe waiting at the end of the day.

She was staring straight at him, straight through him, and it occurred to him that the music carrying him back to those forests of the past might have done exactly the same to her. His impulse was to turn and run, but he controlled it. His disguise was reliably impenetrable. Still, he did not mean to linger.

"Madam." He bowed. "Pray forgive the intrusion, I was caught by your music. I will leave you."

"Stop," she commanded, and he paused reluctantly. "You are Dr. Flambeska?"

Tradain inclined his head.

"You have attended the Regarded Kwieseldt?" She was inspecting him with disquieting attentiveness.

"I have."

"They will not allow me to—" She broke off. "Please tell me what's happened to my guardian."

Her guardian. She almost sounded affectionate. Surely, she couldn't know the truth, or even suspect it.

"He tripped, fell, and cut his brow. The injury is minor, there is no cause for alarm."

"Are you quite certain, Doctor? For some weeks, his state of mind has seemed—"

"The Regarded Kwieseldt suffers a mild excess of the melancholy humor. I have devised a course of treatment that is likely to prove effective."

"What treatment?"

"I am not at liberty to say, madam."

"No—no, of course not. I understand. Only tell me, Doctor, is there anything that I might do to speed his recovery?"

Her obviously genuine concern was almost painful to witness. And there was still that disturbingly intense gaze, boring straight through the weak barrier of his dark glasses. He wanted to be away from her, as quickly as possible.

"Allow him rest and peace. See to it that he is neither troubled nor overly stimulated. An extended period of tranquillity will serve him well."

"I hope so. Thank you, Dr. Flambeska. You've been most kind."

"Not at all. And now, madam, by your leave, I will—"

"Return to Solemnity Square?" Her face was quite expressionless. Her gaze never faltered. "I gather you've a busy practice."

"Exactly so."

"And swiftly established, I believe. You are a newcomer to Lis Folaze, are you not?"

"I am fortunate in the welcome I have found here, madam."

"Well deserved, no doubt. And before you came to this city—?"

Idle curiosity? Or something more?

"I lived and worked where fate willed, but largely in Strell." His face and voice were equally unrevealing.

"Fate. Ah. But you have visited Upper Hetzia in the past, surely?"

"Never."

"That is curious."

"How so?"

"I've a very strong sense that I've seen you before today, and I am rarely mistaken in such matters."

"Quite possible, madam." He allowed no sign of perturbation to touch his face. "Often I walk the streets of your city. I have lingered in the public gardens, I have gazed upon the river from various bridges. It is not at all unlikely that you have glimpsed me."

"No, that's not what I mean. I am thinking of the past, the far distant past."

"Another life, perhaps?" His smile was daunting.

"Not quite that distant," she returned dryly. "When I was a child—"

"I was far away, in Eschelleria. Unless you were there as well, then you are surely in error. And now, madam, if you will grant me leave to depart—"

"I am not in error," Glennian observed mildly. "Give me another moment, and I will solve the puzzle. My memory is not at all bad."

Her memory. His own had surely slept, for he'd forgotten that she'd been a gifted child, possessing prodigious powers of recollection. She'd been capable, at age nine, of glancing briefly at the pages of a book she'd never seen before, shutting the volume, and then reciting the text aloud, without an error, for minutes at a time. This, in fact, was a trick she'd often performed for the benefit of her father's guests, and she'd been inordinately vain of it. Her extraordinary, damnable memory.

He should never have let her catch sight of him. He would take care not to repeat the mistake.

"I would linger in hopes of a revelation, but a thousand duties prevent—"

"I am cold," she interrupted abruptly. Rising from the harpsichord, she glided across the parquet floor to the nearest fireplace.

She was very slender, but nicely molded, he observed. She moved well. Her complaint was frivolous, for the music room was not at all chilly, or at least did not seem so to him. But perhaps thirteen years' residence in Fortress Nul had affected his standards of judgment.

The fire was burning well and wanted no adjustment, but for reasons best known to herself, Glennian liTarngrav was fooling with the damper, and she ought to have left it alone, for she didn't know what she was doing. Metal clanked behind the mantel, and heavy smoke began to gush from the fireplace.

Coughing violently, Glennian beat at the smoke with her hands. Much good that was likely to do. Why hadn't the silly girl simply summoned a competent servant?

He hurried to her side. Thick black clouds swirled about him. He coughed, and turned his face aside. Groping blindly beneath the mantel, he found the lever and pushed the damper wide open. The smoke subsided at once, and the fire leaped.

"How clumsy I am," Glennian murmured. "These domestic mechanisms are far beyond me."

Tradain blinked. The room had gone dark. Black soot thickly coated his spectacles.

"Forgive me, Doctor," Glennian implored. "I've a handkerchief, let me make amends."

"That will not be necessary. I would prefer—"

"Nonsense, it is the least I can do," she returned, and in one unexpected motion reached out a hand and drew the spectacles from his face.

It took an almost physical effort to refrain from snatching them back. Too late for that. She made no pretense of cleaning the soiled lenses, but dangled the spectacles between thumb and forefinger, while staring straight into his eyes.

"Yes," she said.

"I must ask you to return my property at once," he essayed. "I am troubled with an ocular morbidity, and the daylight is acutely painful to me."

"I am sorry to hear it. Is the problem of recent development? For there never used to be anything wrong with your eyes, Tradain, and they look now very much as they always did. They are quite recognizable, as you know, else you wouldn't have troubled to hide them."

"I must confess, your pleasantries bewilder me, madam." His expression never altered, but his heart raced. "Perhaps I shall better appreciate the jest when my present discomfort has subsided. If you would be so good as to—"

"Your eyes are neither watery nor bloodshot," Glennian observed calmly. "They exude no rheum, and exhibit no sign of swelling or discoloration. I really don't think there's anything wrong with them, Tradain."

"What name do you pronounce?"

"Your own. Tradain liMarchborg. It's been a long time, but I've never forgotten it."

"You amuse yourself at my expense, madam. Or else you simply mistake the matter."

"I believe not, but the issue is easily resolved. Do you know, there are several among the older household retainers whose term of service dates back twenty years and more. They were here when you used to visit as a boy. Shall I summon two or three of them, and ask if they recall the blue eyes of Dr. Flambeska?" She smiled amiably.

"That won't be necessary." Denial was useless, and he let the Strellian accent slip. "You are right. I am Tradain liMarchborg." He saw her eyes widen. Perhaps she hadn't anticipated such an easy victory. He found himself less alarmed than he might have expected. There was something strangely pleasurable in this act of self-acknowledgment. Moreover, his powers armed him against any threat offered by Glennian liTarngrav. This so, he awaited her reaction with a certain detached curiosity.

She found her voice. "I thought you were dead."

"I was. The condition proved impermanent."

"What happened to you?"

"Nothing, for many years."

"Where have you been?"

"I have not been. Existence resumed in Solemnity Square."

She blinked at each of his answers, as if he had slammed three doors shut in her face. There was a pause, and then she asked, "What are you doing here?"

"I was summoned to treat the Regarded Drempi's fearful wound."

"Are you really a physician?"

"My patients choose to regard me as such."

"I see. When I asked what are you doing here, I actually meant here in Lis Folaze."

"Where else should a liMarchborg take himself, but to his ancestral home?"

"Yes, but for you—your family—the Tribunal's judgment—surely it is dangerous," she concluded, in some confusion.

"Not so long as I go unrecognized," he returned. "But you have penetrated my disguise, and the secret now rests in your hands." He did not think it necessary to point out that a certain expenditure of sorcerous power could empty her famous memory of secrets, along with everything else it might contain, should he so choose. "What do you intend to do with it?"

She was still staring at him. Her eyes, he noted impersonally, were really quite astonishingly beautiful.

"You don't appear greatly concerned," Glennian observed at last.

"I've little to lose."

"That's scarcely true. Your freedom—"

"Is essentially a quality of mind."

"Debatable. Apart from that, you're still young, and your life—"

"Hardly signifies."

"Nevertheless, you won't lose it through my agency. I will keep Dr. Flambeska's secret."

So it wouldn't be necessary to purge her memory. Unexpected relief flashed through him. He realized then that the prospect of tampering with the young woman's mind was distinctly repugnant. *To rule the intelligence of others is costly,* Xyleel had told him, but his reluctance transcended mere considerations of economy. He did not know exactly why.

"On one condition," Glennian concluded.

He waited.

After a moment she resumed, "On condition that you tell me all I want to know. Tell me what happened to you thirteen years ago. Tell me how you've spent those years, which seems to have changed you so very greatly. Tell how you became 'Dr. Flambeska,' and why you've come back to Lis Folaze in disguise. Tell me everything, and tell me the truth."

Tradain reflected. He most certainly wouldn't tell her everything, but perhaps there was no great harm in telling her part of it. He discovered that he wanted to tell her. In view of his powers, the risk was affordable, and he found it oddly satisfying to speak in his own voice. Yes, he could allow himself that luxury, for once.

"Agreed," he said. They seated themselves upon a gilt and brocade bench beside one of the arched windows, and he began to talk. It was far easier than he had expected. There was something in her air of intelligent sympathy almost dangerously encouraging. The memories bottled for so many years were flowing out of him, too freely, and caution dictated control of that verbal stream. Thus, he told her of the tower room in the Heart of Light, but never mentioned the cellars; spoke of watching the executions, without describing the details; told something of the Boneworks at Fortress Nul, but nothing of Sergeant Gultz; described Fangs as a kindly old friend and benefactor, without speaking of the sorcerous tutorials; glossed lightly over the solitary dungeon years; described the prisoners' riot, the escape from Fortress Nul, and the flight to the mansion of Yurune the Bloodless in some detail, but never hinted at his own discoveries in Yurune's workroom.

Even this pallid version of the truth sufficed to moisten her eyes with tears of grief and horror. The spontaneity of that reaction exerted a curious effect on him. Some dam inside him seemed to break, the too-revealing words pressed for utterance, and he had to tighten his lips to hold them in. *Unsafe.* To make matters worse, she was still asking questions, which now verged on dangerous areas. How had he acquired such learning? Where had he learned a physician's skills? What was his purpose in returning to Lis Folaze? He'd find himself telling everything, if he didn't get away from her now.

"I must return to my lodgings." Tradain stood up. "I've above a dozen appointments."

"Then meet with me another day."

He hesitated only a moment, and then heard himself tell her, "I promise."

Past merged with present, and Glennian commanded, "Spit twice on it."

Sixteen

Premier Jurist Gnaus liGurvohl sat at the head of the conference table. Below him sat the lesser judges of the White Tribunal. LiGurvohl discoursed at length. His colleagues nodded like flowers in the breeze. Concord was complete.

This perfect harmony touched no answering chord in the heart of Drempi Kwieseldt. Scowling, Kwieseldt squinted hard into the depths of the Iron Vigilance. But the image within was already distinct, and no amount of effort could win him what he really wanted—the power to hear the Premier Jurist's silent words.

Sighing, he set the black sphere down on the desk before him, bowed his head, and massaged his brow. He felt another headache coming on. Not a bad one, nothing that a little relaxation wouldn't banish, but vexing all the same, for not long ago, he had imagined himself permanently relieved of such inconvenience.

For the first fortnight or so, possession of the Iron Vigilance had seemed the cure to every ill. The device had fulfilled all of Dr. Flambeska's promises, allowing its new owner unlimited observation of the currently imprinted subject. There were no walls thick enough to block surveillance, no midnights black enough to foil the invisible eye. Thus, the Regarded Kwieseldt had watched the Premier Jurist at work and at home, awake and asleep, alone and in company, and for a while that had been enough.

No doubt about it, Gnaus liGurvohl was a disciplined, methodical, energetic, and highly industrious public servant. He worked constantly, such was his devotion to humanity's welfare, and his every day was crammed with conferences, interviews, and court sessions. When alone, he toiled ceaselessly at his paperwork. From the viewpoint of the Regarded Kwieseldt, these activities were largely unthreatening, or so they had initially appeared.

With the passing of the days, however, and the first early breath of spring softening the air, Kwieseldt's early assurance had somehow begun to erode. He had watched the Premier Jurist engage in silent conversations, issue silent orders, express silent expectations, and at some point—he could hardly have said when—that fraught silence had begun to prey upon his mind. LiGurvohl's actions appeared humdrum, but his intentions remained obscure, and Kwieseldt's insomniac imagination had lately begun to suggest the most hideous possibilities.

Gnaus liGurvohl wanted him discreetly dead. The White Tribunal was not to involve itself officially in the removal of its own long-standing ally—perhaps the lesser jurists didn't even know of their master's design— and therefore, the murder would be quietly committed, possibly even made to appear an accident. A few attempts had failed already, but there would surely be others.

The terrors, encased in headache, struck at any hour of the day or night, but displayed a decided preference for the sleepless environs of midnight. As for the visions vouchsafed by the Iron Vigilance, they roused more fear than they allayed. Kwieseldt knew it, but the insight didn't suffice to keep his fingers and eyes off the sorcerous sphere.

He lifted his head. His hand sought the Vigilance almost unconsciously, found it, and raised it to his eye. Inside the sphere, the members of the White Tribunal were passing some sort of document around the table. Each jurist perused the paper briefly, affixed his signature, then handed it on to his neighbor.

Death warrant?

Kwieseldt tilted the Vigilance this way and that, seeking a better view of the document. He discerned a vertical column of script—it looked as if it might be a list of names—but he really couldn't be certain. Frustration pricked him, and he contained his impulse to hurl the sphere across the room. Rather than so giving way, he fixed his attention upon the Premier Jurist, as if by sheer intensity of observation, he might read the mind behind the face.

It was a dreadful face, he decided. Icy, remote, inhuman as the image of a malevolence conjured by some sorcerer. How ridiculous that he should apply such a comparison to the great enemy of all things sorcerous. Still, a fearsome face to threaten a terrified world.

The world might be better off, relieved of such a face. Certainly, Drempi Kwieseldt would be better off.

Someone knocked at the study door. Instantly Kwieseldt thrust the Iron Vigilance into a desk drawer, which he slammed and locked.

"Come," he invited.

The door opened, and Pfissig entered, attired in persimmon brocade. Perhaps not the best shade in the world for a pink complexion, Kwieseldt reflected, and yet, surely such a color lent his son *consequence*.

"Father, I've come to warn you," Pfissig nasally announced.

Kwieseldt's full attention was at once engaged.

"There are matters demanding your immediate attention, sir," the young man continued. "I am sorry to trouble you with ill tidings, but conscience demands no less. It is only fitting that the master know the full state of affairs in his own house, and therefore I feel it my duty to inform you at once of Glennian's misbehavior."

"What's she done?"

"She has presumed to place a very large, very conspicuous padlock upon her bedroom door. There is no question in my mind that she far exceeds her license as a dependent in this house to—"

"No she doesn't," Kwieseldt interrupted. "I gave her permission to do that, several days ago."

"I see. Well." Pfissig brooded briefly, and then complained, "Perhaps I grant a trivial incident undue significance, yet I cannot help but perceive her actions as deliberately *insulting*—"

"You are too sensitive, my boy. The matter is beneath your notice."

"When it is a question of protecting *your* interests, Father, nothing is beneath my notice," Pfissig returned soulfully. "But let us forget Glennian, for I've discovered other infractions. In the kitchen, for example. I performed a discreet inspection only this morning, and what do you think I found there? A candle, sir—a beeswax candle. Sitting right out on the table, in plain sight!"

"Well?"

"A *beeswax* candle. *Pure* beeswax! Do you know how much such things cost? Beeswax isn't meant for the kitchen, tallow's good enough. One of the servants must have taken that wax candle from an upstairs chamber. Stolen it, Father! We must identify the thief."

"You would have made an excellent steward, my boy. You've natural talent. But I've worse on my mind at the moment than misplaced candles."

"There is more, Father. There is really no limit to the grasping, mendacious laziness of the servant class. What do you suppose I've found in the garden? Nothing less than a lair, sir!"

"A what?"

"Behind the stand of ornamental juguberries, I have discovered a small canvas awning, cushions, a grill, gnawed chicken bones, and a couple of empty wine bottles. Here, it is obvious, one of the gardeners takes his ease—his *ease*, Father—at your expense!"

"Bones and bottles, littering the garden?"

"It is not to be borne. I will show you, sir—you must see with your own eyes."

Pfissig was literally tugging at his arm. Kwieseldt shrugged and followed. Through the splendid corridors they hurried, out the door and into the great courtyard, with its fountains, statues, and elaborate plantings.

Early spring was soft in the air. The new shoots were pushing out of the soil, while the branches of shrub and tree were studded with small, incipient greeneries. Overhead, the sun shone in a sky miraculously blue. For once, there was scarcely a shred of mist or fog. Kwieseldt's lungs expanded to drink the fresh breeze. He hadn't set foot out-of-doors in a very long time, he realized. Fear had made a prisoner of him, for weeks. Already, the confinement seemed endless. Was he doomed to a lifetime of the same?

"This way." Pfissig strode resolutely on along one of the curving paths.

These were his own gardens, Kwieseldt reflected as he walked alongside his son. His, and he hadn't even looked at them, much less trod their paths, since that awful moment—upon the balcony—

He couldn't bear to think about it.

In any case, the thought was interrupted. Kwieseldt heard a low snarl, and spun to face the sound. Pfissig did likewise. Father and son confronted a gigantic, brindled mastiff. The creature's fangs were exposed, and they were enormous. Its yellowish eyes blazed, and the short hair bristled along its spine. A light slaver frothed the great jaws.

Rabid?

Both men froze. The deep-throated canine snarls rumbled. The mastiff, head down and muscles tensed, stood motionless.

It was all wrong. The dogs, trained to disassemble intruders, were supposed to remain chained until sunset. The handler had been *ordered*. Moreover, the animal ought to recognize its own true master's authority.

"Here, you—sit," the Regarded Kwieseldt commanded. Even to his own ears, his voice sounded feeble. "Sit, sir!"

The snarling dropped in pitch, but rose in volume. The dog made a little, stiff-legged rush at its own true master's leg. Its jaws snapped, and Kwieseldt heard the click of the teeth. He stumbled backward a few paces, then turned and ran. Behind him, he heard the sinister patter of pursuit, and also heard his son's voice, upraised in shouts for help.

Down the curving path he fled, his short woolen cloak flapping behind him, and then he felt his flight arrested as the dog grabbed a mouthful of fabric. The Regarded Kwieseldt struggled violently, heard cloth tear, and then he was free and running again, with the mastiff worrying at his heels.

Before him rose an ornamental whikilpoy, with bare, low-hanging limbs. Seizing the lowest branch, and bracing his feet against the trunk, Kwieseldt miraculously managed to haul himself up into the tree, where he crouched, panting and shivering. A few feet below, the mastiff paced and drooled.

Assistance was not long in coming. The handler arrived, bearing a club, with which, following an astonished glance, he beat the offending animal off.

The Regarded Kwieseldt descended from the tree. Shrill fear and fury sprayed violently out of him. Some minutes passed before the handler was granted opportunity to reply.

There finally came a lull in the boiling flood of words, and the handler seized his opportunity to inform the master that the brindled mastiff roaming the gardens was no rightful denizen of the Kwieseldt kennels. The animal, though similar in type to the household guard dogs, had never before been seen upon the premises. *Not ever.*

Its origins were entirely unknown.

This revelation dampened Drempi Kwieseldt. In sickly silence, he reentered the house, dismissed his anxious son, and dragged himself back to his own apartment, whose door he locked behind him.

Once safely immured, he scurried for the study, the locked desk drawer, and the Iron Vigilance. Lifting the sphere to his eye, he gazed into its depths.

Premier Jurist Gnaus liGurvohl labored over his never-ending paperwork.

The hypocrite. The two-faced, virtue-vending, homicidal *fraud.*

The bile rose to burn Drempi Kwieseldt.

"I know you," he whispered to the unconscious image within the sphere. "Look as pious as you please, you sanctimonious son of a bitch, but I *see you!*"

He set the Vigilance aside with a shudder, and buried his face in his hands. The pressure upon his closed eyelids turned his internal vision red. He saw the package of Golden Trueleaf, the knife quivering in the tree trunk, the falling stone, the spider upon his pillow, the dagger-fanged mastiff. He saw the Premier Jurist's face.

It had to end. He could endure no more.

The Regarded Kwieseldt sat very still.

It had to end.

❧ ☙

He wasn't sure exactly when it was that terror and misery hardened into desperate purpose. He couldn't have named the exact moment that he began his mental review of the household retainers. He needed someone brave, strong, resolute, reliable, intelligent, resourceful, and, above all, demonstrably devoted. Face after face flashed into his mind, each to be rejected in turn. Not a one of them seemed to possess all the requisite qualities. But at least, one came reasonably close.

His mind winged back to the ghastly spider incident. He recalled the courage, determination, and demonstrable devotion of the servant answering his screams for help upon that awful morning. He remembered the efficiency with which the servant had squashed the intruding spider. What was the fellow's name? The Regarded Kwieseldt thought hard. Retz? Detz? Dretetz? No. DeTretz. *Yes.* Surprising that he could have let such a good man's name slip his mind even briefly.

He issued a summons, and DeTretz appeared. And there was the blunt-featured, ruddy face, the bowl-cut blond hair, the sturdy frame, and the air of cheerful confidence that the Regarded Kwieseldt remembered.

An intensely secret discussion ensued, and DeTretz's air of good cheer faded. It seemed that his devotion, although demonstrable, could hardly be categorized as unquestioning. Indeed, the tiresome questions boiled out of him. He was a fine servant, but not intelligent enough to understand that duty demanded perfect, unhesitating obedience.

The Regarded Kwieseldt sighed internally. He himself had never ventured to question any command of the High Landguardian Jex liTarngrav, prior to that worthy's early demise. Patiently, he explained the concept of perfect duty to his own imperfect servant, and in the end, DeTretz seemed to understand, after a fashion. At least he nodded his blond head, and said that he understood.

The Regarded Kwieseldt had to trust in that. There was no better alternative.

Time passed. Impossible to measure the hours, days, or weeks; Kwieseldt could only know that the moment had come at last.

It was the thin, sharp middle of a night in early spring. The Regarded Kwieseldt sat alone in his quiet study, with the Iron Vigilance glued to his eye. All about him, liTarngrav House—*Kwieseldt Mansion!*—slumbered. All the city of Lis Folaze slumbered, or nearly so.

The Premier Jurist Gnaus liGurvohl slept the sleep of the just. This, Kwieseldt saw clearly. His unnatural vision halted at the boundaries of liGurvohl's bedchamber, but he knew well what was happening beyond the realm of his sight.

∞ ∞

Through the chilly streets crept the demonstrably devoted DeTretz, armed with a poniard and high ideals. His master had explained matters carefully. There could be no question where his duty lay. His was less a fervent nature than simply unimaginative. He never thought of disobeying the master's commands.

The house of the Premier Jurist loomed before him; a dignified, austere, but hardly overwhelming edifice, with little about it suggesting re-markable significance. DeTretz knew better than to approach the highly visible facade, the well-guarded rear, or the virtually unassailable northeast side. The southwest face of the house, masked in ornamental shrubbery, offered the only possible point of entry. Here, he had been instructed, the armed sentry passed but once in every eight minutes.

Buried in shadow, DeTretz awaited his chance. The sentry passed. Eight minutes of opportunity presented themselves. He darted forward, gained the shelter of the bushes, and addressed himself to the ground-floor window. Shuttered and locked, of course, but his knife point made quick work of the simple, old-fashioned fastening. The shutters parted, revealing an expanse of small, lozenge-shaped glass panes. Discreetly breaking a single pane, he reached in, unlocked the window, opened the casement, and climbed through, closing the shutters behind him.

He stood in total darkness, but he knew just where he was, for his master had required him to memorize the entire floor plan of the house. He had broken into the dining room. Straight ahead of him, clearly visible in his mind's eye, stood a door, opening upon the entrance hall, where he would find stairs leading to the second story, and the Premier Jurist's bedchamber.

Advancing blindly, DeTretz encountered the dining-room table, which he felt his way around. Another few hesitant paces, and he reached the door. Opening a cautious crack, he peeked out into the hall, wherein wall sconces supported a couple of blessedly burning candles. And there were the stairs, just where they were supposed to be.

No servants or guards in sight.

Excellent. He had never quite believed that a personage so august as the Premier Jurist of the White Tribunal might prove so astonishingly vulnerable, but the Regarded Kwieseldt had insisted otherwise, and rightfully so.

Slipping silently from the dining room, DeTretz mounted the stairs, and despite a generous measure of trepidation, his confidence rose as he ascended. Everything was going exactly according to plan. The master would be so pleased.

Drempi Kwieseldt was sick of watching Gnaus liGurvohl sleep. He felt as if he had sat trapped in his study, eye glued to the Iron Vigilance, since the beginning of time. And there was so little to see. The Premier Jurist slumbered soundly, and that was all. The hours passed, the Regarded Kwieseldt's own nervous tension reached sickening levels, and *nothing happened.*

And then, in an instant, everything changed.

Kwieseldt saw the bedroom door swing wide. His breath caught. He saw DeTretz's sturdy figure framed in the opening, and he saw the poniard in his servant's hand. All this was clearly visible to him, by grace of the sorcerous sphere, but DeTretz was not similarly advantaged. It was dark in the bedroom, a point that the Regarded Kwieseldt had failed to consider when formulating his plans, for he himself slept with a night-light. Not totally dark, however. There must have been some small lamp or candle burning in the corridor, for a little faint light leaked in through the open door. DeTretz need only bide his time for a few moments, and his eyes would adjust.

But DeTretz was not waiting. Amateurishly eager to finish the job and be gone, he was groping his way toward the bed. A low table supporting a heavy candelabrum stood in his path. He seemed not to see it.

"Watch out," the Regarded Kwieseldt advised aloud. "You bungling idiot, *watch out!*"

His urgency was useless. DeTretz, hearing nothing, pressed on doomfully. As Kwieseldt watched in impotent horror, the inevitable collision occurred. The table toppled. The unheard crash was probably tremendous. DeTretz staggered, and came close to falling. His mouth opened and shut; almost certainly, a cry escaped him. An equally terrified cry burst simultaneously from the lips of Drempi Kwieseldt.

The Premier Jurist Gnaus liGurvohl awoke and sat up in bed. His pale eyes, evidently requiring little illumination, were at once aware. Almost without haste, he twitched the bellpull beside the bed. A brace of armed guards instantly answered the summons.

"Finish yourself off!" the Regarded Kwieseldt begged his servant. "With the knife, imbecile! Do it!"

The master's pleas went unheard. DeTretz was simply standing there paralyzed, broad face red with an incongruous embarrassment. The guards disarmed him without difficulty, and the opportunity fled forever.

Gnaus liGurvohl rose unhurriedly from his bed. He wore a long, white nightgown whose loose cut uncannily recalled the judicial robes of the White Tribunal. Only the gold chain of office was lacking. Circumstances notwithstanding, he had lost none of his power to inspire terror.

The Premier Jurist's lips moved. The watching Kwieseldt only too easily guessed the tenor of the silent questions.

"Say nothing!" he commanded his unhearing emissary. "Die under torture if you must, but say nothing! Now is the time to demonstrate your devotion!"

But the demonstration furnished little reassurance. DeTretz fell to his knees before Gnaus liGurvohl. His lips moved rapidly and ceaselessly. Silent confessional torrents spewed forth.

Kwieseldt's own scream of despair fought for utterance. He managed to keep it down to a muted whimper. His eyes screwed themselves shut, and the hand clenched upon the Iron Vigilance trembled.

The Iron Vigilance, that hateful sorcerous sphere. It had brought him nothing but misery. He wished he'd never glimpsed its abominable depths.

Even so, the blindness was insupportable. One eye popped open, and Kwieseldt beheld the abject and tearful DeTretz, crouched on the bedroom floor, mouth flapping, flapping, disastrously flapping . . .

The Regarded Kwieseldt sprang to his feet. Within minutes, he realized, they would be coming for him. The Soldiers of the Light . . . the closed wagon . . . the inevitable destination. Already, they knew he had attempted the life of the Premier Jurist. They knew nothing, however, of the Iron Vigilance. He needed to rid himself of the vile thing, at once.

Get it out of the house.

Stuffing the sphere into his pocket, Kwieseldt paused only long enough to wrap himself in a woolen cloak, before hurrying from his apartment, along the corridor, down the stairs, across the hallway, and straight out the great front door.

The guards and sentries marked the master's passing, but wisely asked no questions.

The fresh, cold night air bathed Drempi Kwieseldt's burning face. It felt good, and it helped him to think.

Where?

Only one place, obviously.

It wasn't a long walk to the river. All the best houses in the city were built almost within a stone's throw of the Folaze. His own wealthy neighborhood was well lighted, and he had no trouble finding his way through the nocturnal fog. Soon he came to the eastern bank, and Marbleflower Bridge, but that was no good, it was too close to liTarngrav House.

His mechanical footsteps directed themselves downstream, and he had no idea how long he walked before he came to another bridge, this one hung with big, mirrored lanterns. Brilliant Bridge, it was, and he supposed it would have to do.

Out onto deserted Brilliant Bridge hurried the Regarded Kwieseldt, and paused halfway across. Scarcely pausing to survey his surroundings, he drew forth the Iron Vigilance, and hurled it down into the swollen stream below.

Done. Nobody would ever find the incredibly incriminating item, now.

His purpose accomplished, the Regarded Kwieseldt remained motionless, glazed eyes fixed upon the roiling springtime waters.

What now?

What indeed? Where could he go, what could he do? Brilliant Bridge was quiet and empty. So too were the streets beyond. Lis Folaze seemed tranquil, stable, unchanged. It took a certain effort of will to recognize the truth that, for him, everything had changed forever. It didn't seem real, as yet.

The Regarded Kwieseldt stared down at the racing river, and remembered that the Landswoman Aestine liHofbrunn had stood upon just such a bridge, gazing down at these same waters, not so very long ago. She had launched herself from Singlespan Bridge, thereby eluding all persecutors and prosecutors. Not such a bad example to follow.

With some difficulty, the Regarded Kwieseldt clambered up onto the guardrail, where he sat watching the river. It looked cold, merciless, ferocious. He thought of that muddy water, filling his lungs. He thought of the agony and terror. He thought of how awful he would look, fish-nibbled and disgustingly distended, when they finally plucked him forth. He considered all of it, and fear froze his limbs.

He couldn't do it.

No use reminding himself of the unpalatable alternative. With the Folaze raging a few feet below, alternatives offered but little deterrence. In any case, he reminded himself, no one had hurt him as yet, hope was not dead, and there always existed the possibility that some last-minute miracle would intervene to save him. Perhaps Autonn would interest Himself in the matter; such things did happen, sometimes, and the Regarded Kwieseldt was surely worthy of the Benefactor's attention.

He sat there for a very long time, until the cold began to work its way into his bones.

Kwieseldt dismounted from the guardrail. As if in a dream, he betook himself home to liTarngrav House, where he ordered a big, hot meal—the first he had been able to swallow in days—a hot bath, a haircut, shave, and massage. These pleasures savored, he laid himself down upon fresh, lavender-scented silken sheets.

They came for him at dawn.

The soldiers, the irons, the wagon, the clattering transport to the Heart of Light—it was all just as he had foreseen. The Regarded Kwieseldt gazed dully around him. There was little to see. He sat huddled on the straw in the corner of a dank stone cell. The walls were bare. The barred window overlooked a featureless courtyard. The window was unshuttered, and there was no fireplace, but he hardly noticed the cold. They had taken away his manacles, but left him his woolen cloak.

He felt little, and vaguely hoped that anesthesia might continue. The entire scene and situation retained its air of unreality, and he hoped that, too, would continue.

The hours passed, and he never stirred from his corner. Around noon, an unseen hand thrust bread and water into his cell, but he didn't trouble to turn his head. He sat quite motionless until the late afternoon, at which time the lock scraped and the door opened.

Kwieseldt looked up unwillingly, and then literally cowered as the Premier Jurist Gnaus liGurvohl swept whitely into the cell. LiGurvohl was alone. Presumably, he required no armed assistance in dealing with the Regarded Drempi Kwieseldt.

For an eternity, the Premier Jurist stood staring down at the prisoner. Unable to meet the lambent gaze, Kwieseldt looked away. His eyes roamed in search of refuge, of which there was none. LiGurvohl spoke at last.

"You have betrayed me," he observed.

The prisoner shrank in on himself. He studied the floor minutely.

"I raised you from obscurity and servitude," liGurvohl continued. "I conferred honor, rank, and wealth upon you. I demanded no return beyond your loyalty. Now, you have sought the death of your benefactor. Such depravity all but defies understanding. I come here today to school myself in the nature of your evil."

Somehow, it never occurred to Kwieseldt to deny his own guilt. Lifting haunted eyes to the other's face, he swallowed hard and replied, "You gave me no choice."

"Explain yourself."

"You gave me no choice," Kwieseldt insisted, and rising indignation seemed to loosen the constriction in his throat. "The various attempts on my life—the poisoned pipeweed, the dagger, the invasion and sabotage of my home—I was forced to defend myself."

"You seek refuge in feigned madness?"

"No madness, Premier Jurist. We both know that the attacks were real. My servants will confirm it."

"Your servants prove themselves useful in many capacities."

"The mastiff might easily have killed my son, you know. Had you no care for the innocent?"

"You rave."

"What, will you deny it still, Premier Jurist? You have me where you want me, at last. There's nobody to overhear. What harm now in owning the truth?"

LiGurvohl bent a piercing analytical regard upon the prisoner. The rainwater eyes probed the recesses of mind and heart. At last he conceded, "You do not feign. The power of malevolence has triumphed, and the madness that possesses you is genuine."

"My only madness lay in trusting you, a treacherous villain." Kwieseldt had forgotten his customary prudence. A headlong, exhilarating recklessness seized him. For once in a lifetime, he spoke freely. "See where it has got me."

"You speak the truth as you perceive it." The Premier Jurist's expression reflected academic interest. "Else you would never dare utter such words to me."

"Yes, I speak the truth! Will you not do the same? What difference does it make now?"

"Perhaps more than your small mind conceives. Let us concede the possibility that attempts upon your life have indeed occurred. How have you persuaded yourself that I am the author?"

"Shall we have no end to this fencing? Who else has your motive?"

"To what motive do you allude?"

"We both know what we know of past events. Are you going to pretend that you've forgotten?"

"I have not forgotten that once you did your duty, as a morally sentient member of the human race, to assist in the removal of a sorcerous menace. Nor have I forgotten that you were well rewarded for your service."

"And I've not forgotten that I lied under oath, at your behest. My master died, as a result. I was guilty of perjury, you of subornation. It's galled your heart for thirteen years that I know what you are, and you want me dead for it! Well, you'll shortly have your wish. Happy now, Premier Jurist, moral arbiter of the nation?"

Gnaus liGurvohl's look of detached interest never wavered. "What tragic misjudgment," he observed at last, his beautiful voice slow and sorrowing. "How pitiful to witness a mind overturned by malevolence. My heart holds sadness for a spirit too weak to arm itself against supernatural deceit. For you are indeed grossly deceived. Never have I, or any agent of mine, lifted a hand against you."

"I don't believe you." This was not quite true. A hideous doubt was already gnawing at Kwieseldt's convictions.

"Is it possible that you imagine me capable of falsehood?" The Premier Jurist sounded more astonished than offended.

"I watched you." The Regarded Kwieseldt's sickening doubts deepened. "I watched you for days, and your actions suggested—suggested very strongly, in fact—"

"Watched me? What new delusion is this?"

"No delusion. I saw you. I was furnished a device—I've no idea how the thing worked—but it let me watch you. Anytime I liked." There was no reason to hold back now, he was doomed whatever he might say. "Mind you, I heard nothing, for it didn't transmit sound, but I could always see you, and your immediate surroundings."

LiGurvohl surveyed the prisoner, whose demeanor suggested an almost wild freedom from customary restraint. "Produce this device," he commanded.

"Too late. I threw it into the river. You'll have to take my word for it. But let me assure you, what I saw was—" *Was what?* Kwieseldt paused. What, indeed, had he truly seen? What had it all meant, if anything?

"Where did you obtain such an object?"

Had fear goaded imagination to a frenzy? Had he in fact thrown his life away over a *mistake?* That detestable, deluding sphere. Its demonic, destroying donor.

"Who sold or gave it to you?" The Premier Jurist's voice and eyes compelled.

Kwieseldt didn't remember to bargain, and the truth spilled out of him. "That Strellian, Dr. Flambeska. He said it would help me. I believed him."

"Ah." LiGurvohl nodded, as if to himself.

"He's brought me to this. He's ruined me."

"Why should he do so? Has this foreigner some grudge against you?"

"Not at all. We're strangers." Doubt and confusion blunted Kwieseldt's anger. "Perhaps, after all, Flambeska acted in good faith."

"His possession of a sorcerously tainted artifact suggests otherwise. But that is no longer any concern of yours."

"No."

"You have spoken openly, condemning yourself with your own words." The Premier Jurist addressed the prisoner as if from the heights of the bench. "I recognize your present candor, and therefore will regard you as sincere in your erroneous beliefs—lamentably misguided rather than willfully vicious. Although this distinction carries no legal weight, yet it must to some degree mitigate the enormity of your moral failing. Perhaps you will take comfort in that."

"Oh, great comfort."

"So sudden and complete a fall from grace must stand as a warning and a lesson to all men," liGurvohl intoned. "For the spectacle is pitiable as it is repugnant. Once, not long ago, you were respected, honored, even admired. In recognition of your former eminence, I offer you a measure of mercy."

Kwieseldt lifted avid eyes.

"As you perhaps surmise, this attack upon a jurist of the White Tribunal, an act suggestive of sorcerous leanings, warrants recourse to the Grand Interrogation."

Kwieseldt shuddered.

"Upon conviction, your property is forfeit to the court. I am willing to spare you the Grand Interrogation, however, and I will also guarantee the immunity of your estate, provided that you affix your signature to a full confession. You will sign immediately, without complaint, argument, or attempted negotiation, else the offer is withdrawn."

As if by sorcery, a document had materialized in the hand of Gnaus liGurvohl. Kwieseldt could hardly have said where it came from. LiGurvohl extended the paper. Kwieseldt mechanically took it, and scanned the contents. He discovered a concise and straightforward statement, affirming his deliberate attempt to murder the Premier Jurist of the White Tribunal. So violent an attack, apparently devoid of sense or motive, could only find its origin in the will of malevolences, whose voices had befuddled, deceived, and led him astray . . .

The confession never touched upon acts of true, conscious sorcery; an omission beneficial beyond expression to himself and his family members. The Premier Jurist's generosity exceeded reasonable expectation. Brief cogitation suggested a possible cause.

Jex liTarngrav. Ravnar liMarchborg. Condemned by false witness, thirteen years ago.

Gnaus liGurvohl desired discretion, and he was willing to pay for it. The price was more than right.

"I will sign," Drempi Kwieseldt whispered.

The Premier Jurist rapped upon the door. A guard entered, bearing quill and inkpot. Kwieseldt dipped the quill and signed. The guard withdrew. LiGurvohl caused the confession to disappear. The thing was done.

The Premier Jurist departed, and Drempi Kwieseldt found himself alone in the chilly silence. All things considered, he was getting off easily. There would be no detour to the subterranean torture vaults. Pfissig would safely inherit liTarngrav House. *Kwieseldt Mansion!*

LiTarngrav House.

His impending confrontation with the White Tribunal, potentially so devastating, now reduced itself to an awkward unavoidable formality. The aftermath would be unpleasant—horrifying, actually—but brief.

Really, it might have been far worse.

And yet, he couldn't forget how few hours had elapsed since he had been the Regarded Drempi Kwieseldt; rich, respected, and secure. Surely, that was his real life.

Kwieseldt let himself fall back on the straw. He turned his face to the wall. Catastrophe seemed to have struck him almost randomly, sudden and inexplicable as disease. He couldn't fathom how he had come so quickly to such a pass, by whose agency, or why.

He lay vainly striving to discern some pattern or purpose. The tears scalded their way from his eyes.

He understood none of it.

Seventeen

The waiting room and office were empty, for Dr. Flambeska had scheduled no appointments. Thus, it was safe for once to open the curtains and set the dark glasses aside. Tradain sat at his desk. Two pieces of paper lay before him. One of them was the latest issue of the Blowflies' notorious newsletter, *The Buzz*. The other was a note from Glennian liTarngrav, requesting him to meet her at Immemorial Bridge, in the early afternoon.

It was easier to consider *The Buzz* than the note. He scanned the newsletter for perhaps the twentieth time since its appearance upon his doorstep some days earlier. The front page was given over to a cartoon certain to catch the eye of every beholder, literate or otherwise. There at the center cringed a dwarfish, terrified figure, easily identifiable as a caricature of the Regarded Drempi Kwieseldt. The Regarded Kwieseldt was ridiculously festooned with white cockades. The emblems of judicial favor wreathed his head, garlanded his neck, dotted his garments, and decorated the iron manacles confining both his wrists. Thirteen gigantic, absurdly ferocious jurists menaced the wretched prisoner, who balanced precariously upon the rim of a cauldron engraved with a small image of liTarngrav House.

The next couple of pages contained an essay entitled "Asinine Assassin," which described the bungled attack upon the Premier Jurist, then went on to question the motives of Drempi Kwieseldt, longtime lackey of the White Tribunal, in turning so violently upon his master. The Regarded Kwieseldt's own confession cited the fatal if vague influence of malevolences, an explanation somewhat less than informative. The essayist concluded the piece with a demand for an investigation of judicial activities, followed, should findings so warrant, by the suspension of the entire White Tribunal.

A bold suggestion indeed, and one greeted with popular interest and enthusiasm unthinkable in former decades. At the Fogchaser, they had talked of nothing else for days. And Master Einzlaur was forever turning up to relate some new anecdote or rumor touching upon the Kwieseldt scandal. The latest involved a confrontation in the street between Jurist Fenj liRohbstat and a gang of angry, vociferous citizens. It was said that the thoroughly shaken liRohbstat had barely escaped a serious mauling.

Tradain hoped that it was true. As always, he wished the Blowflies well, but suspected that they'd overshot their mark with this latest essay. Sedition so inflammatory invited retaliation, and hereafter, civic surveillance was bound to intensify. Sooner or later, the anonymous journalists were sure to be caught, and their collective fate would not be pretty.

Unfortunate, Tradain reflected, but no concern of his.

The same could hardly be said, however, of Glennian liTarngrav's note. Outside, the bells were tolling the hour of twelve. Time to make the decision he'd been postponing since the invitation, or rather the summons, had arrived. He'd do better, he knew, to stay away from Glennian. Within seconds of meeting him, she had penetrated his disguise, and now she held the dangerous secret of his identity. With her sharp wits and insatiate curiosity, how many other secrets was she likely to ferret out? Eventually, in sheer self-defense, he'd find himself obliged to wash her memory clean. On the other hand, he had promised to meet her again, and if he refused today, she'd pester him relentlessly until she got her way. It might be best simply to get it over with. Moreover, he realized, some part of him wanted to see her and hear her voice again. Perhaps that part was responsible for holding the afternoon free of appointments . . .

The final stroke of noon sounded, and Tradain rose from the desk chair, his decision made. Resuming his dark glasses and wide hat, he hurried from the house, making his quick way through the streets toward Immemorial Bridge. So intent was he on his destination that he never noticed the nondescript figure of a groundskeeper detach itself from the little park at the center of Solemnity Square, to follow discreetly in his wake.

She was already waiting there when he arrived. A long cloak of dark blue enveloped her slight figure, and she stood with her back to him, gazing out over the river, but the glinting mass of red-brown hair was recognizable at a distance. Tradain advanced to her side, and she turned to face him. She was pretty as ever, he noted, but looking a little tired, with faint shadows under the wide-set greenish eyes.

"I thought perhaps you wouldn't come," said Glennian.

"I spat twice on it, didn't I?"

"I wasn't certain that you'd regard saliva as legally binding. No matter. I wanted to talk to you today because of your special, unusual knowledge."

He went cold. Not a muscle in his face moved. She knew. Somehow she had guessed his magical expertise. He had no idea what sort of logic or intuition had penetrated the darkest secret of all, but *she knew*. And now, no matter how distasteful the prospect, he would have to purge her memory, empty it *completely*—

His expression reflected nothing beyond polite incomprehension as he prompted, "Unusual knowledge of—?"

"That." She pointed.

Reluctantly, his eyes followed the pointing finger across Immemorial Bridge to Lisse Island, where the Heart of Light stabbed at the heavens with its pitchfork tower.

"You are the only person I know—perhaps the only person to be found—who's been a prisoner in that place and lived to speak of it," Glennian explained. "My guardian, Re'Drempi Kwieseldt, is in there now. I would like you to tell me what's happening to him."

No you wouldn't. The worst of his alarm ebbed. She had not divined his sorcerous knowledge.

"You sound," he temporized, "very fond of your guardian."

"Re'Drempi and I are not close. But he's given me a home, since the death of my parents, when otherwise I'd have had none. He's been kind, and generous, and I am grateful. I owe him a great deal."

You don't begin to realize what you owe him. He said nothing.

"And I'd like to help him now, if I can," she concluded.

"I fear there's little hope of that. They'll allow him no visitors, packages, or correspondence."

"What will they do to him, in there?"

"Lock him up, probably alone, until he goes to trial. He's not, so far as I know, accused of sorcerous crime. But he's believed to have attempted the life of the Premier Jurist, and will almost certainly face the White Tribunal."

"Whose leader will then proceed to pass wholly impartial, disinterested judgment upon him. Oh, what a travesty!" she exclaimed.

"Take care," he advised.

"Very well, I'll lower my voice. Discretion, by all means! Will they hurt Re'Drempi?" she demanded bluntly.

"He'll be strongly encouraged to sign a confession. Should he capitulate promptly, they'll have no particular reason to hurt him." *Beyond simple pleasure in brutality*, he concluded internally.

"Then he'll cooperate, beyond doubt. He's probably already signed the confession. Poor Re'Drempi! It's so unfair, so horrible!"

"What, you believe him innocent?" Tradain inquired. "I'd gathered that the evidence against him is very strong."

"I can't claim that I quite believe him innocent," she admitted. "But I will say that I don't understand behavior so utterly out of character. My guardian isn't a violent man, nor even quarrelsome. Indeed, he's quite timorous, and he's absolutely terrified of Gnaus liGurvohl. That Re'Drempi should launch such a senseless attack against the Premier Jurist, of all people, is—well, it's almost inconceivable. If he did it, he must have been temporarily deranged, or delirious, or deluded. Certainly his nerves had been bad for weeks prior to the incident. I don't know why, he'd tell me nothing. One thing I do know, though—some sort of influence must have been at work on him. I mean to discover what or who that was."

"To what purpose?"

"Relief of mental itching. Beyond that, if others are truly responsible, is it just that Re'Drempi suffer alone?"

The conversation had taken an unfortunate turn. An outbreak of shouting upon Lisse Island spared Tradain the necessity of reply. He turned to face the sound, and Glennian did the same.

A sizable crowd had gathered before the great central gateway in the wall girdling the Heart of Light. Apparently the citizens desired entry, but the vast portal remained closed and barred against them. Frustration exerted its customary effect, and the furious voices rose. Complaints, reproaches, and vituperation winged out over the Folaze. Presently, stones and rotten vegetables began to pelt the gate.

"I never believed they would dare," Glennian breathed.

"Neither did I." His surprise equaled hers. "That latest Blowflies circular must have stirred them up. It's everywhere about. Have you read it?"

She nodded.

"Audacious characters, these Blowflies," Tradain opined. "But they'll end in the cauldron, over nothing."

"Nothing?" Glennian's brows lifted.

"Over a high but hopeless cause, then."

"So certain it's hopeless? You see the results of their efforts, right over there, before your very eyes."

"A rock-throwing rabble? They'll scatter quickly enough, when the guards come."

As if in response, a line of Soldiers of the Light appeared at the summit of the wall. Commands were issued, and gunfire crackled. The soldiers must have aimed deliberately high, for nobody fell, but the chastened citizens shrank back from the wall and quickly began to disperse.

"There, you see?" Tradain observed indifferently. "It amounts to nothing."

"You're wrong, it's more than that. At least those people tried to do something."

He fancied she spoke with a hint of accusation, or even disdain. She'd been like that as a child, he remembered—always keen to act, to *do* something. The quality was simultaneously alarming and appealing. But she was only a young woman, he reassured himself, and daughter of a proscribed House, at that. What could she possibly do?

The first of the retreating rioters were already out on Immemorial Bridge. Should the Soldiers of the Light choose to follow, the western riverbank might witness conflict.

"We'd better go." He touched her arm lightly.

She looked up into his eyes and nodded. They walked off together, quite unaware of the consummately nondescript figure, trailing not far behind.

❧ ❦

Sergeant Orschl of the Select Squadron was pleased. For once in his dreary life, the Clockwork was varying his deadly routine. Flambeska had actually allowed himself an afternoon off from work. He'd walked to Immemorial Bridge, a locale he'd hitherto shunned, and there—best of all—he'd rendez-voused with a woman. A young and fetching one, at that. Perhaps the doctor was more or less human, after all.

Then again, perhaps not. For the two never repaired to the nearest inn, tavern, or patch of ground behind the handiest bush, as Orschl might naturally have expected. They didn't kiss or fondle, they didn't even hold hands. They simply talked, with considerable animation, but no suggestion of established intimacy.

There had to be something wrong with that doctor.

And the woman? Orschl was an experienced observer, but he found her difficult to categorize. She was dressed in simple but unmistakably ex-pensive garments. Her appearance, bearing, gestures, and expressions all screamed quality. In which case, what was she doing, gadding off on her own to meet a man? Was she some High Landguardian's errant wife, or daughter, intent upon illicit adventure? Poor little kitty. The Clockwork was sure to disappoint her.

Shortly thereafter, the mystery partially resolved itself. Musket fire popped on Lisse Island, the rioters fled across Immemorial Bridge, and the Clockwork and his companion wisely withdrew. Off they went along the Folaze, chattering all the way. Certainly, they had a great deal to say to one another, all of it inaudible. Their expressions suggested mutual absorption, and yet they didn't touch. At last they turned away from the river, and into a small side street, where the woman's conveyance awaited; a small, rich car-riage, blazoned with the single letter K. The monogram was gilded, choked with curlicues, embellished to the verge of extinction. Orschl recognized that vaunting K at a glance. It belonged to the Regarded Drempi Kwieseldt, presently incarcerated and awaiting trial. That insight revealed the passen-ger's identity. She had to be Kwieseldt's ward, the liTarngrav girl, daughter of the infamous sorcerer.

The couple parted, without so much as a handshake. The carriage rattled off toward Kwieseldt Mansion. Flambeska stood watching it go. The doctor might be an automaton, and yet, Orschl would have bet money that something or other was going on. The carriage vanished. Flambeska and his shadow returned to Solemnity Square.

Once again ensconced in his customary bower at the center of the square, Sergeant Orschl smiled to himself. At last, something interesting to report.

ॐ ॐ

A knock shook the office door.

"Come," Gnaus liGurvohl commanded, and his clerk entered, bearing a couple of sealed missives. One of them flaunted the golden insignia of Dhrevian correspondence, at sight of which the crease between the Premier Jurist's brow deepened. The other bore no identifying marks.

Neatly depositing the letters on the desk before his master, the clerk moved to withdraw.

"One moment," liGurvohl ordered.

The clerk paused reluctantly.

"What is this?" liGurvohl tapped the anonymous missive with an impatient forefinger. "It is damp."

"It has been cleansed, Premier Jurist."

"Explain."

The clerk fidgeted, but there was no point in delay, for his master brooked neither falsehood nor evasion. Taking a deep breath, he confessed, "The document was collected from the Hungry Man's mouth just before dawn, and it appears that the Hungry Man has been—attacked."

LiGurvohl regarded his underling in expressionless silence.

"Vandalized, Premier Jurist," the clerk answered the other's look. "It seems that some unidentified hooligan has doused the Man with blood-red paint, and stuffed his mouth full of—er—excrement, sir." Still his master said nothing, and he babbled on nervously, "There was no serious damage, for the paint hardly adhered to the bronze. The Hungry Man has already been purified, inside and out. The sole communication reposing within the mouth has been—rehabilitated, Premier Jurist."

Some moments passed before liGurvohl replied. "Instruct Zegnauer to set discreet guard upon the Hungry Man," he commanded at last. "Now leave me."

The clerk thankfully withdrew.

Alone again, Gnaus liGurvohl sat motionless, unseeing gaze fixed on the wall before him.

"Malevolence," he murmured aloud. "Dire malevolence, continually striving. The battle never ends."

Breaking the seal of the moist document, he unfolded the paper and scanned a smeared, barely legible report from Sergeant Orschl of the Select Squadron. It seemed that the eccentric and highly questionable Strellian physician Flambeska was connected in some way other than the obvious to Drempi Kwieseldt's conscience-sop, Glennian liTarngrav; dispossessed daughter of an Enlightened sorcerer, ward of a would-be murderer. A suggestive association indeed, and worthy of close scrutiny.

At the moment, however, matters of greater urgency claimed the Premier Jurist's attention. Setting Orschl's report aside, he addressed himself to the Dhrevian communication. His frown deepened as he read. As he had feared, the Dhreve Lissildt—customarily acquiescent, but recently exhibiting signs of an unseemly officiousness—wrote to intercede on behalf of the condemned sorceress Issko liJeinzko, scheduled for Disinfection within the next week. Issko liJeinzko had been convicted upon the flimsiest of evidence, according to the Dhreve, who now ventured to recommend a retrial.

Intolerable presumption. Lissildt, though rightful hereditary ruler of Upper Hetzia, lacked authority to meddle in the internal affairs of the White Tribunal. That judicial body—created to defend the Eternal Benefactor Autonn against the evil deeds of vile men, as Autonn Himself defended humanity against the others of His own kind—was answerable to no human Dhreve. The White Tribunal owed homage to the Benefactor alone.

In the past, Lissildt had comprehended and accepted this truth. Lately, matters had altered unpleasantly with the Dhreve, as they had altered with so many others throughout the land. The origins of change were no doubt diverse, complex, and obscure, but one baneful influence was entirely apparent.

Those impious, jeering, anonymous journalists. Those malignant calumniators rightly calling themselves the Blowflies.

The pests demanded immediate extermination, at any expense of money and manpower. This pressing matter resolved, there would be time enough to deal with the enigmatic Dr. Flambeska.

Summoning the appropriate officers to him, Gnaus liGurvohl issued the necessary orders.

In the days that followed, the Soldiers of the Light were to be seen everywhere about Lis Folaze. Those in uniform were impossible to overlook. The ones in civilian garb were harder to spot, but observant citizens did not miss them. The muscularity and extreme cleanliness, combined with an attitude of watchful nonchalance, were dead giveaways. The most sportive among interested Folazers took to competitive Sight-the-Light, upon whose outcome it was possible to place wagers. The more cerebral considered cause, and probable purpose. Following the fruitless pursuit of several youthful, illicit runners, or "Blowfliers," as they were commonly known, the purpose revealed itself. The Soldiers of the Light waged an intensive assault upon the authors of *The Buzz*.

Why such effort just now, in particular?

It wouldn't be happening, the wise concluded, if somebody definitely high up didn't see the matter as urgent.

Spoke very ill or very well for the Blowflies, depending on your point of view.

Lis Folaze watched with interest. The young Blowfliers were resourceful, beyond question. Time after time, they managed to distribute their wares, a feat accomplished largely by dint of imaginative unpredictability. Once, on a particularly windy day, a basketload of fliers was tossed from the summit of the Longshanks bell tower, to send the white sheets fluttering everywhere. Another time, ripped pouches full of paper were tied to the tails of at least a score of stray cats, subsequently loosed to scamper through the streets, trailing newsletters as they went. There was no end to the Blowfliers' tricks. Never were the pamphlets or cartoons deposited twice in the same spot. Never were the big broadsides tacked up twice in a row before the same inn, tavern, or public well. Yet they turned up everywhere, every day, their message infusing throughout the city and beyond.

And the message itself? Appealing to those tired of midnight visitations, sudden disappearances, and the smell of boiled flesh. Suspension of the White Tribunal. A thorough scouring of the Heart of Light. Reexamination of existing laws. Revision as appropriate. Those of shallow mind and weak character were all too capable of responding to such pleas.

Springtime flowered into pastel glory. The atmosphere warmed and softened. The Blowflies showered the city with paper. The Blowfliers darted unscathed, while the gamesters honed their skill in Sight-the-Light. So matters might have continued indefinitely, had not a single youthful runner chanced one morning upon misfortune.

The boy was new, too eager to impress his colleagues with his daring, too willing to take chances, and too inexperienced to know when he was in trouble. Certainly he never dreamed that anyone had spotted him at dusk, dropping pamphlets into the various boats moored at the riverside wharves. He never knew that he was followed back to the tailor's shop wherein he toiled as an apprentice, nor did he note, in the days that followed, the unobtrusive, loitering presence of a highly accomplished officer of the Select Squadron. He had no idea at all that his next meeting with the superintendent of his gang was observed; nor did that superintendent in turn ever dream, some evenings later, that she was followed through the streets to the northern edge of the city, where the eerie white light of the Melt bathed the ramshackle dwelling of Meustri Vurtz, the Tocsin.

❧ ❧

"We need to expand," the Tocsin insisted. A meeting of the Blowflies superintendents was in progress. He had harangued his colleagues for the past fifteen minutes, and their lack of enthusiasm was beginning to gall him. "More pamphlets, more broadsides, extra editions of *The Buzz*. New and bolder runners, wider distribution. We've seen results lately, it's time to push harder." He surveyed his listeners, noted their reserve, and glared. "What's the matter? Too much work for you? More bother than it's worth, eh?"

There was an embarrassed stirring, and the White Gardenia spoke up placatingly. "It's not a question of *bother*, Tocs. We're all of us here willing to work, you ought to know that by now."

"Well, then? What's the matter with you people?"

"It's just that the idea of expansion doesn't seem altogether practical," the deceptively effeminate-looking Brimstone hazarded. "The city's already saturated with our publications. There's scarcely need, or even room for—"

"Idiot, you've no idea what you're talking about!" the Tocsin exploded. "There's a very real need, and I can't understand why none of you have got the sense to see it! What must I do to get it through your thick skulls that—"

"The Tocsin is certainly justified in calling for change." The calm voice of the Chair effortlessly made itself heard. "We've made some progress, but advanced to the limit of our present path. To my mind, though, the necessary alteration involves direction. I see little good in higher production. Our current quantity is ample, but we'd do well to concentrate upon reaching the readers whose support is likely to prove most valuable. I am thinking of the greatest courtiers, the closest intimates of the Dhreve, and even the Dhreve himself—"

The audience was intent and receptive. Rapt heads nodded. Even the Tocsin appeared sourly approving. The collective mood was optimistic. Nobody's instincts sang out in warning, nobody expected disaster.

The Blowflies were taken entirely off guard when the front door banged open, and half a dozen Soldiers of the Light entered in a wash of white Meltlight. At the same instant the back door gave way under a violent assault, and another half-dozen soldiers burst in, bellowing. The majority of astounded journalists simply froze. Some four or five, possessed of youthfully quick reflexes, raced for the cellar stairs.

"HALT!" Several shots rang out, and the Blowfly known to his colleagues as Bootstraps fell dead. The four surviving fugitives reached the stairway, which they descended expertly, in total darkness. Behind them stumbled the cursing soldiers, the swiftest of whom managed to lay hands upon a frantic, invisible form. A sightless struggle ensued, culminating in a yell of alarm, followed by the thud of a heavy body rolling down the stairs.

One of the pursuers had wit enough to grab the lantern from its hook in the hallway. Tremulous orange beams pushed down into the cellar, to reveal the printing press, the stacked copies of *The Buzz*, and the fleeing Blowflies. A lone cloaked figure at the bottom of the stairs cleared the corpse of her broken-necked assailant at a bound, and sprinted for the open cellar window.

Her comrades had unlocked and thrown wide the heavy shutters, and now the last of them was wriggling out into the Meltlit little alley that separated Meustri Vurtz's house from the tumbledown warehouse that was its nearest neighbor.

A useless exercise, or so it seemed, for that alley was guarded at both ends.

While a couple of soldiers paused to smash the printing press, the others climbed out the window to secure the trapped Blowflies. To their unpleasant surprise, the pursuers beheld their quarry disappearing through the small side door of the neighboring warehouse, evidently left unlocked to accommodate entrance and exit of squatters and transients alike.

The Soldiers of the Light followed, and found themselves in a vast, lofty space, eerily aglow with Meltlight pushing in through the high, narrow windows. The cold light caught and gleamed upon a liquid host of watchful eyes. The wavy brick floor was all but covered with threadbare blankets, heaps of rags, and even piles of limp old straw, upon which sprawled or curled the nightly population of those too wretched or desperate to fear the white glow of the Melt. Most of them slept, some probably feigned slumber, but many were unabashedly awake, staring eyes fixed upon the intruders.

At the far end of the enclosure, the big front doors stood wide open. The space beyond drowned in pallid luminescence, into which the four fleeing Blowflies were flinging themselves, one after another.

If they thought it as easy as that, they were wrong. The bitch in the grey cloak wasn't about to get away. She'd killed Captain Zegnauer.

Ignoring the recumbent bodies beneath their boots, the Soldiers of the Light gave chase.

Following the first few seconds of shock, the paralyzed Blowflies in Meustri Vurtz's parlor came back to life. They unfroze to find themselves trapped and helpless. There was nothing at all that they could do to save themselves, but this reality did not keep them from trying.

Seizing the nearest chair, the Blowfly known as the Pickax sent the piece flying straight into the faces of two soldiers standing between himself and the door. The armed men tumbled, and the Pickax dashed for the exit. A well-aimed shot from behind brought him down. He jerked convulsively, and died.

A furious, terrified shriek escaped the White Gardenia, and she aimed an annihilating kick at the killer's groin. A couple of blows of some-one's musket butt clubbed her to the floor. She stirred feebly, tried to raise herself, and a third blow to the temple struck her down again, this time permanently.

The Apricot and the Gargoyle both ran for the kitchen, and possible escape by way of the great chimney. A brace of nearly simultaneous shots dropped them both in their tracks.

Ninetoes managed to dispatch herself with a beautifully precise dag-ger thrust, before anyone could move to stop her.

The Tocsin was not so fortunate. A powerful soldierly grip closed upon his wrist, arresting the progress of a hand from pocket to mouth. The hand was pried open, and a small ampoule was discovered therein. The contents of the ampoule hardly demanded analysis.

The Tocsin's lips drew back over his teeth. Something between a snarl and a groan escaped him.

The surviving Blowflies were dragged from the house and loaded into a closed wagon, which then set off for the Heart of Light.

Eighteen

The hour was far too late for scheduled appointments, and social callers he had none, yet someone was at the door, knocking very insistently. It had to be some emergency case, a patient in dire need. Pausing only long enough to resume his dark glasses and wide hat, Tradain opened the door to confront a slight figure wrapped in a hooded cloak colored to match the fog. The visitor looked up, and he recognized Glennian liTarngrav. She looked unwell. Her face was flushed and perspiring, despite the coolness of the night air. Her breath was distressed, and she was actually trembling.

Fever? Unwonted alarm shot through him, then vanished, for his powers sufficed to cure any physical ill. In this particular case, he wouldn't mind the expense of limited arcane resource. In fact, the thought of restoring her to perfect health was remarkably attractive. He realized that he was smiling, an entirely inappropriate reaction to the situation.

"Come in." He took care to suppress the smile. Voice and face expressed the proper concern.

She walked in, allowing him to take her cloak, and to install her in a comfortable chair. She was oddly disheveled—her long hair had somehow escaped its fastenings—and visibly nervous. Her hands were clenched, and her green eyes darted everywhere. For a while he waited, but she said nothing, and at last he prompted gently, "You are ill?"

"Ill?" she echoed, for once in her life looking almost stupid.

"Tell me what troubles you. Perhaps I can help."

"Oh." She stared at him for a long moment, and then apparently regained her wits, along with her tongue. "Perhaps. You're an excellent physician, people say. I came to you tonight because—because I am so tired all the time, and my hands shake, and the smallest exertion robs me of my breath, as you can see. I'm sorry to burst in on you unannounced, at this hour of the night, but quite suddenly such a desperate terror seized me that I felt I couldn't wait another instant to find help. You understand me?"

"Not entirely. When last we met, not long ago, you displayed none of the symptoms you describe."

"They've come upon me recently. Illness does so, does it not? Perhaps the constant fear accounts for it."

"You need fear nothing. I can promise you that."

"But can you promise the same to Re'Drempi? My guardian faces the White Tribunal within days, and there can be but one outcome. It is his plight that preys upon my mind."

"I am sorry." *Not for Kwieseldt.* She was looking, he noticed, more uncomfortable and uneasy than ever. Her eyes were fixed on the nearest window. The shutters were open, but fog obscured the world beyond the leaded glass panes. Her breathing continued curiously rapid, and her death grip on the chair arms never slackened. He himself was to blame. He had only intended to punish the guilty, but innocent bystanders were inevitably burned. He could compensate Glennian liTarngrav, however. What were sorcerous powers good for, if not to mop up a few moral messes, here and there? Someday, he would see liTarngrav House returned to her. In the meantime—

"There are draughts aplenty to calm your fears, but I don't advise you to use them," he told her. "You would be far better off to—"

A commotion at his door interrupted the recommendation. Someone was knocking—pounding, in fact—and imperative voices resounded outside. Glennian jumped to her feet. Her face was white, and her eyes enormous. She shot him a scared, imploring glance.

"What is it?" he demanded.

The loud knocking repeated itself, and Glennian flinched.

"*Please,*" she whispered.

"Didn't I promise only moments ago that you need fear nothing? Believe it."

She hardly looked as if she believed it. Her eyes flew to the window.

"Stay where you are," Tradain advised, and left her, closing the office door behind him. He had no idea whether she would obey. Through his rooms he hurried, to the marble foyer, where the outer door shook beneath the assault of impatient fists. He opened up, to find three uniformed Soldiers of the Light upon his threshold.

"Gentlemen?" Dr. Flambeska inquired courteously.

"We're on the trail of four fugitive seditionists," the commanding sergeant announced without preamble. "One of them, female, was spotted in Solemnity Square, and we're checking every house. She's probably young, light and fleet, and she's wrapped up in a long, hooded grey cloak. Seen such a woman?"

"Sergeant, I have scarcely glanced out the window in hours."

"And nobody at your door claiming illness, trying to get the doctor to let her in off the street?"

"I scarcely accept random, nameless patients—off the street. Particularly at this hour."

"I guess not. Send word if you spot her, Doctor. She's at the top of the list."

"I shall cooperate to the fullest, Sergeant."

The Soldiers of the Light withdrew to continue their search, and Tradain returned to his office, unsure of what he would find or not find there. She'd been terrified, and unwilling to trust in his ability or inclination to deflect the soldiers, she might well have exited by way of the window. If so, it would be the greatest mistake she had ever made.

He walked into the office, where suspense promptly gave way to anger. She was still there, just where he had left her. She looked frightened, as well she might. The reckless, headstrong, little idiot savant.

"They're gone," he told her.

"I know, I heard. Thank you." Her face was very pale. Her voice was even, but she stood with every muscle tensed, as if bracing against attack.

She had reason.

"Fugitive seditionists?" Tradain inquired, too calmly.

She nodded.

"That is an imposing title. Far more resonant than the humdrum, insectile 'Blowflies.'"

"Ummm."

"You *are* one of the Blowflies, aren't you?"

"I can't answer that."

"No, of course not. Oaths of deepest secrecy, sealed in blood. Loyalty unto death, and all that. Never mind, your silence answers."

"Silence admits to nothing."

"Wonder if the jurists of the Tribunal would agree?"

"Are you really in any position to threaten me, Tradain liMarchborg? Excuse me, I mean, Dr. Flambeska."

"Sheathe your claws, I don't threaten you. I'm trying to help you, if possible. Tonight, you were lucky. Next time, there'll be nobody to stand between you and the Soldiers of the Light. Unless, of course, my concern is misplaced, and colorful martyrdom is your aim."

"Not really."

"Then what do you think you're doing?"

"Some good, I hope."

"Oh, let's dispense with the juvenile, rose-colored platitudes."

"That's all you hear? I must pity you. Something is dead in you, or else it is asleep."

"The only thing asleep is your intelligence. Have done with these sentimental and heroic fancies. This is no afternoon at the playhouse, full of mock peril. The risk you run is real. When you're caught—and you will be—your death will be real, and painful, and permanent. You're too young, too gifted and beautiful, to throw your life away over nothing."

"Nothing. You must be fond of that word, you seem to use it so often, and so carelessly. I myself am not so despondent, so embittered, or so hopeless and empty that I admit no possibility of positive change in the world."

"Leave positive change to others, preferably those equipped with armies. You and your playmates will accomplish nothing beyond your own destruction."

"That remark's not worth the loss of my temper. Your condescension is as hollow as you are. Do you care for nothing? Is there nothing in the whole world that you believe worth some effort and risk? Nothing at all?"

"Now who's using that word to excess? But this digression is pointless. We were speaking of the Blowflies, and their inevitable ruin. We were speaking of your own precarious hold on existence."

"Strange words, coming from you, Doctor." Her green eyes bored straight into him. "What about your own precarious hold? Should your true name discover itself, how long before you find yourself sharing straw with the fleas in the Heart of Light? All things considered, the city of Lis Folaze is the last place in the world you should show your face, even behind dark glasses. And yet, here you are. You know the risks, you undertake them of your own free will, and there must be a reason. What is it?"

"In my case, unlike yours, the risks are negligible."

"How so?"

"I've been absent for thirteen years. My name and face are forgotten—"

"Did I forget them?"

"Your memory, as you have so often been at pains to observe, is exceptional."

"But hardly unique. In returning to this place, you've deliberately jeopardized yourself, and you must regard the dangers as acceptable. Why won't you accord me the same privilege?"

"The two cases are hardly comparable. I live quietly, while you court disaster. You dabble your fingers in the cauldron, with every new edition of *The Buzz.*"

"And then there's the matter of the physician's disguise," Glennian continued, apparently oblivious to his complaints. "You are by all reports an excellent doctor. Where did you acquire your skills? Where, for that matter, did you acquire the funds to set yourself up in such an establishment as this? These are very handsome lodgings, and I can't help wondering—"

"I can't help wondering how we've drifted so far from the topic of real importance. Glennian, you must abandon this Blowfly folly. Promise me that you will."

"It may be that the Blowfly folly has abandoned me. Tonight, the Soldiers of the Light raided the meeting house. It was horrible—unimaginable. Only a few of us escaped into the streets. Someone grabbed me in the dark, and we struggled, and he fell down the stairs, so I got away, but most—" Her composure wobbled. "Captured or dead. The organization has been shattered."

Unfortunate, but at least you're safely out of it. Aloud, he observed simply, "I am sorry."

"Are you?"

"Yes." He discovered that it was at least partially true. "They did good work. It's a sad ending." *But predictable.* She said nothing, and he looked at her sharply. She was staring into the fire quite expressionlessly, and something prompted him to inquire, "It *is* the end?"

"How could it be otherwise?" she returned.

The reply failed to satisfy him. "I hope you're not considering—"

"I'm too tired, frightened, and miserable to consider much of any-

thing at the moment. The soldiers must be gone by now. It's time for me to
leave."

"How will you get back to liTarngrav House?"

"Boat hire as far as Marbleflower Bridge, and then walk."

"Unsafe. My landlord allows me occasional hire of his carriage.
You'll ride home, and then, promise me that you'll rest."

"I promise."

"Good. And promise me as well, from now on, to forgo dangerous
escapades."

"I promise to undertake no unnecessary risk."

"You equivocate."

"You know, I've never heard anyone actually use that word in conversation before. You never did tell me where you picked up all that learning.
Or why you've come back to Lis Folaze."

"Didn't I?" She was a menace, he reflected. She always had been.
"Another time. Come, I'll walk you to the carriage. This way." He led her
back through his rooms, and as they went, he couldn't forbear asking the
question that had been gnawing the edges of his mind ever since she'd told
of the evening's disaster. "Glennian. Among those Blowflies, how many
know your real name?"

"Only one." Her voice and eyes were somber. "And he will never
betray it."

❧ ❦

"It is no betrayal," Gnaus liGurvohl corrected, patiently, but with some
sternness. "It is only a portion of that reparation you owe wronged humanity.
It is an opportunity to atone in measure for your past crimes."

"Look to your own crimes, Blood-boiler," gasped Meustri Vurtz, formerly known to his colleagues as the Tocsin.

"Insolence—defiance—deceit—arrogance—malice. Here, at the
heart of the Heart, you will purge yourself of such faults," liGurvohl promised. "In the end, you will emerge morally whole." He surveyed the prisoner
consideringly.

Nude and scrawny, Vurtz stood with his back pressed to a heavy
panel of splintery raw planking. Iron clamps attached him closely to the
wood at wrists, ankles, and throat. The atmosphere of the cellar was dank
and frigid. His naked limbs shook as much with cold as with fear and pain.
His jaw was set, and his eyes like stone. The man had much to learn.

"Speak the names of your fugitive associates," liGurvohl instructed.

"Speak but one of them. Whisper it, and only I will hear. By this sign, I shall perceive that your truest self desires salvation."

"I don't know the names," Vurtz returned, flinty gaze aimed straight ahead. "We used aliases. We didn't know each other's names."

"Ah, but surely the leader, the arch-seditionist, must have known."

"That does you no good. He's dead. Your ruffians murdered him."

"Falsehood is useless as it is contemptible. The eyes and ears of the White Tribunal do not fail. In time you will come to learn that it is impossible to deceive me. You are master of the Blowflies organization. This fundamental truth, touching upon yourself alone, honor compels you to acknowledge."

"It's a lie."

"You have been identified by one of your own colleagues."

"That's a lie too, White-shit. Go crawl back into your cesspool."

"You are discourteous, Master Vurtz."

The Tocsin replied with an expressive obscenity.

"And unregenerate, as yet. In this place, however, you will acquire education." LiGurvohl lifted a finger in silent signal.

A faceless figure crouched above a glowing brazier instantly reached forth a gloved hand to draw from the coals a long steel spike about the thickness of a knitting needle. The sharpened point of the spike shone dull red. Taking up a heavy hammer from its place on the floor beside him, liGurvohl's minion advanced upon the immobilized prisoner.

A faint sneer curled Vurtz's colorless lips.

Touching the point of the spike to the fleshy part of the prisoner's forearm, the torturer plied his hammer with no great force, to drive the steel slowly through muscle and sinew, deep into the wooden planking. The red-hot metal cauterized the wound it created, and remarkably little blood flowed.

Vurtz's breath whistled, but he allowed no other sound to escape him. He could not control a grimace of deepest anguish. After a moment his eyes opened, and dropped involuntarily to the spike transfixing his right forearm. It was the third such instrument to pierce that limb within the space of the last quarter hour or so. Similar spikes protruded from his left arm, and both legs.

Meustri Vurtz met the rainwater gaze of the Premier Jurist. Bending his stiff lips into a parody of a smile, he whispered, "Come, you'll have to do better than that."

"*We shall.*" The Premier Jurist gestured, and his minion proceeded to drive a redly radiant spike through the prisoner's shoulder.

"The names," liGurvohl commanded. "Speak but one of them, prove yourself worthy, and you will return to your cell."

The Tocsin cursed at him.

LiGurvohl's hand signal altered almost imperceptibly, but his underling did not miss the change. The next spike, forcefully hammered, drove straight into the prisoner's left kneecap, splitting the bone.

A shriek of mortal agony reverberated through the cellar, whose stone walls had contained and deadened thousands of such cries. Vurtz's head thrashed from side to side. All other portions of his anatomy were pinned immovably to the wooden panel. Eventually the abortive contortions ceased, and his head fell forward, within the confines of the iron collar.

"Your folly saddens me," reproved the Premier Jurist. "I desire to assist you, yet your obstinacy thwarts my efforts."

A feeble string of curses droned indistinctly from the semiconscious prisoner.

"I do not abandon hope, however. Autonn may yet soften your heart. Let us try again. We will speak of the Winter Commendation, so accurately described in one of your pamphlets, some months ago. Your informant numbered among the guests or servants. So much is known."

"Dolt, ass, you know nothing," the Tocsin mumbled, without opening his eyes. "She was not even there."

"She?" The Premier Justice nodded. "Indeed. She questioned one of the guests, I presume?"

The prisoner was silent, and limp in his bonds. His breath rasped annoyingly. A spike driven through his right kneecap elicited nothing more than a couple of low moans, followed by a lapse into complete unconsciousness.

"Revive him," liGurvohl commanded.

The efforts of his underlings were ineffective.

"He's through," one of them reported.

"You took care to touch no vital organ?"

"Clean as a boiled bone, Premier Jurist. But he's old and undernourished. Sometimes, the heart just quits. It happens."

So it did, and not infrequently. The Premier Jurist knew that well.

"Unfortunate," he observed. "And yet, Autonn has willed that he should not die in vain."

Within hours of Meustri Vurtz's death, the Premier Jurist's impressions were reinforced by the arrival of a report from Sergeant Reschbek of the Select Squadron. Upon the night of the Blowflies raid, the Strellian physician Flambeska had received a call at an unusually late hour from an agitated lone female identified as Glennian liTarngrav.

The air of late springtime was mild and fragrant upon the morning the Regarded Drempi Kwieseldt finally came to trial. The proceedings of the White Tribunal always took place behind closed doors, but closed doors scarcely impaired the sorcerously enhanced vision of Tradain liMarchborg.

Tradain watched it all from the silent sanctum of his own office, by means of a Vigilance similar to that employed by Drempi Kwieseldt, but capable of transmitting sound. Dr. Flambeska had left the entire day free, but this allowance proved excessive, for the trial was a perfunctory affair, concluded within minutes. The Regarded Kwieseldt had, after all, voluntarily signed his name to a full confession, weeks earlier. Assuming the defendant attempted no desperate last-minute recantation, there was really little to be said.

Kwieseldt clearly intended no such futile recantation. His face was pale, his aspect wanly resigned, as he listened to the confession read aloud to the jurists. His eyes remained fixed on the floor throughout the lengthy recitation of offenses, lifting only once, as the words "confess to treachery in the direst degree" droned out in the flat monotone of the court clerk. At the conclusion of the reading, the defendant's statement was demanded.

Kwieseldt stood.

"I am guilty," he announced firmly, and resumed his seat.

Conviction followed, almost without delay. The prisoner waived his right to plead for mercy, and Premier Jurist Gnaus liGurvohl calmly condemned him to death. Kwieseldt was escorted from the courtroom, and the White Tribunal turned its attention to other matters.

It was over. Tradain set the Vigilance aside. Justice of sorts had prevailed, yet the spectacle had furnished astonishingly little satisfaction. The glow of victory he might naturally have expected to enjoy somehow failed to warm him. Quite the contrary, he was decidedly cold inside. Perhaps it had something to do with the impersonal, almost mechanical nature of the trial itself; or else the doomed man's demeanor—resigned, hopeless, yet composed—somehow invited pity in a manner that precluded justifiable enjoyment.

Whatever the reason, he took no more pleasure in Drempi Kwieseldt's destruction than he had found in Aestine liHofbrunn's dreary ruin. But no, the comparison was surely invalid, for the two culprits were quite dissimilar. Unlike Aestine, Kwieseldt was capable of comprehension, certain to manifest itself as execution drew nigh and the reality of his fate impressed itself upon the condemned man's mind. And then at last, Tradain liMarchborg would know satisfaction. In the meantime, the chilly serenity that filled him was tolerable enough.

It was not yet noon. The day stretched before him, empty and featureless. He wished that he hadn't canceled Dr. Flambeska's appointments,
for now there was nothing to keep him occupied, nothing to exclude unwelcome or uncomfortable thoughts, and above all, nothing to banish the in-
candescent visions of the torment ultimately awaiting him. He had made his
bargain; regrets and terrors were equally pointless.

He busied himself as best he could, with the doctor's paperwork and
correspondence, with replenishment of dwindling medicinal supplies, with
a lunch that he hardly tasted, followed by a long walk. The afternoon was
well advanced by the time he returned to his lodgings, but hours still remained. He went back to his office and his paperwork, but found his eyes
and thoughts drifting continually to the lower left drawer of the desk. The
drawer contained a false panel concealing a hidden compartment, proudly
displayed by Master Einzlaur shortly after the Strellian physician had taken
up residence at Number Sixteen Solemnity Square. Tradain rarely opened
the compartment, despite the fact that its contents often preyed upon his
mind. His reluctance was understandable, but not to be indulged, for certain realities demanded periodic attention.

He opened the drawer and forced himself to slide the false panel
aside. Faint blue light spilled from the secret compartment. Drawing the
hourglass forth from its hiding place, he set the device before him on the
desk, looked at it, and froze.

A *mistake*. The hourglass was malfunctioning. Nothing else could
explain the massive loss of luminous matter from the upper chamber. The
pile of lightless granules lying dead at the bottom of the glass suggested a
prodigal expenditure of power. Prior to this morning's surveillance of the
White Tribunal, however, he hadn't resorted to sorcery in weeks. He had
been careful, he had been thrifty; he always was.

His mouth was dry. There had to be a mistake.

Or a cheat.

Malevolences were said to hate mankind. Malevolences deceived
and destroyed. Xyleel had cozened him. Outrage flared then, and his hand
clenched on the hourglass. The impulse was strong to crush the damnable
thing underfoot, but he restrained himself. The consequences of such an act
were unclear, but potentially catastrophic. For all he knew, the spillage of
those remaining luminous granules might propel mind and body instanta-
neously from the plane of mankind, leaving his great task uncompleted.

Great task?

The hourglass stood before him, its heap of lightless matter a mocking memento mori. Leaning back in his chair, Tradain strove to penetrate
the mystery, but alarm and confusion hampered logic. The glass taunted

him in silence. He couldn't bear the sight of it, and his gaze strayed, soon to light upon the Vigilance whereby he had observed the morning's session of the White Tribunal. He brushed the Vigilance with his fingertips, and he understood.

He had furnished the Regarded Drempi Kwieseldt with a sphere of similar type. Each vision vouchsafed by the Iron Vigilance, he belatedly realized, demanded a certain outlay of sorcerous power—his own power. That was a detail easily overlooked, in the heat of the device's creation. The Regarded Kwieseldt must have employed the Vigilance almost continually, over the course of weeks.

Tradain sat very still. The error was less than lethal, but he could hardly afford another such. He was amply equipped for the work immediately ahead, and when that work was completed, the state of the hourglass would no longer matter. There was no cause for clammy hands and icy limbs.

He waited, eyes shut, but the frigid sensations only deepened. The hairs stirred at the back of his neck, a sense of overwhelming dread oppressed him, and he knew then that he was not alone.

The Presence Xyleel was with him.

He opened his eyes to gaze again upon that inconstant, insupportable form, its vastness impossibly contained within the finite volume of the chamber. Once more, he submitted shudderingly to the alien occupation of his mind, and the methodical examination of its contents. There was no point in attempting resistance.

Moreover, he was learning that voluntary acceptance of the invasive intelligence carried certain rewards of its own, including an increased understanding of the Other's nature. Accordingly, he threw wide the portals of selfhood, and at once received an impression wholly familiar in terms of human experience:

Curiosity.

Impersonal, foreign, and infinitely remote, but recognizable curiosity, of which he himself seemed to be the object. He could not imagine why. His own incomprehension must have communicated itself, for the radiant voice replied in silence.

You have punished the guilty. You have achieved a measure of justice.

Tradain's response, immediate and spontaneous, framed itself aloud. "Why do You so often repeat those same words?"

The question was not excluded from Xyleel's awareness, but there was no direct reply, in words or any other medium of communication. There was only an intensification of that alien curiosity. Tradain sensed the inquisitive effulgence insinuating itself coldly through the levels of his consciousness, but caught no echo of successful conclusion. Whatever the malevolence sought, He did not find.

The mental ransacking was intolerable. Words might put a halt to it.

"Why have You come?" asked Tradain.

Curiosity. *You have punished the guilty.* Knowledge? Volition. Justice? *Autonn.*

A seemingly random jumble of impressions, obscurely linked. Tradain strained to open himself wider, to admit all, to capture and to hold every shadow of sensation.

Punished the guilty. Knowledge. Autonn.

He caught the intimation of Autonn quite clearly, and then he actually experienced Her through the mind of Xyleel, beheld Her mutable luminescence, and knew that She was near, even present upon the Netherly plane of mankind's existence, though beyond the realm of ordinary human perception. But he could see Her, for this one moment, and he could even faintly sense Her urgency.

Sentient Symbiosis.

The words welled from the bottom of his brain. Their precise meaning eluded him, but he grasped the general sense of communion.

The Radiant Level, flooded with Netherly poison, darkened forever. The great chorus of shared consciousness, silenced forever. *Punish the guilty.* Anomaly. Exile. Autonn.

The images, words, and sensations bombarded him, and Tradain finally knew what the great Presence Xyleel sought in his small human mind: knowledge of justice, or vengeance, two frequently indistinguishable concepts. Both of them equally exotic to the Aware of the Radiant Level, whose collective perfection admitted of no disharmony demanding drastic measures of correction. Or so the telepathic body of Awareness perceived itself.

But the Presence Xyleel was an Anomaly; by definition, warped of viewpoint. The Presence Xyleel desired knowledge of justice and vengeance, information with which to arm Himself against the arguments and exhortations of Autonn, with whom He currently communed. He might reasonably expect to discover some of what He sought in the mind of Tradain liMarchborg.

Satisfaction? Fulfillment? Certainty? Peace?

He would find none of them. What would He actually find?

Disappointment? Melancholy? Inexpressible fear of the future?

Yes. Much good they would do Him.

He had no encouraging insight to offer Xyleel, nothing with which to silence the telepathic plaints of Autonn.

You have achieved a measure of justice.

"And it has been empty so far, but all of that is about to change."

He wasn't certain if he had spoken the words aloud, or only in his own mind, and there was no time to ponder the matter, for the creak of the office door arrested his attention. He turned to watch with an almost detached interest as the door swung open.

Nineteen

Shortly before noon, the news of Drempi Kwieseldt's conviction and condemnation reached liTarngrav House. The announcement was not unexpected, yet the finality of it was shocking.

The household members each reacted characteristically. The Regarded Madam Kwieseldt retired to her bedchamber, there to soak her pillow with tears. The heir apparent, Pfissig Kwieseldt, sought the great study, where he spent the afternoon composing a long and florid plea for clemency, addressed to the Dhreve Lissildt. And Glennian liTarngrav, as was her wont in time of trouble, fled to the music room.

Seating herself at the harpsichord, she let her fingers move at will, and the sadness poured out, expressing itself in restless melody spiked with startling, dissonant chords. Thus she often purged her-self of corrosive emotion, thereby occasionally discovering musical inspira-tion. Not this time, however. The grief and confusion deepened as she played.

There was nothing confusing in the bare facts of Drempi Kwieseldt's case. He had attempted the life of the Premier Jurist Gnaus liGurvohl, failed through a combination of incompetence and ill luck, confessed his crime voluntarily, and now, inevitably, faced execution. His motives, however, remained obscure. More than obscure—downright unfathom-able.

Her sense of unseen influence at work was stronger than ever, and for the first time, Glennian thought to connect her guardian's inexplicable self-destruction with the reappearance of Tradain liMarchborg. The idea sprang from nowhere, she couldn't have said why. It was as if her own music had somehow suggested it. She hadn't a shred of evidence to support the theory—or, rather, the wisp of intuition—but found that she couldn't let it go.

Her fingers stilled themselves. She stared blindly down at the keys. Tradain liMarchborg, tortured victim of the White Tribunal. "Dr. Flambeska." Certainly he had every reason to desire the Premier Jurist's death. Perhaps he had even come back to Lis Folaze specifically to avenge himself upon liGurvohl. But why, in that case, would he lure Drempi Kwieseldt, of all people, into his scheme? Perhaps he'd needed an accom-plice of sorts, but the timorous and circumspect Re'Drempi seemed an unlikely choice. And it wasn't as if any personal connection existed between Tradain and the former liTarngrav steward; thirteen years earlier, the two had barely known each other. Did it suffice, for Tradain, that Re'Drempi was a famous friend of the Tribunal and a member of the League of Allies? Perhaps, but the League comprised scores of members, many of them far better suited than hapless Drempi Kwieseldt to homicidal endeavor.

No, it simply made no sense. She had to be mistaken.

Very difficult to forget, however, that all of Re'Drempi's troubles had commenced within months of Dr. Flambeska's descent upon Lis Folaze. Coincidence? Perhaps. Easier to judge, if she knew the actual purpose of Tradain's return. She had never succeeded in prying that out of him, and something in those glacial blue eyes of his discouraged her from pressing the issue. They weren't always glacial, of course. A few times, the eyes had warmed, the impassive face had come to life, and she'd glimpsed traces of the boy she'd once known, the boy she'd trailed everywhere, even while fiercely disclaiming all weak sentiment. At such moments, she knew that he enjoyed her company, liked her, even let himself trust her a little; but not so much that the slightest infringement upon his precious privacy wouldn't meet with a courteous but granite-solid rebuff.

She'd never manage to break down that reserve. No point in trying.

But she would keep on trying, all the same. Some things didn't change, even in thirteen years.

She told herself she simply pitied his misfortunes. That, she knew, was a lie.

Glennian willed her hands to move, and music filled the room. Her thoughts raced, and presently she noticed that melody had given way to horrendous discords. She was unconsciously pounding the keys. Irresponsible. She'd damage a very fine harpsichord if she didn't take some care. Rising abruptly from her bench, she crossed the room to the fireplace—the same whose damper she had deliberately closed, to send smoke pouring into the face of Dr. Flambeska, upon the occasion of his first visit. She couldn't seem to stop thinking about the good doctor, but that was better than thinking of poor Re'Drempi, locked up in the Heart of Light, awaiting Disinfection. Or were the two apparently disparate subjects linked?

Music, her accustomed solace, would not help her today. She went back upstairs to her own room, and there unsuccessfully attempted diversion by way of books, lunch that she couldn't bring herself to eat, perusal of liVauptof's score to *The Masque of Black Nightingales*, a hot bath, and more books. None of them worked. The hours crawled, and her unhappy thoughts darkened.

In the late afternoon, she gave up the struggle. She couldn't control or resist the avalanche of her fears and suspicions. Now, she yielded.

Glennian glanced out the window at the shadows lengthening along the ground below. The afternoon was wearing on, but her one appointment of the early evening was still hours off. Time enough remained. She would do it. She couldn't not do it.

The spring weather was bright and unseasonably warm. Her gown was of summer-weight silk, dark green as the deep woods; good enough to purchase respect, but not so grand as to draw unwelcome attention. She checked the little purse hanging at her waist, discovering adequate funds for transportation, and more, for poor Re'Drempi had always been generous. Pausing only long enough to adjust one of the tortoiseshell combs anchoring her mass of hair, Glennian departed liTarngrav House.

In the late afternoon, Pfissig Kwieseldt returned from the palace of his neighbor, the Dhreve Lissildt. He had spent hours waiting in one of the grand antechambers, along with the usual horde of petitioners, both humble and exalted, always to be found there. The Dhreve, trailed by a brace of basket-bearing flunkies, walked through that antechamber every day, thus according his importunate subjects opportunity to present their various requests, suggestions, and demands. Most of the sealed or scrolled missives found their way straight to the baskets. But the Dhreve always accepted a few directly into his own hands as he walked, and it was generally believed that these favored petitions enjoyed immediate attention, and a high probability of favorable response.

Pfissig had arrived early enough to secure a good position near the door. He had waited resolutely, and when the moment came, he had pushed, shoved, elbowed, trodden toes, even aimed a furtive kick or two; in short, fought with all his strength to win his way to the Dhreve's side. He was by nature disinclined to competitive physical effort, but the situation demanded extraordinary measures, and in the end, his determination had borne fruit. He had flapped his written plea on his father's behalf like a banner before the Dhreve's face. Lissildt had checked for a startled instant, then accepted the paper and moved on. It was done. Nothing remained but to wait and hope.

Pfissig walked on home. He was not accustomed to walking and not fond of it, but use of the ornate Kwieseldt first-carriage, under the present dismal circumstances, struck him as tasteless, perhaps even improper. As he went, he mentally reviewed the recent scene in the antechamber, and certain details sprang to the fore. That fleeting expression in the Dhreve's eyes, at the instant he accepted the petition. Recognition? Did Lissildt recall the face of the Regarded Drempi Kwieseldt's only son? Would it make a difference if he did?

Pfissig was nearing Kwieseldt Mansion when his cogitations were interrupted and his attention caught by the emergence of a slender, green-clad figure. He stopped dead in the discreet shade of an old redtooth to stare at Glennian liTarngrav, trotting out on her own, and not for the first time, either. Off she went, without so much as a maid to attend her, and it didn't look well, particularly not at such a time as this, but Glennian wouldn't trouble her head about appearances. She was an aristocratic liTarngrav, far above such petty considerations as feminine modesty and propriety, or *so she thought*. But unseemliness was unseemliness, in Pfissig's opinion. It didn't matter what her last name was, or how blue her blood, such careless solitary gadding was worse than unladylike—it wasn't even respectable.

Through the gate she hurried, and on along the street, her pace quick, and her air unattractively purposeful. Had the creature no care at all for the Regarded name of Kwieseldt, already so grievously injured? Where did she think she was going, anyway?

This time, he meant to find out. As new head of the household, he had every right to know. Should it happen that she hurried to the arms of a secret lover, then duty compelled him to confirm her guilt, and the ocular proof was required. Perhaps he might contrive some means of direct observation. The thought of watching Glennian couple with some lowborn muscular swain sent delicious warm ripples all through him. He would see them both disrobe, feverishly or languorously. He would see big, sun-browned hands stroking her white flesh. He would see—

The warm ripples swelled at the mere thought. How much sweeter the reality?

This afternoon, perhaps he would learn. And if it happened that she had brought shame to the House of Kwieseldt, then he would take the course that duty demanded, and put her out on the streets. Conscience demanded no less.

Along the avenues he furtively followed her, straight to Marbleflower Bridge, where she engaged a boat. Pfissig did likewise, disembarking close behind her downstream at Singlespan Bridge. Thereafter, he trailed her through the Eastcity, as far as Solemnity Square, where she knocked at the door of Number Sixteen.

Something familiar about that address. Oh, yes. Number Sixteen Solemnity Square was the much-publicized address of that Strellian physician fellow, Flambeska. Why should Glennian come here? Could she harbor some gruesome disease—possibly contagious? She appeared healthy enough, but women seemed to suffer an astounding assortment of the most indelicate and indecent ailments. He didn't understand why the creatures couldn't manage to keep their internal organs in better order.

The door opened, and Pfissig saw a man, not Flambeska. Glennian was admitted, and the door closed behind her.

Pfissig scowled. He couldn't go to the windows, the house was far too exposed. He could, however, approach for a better view. The little park at the center of Solemnity Square offered an excellent vantage point. Straight to the pretty patch of greenery he made his unobtrusive way, and, despite the pleasant weather, found the place empty save for a silent, nondescript groundskeeper, who eyed him askance as he drew nigh. Really, the lout looked as if he thought himself owner of the park. Ignoring the disgruntled menial, Pfissig settled himself upon a low marble bench, and fixed his attentive regard upon the abode of Dr. Flambeska.

Glennian knocked, and the door opened. A ruddy-faced man, probably the landlord, blocked her way. He had not been in evidence upon the occasion of her previous visit. Fortunately.

"Dr. Flambeska, please," she requested.

He ushered her in with a gallant bow and a knowing smile. She wondered briefly if Tradain received many female callers, arriving alone and on foot at the end of the day, and found the thought remarkably disturbing. Well, it was really none of her business.

She stood in a glossy little hallway, before Tradain's own apartment. The ruddy-faced individual retired, and Glennian knocked. There was no response, and she tried the door. It yielded, and she went in.

She had heard that the fashionable Dr. Flambeska enjoyed a busy practice, and she'd wondered if she might arrive to find his waiting room thronged with patients, but the place was empty. Perhaps Tradain was absent. If so, she could either wait for his return, possibly hours hence, or else come back another day, but neither alternative appealed. She had worked up her courage to confront him with her questions, she was ready to fight for answers, and she wanted to do it at once, before determination flagged.

Last time, he'd been in his office. Perhaps he was in there now. Preoccupied or even asleep, he might have missed her knock. The office door was shut. As she approached, she caught the mutter of a voice, *his* voice. He was in there, all right, and evidently not alone. She paused to listen to him speak—a question, she thought, but couldn't distinguish the words—and heard no reply. Several moments of silence ensued, and then he said something else, she wasn't sure what. Again, there was no answer. Apparently he was alone, after all. Talking to himself?

She lifted a hand to knock again, and halted. Should she advertise her presence, he might tell her to go away, and she wasn't about to give him that opportunity. Her heart was hammering. She realized that she was very afraid. Surely not of Tradain liMarchborg. He had changed greatly over the course of the years, and she no longer fathomed his thoughts, but somehow she knew to the marrow of her bones that he would never harm her. Yet the formless terror was rising.

She took a deep breath, and made herself open the door. The office beyond was filled with light so dazzling that her eyes shut involuntarily, and she turned her face away. In that moment of blindness she thought she heard music, or something like it; a great chorus of inhuman voices, rising and blending in a concert of disturbing beauty. But the voices were somehow silent, and she heard them not with her ears, but with her mind. It was perhaps the loveliest and most terrifying music that she had ever encountered, awakening exultation and despair, and it took her in its grip, bent her as it would, and forced her eyes open to gaze upon itself.

She looked straight into the light, to behold a vast and mutable form, too brilliant for human eyes, too alien for human minds. She blinked, and the tears coursed down her face, but this time she refused to avert her gaze. She saw unimaginable vastness, inconceivable force and will, impossibly contained within a finite space. Intelligence and dark intention radiating from that effulgence caught her flying imagination, and she stretched forth her arms, but it was too late, for the light was already fading. She heard herself cry out, begging it to stay, but it dwindled out of being, and was gone. The confusion of relief and loss was almost more than she could bear.

Confusion ebbed, and her mind cleared. She found herself alone with Tradain liMarchborg. He was watching her. She looked straight into his eyes, and asked, "Will it come back?"

"Yes," he said.

"When?"

"I don't know."

"Soon?"

"Maybe."

"Did you call it?"

"Not this time."

She walked into the office, and let herself sink into a chair. He offered her a glass of water, and she drank it. The mental paralysis loosened, and when she was more or less herself again, she looked at him and asked, "That was a malevolence?"

"A presence," he told her, his tone quite flat, almost uninterested. "An awareness."

This seemed less a contradiction than a correction. At least he wasn't trying to convince her that she'd been imagining things. Just as well. The supernatural manifestation that answered so many questions, completing such a clear picture, could hardly be denied.

"Your return from the dead—your knowledge and skills—your wealth—"

He said nothing.

"All of these miracles are now explained. All of them, granted by—that—?"

Still no answer, but he denied nothing.

"At what price?"

"You shouldn't have come bursting in here," he told her. "Something could have happened."

"At what price?"

"Don't concern yourself."

"The old stories are true, then. You have sold your life-force."

"I don't know what's meant by that term. Now go home, Glennian. I don't want you here."

His expression was bleak as midwinter, but she didn't altogether believe him. "Years ago, you were always trying to tell me when to go home. It didn't work then, and it won't work now."

"And you are no longer a child, and this is not a game."

"What is it, then? Please explain. What is your connection to—*that?* What have you done, and why?"

She didn't really expect him to answer, and he didn't. The office was filling with shadow. Outside, the sun was setting. In silence, Tradain lit a couple of lamps. Even by that warm-colored light, his bloodless pallor was evident.

It had to be something terrible, to make him look like that. She tried hard not to let her own fears show.

"What's brought you back to Lis Folaze, Tradain?" she persisted, relentlessness offset by the softness of her voice. She didn't think he'd answer that one, either, but finally he did.

"You've seen the sign in my window. 'Systemic Imbalances Corrected.'" He smiled without mirth. "An imbalance exists. I am here to correct it."

Imbalance. He was deliberately obscure, but she knew something of his history, and could only assume that he referred to injustices of personal concern. His father. His brothers. His own nightmare years. If he desired redress, he could only seek it of the White Tribunal.

"LiGurvohl?" she asked.

"You were always quick."

"But that doesn't explain why that—"

"Presence."

"Does it own you?"

"Not yet."

"Yet? What do you mean by that? Speak plainly—have you sold your life-force to a malevolence?"

"I have bartered my sentience, a commodity the Presence stores against future need."

"And in exchange?"

"Certain unusual abilities."

"Which you will use to exact vengeance upon the Premier Jurist?"

"And a couple of others."

"That's paltry."

"To me, it is vast and consuming. So it must be, for without that purpose, there is nothing."

"There are far worthier goals, and far higher aims. There are other people to think of—great ills in the world that demand change—battles of true importance to be fought—"

"These things are no concern of mine."

"Then you are scarcely human."

"And you are scarcely qualified to judge me. Had I not chosen as I did, submitting to the Presence, then I would now be dead, else buried alive at the bottom of Fortress Nul. I never told you much of the fortress dungeons, and you may count yourself fortunate for that. Even at the last, in the workroom of Yurune, when great Xyleel came to me with His offer of freedom and power, I might have refused, had He not granted me knowledge of the treachery that destroyed my House. Ravnar liMarchborg was sold for a pittance, you know. His wife, suborned by that master of misery liGurvohl, bore false witness against my father. As a result, Ravnar and his two older sons died in agony, while the youngest son was consigned to torments less intense, but infinitely prolonged."

And did Drempi Kwieseldt somehow share in the responsibility? Glennian wondered. She hardly dared ask aloud, for the implications of an affirmative reply were too painful to contemplate.

"Since that night," Tradain continued, "the hope of punishing those crimes has lent meaning to my life. When that purpose is accomplished, I will yield myself gladly to the malevolence, and He may do with me as He wills."

She had never seen a face so empty, the eyes dead, and the sight terrified her.

"Tradain," she appealed, "it can't be as hopeless as that. You turned to the malevolence in a moment of desperation. It wasn't really your fault, and it can't be too late to save yourself. Turn away from Him—relinquish your powers, change your way of life, and make it known to Him that the agreement is voided."

"As easily as that? You don't understand. The recollection of our bargain is imprinted upon my memory. It is not within my power to erase it, or to alter it in the slightest. So long as the imprint remains—and it is permanent—I may not deny my obligation to the Presence Xyleel."

"Surely there's something you can do. What about the power of Autonn? Have you called upon Him? Perhaps He—"

"Autonn." Tradain produced a smile of lifeless amusement. "Don't ask me to explain, but only believe—I may expect no assistance from Autonn."

His leaden conviction convinced her, and she attempted no argument, but only asked, "And if you could escape your bargain with the malevolence, would you do so?"

"There is no escape." His nonexpression did not alter. "The question has no meaning."

That silenced her for several moments. At last she asked hesitantly, "Will you not at least consider turning the powers at your command to some better use than the simple destruction of your enemies?"

"Better use involving some cause of the sort favored by your journalist friends?"

"You might do much, for many."

"Did I tell you that my powers are limited in quantity, and reduced by expenditure? When they are exhausted, Xyleel claims me. Still so eager to see me use them up?"

"No, then don't use them at all, *never* use them. Take care never to exhaust them, and—"

"Eventually, my natural term of existence ends. At that time, if not before, Xyleel claims me."

"What happens then?"

"My consciousness persists, indefinitely, in bondage, and in some—discomfort."

"Oh," she cried, "however could you have landed yourself in such a trap? There's nothing in the world worth such a price as you'll pay!"

"It's a little late for regrets. I can only make the most of this bargain I have chosen."

"By hunting your enemies to the death? Your situation is already wretched, and you'll only make it worse. Please, Tradain, stop now."

"I cannot. I will not."

"Then I pity you, and I fear for you." Immediately she regretted the words, for he froze as if she'd sunk a dagger of ice in his heart. She couldn't endure the cold, lost look in his eyes, but there was no denying that he was lost, beyond hope of salvation. There was nothing she could do for him, nothing anyone could do for him.

Her face was stiff and hot. In another moment she would start to cry. Best to leave, immediately; in any case, she was shortly expected elsewhere.

"Good-bye," she said, almost surprised at the spurious calmness of her own voice. Expecting no reply, she was startled when he spoke.

"Will you come back?"

"Yes." Until the word emerged, she hadn't known what she would say.

She turned from him, and walked out.

Pfissig Kwieseldt mopped his brow and sighed. The drunk beside him on the bench stirred and snored, a disgusting sight and sound. Around sunset, Pfissig had imagined himself liberated by the withdrawal from the little park of the sullen groundskeeper. That nondescript individual's departure, however, had preceded literally by moments the arrival of the seedy, smelly, generally repulsive inebriate polluting the seat beside him. There was no relief, it seemed.

Despite all discomfort, Pfissig's eyes remained fixed on the dwelling of Dr. Flambeska. The shutters were drawn, blocking the view from his present position. The big, bright lanterns of Solemnity Square furnished excellent illumination, killing all hope of a surreptitious descent upon Number Sixteen. He could see and hear nothing occurring within, and thus his imagination was free to conjure the most luscious possibilities.

Glennian liTarngrav and that peculiar foreign physician, alone together. A detailed medical examination, the probing of her unclothed body, the inevitable progression of events . . . and, in all likelihood, Flambeska never removed those famous dark spectacles of his, not *ever* . . .

Pfissig shivered pleasurably, despite the warmth of the evening. His agreeable fancies were cut short by the sudden gleam of orange-yellow light spilling from the house as the front door swung wide. Glennian liTarngrav came out, and the door closed behind her.

He was too far away to read her expression by night, but the droop of her shoulders suggested dejection. Apparently, her tryst with the doctor had failed to satisfy. Pity. She lingered there for a moment, seemingly lost in unhappy thought, until the chimes of a distant clock roused her from her trance. She straightened with a decisive jerk and strode off, moving with the purposeful air that Pfissig so deplored. Didn't she realize how unattractive it was?

He followed discreetly. At first, he had assumed she would hurry straight home, but soon discovered his mistake. Through the clean and well-lighted avenues of the Eastcity Glennian liTarngrav led him, and into the realms beyond, where the streets narrowed, the light dimmed, the refuse lay everywhere, and the air was thick with unpleasing odors.

Not the very worst of neighborhoods, not exactly the sump of the city, but certainly not a place for a respectable woman to show herself, alone, and after dark; or before dark, for that matter. At the very least, for appearances' sake, she ought to hire herself a linkboy. But she, careless or *loose* as always, predictably neglected such measures.

She hardly seemed to note, much less fear, her disreputable surroundings. Perhaps she hoped to be accosted, perhaps she *invited* it. He wouldn't have put it past her, not for a moment, but at least her preoccupation offered one benefit—she never noticed that she was being followed.

On she went, down an alarmingly dark passageway, emerging at the other end into a shabby, cramped little alley, lined with anonymous tenements. Surely not her destination; or so he imagined, until he saw her beeline for the smallest, oldest, dreariest house in sight. She knocked, the door opened at once, and she slipped on through.

Well.

Pfissig eyed the house and its surroundings. Windows dark, save for a ground-floor glow at the rear. Night-smothered alleyway, conveniently deserted. He glided silently for the glow, and as he drew near, internally blessed the unseasonable torrid weather that obliged the inhabitants to leave the window open a crack. They'd drawn the curtains, but the cheap, skimpy panels gaped at the center, and he could see between them.

He peered into a kitchen drab and mean as the exterior of the dwelling suggested. Glennian liTarngrav sat at the head of an unpainted pine table. Three others sat with her: one female, one male, one indeterminate. Frowning, Pfissig squinted at the androgyne; glinting fair curls, pink and white baby skin, delicate features, large hands, large larynx—he supposed it must be a male, of sorts.

Glennian was speaking, her voice and manner quietly authoritative. Certainly, she was the ranking member of this little group. If he listened very closely, blocking extraneous city clatter from his consciousness, he could pick up most of her words.

". . . are the only ones left," she was saying. "The others are all dead, else locked up in the Heart of Light, and good as dead. Their respective gangs are dispersed, and the identities of the individual runners lost, which is probably just as well. The boys, at least, are safe."

Runners? The boys?

"As second to Tocsin, I ran no gang of my own," Glennian continued. "That leaves the three of you to represent our entire remaining force. How many runners do each of you direct? About eight or nine apiece?"

Mutters of affirmation around the table.

"Enough for a drastically pruned operation, should we elect to continue. And that is the question. Shall we continue? Is it desirable, or even practical? We've sustained immense casualties, lost our leader and our comrades, lost our press and supplies, and lost the former haven of Melthouse. May we hope to survive such a blow? What have you to say?"

There was silence for a while, until the other woman present— rounded, brown-haired, brown-eyed, bespectacled—remarked calmly, "I've a friend whose sister's husband's nephew may know where to acquire a secondhand press at a good price."

"I'm not the artist that Gargoyle was," confessed the androgyne. "But I'm game to try my hand at the cartoons."

"And—?" Glennian prompted the last, hitherto silent member, an elegantly grey-clad, grey-haired gentleman of middle years.

"Continue," came the immediate reply. "And you, Chair?"

Chair? What a queer game Glennian and her friends seemed to be playing.

"Continue. We are unanimous," Glennian observed with apparent elation. "The Blowflies live on."

Blowflies. Comprehension dawned, and Pfissig could hardly forbear hugging himself with pleasure. His concentration faltered, and he missed a few moments of illicit exchange, then managed to refocus his attention in time to witness the birth of the most stubbornly optimistic schemes. The broken band of proscribed journalists meant to regroup, recover, and ultimately expand to its former size. In the meantime, publication must shrink, but not cease. If all else failed, the fanatics were prepared to hand-letter notices, scores at a time, and post them all over town, for the Blowflies wouldn't give in, and they wouldn't give up.

Idiots, in Pfissig's opinion, *wicked* idiots, mindlessly evil and annoying as the insects whose title they bore. Just what he might have expected of Glennian liTarngrav, that down-your-nose, blue-blooded, bluestocking strumpet. She'd always been so superior, so contemptuous. A little *toad*, she had called him, and worse. But he had her now.

He had her now.

The meeting trudged to its conclusion, and Pfissig buried himself in shadow. Glennian emerged, and he followed her home to Kwieseldt Mansion, where she locked herself in her own chamber. As acting master of the house in his father's absence, he might easily have ordered her forth, but chose otherwise, for his mood embraced warm generosity, so delighted was he with the fruits of the evening's endeavors.

Twenty

Sergeant Orschl of the Select Squadron was pleased, for his newest set of orders offered welcome, if puzzling, relief from tedium. He did not know why he should receive such improbable commands to raid the lodgings of Dr. Flambeska. The doctor appeared to lead a boringly inoffensive life, but the Premier Jurist evidently regarded that appearance as deceptive. No doubt liGurvohl had his reasons, he always did, and it was hardly a sergeant's place to demand explanation. Nevertheless, it was only human to wonder, and the rumors were rattling among his fellow Soldiers of the Light.

The consensus seemed to be that the recent Dhrevian proscription of the broken Blowflies organization—a writ authorizing immediate execution of any known member, without recourse to the formality of a trial—had freed the Premier Jurist's attention to focus upon lesser annoyances. It was also said that the proscription had been purchased at the price of liGurvohl's cooperation in the matter of the Dhreve Lissildt's request for a commutation of the Regarded Drempi Kwieseldt's death sentence. If past history was any indication, the Premier Jurist was unapt to relinquish his prey, but he was capable of politic temporization. No mere mortal could hope to fathom the mind of Gnaus liGurvohl, but one fact was clear; the weeks passed, spring had given way to summer, and the Regarded Kwieseldt lived yet.

Shortly after sunset, Orschl and his men brought the closed wagon into Solemnity Square. At such an hour, vehicular and pedestrian traffic had thinned. Better yet, the doctor's appointments were finished for the day. The clutter of carriages no longer blocked access to Number Sixteen, and the waiting room presumably was clear of fluttery female patients, ready to scream and faint at sight of a musket.

They halted the wagon and disembarked, indifferent to the apprehensive, inquisitive glances of passersby. Straight to Number Sixteen they hurried, and kicked the front door open, with a crash that brought the landlord scurrying from his own apartment.

Instantly the astounded Master Einzlaur was seized, shackled, hustled on out to the wagon, and deposited therein.

Dr. Flambeska's door was unlocked. Orschl led them into the empty waiting room, and then through the rooms beyond. They discovered their quarry in his office. Unlike so many others, the Clockwork neither sought ridiculous concealment behind an arras, nor attempted escape by way of the window or chimney. Rather, he sat calmly at his desk, regarding the intruders without apparent fear or even surprise.

"Flambeska of Strell," Sergeant Orschl announced, "I arrest you in the name of the White Tribunal."

"Sergeant, I submit to your authority," Flambeska returned obligingly. "May I know the charge?"

"You will be informed in due course," Orschl told him.

"I understand. The nature of my crimes has yet to reveal itself." The Strellian nodded gravely.

His expression was all but lost in the shadow of the wide hat and the dark spectacles, and yet, Orschl could almost have sworn, the Clockwork communicated something resembling amusement. Odd, but probably meaningless. Malefactors confronting the ultimate disaster not infrequently attitudinized. Fortunately, Flambeska's posturing did not extend to the extreme of resisting restraint, and the manacles closed swiftly and smoothly upon his wrists.

Thereafter, the doctor stood silent and passive between a brace of his captors, while the Soldiers of the Light conducted a thorough search of the apartment. Sergeant Orschl believed in allowing or compelling the prisoner to observe the investigation. In his experience, the inconvenience of enduring complaints, reproaches, accusations, pleas, curses, taunts, and tears was more than offset by the revelations of changing expression.

Not this time, however. Flambeska never so much as blinked. Not when the soldiers searched through his office drawers, shelves, and cabinets. Not when they bayoneted the hangings, cushions, and padded hassocks in his waiting and sitting rooms. Not when they rifled the contents of clothespress and chests in his own bedchamber. Not even when one of those violated containers yielded a piece of evidence likely to carry its owner to the cauldron.

Deep at the bottom of a lion-footed coffer, buried beneath a hundred odds and ends, lay an object carefully wrapped in black velvet. Orschl himself drew it forth, and instinct informed him that he had discovered a prize.

He stripped the dark wrappings away and found himself holding an oval mirror, encased in a simple steel frame, incised with unfamiliar symbols. Foreign alphabet—glyphs—meaningless ornamentation—he didn't know just what they were. For a moment Orschl was disappointed—the expected treasure was only a commonplace trinket—and then he glanced at his own reflected image, and his interest reawakened. The face in the glass was curiously distorted—eyes, nose, and ears hugely exaggerated; forehead, mouth, and chin all but nonexistent. Nothing so astonishing in that—he might spend a copper to see as much at any fair. Although, he recalled, the undulant metal mirrors of his experience furnished wavering, dim reflections at best, while this one was extraordinarily distinct, its colors brilliant to the point of luminosity.

Well, he simply confronted a glass of unusual optic quality.

Very unusual, Orschl discovered, when the image began to change. He watched in disbelief as the glowing outsized eyes bulged from their sockets, the nostrils broadened and gaped cavernously, while the ears unfurled like great bat wings, sprouting spiky points and ruffled efflorescences as they grew. Small, dark pimples popped out all over the mirrored face and hairless scalp. Swiftly the pimples swelled, sloughing their fleshy coverings to disclose countless staring eyes, lidless and slit-pupiled like a lizard's. Presently, a gelatinous cluster of yellowly glittering eyeballs, surrounding a brace of black nostril pits, and framed in frilled leather ear-wings, stared out from the depths of the glass.

He was awake and dreaming, or else he was going mad. Orschl shook his head, but the picture did not change. He rotated the mirror experimentally, to no effect, until he chanced to catch the reflection of one of his subordinates—a massively muscled, crop-haired recruit, whose name he did not immediately recall. The youngster's actual appearance was unremarkable, but there in the glass, Orschl spied a porcine snout, undershot jaw armed with protruding tusks, a wiry bush of lice-ridden hair, and a moist greyish complexion, slicked with the faint iridescence of rotting meat.

He looked up to find the prisoner watching him.

"What is this?" Orschl demanded.

"Sergeant, I will not tell you," returned Flambeska.

"Please yourself, for now. At least you needn't wonder any longer about the charges." Replacing the velvet cover, Orschl slipped the mirror into his pocket. Inwardly, he was surprised. He wouldn't have believed that the Clockwork had it in him.

There was no further conversation as the Soldiers of the Light completed their search. No additional evidence was discovered, but certainly none was needed. When they were done, Orschl and his men took their leave, steering their prisoner through the door and out of the house, past the knot of interested spectators gathered to witness the astonishing arrest of the fashionable Dr. Flambeska. There were catcalls and taunts, and Orschl realized to his indignation that the hostility was directed toward captors rather than captive. Ungrateful slum scum, didn't know what was good for them. He shut his ears against the angry voices.

Straight to the wagon they hurried Flambeska, and locked him in alongside his erstwhile landlord, whose reaction was not observed.

Carriage, prisoners, and Soldiers of the Light departed Solemnity Square.

To Sergeant Orschl, the relatively short journey to the Heart of Light seemed endlessly prolonged, for the mirror in his pocket weighed upon his mind, and he longed to rid himself of the unnatural, blatantly sorcerous gewgaw. He could hardly wait to transfer the contaminated burden to the one back undoubtedly strong enough to bear it, that of the Premier Jurist.

Summer light and warmth spilled in through the open windows of the music room, but Glennian liTarngrav scarcely noticed. She sat at the harpsichord, head bent over the keys, fingers moving of their own volition, and the melody that filled the chamber was darkly agitated as the thoughts that filled her head. But it came to her, as she played, that the sweet, delicate notes of the harpsichord quite failed to convey the intensity of the emotions she sought to express—for that, an entirely different instrument was required, something of altogether greater power, range, and depth. So far as she knew, no such instrument presently existed. Perhaps she needed to invent one herself.

Glennian's moving fingers halted. Never before had it entered her mind to invent a new musical instrument. Never before had she found those currently at her service in any way inadequate. But they were inadequate now. She had felt it repeatedly during the last several days, ever since the news of Dr. Flambeska's arrest had reached her.

Tradain liMarchborg arrested, like his father before him, on charges of sorcery. Unlike his father, unlike almost all thus charged, Tradain was actually guilty. She ought to detest and despise him for that, but she did not. There were extenuating circumstances, after all, for what choice had he really possessed? Whatever he'd done, he wasn't altogether to blame, but the White Tribunal was unlikely to see it that way. The jurists wouldn't care anything for excuses, weak justification, obfuscation; they wouldn't trouble to look beyond the fact that "Dr. Flambeska" had dealt with a malevolence, and so acquired sorcerous powers.

Powers that surely ought to protect him.

Glennian wrapped her arms around herself, cold despite the humid warmth of the air. The questions popped in her mind, the same questions that had repeated themselves tirelessly throughout the recent days. Why had he allowed them to arrest him? Why had he let them drag him off to the Heart of Light, and why did he let them keep him there? For he had the means to save himself, she knew that beyond question, had known from the moment that she'd stumbled in upon his communion with that thing, that being, that—

Presence, he had called it.

She thought of that evening, remembering her own astonished experience of an alien chorus, a gigantic music of the mind, impossible to reproduce upon existing instruments, but perhaps someday . . . The opening chords of a great composition crashed in her mind. That silent miracle had flown to her straight from the intellect of the Presence, and she found that she couldn't believe entirely ill of an entity encompassing such splendor. No matter what the White Tribunal had to say about it.

The Presence had granted power, and Tradain should be able to liberate himself, assuming he was not already mentally shattered or dead; two very real possibilities. Also assuming that his finite resources had not yet exhausted themselves.

He could die in the torture vaults, and she might not hear about it for months, or she might not hear about it at all.

Don't think about it. Glennian resumed her attack upon the

harpsichord. The pretty tones were actively annoying, but better than silence, and so she played on until the squeal of old hinges spun her around
to face the door.

Pfissig entered. He was clad in sober black, in recognition of his
father's gloomy state, but the obnoxious little smile—smirk, actually—that
she abhorred curled his lips. Glennian suppressed a flash of irritation. Her
guardian's son rarely entered the music room. Here, if nowhere other than
her own bedchamber, she considered herself free of his grating presence.
She came within a breath of ordering him out, but managed to swallow the
words. She had no right in the world to issue any such command; quite the
contrary. Pfissig Kwieseldt, as heir to his father's estate, could order *her* out,
should he so choose; out of the music room, out of liTarngrav House itself.
Very likely, he intended exactly that. *And then what?* For she had lived safe
from want only so long as Re'Drempi extended his—hospitality. *Charity.*
She could feel the flush of rage and shame suffuse her face.

"My foster sister," Pfissig intoned ceremoniously.

She stiffened visibly, and saw his smirk widen. The little toad.

"Dear Glennian, in this the hour of our shared grief, I feel it my
duty, as acting master of Kwieseldt Mansion, to strengthen you as best I can
with words of comfort and counsel."

"That is kind." She managed a semblance of graciousness. *Counsel?*
Just what did the pompous twit think he was talking about?

"There is nothing I can say to lessen the pain of my father's loss."

His expression altered, and she believed him sincere at that moment.
But there was more in store, she would have bet her life on it, and sure
enough, the little smile reappeared.

"It is possible, however—and very much to be hoped—that my advice at this time may be of some service to you, in preventing the recurrence
of certain no doubt innocent indiscretions."

"What do you mean?"

"Mind you, *I* should never think ill of you, despite all appearances,
for I know your upright character, and cannot doubt your honor."

Her brows rose.

"Alas that others are petty of mind, filled with scurrilous suspicion,
and always eager to blacken the fairest reputation." Pfissig shook his head.
"Alas that slanderous tongues are heeded, and that the world's sorry judgment cannot be ignored, particularly by those among us most unjustly perceived as guilty by association—"

"Pfissig, would you please just say what you have to say?"

"As you wish. My dear, a word of warning. All the town knows of the arrest of that foreign physician fellow Flambeska, upon charges of sorcery. Far fewer are aware, however, that you have been seen visiting this accused sorcerer's lodgings, and it is better, I think, that the world remain ignorant of so questionable an association."

"Dr. Flambeska is popular and fashionable." Glennian permitted herself an easy shrug. "He has many patients, hence many visitors."

"But how many of them call at the end of the day, when the doctor's scheduled appointments have concluded? And how many are young, unmarried women, gadding about town all alone? And how many of such women share an unfortunate family history, likely to magnify the significance of even the smallest transgressions?"

"Why, I don't know, Pfissig. *How* many?"

"Ah, Glennian." Pfissig's smirk took on a wrinkle of rueful amusement. "It is good to see that trouble cannot quench your spirit. Mind you, I speak as your friend, as your acting guardian—"

Little toad. Wart king.

"As one much concerned for your welfare," Pfissig concluded. "Therefore, let me hasten to assure you that your secret is entirely safe in my hands."

"There is no secret. Yes, I paid a visit to Dr. Flambeska. You may shout that from the rooftops if you wish."

"But I do not wish to shout it from the rooftops, my dear, any more than I should wish to see the news published in the next edition of *The Buzz.*"

A qualm stirred her insides. She kept her face blank.

"It is the appearance that concerns me," he continued feelingly. "The mere appearance of wrongdoing, by which the shallow world too often wrongly condemns, particularly in circumstances so unfortunate as your own. Oh, *I* am certain that you have nothing to hide, *I* am certain that your blameless life might support the most intense public scrutiny, *I* know you are innocent as a rose—but *others* lack my faith, and it is *their* malice that I fear on your behalf. Therefore, be assured that you may rely upon my constancy and my silence."

Glennian nodded, bending her lips into the lackluster imitation of a smile. She wasn't at all sure what he was driving at, or how matters stood between them. He seemed to be dropping all sorts of vaguely threatening hints, that might be neither threats nor hints. It wasn't clear what he actually knew, beyond the fact that she had visited Dr. Flambeska, which in itself meant little. If he knew that, however—in short, if he had been spying on her, as he'd always delighted in spying—then what else might he know?

That casual reference to *The Buzz*—meaningful, sinister, or pure coincidence? She couldn't tell, but one thing she could see—Pfissig was enjoying himself immensely.

"For we are friends, are we not?" He was still rattling on, with an air of sickeningly soulful candor. "Comrades, allies, almost brother and sister, if you will. I trust you recognize the quality of my devotion."

"I believe so."

"That being so, I dare to hope that I may similarly rely upon your lasting affection and loyalty."

The little brute was mocking her, but she wasn't about to challenge him. Inclining her head briefly, she met his eyes with a faint, cool smile.

Pfissig appeared to take it for assent. Bowing gallantly over her reluctant hand, he departed the music room, closing the door behind him with care. Glennian sat quite still. Her heart throbbed, and her blood raced. After a moment she turned and attacked the harpsichord keys with renewed fury.

The steel-framed mirror was glaringly sorcerous in origin, product of malevolent forces, yet the Premier Jurist did not fear it. His own virtue, strengthened by his trust in the protective power of Autonn, shielded him against evil. Thus he was free to examine the mirror at length, to handle and hold it, even to investigate the character of its magical properties. Such study, distasteful though it was, armed him with precious knowledge. He owed it to mankind and Autonn to educate himself.

In some respects, the task proved almost disconcertingly easy, for the mirror yielded its secrets willingly. There was no mystery surrounding its function. The glass obviously offered visually metaphoric reflections of essential reality. Thus it was possible to glimpse the true evil underlying so many a bland and guileless facial mask; a most desirable tool, almost invaluable to the jurist whose task in life it was to observe minutely, to uncover the truth, and to judge his fellow man. No secret malefactor could hope to escape his notice or his justice—no seditious journalist toiling in shadow, no sorcerer concealing vileness behind a virtuous facade. This mirror, properly employed, could cleanse a nation, and serve all humanity.

Something approaching a smile softened Gnaus liGurvohl's beautifully drawn lips. How easy it was to recognize the stratagem whereby the miserable Drempi Kwieseldt had been ruined! Just such an alluring sorcerous device as this one—and of identical origin—had led Kwieseldt astray, deceived and ultimately destroyed him. Almost liGurvohl could find it in his heart to pity the poor wretch a little, for now he understood the seductive power of the temptation.

Fortunately for the nation, however, Gnaus liGurvohl was no Drempi Kwieseldt, foolish and weak at center. Nor would pity for the fallen man blind the Premier Jurist to his duty. For days, even weeks, he had humored the Dhreve Lissildt's caprices, postponing Kwieseldt's execution, but the time for such indulgence was past. Taking up his quill, liGurvohl scribbled out the order of Disinfection, set a date, signed the document, affixed his seal, and rang for his clerk.

Moments later the clerk appeared, and liGurvohl glanced down at the mirror on his desk, angled to reflect the office door and all who entered thereby. He saw the clerk's image, and very peculiar it was, with a meek, lamblike countenance, dull eyes tiny as raisins, little woolly ears, hands terminating in slender transparent tentacles, and a host of crawling black flies, of which the host appeared unaware.

LiGurvohl issued the appropriate commands. His clerk accepted the sealed missive, bowed low, and withdrew.

The mirror reflected an empty office, in perfect, sharp detail. The Premier Jurist could see austere stone walls, monastically sparse furnishings, uncurtained open window, and, through the window, the towers and tripartite domes of Lis Folaze.

What he could not see, however, was his own reflection. Twist and tilt the glass though he might, his face never graced its depths.

The flaw was not in his vision. The office contained no other mirror, but there was a salver of polished silver, and this bright surface showed him his own visage, indistinct but unequivocal. There was something wrong with the sorcerous glass; or else, the elemental force of a wholly righteous subject simply suppressed the power of malevolence.

One way or another, he couldn't see himself.

He had spent some time experimenting with locale and lighting, but the results remained consistent, and his own invisibility seemingly invincible. He did not need to view his countenance, for personal vanity was truly not his failing. Yet the puzzling anomaly rankled, and at length he resolved to satisfy his curiosity. An ambition easily achieved, for the source of knowledge lay close at hand.

Summoning a captain of the Light to him, the Premier Jurist issued orders. The captain saluted and vanished. The minutes passed. Presently Dr. Flambeska entered, in shackles and flanked by guards. LiGurvohl gestured, and the soldiers withdrew. Prisoner and Premier Jurist inspected one another in silence.

Dr. Flambeska, whose patients numbered among the wealthy and titled, had clearly received preferential treatment. His garments remained undamaged, his flesh unbruised, and he had even been permitted to retain his personal belongings, including the dark glasses that so effectively disguised his expression. He might retain them yet, for the Premier Jurist, whose powers of penetration were hardly to be thwarted by so flimsy a barrier, disdained to command an unmasking. LiGurvohl did allow himself a quick glance at the doctor's reflection in the sorcerous glass, but saw there only a dense concentration of shadow, shaped like a man.

He could almost imagine that he had seen the shadow in the past, somewhere, sometime.

Unlike the majority of prisoners, the doctor displayed no sign of fear, hostility, effusive complaisance, or even mild unease. The doctor, in fact, revealed nothing at all; but this was a mask not unfamiliar to the Premier Jurist.

"Flambeska of Strell." LiGurvohl shaped his beautiful voice to express a gravely benevolent authority. "You stand charged with numerous offenses. Chief by far is the charge of sorcery, a crime against humanity deserving of the ultimate penalty. So great is the transgression, and so extreme the punishment, that justice must grant the accused opportunity to answer, prior to his trial. Therefore, I am willing to declare that the strongest evidence against you resides in this mirror—" LiGurvohl's finger tapped the sorcerous glass. "Discovered in your lodgings. What have you to say?"

For a time it seemed that the doctor might not trouble to reply, but at last he spoke. "The Premier Jurist has observed the mirror's singular properties?"

LiGurvohl inclined his head. The Strellian's voice, he noted, although muted and exotically flavored, seemed indefinably familiar.

"Then it is clear how greatly such a device must aid a physician, granting him immediate comprehension of his patients' various complaints."

"You imagine this end justifies recourse to sorcery, Doctor?"

"I have not spoken of justification."

"Is the device of your own manufacture?"

"I am not an artisan."

"An artist, then?"

"A physician."

"That is only part of the truth. Presently we shall discover the entirety. Where did you acquire the mirror?"

"Here in Lis Folaze, at the bottom of a barrel of odds and ends, purchased at the Pigeon Stalls."

"Could you recognize and identify the vendor?"

"I fear not."

"That is unfortunate, for all concerned. Do you claim ignorance of this object's sorcerous character?"

"I claim nothing, Premier Jurist."

"If you purchased the mirror in innocent ignorance, as you describe, then why did you not report the matter to the appropriate authorities?"

"Was I legally obligated to do so?"

"You are a foreigner among us. Do you pretend ignorance of our laws? Or do you believe yourself above them?"

"Your laws have influenced my life profoundly."

"Who revealed the mirror's function to you?"

"Nobody, Premier Jurist. It is possible to learn without assistance. Have you not done so?"

"Well enough to satisfy myself that Autonn does not permit sorcery to operate unimpaired in the world, nor so execrable an object to exist free of significant weakness."

"I am aware of none."

"Perhaps no mind or character among your patients has ever challenged the unnatural capacities of this device. You will note, however, that the glass fails to reflect my image."

Dr. Flambeska stretched forth his manacled hands to adjust the mirror's angle. "I perceive no such failure," he said.

"Your case is singular. You yourself awaken my interest." LiGurvohl steepled his fingers. "I am disposed to grant mercy, even to the extent of sparing you the Grand Interrogation, but such largess can only reward your full honesty and unreserved cooperation. Therefore, cease this vain and puerile sparring, abandon the pride and insolence that cannot serve you in this house of truth. Confess freely, disclose all, and convince me of your worthiness."

Dr. Flambeska maintained silence for some expressionless seconds. At last he answered, "The mirror continues to function. The flaw lies not in the glass, but rather in the beholder's inexperienced vision. Your eyes and mind, Premier Jurist—unaccustomed to stimuli of this nature—fail to register and recognize every visual subtlety."

"Presently you will come to learn that my eyes are never deceived."

"And yet they are untrained in certain forms of observation. It is possible, however, by means of fairly simple procedures, to cleanse the mirror, thus clarifying the images presented to the uninitiated."

"If you are capable of repairing this object, you will do so at once."

"Willingly, Premier Jurist."

Dr. Flambeska's pockets yielded an assortment of small vials, containing pungently aromatic fluids. Gnaus liGurvohl did not recognize the odors, and did not demand explanation. Nor did he choose to observe the details of the physician's sequential application of fluid to glass, deeming such borderline sorcerous proceedings an affront to the purity of his vision. The stinging odor intensified, and he fastidiously turned away from it. He heard the clink of the little vials, the swish of a polishing cloth, and then Flambeska's voice.

"It is done."

Something in those tones struck him. It seemed then that the prisoner's Strellian accent had diminished, or even vanished, but three small syllables furnished inadequate evidence whereby to judge. He turned back to face Flambeska, who wordlessly extended the mirror. LiGurvohl took it, and gazed intently into the newly clarified depths. Still he did not discover the reflected image of his own present reality, but there was a good deal else to see.

Small figures, quite distant, stirred at the bottom of the glass. They moved in a misty world of field and forest. The figures sharpened into focus, and Gnaus liGurvohl beheld the past.

There were three of them, all very young. A slender, fair, rather frail boy, in whom he recognized his youthful self, and two others. A stocky, ebullient, heedless, redheaded lad, equipped with the best clothes, the best gear, the best of everything—young Jex liTarngrav, heir to the family title and vast fortune. And the other, with the black-haired, blue-eyed good looks that garnered such favor and attention everywhere—Ravnar liMarchborg, likewise heir to a High Landguardianship.

Three boys, friends and equals, despite the disparities of fortune. Well, perhaps not entirely equal, for the other two, Jex and Ravnar, were certainly hardier, stronger, faster, and more agile than the youthful Gnaus. Not bolder, however. They didn't possess a jot more courage than he, no more daring or resolve. Sometimes, in fact, they scarcely ventured to follow where he was willing to lead, for there was really no limit to his determination to impress them, particularly Ravnar. For all of that, he could not rid himself of the suspicion that they liked each other better than they liked him.

Time passed, and suspicion hardened into certainty. The other two, Jex and Ravnar, the two future High Landguardians, certainly preferred one another's company, and Gnaus could scarcely comprehend Ravnar's lapse in judgment, for any impartial observer must have acknowledged the inferiority of Jex liTarngrav's intelligence. Jex had nothing to give, nothing remotely approaching the treasures of intellect or the heartfelt devotion that Gnaus was prepared to bestow, but somehow Ravnar seemed hardly to appreciate the worth of the offering. Ravnar was shallow and ungrateful. Gnaus perceived it clearly, but resentment scarcely dampened the quiet intensity of his affection.

The youths in the mirror matured into young men, and they never excluded him, but self-respect obliged Gnaus to busy himself elsewhere, and thus he had gravitated to the great cause that served humanity and lent meaning to his life. He had enlisted in the struggle against the powers of malevolence, he had devoted himself to the destruction of all things sorcerous, and he had discovered that he possessed a natural gift for such work; a talent that swiftly distinguished him, first as an agent of the White Tribunal, and later as a dedicated jurist.

Within the very first year, his personal efforts resulted in a score of Disinfections, and no less than three Enlightenments. His achievements and service were altogether praiseworthy. But somehow, astonishingly, Ravnar and Jex failed to appreciate either. Rather than the commendation and admiration he deserved, Gnaus endured the most galling of criticism. There were complaints, exhortations, debates degenerating into arguments increasingly acrimonious. At last, the Disinfection of the convicted sorcerer Hirj liGeinzlor's entire staff of household servants—all of them, demonstrably accessory to their master's crimes—had ignited the hottest of quarrels. The accusations had flown in both directions, the epithets had burned, unforgettable and unforgivable words had been uttered by all, but especially by Ravnar, who was false, ignorant, vicious, and unworthy. By *Ravnar*, who understood *nothing* . . .

And after that, there was no pretending that Jex and Ravnar were anything other than enemies of Gnaus liGurvohl, and enemies of all mankind.

The years hastened, and the images in the mirror kept pace. Scene after scene flashed by, as if dredged up from the depths of his memory. The Premier Jurist saw the courtroom of the White Tribunal, and the ashen, set faces of the accused. He saw the terror behind the brave stillness, the bewilderment, the incredulity, the incomprehension and horror. He saw the torture vault at the bottom of the Heart of Light. A host of faces blinked in and out of existence; a multitude of screaming mouths and lunatic eyes, a gorgeously colored rush of blood. He could see it, he could hear and smell it, because he was there again, and this time cursed with a greater acuity of vision than he had ever known. This time, he perceived innocence.

The scene shifted to Radiance Square, and he saw the fires, the cauldron, the crowd, the Soldiers of the Light, and the condemned, the numberless condemned. Innocent victims, dying in torment. No—enemies of Autonn and of mankind, necessarily purged from the world. The defense of humanity demanded such sacrifice, but still, their expressions and contortions were dreadful to behold. The mouths were wide open, throats corded, and somehow he seemed to taste the screams that he had never chosen to let himself hear.

The Premier Jurist noticed that the images were shuddering; the hand that held the mirror was trembling. The pictures blurred briefly out of existence, and when the scene again resolved itself, he saw the contemptible little face and form of the treacherous steward, Drempi Kwieseldt. The mirrored lips moved, and the remembered words rang through his mind: *"I am ready and eager to serve the White Tribunal . . . But I do not quite grasp what is required of me."* And he had told Kwieseldt what was required, and the miserable little insect had complied, but that was no reason to dismiss the testimony as unreliable . . .

The image shifted again, and he saw the sallow, unattractively swollen, and tearstained visage of Aestine liHofbrunn, or Aestine liMarchborg as she had still been at that time, and he heard her choked and stumbling voice: *"Never once have I actually seen or heard my husband engage in any sort of forbidden practice."* But the woman had been a noisy lackwit, incapable of recognizing and relating the truth. She had required instruction, the guidance of a stronger mind, and he had provided it. He had helped her to serve mankind, and she had repaid him with betrayal. The universe had exacted its vengeance upon her, but that was no reason to doubt the truth of her testimony against her husband.

Ravnar liMarchborg was guilty, evil, and deserving of punishment. The deficiencies of his wife's character hardly altered that fact.

Briefly, he glimpsed the torture vaults again; the youngest liMarchborg son, an arrogant adolescent echo of his father, freezing and drowning. That spectacle had wrenched the necessary confession out of Ravnar. Even thus, Autonn the Benefactor contrived to arm His servants . . .

The scene shifted again to Radiance Square. There he viewed the dais, the cauldron and fire, the attentive rabble, the unwavering fellow jurists. There was middle-aged, spreading Jex liTarngrav, striving to conceal his own terror, and beside him there was Ravnar, likewise middle-aged, but slim and upright as always, still beautiful, and innocent of wrongdoing. Entirely innocent.

Impossible.

The Premier Jurist raised his eyes to encounter the black glass regard of Dr. Flambeska. "This object is an instrument of malevolence," he declared, and failed, for once, in suppressing every visible indication of anger.

"The visions that it offers are fraudulent and filthy, designed to delude the unwary."

"I myself have never found cause to fault its accuracy," the doctor returned, and this time, there could be no doubt, his voice had freed itself of every Strellian inflection.

Almost upon instinct, liGurvohl slanted the glass to catch Flambeska's reflection, and saw the face of Ravnar liMarchborg; a relatively youthful, but pale and haggard Ravnar, clad in the grey gown of a Strellian physician.

Ravnar was dead, and the mirror a vessel of deceit.

The Premier Jurist subjected the prisoner to an unhurried scrutiny. "Remove your hat and spectacles," he commanded.

Dr. Flambeska obeyed, uncovering Ravnar's face, Ravnar's eyes, exactly as mirrored. Something approaching horror chilled the Premier Jurist for a fraction of a second, before trained intellect resumed its accustomed sway.

"Ah. I see. The youngest son, recipient of our mercy." LiGurvohl thought for a moment, and the name came back to him. "Tradain liMarchborg."

"The Premier Jurist's powers of recollection are formidable."

"Did I not promise that we should discover the truth in its entirety? Presently we shall have it all. Your identity is known, and you stand revealed as a fugitive felon."

"Felon, Premier Jurist? How so? I was convicted of no crime. I received no trial. I was not, insofar as I know, ever formally charged."

"Ravnar liMarchborg's own son, to the very marrow, and doubtless deserving of the same fate."

"What was Ravnar's desert, Premier Jurist? Has the mirror afforded no insight?"

"Its presence in your lodgings marks you as a trafficker in sorcerous goods, at the very least. No doubt there is more to be learned. As for the images within the glass, they are so much visual poison, meaningless and false abominations."

"There you are mistaken. The mirror reflects only the truth, in my experience."

"Your experience warrants the Tribunal's closest attention."

"I have cleansed and clarified the glass," Ravnar's son continued almost conversationally, as if unaware of his own doom. "There is no reality now hidden from the eyes of the Premier Jurist."

The ersatz doctor appeared to issue some sort of obscure challenge, but Gnaus liGurvohl reckoned his own personal strength proof against the forces of malevolence. They could not touch him, he did not fear them.

He raised the mirror to his face, and stared straight into it. This time, as Ravnar's son had promised or threatened, he was able to see himself.

And such a self. Corrupt, almost liquescent flesh, faintly green in color, alive with maggots. Distorted features. Mouth vastly distended, stretching from ear to ear and farther, around to the back of the skull; all but lipless, equipped with steel fangs—a mouth wide open and eternally hungry as a baby bird's. Pointed, tufted ears. Eyes filmed with fiery cataracts. Skeleton hands of old-ivory bone, grasping at everything and everybody. Grotesqueries too numerous to encompass at a glance. But it was the impossible mouth that irresistibly fixed attention upon itself; the mouth gaping to swallow the world, yawning wide enough to split the skull in two, revealing the bottomless vortex within.

Certainly as ghastly a vision as ever devised to confound the judgment of Autonn's servants. Not ghastly enough, however, nor real enough, to cloud the sight of the Premier Jurist Gnaus liGurvohl; at least, not for more than an instant.

For an instant only, liGurvohl confronted the monstrosity, recognized and admitted it. In that moment, his hand moved of it own volition to smash the mirror down upon the desk, shattering the glass into a thousand fragments. The prisoner's gaze pressed upon him in silent anticipation of devastation, and almost the Premier Jurist sensed his own moral identity shuddering upon the verge of violent dissolution. Then the weakness passed, he conquered it and was himself again, contemptuous of the malevolent cheat.

"The strongest evidence," Ravnar's son murmured, never acknowledging the failure of his sorcerous assault.

"Hardly signifies," liGurvohl informed him. "Your own confession, rendered unreservedly, furnishes all the evidence required."

"The matter is all but concluded, then?"

"Beyond doubt. Thirteen years ago you visited the cellars, and your youth purchased gentle handling. Now, you may expect no such forbearance. The enemies of mankind and Autonn must come at last to acknowledge the reality of their guilt, and you are no exception. Down below, you will reveal the deepest secrets of your heart. The way may be lengthy and taxing, but at last, like your father before you, you will yield all."

The Premier Jurist rang, and his Soldiers of the Light answered the summons.

"Below," liGurvohl commanded. "We have dallied too long. It is time to make an end."

Twenty-one

Astonishing how familiar everything seemed. The spiral stairways, the reeking corridors, the airless subterranean passages, the black iron door sunk deep in an oozing stone wall—it was as if he had seen them all yesterday. And beyond the door—the big cellar room, awash with weak reddish light. The instruments of nameless function, the braziers, the blades and cords, the cages and tanks—all just as he remembered.

There was the great glass aquarium, above which Rav liMarchborg had dangled. There was the wire cage in which Zendin liMarchborg had crouched among the constrictors. There was the great glass cylinder, in which he himself had nearly drowned; empty at the moment, but suggestively beaded with moisture. And there was the great oaken armchair, once occupied by the High Landguardian Ravnar liMarchborg. He could still see his father sitting there, still remember the eyes.

LiGurvohl's minions were hurrying him toward that same chair, removing his manacles, strapping him in, and buckling him down. He did not resist, there was no need to resist. He retained his physician's robe—evidently, he was not to echo Ravnar's torments.

A leather strap encircled his brow, binding his head to the back of the chair. A glass dropper filled with colorless fluid approached his face. Impossible to turn away from it. A couple of heavy dollops splashed his eyes. The excess spilled down his cheeks. Eyes and face commenced to burn. He blinked, and the fire intensified. A voice flew from the heart of the fire, a sonorous and well-remembered voice.

"The acidic solution," Gnaus liGurvohl instructed, "presents itself to you in its mildest form. Obduracy and defiance serve only to increase the intensity of subsequent applications. The pain, and the progressive diminution of vision, fulfill a constructive purpose, perhaps incomprehensible to you at this moment. It is my hope, however, that the deepening physical blindness must at last awaken the inner perceptions that sleep within the unregenerate heart and mind. Thus recalled to a sense of your own iniquity, you will long to cleanse yourself."

"How shall I do so?" inquired Tradain.

"Confess all," liGurvohl commanded. "Explain your purpose in returning to this city. Describe in full your dealings with Aestine liHofbrunn, Drempi Kwieseldt, and others, including Glennian liTarngrav. Ah, that last name has touched you, I think. Above all, speak of your sorcerous crime, omitting no particular. Do so, and your sojourn in this cellar is swiftly concluded."

"I see." Tradain was unable to nod. A slight, chill smile bent his lips. "Premier Jurist, in all the years that you have conducted the Grand Interrogation, has it never occurred to you that a prisoner truly guilty of sorcery possesses power to defend himself?"

"That is a commonplace quibble, superficially rational, yet unsound at its core. For the power of sorcery, though boundless in its malignity, cannot match the vast, benevolent strength of Autonn. And we—the jurists of the White Tribunal, the Soldiers of the Light, all of us sworn to the service of our Defender—are well shielded against the forces of darkness. Here in the Heart of Light, all sorcerous shadows are dispelled."

"Possibly. Let us put it to the test." Tradain focused inwardly. So proficient in its use had he grown that no spoken words were required to access his store of arcane power. In stillness and silence, he performed the necessary mental contortions, and when he was done, his eyes had cleared and soothed themselves, while the straps holding him to the chair had dropped away. He rose slowly to his feet.

Some half-dozen guards, torturers, and attendants backed hastily away from him. Gnaus liGurvohl, apparently undismayed, stood his ground.

Tradain liMarchborg spoke inside his own head, sensed the internal radiance of extradimensional force, shaped and aimed it. The oaken chair behind him burst into flame. Vaguely, he heard the cries of alarm arise around him, but scarcely listened. A pair of iron braziers crumbled away in a cloud of rust, scattering their cargo of red embers across the floor. The wooden ladders, scaffolding, and barrels simultaneously ignited, and fires leapt everywhere about the cellar. When the heat grew oppressive, a mental slash split wide the overhead cistern, and freezing torrents poured down upon all.

Water. Aquarium. Turning to the big tank, he shattered it with a psychic blow, and for a moment watched the hundreds of dispossessed carnivorous fish flopping wildly amidst the glass shards.

Glass. Almost without effort, he smashed the great cylindrical instrument of his own past suffering, and the bright flying fragments vaporized in midair.

One of the guards, apparently frantic, sprang straight for him, truncheon flailing. Tradain spoke, and the guard hurtled backward through the air, to crash against the row of cages lining the wall at the shadowy far end of the cellar. The dazed man slid to the floor, where he sat, back pressed to one of the cages, empty wide eyes fixed on nothing. At once, a leathery grey hand, like a man's but far smaller, and armed with curving talons, snaked its way between the bars to close on the guard's neck.

He had all but forgotten the creatures, lurking back there in the gloom, but he remembered now. The constrictors, and assorted reptiles, the starving rats, and others infinitely worse—the unclean hybrid things, the apelike monstrosities, the nameless spawn of swamp and cavern . . .

He stopped their hearts with a wrench of his will, then turned his attention upon the remaining devices of torture. Several of the most cruelly ingenious he melted where they stood, and one he blasted explosively out of existence, but many he did not trouble to destroy, for he was tiring of the sport, and believed his point had been made.

His gaze traveled slowly over the wreckage of the chamber, pausing from time to time upon a human face, and where his eyes lingered, men trembled and cowered. Only the Premier Jurist sustained the scrutiny unmoved.

"There is the power that you term malevolent," Tradain informed the rainwater eyes. "How many of the others have possessed it? Any of them? Do you begin to understand?"

"Malignancy, your deluding arts must fail in this house of truth." LiGurvohl's rich tones conveyed an almost pitying contempt. "Here, your illusions cannot deceive."

"Your vault of torture lies in ruins all about you. Is this illusion, Premier Jurist?"

"Ah, you may destroy gross mundane substance, if you will. Yet you possess no real power over the minds and hearts of Autonn's chosen servants. You cannot hope to resist true purity of intellect—not you, or your father, or any of your vile ilk. Evil invariably fails to recognize its own weakness. Therein lies the seed of its destruction."

"You have filled the world with misery. You have slaughtered blameless multitudes. Ravnar liMarchborg, whom you murdered, was innocent. This you know."

"I know that Autonn ever rules my judgment. I know that I work His will."

"Are you blind, Premier Jurist? Do you comprehend nothing?" Tradain spoke almost in wonder. A nightmare sense of futility filled him. Perhaps Gnaus liGurvohl had spoken truly in calling him powerless. "Does nothing touch your mind?"

"Your education commences," liGurvohl observed. "You begin at last to perceive the worthlessness of malevolent gifts."

"They are sometimes useful," Tradain replied, and several of his listeners quailed.

Gnaus liGurvohl clasped a small silver medallion, engraved with the image of Autonn, lightly between his long fingers. This medallion he now raised like a weapon.

"Fear nothing," liGurvohl advised his underlings, and his voice reverberated strongly through the cellar. "Only trust in the strength of the Defender. All of you, sworn to the service of Autonn, carry His image. Bring forth those images now, and He will shield you against the forces of malevolence."

His minions made haste to obey, and Tradain found himself confronting an array of small silver amulets, held defensively aloft in hands that shook.

"Now return him to his cell," liGurvohl commanded. "Take heart, for this creature of darkness is powerless before the might of Autonn. He cannot resist you now."

"I would not disillusion you," Tradain informed the Premier Jurist. "But I'll go willingly enough, as our business here is finished, and the exchange has wearied me." This was true. The profound exhaustion invariably attendant upon significant feats of sorcery already assailed him, its effect augmented by his own recognition of defeat. He had not intended to wreak such unrestrained havoc, but emotion had for a time excluded prudence. Now, however, in his mind's eye, without the aid of sorcery, he saw the hourglass, still reposing undisturbed in the office desk's secret compartment, where the Soldiers of the Light had not discovered it. The luminous granules were streaming down from the upper chamber, their brightness extinguishing itself, so many of them, flowing so swiftly, that the fear stirred to life inside him, though he never let it touch his face.

His captors were pushing their pathetic little medallions at him, and the temptation to disintegrate those silvery disks was strong, but he couldn't afford such costly self-indulgence. Only one parting declaration he permitted himself.

"Lest you imagine, Premier Jurist, that our time here has been wasted, let me hasten to acknowledge your triumph. You have succeeded in extracting my confession. I am unable to withstand your righteousness, and therefore must admit freely that I have indeed dabbled in sorcery."

Gnaus liGurvohl deigned no reply.

Anxiously brandishing their medallions, the guards herded Tradain back to his tower cell and locked him in. The hours passed. Down below, the shadows crept across Radiance Square.

Around sunset, the turnkey came to thrust a meager meal on a tray through the slot at the bottom of the door, and to address the alarming captive in tones nervously halting. Evidently deeming a courtroom confrontation unnecessary as well as unsafe, the White Tribunal had sensibly elected to try the accused sorcerer Tradain liMarchborg, alias Dr. Flambeska, in absentia. The defendant having tendered his confession before witnesses, the inevitable conviction had been swiftly secured, and sentence promptly pronounced.

All the city already knew of the Regarded Drempi Kwieseldt's impending Disinfection. Today, word had spread that the modest spectacle was to be immeasurably enhanced by the addition of a highborn sorcerer's Enlightenment.

Tomorrow morning.

The cell was black and cold. The straw beneath him was damp and verminous. The Regarded Drempi Kwieseldt lay motionless, his eyes wide open in the dark. A flea bit, and he slapped reflexively, but hardly noted the discomfort, for his mind was fixed on other matters. It was the last night of his life.

Tomorrow morning they would come for him. They would drag him from his cell, lead him through the grim corridors—carry him, should his legs refuse to function—out onto that dais in Radiance Square, where the cauldron bubbled. No doubt the fires already burned beneath the great iron vessel. By dawn, the water would have reached full boil, and they would toss him in like cooks adding a scrap of meat to the soup kettle; live meat, meat that could feel, and fear, and suffer horribly as long as life continued. And life *did* continue, with remarkable persistence. Sometimes the shrieking victims thrashed for endless minutes that seemed like hours, struggling so fiercely to hold off the relief of death, that spectators wondered at the sight. He had witnessed as much himself, upon many a gruesome occasion, and the sight had wakened his pitying curiosity. But never in his wildest imaginings had it entered his mind that one day he himself would—

Kwieseldt shuddered, and a sob broke from him. His last night, and still he did not understand. Sudden disaster had come roaring out of nowhere. There seemed no sense or reason to it, no cause to explain horrendous effect. He did not doubt for one moment that the Strellian physician Flambeska figured somehow in his calamity, but he couldn't begin to imagine why. He and Flambeska were strangers. He had never even offended the doctor, much less harmed him.

But he had harmed others, many others. The Regarded Kwieseldt didn't ordinarily allow himself to dwell upon such unappetizing topics, but the present circumstances were far from ordinary, and now the insistent memories surfaced like floating corpses. No sooner did he manage to thrust one back down into oblivion than another popped up. There were too many to control, and with them there were faces that he didn't want to see, awful faces, worst of which belonged to the High Landguardian Jex liTarngrav.

No escaping the faces of those he had destroyed, or helped to destroy; all those unfortunates, most of them probably blameless as Jex liTarngrav. It occurred to Kwieseldt then that his own ruin smacked somewhat of supernatural retribution, and he wondered for the first time whether the power of Autonn had not intervened to effect justice.

For just it was, he was finally forced to admit to himself, in the dead of his last night. Just, and utterly merciless.

He hadn't the strength to face his fate. Even now, it was not too late to spare himself the agony and horror. He need only dash out his own brains against the stone walls of his cell. He would do exactly that.

The Regarded Kwieseldt sat up in the dark, extended a searching hand, and found the wall beside him. He bumped his brow experimentally against the frigid stone. It hurt. He would have a bruise in the morning.

No. There would be no morning.

He rose from the straw, and stumbled his blind way to the back of the cell. Bending forward from the waist, he prepared to rush headlong at the opposing wall. A single solid impact ought to split his skull wide open, and there was an end to all trouble.

His legs refused to move. In vain his mind screamed commands. His muscles were so much jelly, his bones like boiled noodles.

Kwieseldt collapsed to his knees. Burying his face in his hands, he gave way to racking sobs. He had thought he'd cried himself dry long ago, but such was hardly the case, for the tears flowed copiously; tears of grief, terror, desperation, and regret for lost opportunities. Not long ago, he recalled, he had stood upon Brilliant Bridge at night, watching the river, so swift and strong, so blessedly *cold*. Not like—

He had stood alone upon that bridge, with nothing to hinder his escape into nothingness. Unlike Aestine liHofbrunn, he'd lacked the nerve to act, and now the chance was gone.

The swirling waters of the Folaze that he beheld in his imagination altered character, bubbled and steamed, and now he was staring down into the cauldron. The eyes of a multitude pressed upon him, and the heat was rising from the water, terrible heat, crueler punishment than even the worst of criminals deserved.

But many, many had endured it, and the majority of them not criminals of any description. A number of those innocents he himself had assisted to their doom. How many victims of his own ambition and fear had lain in the Heart of Light, perhaps in this very cell, suffering as he now suffered? How many had contemplated impending torment, and wept in fear, or vomited, or wet themselves, or found the terrified strength to kill themselves?

He had never let himself think about it before, but here in the dark of his last night, the questions could not be excluded.

It seemed to him then that something in his mind shifted, and he saw the world through eyes other than his own, knew thoughts and sensations other than his own. For an instant it was as if he shared the anguished consciousness of his hitherto anonymous victims, and for the first time, those other than his former master became real, and he understood what he had done.

The sorrow that smote him was like no other he had ever known. His tears evaporated in an instant, for they were wholly inadequate. For long minutes, he knelt crushed and paralyzed, his mind filled with a remorse burning hotter than the fires down in Radiance Square, a remorse that left no room for fear. Forgetting the cauldron, momentarily forgetting the imminence of physical pain and death, the Regarded Drempi Kwieseldt lost himself in thoughts of those formerly faceless deceased.

He had no idea how long he knelt there. At last he grew aware that his body was swaying to and fro, on the verge of collapse, and he felt his way on hands and knees back to his damp heap of straw, where he lay down with a sigh. He hardly expected the boon of oblivion, but exhaustion finally asserted itself. His eyes closed, and he slept.

The dreams that came to him were so extraordinarily vivid and immediate that even in his slumbers, he suspected sorcerous agency. He dreamed at first of Jex liTarngrav, an affable and carelessly generous master, never anything but decent to his retainers, and trusting, fatally trusting. Certainly the High Landguardian had never suspected ill of his faithful household steward. He had gone to his death, ignorant of Kwieseldt's treachery. Perhaps he, too, had wondered at the nature of his own disaster.

Now Kwieseldt saw him as he had stood in Radiance Square thirteen years ago, battered and bruised but unbroken, even affecting an air of nonchalance. And torturous remorse renewed itself at the sight, pursuing the Regarded Kwieseldt through the realms of sleep.

Alongside Jex liTarngrav upon that platform stood the High Landguardian Ravnar liMarchborg, likewise guiltless, intrepid, and doomed. He hadn't thought of the master's friend and ally in years—not, in fact, until the evening of Aestine liHofbrunn's incomprehensible access of public honesty. Since then, the liMarchborg name and face had occasionally intruded upon his thoughts, but never before had he endured so achingly clear a vision of Ravnar's suffering and innocence. It didn't last long, however. Presently the two High Landguardians vanished in a blast of killing light, and nothing remained but the guilt and shame stamped forever upon Drempi Kwieseldt's mind.

The dream changed, and he beheld the foreign physician, Dr. Flambeska. Something in the doctor's aspect suggested the immediacy of revelation, and this impression reinforced itself when Flambeska spoke, in tones devoid of Strellian inflection.

"Do you know me, yet?"

"My enemy," Kwieseldt answered, in his dream. "But I don't know why."

"Then see me." Flambeska's concealing hat and dark glasses faded away.

Sleeping Kwieseldt beheld a familiar face, and whispered, "LiMarchborg's ghost."

"*I am no ghost.*"

"A nightmare."

"*Reality.*"

"His son," Kwieseldt remembered, marveling. "There were three. Only two died. LiMarchborg's youngest son."

"*Now do you understand?*"

"Yes, now. You have avenged your father, your brothers, and my master."

"*I have punished the guilty,*" Flambeska/liMarchborg recited mechanically. "*I have achieved a measure of justice.*"

"Yes, it is justice," Kwieseldt conceded. "Are you satisfied?"

"*It remains unfinished.*"

"I understand you. I wish you success with the Premier Jurist."

"*You turn against your present master, as you turned against the former.*"

"No. LiGurvohl is a sickness of which I am finally cured."

"*It comforts you to imagine so.*"

"It's true. I'd gladly give all I have for the chance to prove it. I regret the past, and hate myself for the evil I've done. I only wish, from the bottom of my heart, that I could undo some of it."

"*You say so now. But your regrets are fragile as your loyalties. A breath serves to shatter either.*"

"People change," Kwieseldt insisted.

"*You dream,*" his nemesis observed dryly.

"People learn."

"*But you remain, in life and death, the same traitor and coward that you have always been.*"

"No," Kwieseldt told him. "No. No."

The prodding of a booted foot nudged him awake. Flambeska/liMarchborg faded from his mind. The Regarded Kwieseldt opened his eyes. Morning light filled his cell. Four Soldiers of the Light stood looking down at him.

"Time," one of them announced superfluously.

"You're a cool one, Regarded," another declared, with an air of approbation. "It's not often we find 'em sleeping."

Kwieseldt stood up, rubbing the film from his eyes. Almost before he knew what was happening, they had him by the arms, and they were hustling him efficiently from his cell, along the corridor, and down the stairs.

There were no manacles, no fetters of any sort, and he remembered that the subjects of Disinfection were never restrained, for the extravagance of their contortions greatly enhanced the visual appeal of the spectacle. The thought stiffened his limbs, but never slowed his progress, for his captors handled him with such skill and speed that there was hardly time for resistance; hardly time for anything beyond a single thought, that he needed desperately to clarify while he still could.

The consequences were significant, they involved Pfissig, and he wanted some time to think, but there was none.

It was all happening so fast.

Down the stairs to a surprisingly small and mean little corridor, where the governor of the prison awaited, all decked out in his feathered hat, and his quasi-military uniform that meant nothing. With the Governor stood a couple of spit-and-polished flunkies, but no prisoners. The loquacious DeTretz had died days ago, and there were no other parties to the crime. Thus, the Regarded Kwieseldt would have the cauldron to himself.

The hallway terminated in a heavy wooden door. Somebody opened it, and the summer sunshine spiked into the Heart of Light. Kwieseldt's eyes closed involuntarily against the light, but he opened them again as soon as he could, for he hadn't seen the world in a long time, and this was the last opportunity. They hurried him forward, and he felt a warmth upon his face, and his lungs swelled to drink the fresh, soft air.

He blinked, and the scene sharpened itself. He stood upon the black and white stone platform abutting the Heart of Light. In front of the platform stood ranged the vigilant Soldiers of the Light. Before him loomed the great iron cauldron, its contents not to be glimpsed from his present vantage point, but he heard the deep grumble of boiling water, and the heat slammed through the air at him. He turned his face away from it. The Governor was reading the record of his crimes, conviction, and condemnation, and he didn't need to listen; it was all too familiar.

At the far end of the dais stood the big thronelike armchairs, occupied by the ocher and black city magistrates and by the snowy jurists of the White Tribunal. The central seat of honor belonged to the Premier Jurist, and for once, Drempi Kwieseldt met liGurvohl's colorless eyes unflinchingly. He had braced himself to withstand hostility, contempt, and menace, but he might as well have saved himself the trouble. The Premier Jurist's gaze was empty of all save impersonal purpose.

Kwieseldt's eyes slid away from liGurvohl's visage to roam the crowd, and what he saw there—or rather what he didn't see—came as a faint surprise. There was little of the collective avid anticipation that he remembered so well. The faces he now beheld were stiff with reserve, discontent, and doubt; not the carnival countenances of the past at all. He even thought to glimpse some sympathy here and there, and the sight heartened him, lending strength to his shuddery resolve.

He would speak. He would—

The Governor was concluding.

His mind seemed half-crippled and numbed with terror beyond comprehension, but he needed to find the words, and there was no time to find them, no time to think, for the guards were leading him up the makeshift stairs to the platform overhanging the cauldron, and they were experts at such work, and it was all going very fast indeed.

They meant to permit no delay. He must make his own opportunity, somehow. He must—

I must— He had thought he was speaking aloud, but no sound emerged, which was a pity, for the audience was intensely silent and he might be heard, if only he could force his voice to obey. His mouth was dry, and he could not moisten his lips, but somehow he managed to swallow, and then the words came out, abrupt and unsteady, but audible enough.

"I want to say something."

A man was entitled to a few last words. A rustling stirred the crowd, a quiet manifestation of powerful affirmation. To Kwieseldt's surprise, his executioners responsively checked. The respite was certain to measure itself in seconds, no more. He swallowed again, and spoke.

"I'm about to die, and I admit I deserve it. Not so much for anything I tried to do to the Premier Jurist, but for what I did to my master, the High Landguardian Jex liTarngrav, thirteen years ago. I testified before the White Tribunal that I saw my master practicing sorcery, alongside his friend, Ravnar liMarchborg. I swore I'd seen it with my own eyes. Well, I never saw anything of the kind. It was all a lie. I made it up because *he*, Gnaus liGurvohl, told me to." Drempi Kwieseldt pointed an accusing finger. His eyes met the Premier Jurist's. What he saw there would have terrified him once, but not now.

"Look at the Premier Jurist, sitting over there like some sort of king of justice on his throne. Let me tell you all, he's a fraud. Thirteen years ago, he was out to get my master and my master's friend liMarchborg, but he didn't have any evidence against them, because they were innocent. But liGurvohl wasn't about to let a little detail like that stop him. So he went to liMarchborg's wife and got her to perjure herself for him, and then he came to me and did the same. I obeyed out of fear and greed. He told me I'd get my master's property if I cooperated, and the cauldron if I didn't."

Pfissig would never have liTarngrav House now. Unfortunate, but Pfissig was a sharp lad, he'd manage all right, and there were some things more important than real estate. Eyes still locked with the Premier Jurist's, Kwieseldt continued, and now the words were coming easily, almost pouring out of him.

"So I did as I was told, and my master Jex liTarngrav died, and Ravnar liMarchborg and his sons died, together with a gang of servants and retainers whose names I never even knew, more shame to me. But that wasn't the end of it, no. After that, I became the Regarded Kwieseldt, a rich man, but it was as if liGurvohl owned me. I had to keep giving him what he wanted, and that meant speaking up for the White Tribunal at court, and joining the League of Allies, and sending I don't know how many innocents to the cauldron over the years. And now I've come here myself, and that's only fitting. I wish my death could right the wrongs I've done, but it won't—nothing can. All I can do to help matters now is to tell the truth.

"That's what I've done, and I'm glad of it." Tearing his eyes from liGurvohl's, Kwieseldt turned to face the spectators, who were staring as if spellbound. "And I swear to you all, with my dying breath, that everything I've said to you is true."

Gnaus liGurvohl signaled the seemingly tranced executioners, and a firm shove thrust Drempi Kwieseldt from the platform.

Kwieseldt's scream was lost in the roar of the crowd. The heat and horror flew at him, and then a merciful blackness swallowed his mind.

Tradain liMarchborg's tower window overlooked Radiance Square, affording an unobstructed view of the dais, the cauldron, the executioners, and the victim. He watched the proceedings with much interest, and when Drempi Kwieseldt paused at the edge of the platform to address the crowd, he clearly heard the condemned man's every word. Those words more than surprised him. He stood staring down at the filthy, bedraggled, but curiously dignified figure of his ruined enemy, and a sharp, unfamiliar pang knifed through him.

He pitied Kwieseldt, he realized. At that moment, he even respected the man, which was all wrong. Drempi Kwieseldt, perjurer and traitor, was finally confronting the fate that he so richly deserved. A brief, belated display of courage and honesty altered nothing. Tradain liMarchborg had punished the guilty. He had achieved a measure of justice, and his hour of triumph had at last arrived.

Remarkable how empty triumph could be, how devoid of sense and meaning.

But surely justice possessed meaning, if anything in the world did.

Intrinsic value had to exist, in order to justify the price he had paid. An instant's agony in the cauldron? What was that, compared to an eternity of the Radiant Level?

Justice was worth any price. So he inwardly assured himself, again and again.

Kwieseldt's remarks concluded, his body hurtled for the cauldron, and Tradain's mind flashed.

To rule the intelligence of others is costly, Xyleel had taught him, and he was aware of no such intention, but found his instincts working almost independently of his conscious will to focus and project the sorcerous power that plunged Drempi Kwieseldt in an instant to the blackest depths of insensibility.

Kwieseldt hit the water, and sank without a struggle. There was no way of judging whether the heat killed him before he drowned. In either case, he felt nothing, and those spectators desirous of sprightly entertainment were disappointed.

But disappointment hardly seemed the prevailing mood. The citizens buzzed and seethed. There was anger or else indignation down there, confusion, intense restlessness, and perhaps some alarm. Probably they sympathized with the victim, perhaps even admired him. Tradain could scarcely read the crowd, or even read himself. He had gone to the ultimate lengths for the sake of justice and/or vengeance. He had let no fear or scruple hinder him, and now, at the very moment of fruition, he had squandered precious resources to spare a guilty foe torture.

It made little sense. He only knew that he felt distinctly better for having done it. But there was no time left to ponder the matter, for the door of his cell was squealing open, and there were the tense, apprehensive Soldiers of the Light, shoving their fanciful little images of Autonn in his face.

He offered no resistance as they affixed the irons to his wrists, ankles, and throat. Once they thought they had him properly secured, their confidence returned, and their tension palpably eased. A couple of them even exchanged uneasy jests as they shepherded the complaisant prisoner from his cell to his doom.

They pushed him through an open door out into sunlight and summer air rich with the smell of boiling flesh. A low murmur swept the crowd at sight of him, and he felt the pressure of countless eyes. Hostile, sympathetic, indifferent—he could not tell. A few feet distant, the boiling cauldron loomed, but they were not taking him to it. At the center of the stage, a great, rectangular flagstone had been removed, and the area uncovered by the displaced stone gleamed black and smooth as polished nothingness. He remembered it well. To this glinting void, the soldiers brought him, chained him closely to staples sunk in the stone, and left him there.

Thirteen years ago, his father had stood upon this spot, and he himself had watched from one of the windows above. From his present vantage point, the place looked different, larger. Radiance Square was packed with humanity, and yet he felt himself standing alone upon a black desert.

The Governor stepped forward to read off the name and title of the condemned, the list of convictions, and the resulting sentence.

"The High Landguardian Tradain liMarchborg—"

The crowd rippled at the sound of that name, and Tradain himself favored the Governor with a startled glance. In all the years, he had never considered his own inheritance of the title that should have gone to his oldest brother. If he had thought of it at all, he would have assumed that the liMarchborg name had been stripped of all rank and privilege long ago, but evidently the Dhreve had never set his seal to the required documents. Amusing time and place to discover it.

The chief charge was sorcery. The sentence was Enlightenment.

The Governor concluded. The Premier Jurist liGurvohl, hitherto motionless, took a single pace forward, lifted his arms, and began to speak.

As the rhythmic syllables of the ancient Invocation poured from liGurvohl's lips, the audience froze into awestruck immobility, and even Tradain caught his breath, impressed despite his thorough comprehension of the mechanism at work. The Premier Jurist did not know it, but the archaic syllables that he accurately parroted in his splendid voice merely activated Yurune's sorcerous black-lens, secreted beneath the dais so many years ago.

As liGurvohl spoke on, the summer air thickened and darkened above the stage; swirled, slowed, and gradually coalesced. When the hidden black-lens caught and focused the collective expectations of the spectators, the mists overhead luminesced, the atmosphere chilled perceptibly, and a visual Receptivity glowed its way into being. And there, once more, hovered the false image of mankind's Benefactor Autonn, with His face of sorrow, strength, and wisdom; His look of suffering benevolence; His countless wounds bleeding darkness in midnight jets.

The crowd sighed, and tears flowed. Even Tradain was struck by the beauty and power of the Receptivity, and for a moment stood fascinated.

Rainwater eyes aglow with intense emotion, Gnaus liGurvohl addressed himself to Autonn's likeness, and the sonorous fervencies rolled out over Radiance Square.

An almost tentative light beaming from the hitherto black space beneath his feet broke Tradain's momentary paralysis. A few feet below, Yurune's device readied itself for replenishment, and such a process, once fairly under way, was not easily halted.

In silent stillness, he exerted arcane force, filling the hidden black-lens with his own desires and assumptions, to the exclusion of all others.

The Receptivity correspondingly altered.

The luminous countenance of Autonn flickered. The strong contours softened, features melting and running like candle wax. Glowing gobbets dropped away. The lower jaw unhinged itself and broke off. The omniscient eyes oozed from their sockets, to slide slowly down the wavering cheeks.

Shrieks of terror greeted the spectacle. The audience roiled violently, and many a citizen fled Radiance Square.

The gouts of shadow spurting from Autonn's multifarious wounds expanded to efface the Benefactor's visage. For some moments a broad spread of blackness lowered above the dais. Then the shadow began to flake away, its remnants crumbling to a dust of darkness that disappeared quickly, uncovering a new image.

The identity was not immediately apparent. The audience beheld corrupt flesh, faintly greenish, and alive with maggots; skeleton hands; dis-torted features—pointed ears, fiery blind eyes, and steel-fanged mouth, gap-ing hugely to swallow all the world. At least a couple of seconds elapsed before the citizens recognized their Premier Jurist as he had appeared in Dr. Flambeska's sorcerous mirror.

⊱ ⊰

Gnaus liGurvohl knew the image at once, and perceived at last the magni-tude of the threat. In vain he signaled his minions to transfer the prisoner immediately to the cauldron. The eyes of the fools were fixed upon the malevolently limned visage glowing overhead. They did not understand their master's commands, or else dared not obey.

But the citizens knew him now, knew him as the forces of darkness might desire Autonn's faithful servant to be known, and their howls con-veyed terrified execration.

Weak-minded, pitiable fools, blinded by sorcerous deception. Such ignorance punished itself. And yet, the popular stupidity was understand-able, in view of the circumstances, for who among these ordinary sheep could hope to withstand the deluding power of malevolence?

It was enough to confound almost any commonplace so-called intel-ligence. Even now, the image overhead was changing, the unspeakable portrait giving way to a seemingly more reasonable, yet far more inflammatory vision of the very recent past.

There overhead, liGurvohl beheld the stage, the cauldron, the condemned, his guards and executioners, magistrates, and jurists. At the center of it all, he saw himself, arms uplifted, lips shaping the syllables of the Invocation. He saw the summer air darken in response. And he saw more.

The low stone wall supporting the pictured dais assumed an impossible transparency, allowing the spectators clear sight of the hollow crawlspace beneath the stage. Within that space, positioned below the translucent expanse supporting the immobilized prisoner, rested an unmistakably sorcerous device comprising a bronze frame and a blackly luminous lens. The lens appeared to pulse, and light flared from its dark heart, to paint pictures on the mists swirling above.

The outrageous implication of trickery was obvious; equally obvious was the imbecilic popular response. Truly, malevolent guile knew neither shame nor limit, yet a faithful servant of Autonn need fear no sorcery.

The angry voices were rising everywhere. The audience had lost all sense of suitable decorum. These gullible, impertinent children had forgotten themselves, and they required instruction.

"Citizens of Lis Folaze." LiGurvohl effortlessly filled the square with his voice. "Hear me. This vision that you see before you now is sorcerous in origin, born of malevolent power, and putrid with deceit. Turn your eyes from it, look not upon it, lest your minds sicken, and your hearts die—"

To his astonishment, the uproar hardly abated at his command. In fact, the shouting increased in volume. The noise and confusion were overwhelming, yet individual voices could still be distinguished, crying out, "The proof! The proof!"

And now a band of riotous citizens rushed forward to attack the low, heavy portal guarding the crawlspace beneath the dais. The door was secured with a stout lock, but they were beating it with stones that seemed to have materialized out of thin air. Someone produced a crowbar, and the old door yielded almost at once. A nameless apprentice boy, lithe as an Oblivion eel, ducked into the darkness beyond, emerging seconds later with the radiant, pulsing black-lens firmly clasped in his hands. Leaping up onto the dais, the apprentice raised the lens and held it aloft, exposed for some moments to the view of the multitude, then flung the instrument down to shatter upon the stone pavement.

The image hovering overhead instantly vanished, and the crowd convulsed.

They had forgotten everything, it seemed; forgotten duty, reverence, order, and civilized restraint—forgotten even Autonn. It was up to a wiser mind to guide and control them. The Premier Jurist advanced a couple of stately paces.

"Blind, foolish, and insolent children," he gravely rebuked his unruly inferiors. "What insensate wickedness is this? Have you forgotten our Benefactor, whose sufferings alone preserve you? Cease this shameful outcry, and lift your voices in entreaty. Implore the mercy of Autonn, humble and abase yourselves—"

The whizzing stone that grazed his forehead took Gnaus liGurvohl by surprise. His voice cut off at once. The hand he raised to touch his brow came away wet with blood, which he regarded in amazement.

Shocked silence enveloped Radiance Square, as if the witnesses could scarcely believe that he would actually bleed. Then the world unfroze, and the furious voices rose anew, countless voices, swelling to a frenzied hurricane roar. The rocks flew, pelting the Premier Jurist and his lesser colleagues of the White Tribunal, where they clustered palely at the far end of the dais.

For a moment longer liGurvohl strove to admonish them, but could not make himself heard. He stumbled backward, arms raised in a futile effort to ward off the rocks. As he retreated, his glance instinctively sought the center of the platform, where the chained prisoner stood watching him. He looked straight into the blue eyes of Ravnar's son, saw there nothing but illimitable emptiness, and knew in a flash of terrible certainty that he beheld no mortal man, but a disguised malevolence, come to work evil in the world.

Gnaus liGurvohl tried to warn them. The impious, ungrateful citizens of Lis Folaze had proved themselves unworthy of his care, and yet he could not abandon them, even now. Thus he strove to speak, but the mob was surging like the sea, the vanguard crashing upon him, and he was caught up, tossed this way and that, beaten, torn, and spat upon. Then their hands were upon him, and they were dragging him up the wooden stairs to the brink of the platform overhanging the cauldron.

He recognized their unbelievable purpose, but knew no fear, for Autonn would surely protect His most devoted servant. It seemed to Gnaus liGurvohl then that time must have slowed or halted, for his staring gaze swept Radiance Square, and in that split second he saw all of it; riotous lunatic crowd howling everywhere, attacking and rending his fellow jurists, assaulting the Heart of Light itself, battering the door down and violating the corridors consecrated to the service of Autonn. And worse yet, *horrifying*, he saw misguided fools striking the fetters from the prisoner, releasing the camouflaged malevolence, blindly loosing the final destruction upon themselves and all the world. LiGurvohl looked at the creature clothed in the likeness

of Ravnar liMarchborg's son, and at last discerned the inhuman reality behind the mask. He beheld a dark and terrible form, grotesque, obscenely
misshapen, with insatiable eyes glaring in triumph.

Nobody else seemed to see it; nobody else possessed sufficient purity
of moral vision to penetrate the creature's disguise. But Autonn would not
be deceived, and Autonn would intervene—

The Premier Jurist felt himself lifted, and flung through the air. The
boiling sea rose to meet him, and he hit the water not far from the bobbing
corpse of Drempi Kwieseldt. For a split second he believed that the Benefactor shielded him against pain, and then it struck, greatly surpassing anything that he had ever imagined. But somehow consciousness persisted. The
seconds lengthened into centuries, the agony continued, and neither death
nor Autonn came to cut his torment short.

He was still fully conscious and cognizant as five of his fellow jurists
dropped screaming into the cauldron, in quick succession. Those others
succumbed swiftly. Their cries faded, and they vanished beneath the churning waters, one after another. But the life spark of a truly righteous man was
not so easily quenched, and the Premier Jurist suffered on. Above him,
edging the cauldron, he could see his misled murderers, faces aflame with
ignorant rage and hatred, contorted mouths spewing abuse in filthy floods.

Directly above, he could still glimpse the soft, cool blue of the summer sky. And then a shriek of bitter despair was wrung from the Premier
Jurist Gnaus liGurvohl, as a vast, expanding darkness seemed to rise, inter-
posing itself between himself and the sky, and he recognized the shape of
victorious evil.

Twenty-two

Tradain sat in his father's study, observing the hourglass that stood before him on the desk. He had spent his powers freely throughout these recent months, never counting the cost to achieve his end, and the glass reflected his prodigality. Lightless ash all but filled the lower compartment. A small quantity of active matter glowed on. He might, with care, hoard the remaining granules for decades to come, consuming them one at a time or not at all. On the other hand, a single significant act of sorcery was apt to exhaust the supply.

So?

He looked away from the desk. His eyes traveled the study. The shelves, books, and sparse furnishings were clean. So too were the rooms immediately beyond, those of the suite once belonging to Ravnar liMarchborg. His own, now.

But were they, really? In the aftermath of the ferocious uprising in Radiance Square, involving the slaughter of some half-dozen jurists, including Gnaus liGurvohl himself—the murder of the Governor, various guards, turnkeys, torturers, and random drudges belonging to the Heart of Light—the liberation of all prisoners, the thorough destruction of the courtroom, and the Dhreve Lissildt's subsequent suspension of the White Tribunal—following all of that, certain legalities tended to blur themselves.

The rightful ownership of the liMarchborg townhouse, for example. In all probability, a petition to the Dhreve would eventually result in the return of the ancestral property to the scion of the original proprietors. Many wrongfully confiscated estates throughout Upper Hetzia were currently undergoing exactly such a process of reversion. Tradain liMarchborg, however, had troubled to submit no such petition, and it seemed reasonable to assume that title to the house rested yet in the hands of the Lady Aestine's second husband, Kreinz liHofbrunn.

But the Honorable Landsman liHofbrunn seemed indifferent. It could hardly have escaped careful Kreinz's attention that the house once deeded to his wife was now occupied, but he chose not to acknowledge, much less challenge, the resident High Landguardian liMarchborg. Perhaps he deemed the battle hopeless, or else intensely distasteful; either way, he kept his reasons to himself.

Thus Tradain was free to live in his father's house, and to do with it as he would, but somehow he could find the energy and will to do almost nothing. He'd had Ravnar's apartment dusted, and he'd brought in his own belongings, collected from his former lodgings. The withdrawal from Sixteen Solemnity Square had been mandatory, for Master Einzlaur, liberated from the Heart of Light during the riot—uninjured but understandably rattled by the experience—had made it clear that the ersatz Dr. Flambeska was no longer welcome. The transfer itself had been easily accomplished, for his great bulk of silver auslins had been changed for paper currency and/or invested long ago, while his personal belongings scarcely filled a single leather valise. Those belongings, such as they were, reposed in Ravnar's rooms.

The rest of the house remained as he had found it. Canvas covers shrouded the furnishings and chandeliers, dust lay everywhere, and the shutters continued tightly nailed against the misty sunshine of autumn. The place resembled a dim, spacious mausoleum. He really ought to open the windows and let some air and light in, for he could use both. He hadn't set foot out-of-doors in—how long had it been, now? Days? Longer? The only human face he had seen in all that time had been that of the delivery boy from the nearest cookshop, and even then, there was no conversation. He ought to do something about that, and he meant to, at some point or other, when he got around to it.

Nothing he could think of doing about it seemed worth the bother. His task was finished, and so was everything else.

He had punished the guilty. He had achieved a measure of justice. In doing so, he had assisted in the overthrow of the White Tribunal, a considerable bonus. Glennian and her surviving Blowfly friends must be so pleased; probably, all of Upper Hetzia was pleased. So he assumed, but could hardly judge with any certainty, for he hadn't spoken or communicated with Glennian liTarngrav since the day she had discovered his connection to the Presence Xyleel.

She had told him then that she would come back, and she never had, but that was certainly not her fault. A half dozen of her notes requesting a meeting lay unanswered on the desk before him. She scarcely deserved such discourtesy, and it wasn't as if he didn't wish to reply. For even as the world beyond the silent confines of the townhouse seemed to recede, assuming a dreamlike insubstantiality, as it had throughout his dungeon years, somehow Glennian liTarngrav managed to retain her reality. He could see her face, and hear her voice, as clearly as if she stood before him. And much as he might wish to grasp the hand she extended, conscience barred him from poisoning her with his touch.

There could be but one conclusion to his presently aimless existence. Whatever the mechanism of his physical dissolution, beyond it lay perpetual agony in the service of Xyleel. And Glennian liTarngrav's generosity could find no possible reward other than contamination.

Best keep her out of it.

He didn't want to dwell on Glennian, but the alternatives were worse. If he didn't fill his mind with her face, then the other faces came. Aestine's, sallow and bloated with tears, unalterably uncomprehending. Drempi Kwieseldt's, weak and avaricious, but ultimately truthful, and filled with unexpected dignity. The Premier Jurist Gnaus liGurvohl, viciously protective of humanity to the end. He had succeeded in destroying them all, justice had been served, and the world was arguably the better for it.

Congratulations.

There was no point in self-recrimination. For him, now, there was no point in much of anything.

Glennian would disagree. . . . *Still young . . . intelligent . . . active . . . much that might be done . . .* He could almost hear that musical voice of hers.

He did not want to hear her, or think of her. He did not want to think at all. Thought burned.

Time to end it.

This idea, he now realized, had been quietly nourishing itself in darkness for some weeks past. He had never before let it seep up into his awareness, but now his mind was ready and receptive.

The right time, the right action.

Repeatedly, the Presence Xyleel had chosen to manifest Himself spontaneously. Only once had Tradain liMarchborg actively sought the entity that men called malevolent. Now, he would do it again.

Last time, in the workroom of Yurune the Bloodless, he had relied upon the stimulus of desperation to boost his mental energy to the necessary level. Now, he would rely upon experience and determination.

His lips were already shaping the arcane syllables. His mind shifted position. He began to speak, and time suspended itself. His concentrated awareness threaded a perilous path between dimensions, and he launched his summons off into the void. Terror of permanent separation from his own body drew his questing intellect home, but not before he knew that his call had been heard.

Tradain opened his eyes. He sat in his father's study, which appeared empty, but he sensed the invisible, chilling proximity of Xyleel. He shivered, and the hairs stirred along his forearms. He did not know why the Presence should so cloak Himself, but who could hope to fathom such a mind?

He need not fathom, but only communicate.

"Great Xyleel." Tradain spoke aloud, as was his usual inclination. "I have called upon You, to make it known that I am ready to conclude. I have done all I set out to do, and now I am prepared to yield myself unto You."

No ghost of a reply, but he thought to catch the vibration of remote curiosity, and knew that additional explanation was required.

"My purpose has been fulfilled, my task completed. Nothing is left to me now beyond memory and the torment of anticipation. I would cut both short."

The Presence Xyleel, although unmistakably near and attentive, vouchsafed nothing.

Tradain found himself afflicted with a senseless urge to explain himself to the silent other.

"It has all been meaningless," he confessed. "I did what I was impelled to do, what I thought would set the balance right—'balance' is as good a way of putting it as any—and I thought that would make a great difference. It has not. I succeeded, but failed."

Still no response from Xyleel, and something constrained him to continue, "I believe I acted for the best, although that was incidental. Be that as it may, it hasn't given me what I wanted or expected. No peace, or rest, or satisfaction. The sum of destruction has brought little beyond doubt, remorse, and a disgust of myself that never fades."

Briefly he awaited the other's answer. There was none. There was nothing at all, and yet Xyleel was present, and listening.

"But that is no care of Yours." The dead air sponged up his words. "You granted me all that You promised, and now I am willing to make good my debt. There is nothing left for me here, and I am very tired. Take me now. We have dallied too long. It is time to make an end."

No answer. No flicker of responsive sentience.

"Xyleel."

Nothing. The renewed warmth stealing along Tradain liMarchborg's veins told him that his visitor had departed.

"Glennian, a word with you, if I may," Pfissig requested.

Glennian suppressed a sigh. An interview with Drempi Kwieseldt's loathsome son was the last thing in the world she wanted, but the confrontation was inevitable, and now was as good a time as any. She nodded with such graciousness as she could muster.

"May we sit?"

"Very well." Her reluctance deepened. His presence in the music room was objectionable as ever. There was much comfort to be found, however, in the knowledge that she would not have to endure it for much longer.

They took a couple of chairs beside one of the tall windows. He had spruced himself up for the occasion, she noticed. He wore the sickly persimmon brocade that emphasized the purple-red of his chronically inflamed and congested nose. Her own nose wrinkled. He was wearing some sort of perfume, too musky, and far too strong. Silently she wondered if there were any way of increasing the distance between them without overt rudeness.

"You are looking quite contented, my dear. Quite—sleek." Folding his hands neatly in his lap, he smiled.

What in the world had he to smile about? Glennian masked her uneasiness with a cool lift of the brows. She said nothing.

"No doubt you have reason." Pfissig paused, but there was no reply, and he continued, "I have been given to understand, by certain well-wishers, that you have petitioned the Dhreve Lissildt for the reversion of Kwieseldt Mansion."

LiTarngrav House! Aloud, Glennian answered simply, "Yes, Pfissig, I have."

"And you are also applying for the return of certain funds, confiscated by the White Tribunal, and diverted to the Kwieseldt coffers, at the time of your father's conviction?"

"His wrongful conviction."

"To be sure. But you have submitted such an application?"

"Yes." *How does he always discover things?*

"And your chances of success are high?"

"I believe so."

"So do I. Well. No wonder you are looking so pleased with yourself these days. An heiress, once again! Allow me to express my very great happiness in your behalf."

"Thank you." She noted his unflagging little smile, and some compunction stirred within her. His situation was pitiable, after all. "Listen, Pfissig. I understand what a painful and difficult time for you this must be. I want you to know that I'll do what I can to ease matters." It crossed her mind to promise him a permanent home at liTarngrav House, but she couldn't bring herself to do it. Half the joy in reacquisition lay in the prospect of Pfissig's ejection. She could offer him money, however. A good cash settlement, or else an allowance, whichever he preferred. That should certainly do. "You won't lack," she promised.

"You are very generous. Very charitable. As my own father was to you, for so many years."

The less said about your father, the better. How dare you mention that lying, treacherous hypocrite to me? The words trembled on the tip of her tongue, but she suppressed them. Pfissig was already bereft, and soon to be impoverished, through no fault of his own. No point in further lacerating his feelings. She could think of nothing to say, but reply was unnecessary, for he was still talking.

"So many, many years," Pfissig continued nostalgically. "Have you ever stopped to consider, Glennian, how many years the two of us have known one another? We have grown up in the same household, and our lives have intertwined since earliest childhood. In recent years, owing to certain reversals of fortune, our intimacy has increased, and we have come to entertain the mutual tenderness and affection of true siblings, have we not?"

"Ummm." Glennian's brows drew together. *Mutual distrust and animosity of true, natural enemies, don't you mean?*

"Of late, however," he confided, "I have come to realize that my feelings for you transcend the simple devotion of a brother. They are deeper, stronger, and more complex. They are, in short, the tender emotions of a faithful admirer, who desires above all things to make you his wife."

His wife! She could not have heard him correctly.

"Dearest Glennian, will you not make me the happiest of men?"

She'd heard him correctly. Was it some sort of joke, or had he gone mad? He wasn't at all stupid, and he certainly recognized her lifelong dislike of him. What sort of strange game was he playing?

Torn between laughter and anger, Glennian stared at him. He didn't look as if he were joking. His demeanor was eagerly expectant, but that obnoxious little smile of his lingered, and the sight set the alarm bells clanging in her head. She didn't know why it should, for she surely had nothing to fear from Pfissig Kwieseldt—not any longer.

"Here we shall live, the two of us together all our days, as master and mistress of Kwieseldt Mansion," he was rattling on rapturously, as if he actually imagined it possible. "Perhaps, in time, if fortune favors us, we shall find ourselves blessed with stalwart sons to carry on the name of Kwieseldt—"

"Stop there," Glennian interrupted. That amorphous sense of danger was stronger than ever, but she wasn't about to let it stop her from terminating the absurd scene. "I appreciate your interest, and I am sensible of the honor you have done me. Nevertheless, I must in all candor confess that I do not entertain for you the appropriate feelings of a wife toward her husband, and I frankly doubt that I ever shall. Therefore, I am obliged to decline your offer. Please accept my regrets, together with my hopes for your future happiness elsewhere."

There. That had been civil enough. At least she'd controlled her natural if unkind inclination to laugh in the little toad's face. How was he taking it? She studied him. He didn't look in the least hurt or despondent. Quite the contrary, in fact. His expression reflected a certain secret satisfaction that disquieted her.

"I am very disappointed, and very sorry to hear that," Pfissig remarked, with patent untruth. "Disappointed for my own sake, and sorry indeed, my dear, for yours."

He was about to say something awful, it was written all over his face.

"For the two of us might have joined our lives, to the greatest possible joy and advantage," he continued. "You might have furnished the tender womanly regard that is so lacking in my solitary bachelor existence. And I might have provided the leadership, guidance, and, above all, the protection that you so desperately need."

"Protection?" Glennian echoed.

"Indeed. As your husband, I would stand as a bulwark between you and the dangers of the world. I'd serve your interests, which would also be my own; shield and protect you, and never be constrained, by any agency of the law, to speak against you."

"And what could you say?" she asked quietly, no longer troubled with the slightest inclination to laugh.

"That directness—I might almost call it bluntness—is not particularly feminine, but I am not without hope that a little kindly instruction will serve to improve. you. I spoke, of course, in a general sense, but if you require particulars, let me see if any specific example springs to mind—" He ruminated briefly, and nodded. "Ah, I have one. As your husband, I could not be compelled to disclose your membership in the Blowflies organization, nor even to reveal the names of your surviving associates. The Regarded Tenzi liMeklinz, for example. Or Leffa Harf. Or that peculiar hermaphroditic person, Joonkul Irtzstro, whom you call 'Brimstone.' "

She stared at him, knowing that the shock showed clearly on her face, but incapable of concealing it, for this was worse than anything she had expected. LiMeklinz, Harf, Irtzstro—he had the names exactly right—no point in trying to deny it, and no doubt, he knew more yet. Their residences, for example—their families . . .

There was only one explanation. Pfissig had shadowed her, at some point or other, to Brimstone's house, and he'd eavesdropped on the meeting, and then he'd set watch on the dwelling and its visitors, quickly gathering all the intelligence he could possibly need or want. And it was her fault—for carelessness, for stupidity and blindness, for never noticing that she was followed—her fault alone. Still, how much difference did it really make, at this point?

"Pfissig, you've outdone yourself," she said slowly.

"You honor me. And it's about time, too. You've always looked down your nose. Maybe now you're finally learning better."

"Maybe. But you're a little late, aren't you? The White Tribunal has been suspended, and *The Buzz* has ceased publication. Who cares anything about the Blowflies, now?"

"The city magistrates care, I can tell you. The Soldiers of the Light care deeply. It seems that a fairly recent raid upon a Blowflies hideaway resulted in the death of one of their most popular officers, a certain Captain Zegnauer. His surviving comrades are most eager to apprehend the murderess."

"Murderess?" Glennian echoed, in disbelief. Such a term could scarcely apply to *her*. She knew that her faceless, hitherto nameless assailant upon that horrible night had obligingly tumbled down the stairs, thus facilitating her escape. Whether she had pushed him, or he had simply tripped, had always been genuinely unclear. She hadn't even known, until now, whether the man had lived or died. She might have made inquiries easily enough, but, she realized, she hadn't really wanted to know. She hadn't intended to hurt anyone, she'd only been desperate to get away. Still—a *murderess*?

"Beyond doubt," Pfissig assured her blithely. "They caught a glimpse of her, you see. A young female, wrapped in a long grey cloak. It comes to my mind that you yourself possess just such a cloak. You have not worn it recently, I think. Perhaps the garment is soiled, or in want of mending? Or possibly you have tired of it, as women will?"

"The weather has turned warm."

"Ah, that explains it. In any case, I'm certain you can well understand the Soldiers' intense desire to apprehend the killer and her accomplices."

"Accomplices?"

"Her companions, her fellow Blowflies."

"What reason to assume that they share in this woman's guilt, if she is indeed guilty?" Glennian inquired steadily.

"They are all of them members of the Blowflies organization, are they not? That suffices," Pfissig informed her. "The Dhreve's proscription still stands, if you'll recall. Under that ruling, all members of the group are subject to immediate execution, upon positive identification."

"The proscription is redundant. The Dhreve is certain to revoke it."

"Possibly, at such time as the matter is directed to his attention. But the Dhreve Lissildt is off inspecting the iron foundries at Ogletz, and won't return before the middle of next week, at the earliest. Of course, a very devoted messenger, provided with excellent horses, might reach Ogletz in as little as two days. And then, should his luck and strength hold, he might be back in Lis Folaze two days after that, with the Dhreve's pardon in his hand. But I am not without influence, and I've assembled the strongest proof. Thus I am safe in assuring you that such a pardon would arrive days too late to save you and your friends from the gallows."

"The Dhreve is unavailable, and that's why you've chosen this particular moment to approach me?"

"Don't whine."

Glennian rose from her chair. Pfissig did likewise, and backed hastily away from her.

"Violence won't help you, if that's what you're thinking!" he cried. "The evidence and accusation, in written form, are safely hidden away, to be handed over to the proper authorities, in the event of my death or disappearance!"

"What, do you imagine I'd murder you, you little coward?"

"If you dared. That look in your eyes right now tells me everything! When we're wed, and I am master here, you'll learn never to look at me like that!"

"Wed?"

"As soon as possible. Tomorrow morning, in fact. Tell your maid to prepare a gown for you, something appropriate to the occasion, handsome but suitably modest, and be certain the neckline isn't too low. And if you mean to run away, you'd best send word to your Blowfly friends before you go, advising them to prepare their testaments."

Glennian could find no words. White-faced, she stalked out, leaving Pfissig Kwieseldt alone in triumphant possession of the music room.

It was evening when she reached the liMarchborg townhouse, and at first she thought the silent place deserted, but a weak light glowing through the closed shutters of a second-story window told her otherwise. She knocked on the door, and waited in vain for a response. She knocked again, much harder, and at last, in desperation, flung a handful of pebbles against the upstairs shutters. The stones struck with a clatter all but impossible to ignore, but just to make sure, she resumed her loud pounding.

The door opened slowly, and Glennian caught her breath. She hadn't encountered Tradain in some days. All the city knew of the High Landguardian liMarchborg's return to his family home, but her written communications directed to that address had gone unanswered, and she had assumed that he simply desired no further contact with her. This apparent disdain had offended and somewhat wounded her, but she found it understandable enough; in all likelihood she discomforted him, simply because she knew too much.

Seeing him now, framed in the doorway, she wondered if she should ascribe his recent silence to illness, for he appeared decidedly unwell. The light of the single candle that he carried flickered upon a pale, haggard, expressionless face and deeply shadowed eyes. He looked as if he hadn't slept in years.

"You've been sick?" she asked.

"No. I'm well." That rusty, unused quality of his voice was more than ordinarily apparent.

"Then why haven't you answered any of my notes?"

"I'm sorry. I thought it best. Why are you here?"

"I came to talk to you."

"There is nothing to say. You'd do well to leave. Go home." He started to shut the door.

"Wait, please! I must talk to you, there's no one else. I'm in trouble, serious trouble, and I need your help."

That halted him. He looked at her, and surprise faintly animated his face. After a moment he pulled the door fully open, admitting her.

Glennian advanced warily, as if exploring a cave. The comparison was not unapt. Tradain's candle furnished the feeblest illumination, but it was enough to show her a marble floor carpeted with dust, shutters nailed tight, and, dimly visible overhead, an eerie pale mass that took a moment to identify as a chandelier shrouded in white canvas.

He led her from the entrance hall into a large, lofty chamber that she recalled from years ago as a well-appointed salon. Dingy old canvas wrapped the furnishings, and the handsomely carved white marble mantelpiece was dark with the accumulated grime of years. The air was cold, musty, and very still.

How can he live here, like this? And why?

Tradain politely pulled the covering from an armchair for her, revealing upholstery rank with mildew and rot. He regarded the wreck a bemused moment, before observing, "It seems I cannot play the host."

"Please don't be offended, but all this worries me. It can't be good for you to mew yourself up all alone in this crypt. I'm sure you'll make yourself ill, if you haven't already. This place seems made for melancholia. Wouldn't you be happier living elsewhere?"

"I doubt it."

"Then won't you at least have the house properly cleaned and aired? You might even—"

"You said that you are in serious trouble," he cut her off, quite gently. "Tell me what it is."

She told him everything, from Pfissig's revelation of knowledge, all the way to the threat of enforced marriage in the morning, withholding only the actual names of her three Blowfly colleagues. Tradain listened closely, never interrupting, and his face seemed to come alive as she spoke.

"So he's got me, you see," she summed up, in conclusion. "I can't run away, or my friends are destroyed. I can't kill him, even if I were willing and able to do such a thing, because he says he's got those papers stashed away somewhere, and I believe him—it would be so exactly like him. I've even thought of doing away with myself, it would be better than submitting to—" She shuddered. "But I think he's spiteful enough to go after the others, if I did that. There's only one hope I can see. The Dhreve Lissildt will soon be back in Lis Folaze, and then no doubt he can be persuaded to repeal the proscription upon the surviving Blowflies. Once that's done, Pfis-sig loses his hold on me. In the meantime, though, I've no choice but to marry him, unless you can think of some other way."

"Oh, yes," he assured her, almost carelessly. "You need seek no such desperate extreme as suicide or marriage. The matter is easily managed."

"Easily? But you've heard everything I've told you, and you know what kind of a trap he's set."

"I've listened, I understand, and I can promise you, Master Kwieseldt presents no great difficulty."

"What must we do, then?"

"You need do nothing. Go home, be at ease, fear nothing for yourself or your friends. In the morning you'll wake to discover the problem perma-nently resolved."

"Really? You're certain?"

"Entirely."

"You make it sound so simple."

"It is."

"Please tell me the truth. It's obvious that you mean to make use of those—those special abilities of yours."

"I can't speak of that to you, it's better that you know nothing. The White Tribunal is gone, but the old laws still stand."

"I'll only ask this, then. You told me that your resources are limited in quantity, and reduced by expenditure, and I wouldn't want—"

"Don't concern yourself. The minor quantity required to deal with Master Pfissig Kwieseldt is nothing I can't easily afford."

"I don't know what to say, or how to thank you. It seems I'm continu-ally begging you for rescue."

"Trust me, I'm glad of the chance to do something useful."

In the dead of night the Visitation came to Pfissig. It came while he slept, and thus he never glimpsed the cold green light that filled his bedchamber, or the nebulous transparent shape, whose true form was in any case invisible to those without senses capable of transcending the mundane dimensions.

Sleeping Pfissig had no inkling of the Visitation's presence, no oppor-tunity to attempt resistance that must, in any event, have failed. He only knew, somewhere between sleep and waking, that something like icy light-ning struck upon his unguarded awareness, and after that, a conquering alien will was inside him and absolute master of his mind.

It was done by the time he was fairly awake, and nothing remained but submission. Some small element continued inviolate, however. Some part of him remained awake, aware, terrified, despairing, and impotently furious, as the Visitation riffled methodically through his recollections, found what it sought, then worked the nerve strings required to lift the puppet host from his bed. Deftly it marched him across the room to that section of wall whose ornate applied moldings enclosed a discreet sliding panel.

Pfissig pushed the panel aside, revealing a recess wherein lay the most valuable of documents. Internally agonized, he watched his hand reach out to grasp the papers. He watched and felt himself carry them to the fireplace, where a few embers smoldered yet beneath a bank of ash, much as his own will smoldered deep inside his head. He tried to balk then, straining to hold himself motionless, but the absurd effort lasted less than an instant and then he saw his hand move again, to thrust the papers deep into the embers. Miserable seconds elapsed before an edge of flame licked the white sheets, and he was permitted to draw his hand out of danger. The fire blossomed, the flames danced, the paper blackened, and soon, the fuel was reduced to a pale film of ash.

Somewhere, below the glaze of alien constraint, disappointment and extreme self-pity raged, but Pfissig scarcely felt either, for the Visitation had not yet done with him. The skilled manipulation of his nerves moved his body back to the bed. He was aware of himself climbing in, and drawing the persimmon silken coverlet up to his chin. He was conscious, for the fraction of a second, of a freezing, consuming light within his mind; an energy that blasted, without pain. But it was over almost before he noticed it, and it hadn't hurt him, and after that, he fell deeply asleep.

He awakened very late the next morning; well rested, fit, alert, and healthy, but with the memories of the last six months of his life wiped completely from his mind.

To rule the intelligence of others is costly . . .

Tradain sat in his father's study. The hourglass stood on the desk before him. Its top compartment was empty. Lightless matter filled the lower chamber. The creation of Pfissig's Visitation had consumed the last of his sorcerous powers, and his debt had fallen due.

The mortal fear that ruled him was almost balanced by his longing to make an end, any end. The Radiant Level, for all its terrors, at least concluded the agonies of anticipation.

The previous night, as he had watched the final luminous granule fall and die, he'd expected the malevolence to claim him then and there. Nothing of the sort had happened. The night had given way to dawn, the morning had advanced to afternoon, and still Xyleel had never manifested Himself. Tradain might almost have fancied himself forgotten, had not the recollection of self-sale imprinted upon his memory burned with increasing urgency throughout the day.

At last, around sunset, he had come to understand what was required of him. Another few minutes, and he would go.

He heard the bang of the door knocker below, and then the rattle of pebbles striking the shutters. Glennian, beyond doubt. She was the only one in the world given to flinging rocks at his window; she was, in fact, the only one in the world given to seeking him out at all. He discovered, almost to his surprise, that a certain pleasure filled him. Seeing her one last time could only underscore the pain of loss, and yet he was glad of the chance to bid her farewell.

Taking up a candle, he went downstairs, opened the door, let her in, and led her to the salon.

Once again she stood among his cobwebs and his mummified furnishings, and it seemed almost a repetition of yesterday evening's scene, except, this time, she was smiling, and those eyes of hers were filled with light. Once, he had thought her pretty, rather than beautiful, but now recognized his error.

"Success," she announced. "Pfissig has lost the last six months. He's perfectly well otherwise, but he remembers nothing. It seems like a miracle!"

"Not quite." He manufactured a faint smile.

"Oh, I know. It's your doing alone, and I don't know how to thank you. There's nothing in the world I can say to tell you how grateful I am."

"You just have."

"I wish I could do more. I owe you so much—"

"You owe nothing. I was glad of the chance to help you. It's been the only time those powers of mine ever served a good purpose. I wish I'd learned earlier to use them better."

"You're sounding rather final about it." Her elation ebbed a little.

"Yes. It's lucky you've come here this evening, I'd have been sorry to leave without saying good-bye. I'm going away tonight."

"Tonight? What are you talking about? You can't start off on a journey at night, nobody does."

"My conveyance is uncommon. Please don't ask me to explain."

"Oh. Oh, I see. How long will you be gone?"

"I'm leaving for good."

"Just like that? This is sudden, isn't it?"

"Not really. I've concluded my business here, and there's nothing to hold me."

"Nothing? Indeed. Well." Her smiles had vanished altogether. "May I ask where you intend to go?"

"I'll travel. Very far, I think."

"And if I hadn't happened to call, you'd just have gone away, without a word?"

"I thought I wouldn't know what to say, or how to speak. Now I find that my fears were misplaced, for I do know what I want to tell you. It's only this—I see now that you were right in so much of what you said. You called my dreams of vengeance paltry—"

"That was presumptuous."

"It was the truth. Helping you is the one worthwhile thing I've done with all that I've been given. The rest has been waste and futility. I've many regrets, so many, and the greatest of all is the loss of the life that I like to imagine the two of us might have shared. I hope it doesn't offend you to hear me say so."

"No," she answered slowly. "It's very strange. When I was a child, forever following you around, you can't guess how often I dreamed of one day hearing such words from you. Now the years have passed, but I find the dreams almost unchanged."

"It was not just my fancy—it might have been real?"

She nodded. "But why do you speak of might-have-been?"

"You have given me something of value to carry away. I will keep that always."

"I don't understand. If what you say is true, then why would you leave?"

"It is far too late to alter my plans."

"Why is it too late?" There was no reply, and the growing dread she strove to conceal drank the color from her face, but she persisted, "You speak of sharing our lives, yet you don't ask me to go with you?"

"No. I must go alone."

"Why? And where? You're starting to frighten me. *Where are you going?*"

"Don't be frightened, there's no need. It is all settled, now."

"What's all settled? What does this mean? Are you running away because you're in some sort of danger? What could it be that your powers don't arm you against? *And where are you going?*"

"It is time for you to leave, now."

"Please, tell me."

"I will tell you that I wish you the greatest good and happiness, and these things can't be yours before you separate yourself from me. Come." He took her arm, escorted her back to the entrance hall, and opened the door. She was staring up at him, wide eyes filled with such trouble and concern that something inside him unfroze at the sight. Without considering the advisability of it, he drew her close, kissed her, and felt her lips part beneath his. When he let her go, the trouble in her eyes was deeper than ever.

"Good-bye, Glennian."

She walked out, and he closed the door behind her.

Time for Glennian to leave, time for Tradain liMarchborg to leave. He had hours of hiking before him, and he'd best get started. Returning to the study, he slipped the lightless hourglass into his pocket, then wrapped himself in a heavy cloak. He took up a lantern, a couple of spare candles, and descended to exit the house by way of the front door.

The autumn air was sharp and chill on his face, and the mists of the season swirled about him. For a moment he paused to look back one last time upon the perfect proportions of his father's house, then turned and walked away. Through the streets of the city he hurried, hardly pausing to note the surroundings that already seemed far removed. Presently he passed beneath the spiky talismans surmounting the open city gate, and found himself amid the merchants' stalls, now empty and closed for the night. Before him blazed the lanterns of the Conquered Malevolence inn, and beyond the inn lay the grassy and tree-lined outskirts of Lis Folaze.

Soon the city lay behind him, and he followed the Dhreve's Highway over misty field and farmland. He walked alone, abroad at night, without weapon, and without sorcerous power. Should he encounter footpad or highwayman, he could scarcely hope to defend himself.

Ridiculous thing to be thinking of, at such a time.

He left the highway to plunge into the fog-smothered woods, and now he would have been all but helpless without the lantern. Over the forested hills he hiked, to the summit of Ziehn's Tooth, and down again, through the crackling sea of fallen leaves smelling of autumn, to the crest of the rise overlooking the ruined mansion of Yurune the Bloodless.

The night was thick and still. He could not pierce the darkness and mists to glimpse the leaden waters of Lake Oblivion, or the fortress rising at its center, nor did he wish to.

Perhaps it would have been better, had he never escaped Fortress

Nul. But if he had not, then the White Tribunal would probably reign yet in Lis Folaze. He might take that consolation with him into Radiance, along with the memory of Glennian.

No point in delay. The mental lash snapped.

Down the slope furred with ashen grasses he hurried, into the sober shade of the bare-branched iron trees, wading through sere drifts of crisped leaves to the foot of the basalt stairway.

The oaken remnants of the door clung yet to the ruined hinges. He walked into the mansion as if coming home; made his way through the ravaged chambers to the well-remembered windowless corridor, and the lofty antechamber, and the doorway into the essence of darkness.

Behind him, clear and unmistakable, he heard the crunch of a footstep on broken glass. In the haunted silence of Yurune's mansion, that faint pop was startling as the bang of a firecracker. Heart contracting, he spun to confront a form that made no effort to conceal itself.

"Glennian." He couldn't decide between anger and terror.

"Herself."

"Might have guessed."

"Didn't, though."

"You followed me."

"Your lantern made it easy."

"Why did you come?"

"I was worried about you."

"Useless. This is no place for you."

"Thanks for the advice, but I choose my own place."

"We've already made our farewells."

"You did. I didn't."

"Do you know what's going to happen?"

"I think I have an idea."

"Then you know how dangerous this is for you."

"No. Dangerous for you. Do you really want to face it all alone?"

No. "Yes."

"Too bad. I'm not going anywhere, other than down those stairs. Don't you remember, you promised we'd see what lies at the bottom, together? You spat twice on it."

"We were children."

"There's an alternative, you know. We could run away, to the very edge of the world, hiding ourselves at the bottom of the ultimate jungles."

"To live as hermits, on berries and rainwater?"

"If necessary."

"There is no hiding from the Presence Xyleel."

"I thought not. Then let us go meet Him."

He couldn't change her mind, and he couldn't chase her away. He might stop her by protective force, knocking her unconscious with a blow of his fist, but that would be as much a violation of her freedom as anything that Pfissig Kwieseldt had ever conceived. It was hard, very hard, but he opted for acceptance. Wordlessly he extended his hand, and she took it.

Down the stairs they went together, as he had promised. Left turn at the bottom, around the corner, and through the splintery wooden door into the workroom of Yurune the Bloodless, awash with faint azure light and crammed with forbidden wonder, just as he remembered. And there at the center of the brightest patch of light was the iron cage containing a folio volume.

He glanced down at Glennian. Her eyes were wide, devouring marvels. She offered no resistance as he led her to the dimmest corner of the room.

"Stay here," he advised. "Don't move, or speak, or try to interfere, no matter what you see."

"What will I see?" Instinctively, she whispered. "What are you going to do?"

"What I must." He spoke nothing but the truth. Within his mind, the memory imprint pressed with overwhelming insistence. Tradain advanced to the iron cage at the center of the room. He had once needed the book, to tell him what to do. He did not need it now, and yet the compulsion ruling him demanded observance of traditional form.

His lips formed the forbidden words. His mind prepared itself. All consciousness of his physical surroundings left him, as his intelligence threaded a path between dimensions. For the last time, he launched his summons into the great void.

Insofar as his intense preoccupation permitted expectation of any sort, he expected a swift response. Judging Xyleel by human standards, he imagined the Presence eager to claim His property. In this, he found himself mistaken. So long an interval ensued that Tradain began to fancy himself unheard and unnoticed. At last, the dawning of vast radiance taught him otherwise.

Reflexively he shrank from the insupportable light, consciousness retreating to the mundane sphere. He opened his eyes upon Yurune's workroom, and beheld the Presence Xyleel. The familiar but eternally alien awareness impinged freezingly upon his own. Behind him, he heard Glennian liTarngrav cry out in fear, or astonishment, or both, and briefly he wondered if she experienced any clear sense of Xyleel's inhuman intellect.

But there was no time to consider the matter, for the goad of his memory told him that the moment had come.

"I am Yours," he said aloud.

He anticipated instant physical annihilation, but again, his expectations were confounded. Nothing happened.

Xyleel did not respond. His immediacy was intense, and yet He communicated nothing. His attention seemed to occupy itself elsewhere, and no glimmering of confirmation or even recognition reached the mind of His human property.

The prolonged psychic silence was torturous as Radiance itself. The terror that he'd hitherto governed was rising uncontrollably, and his agony was acute. A mortal antagonist might deliberately have inflicted torment, but Xyleel was guilty of no such human vice, and His motives remained obscure.

Focus sharpened far beyond its normal limits, Tradain strained for comprehension. He caught a faint vibration from the mind of Xyleel, something akin to an impersonal deliberation. The Presence seemed to ponder, but His cogitations were not to be encompassed by human intellect.

It was unendurable.

"I am ready," Tradain offered, and his voice was even, but couldn't remain so for much longer.

"I am also ready."

He heard Glennian's voice behind him, and her words appalled him, but he realized that he wasn't altogether surprised. He might have known, he *should* have known, that she wouldn't stand by, watching in helpless silence. He'd done her a couple of favors, she fancied herself indebted, and now she intended insane repayment.

He should have known.

He ought never to have let her set foot in this room. Better to have knocked her cold when he'd had the chance, and her freedom be damned. It wasn't too late to rectify his error.

He wheeled to face her and hesitated, involuntarily struck by her appearance. She'd abandoned her dim corner, and now she stood near him, her face and figure bathed in the effulgence that was Xyleel, her eyes reflecting His light. She displayed no sign of fear, but rather wonder, and even something like a delight in discovery.

"Great Xyleel, I believe that You hear me," Glennian addressed the Presence clearly and strongly. "I know what it is that You seek to amass, and I offer all that I have, in exchange for this man You have purchased."

"No. Stay out of it," Tradain told her.

Apparently deaf to his voice, she continued, "Xyleel, You will profit by this substitution. In terms of the human sentience You desire, I am at least the equal of Tradain liMarchborg. Beyond that, I offer a commodity that he does not possess."

"Stop this," Tradain commanded. "You don't understand what you're trying to do."

"I have within me the power to create music," Glennian spoke on unstoppably. "It is a special spark of fiery mind-stuff certain to enrich Your hoard. You must know the truth of this, for music is a part of You, and all those like You, in Your own place."

"Enough! He will not heed you." Tradain grasped her arm.

"He listens." Her whisper thrilled.

"He will not deal with you." He tightened his grip, not caring if he hurt her. If pain could silence her, he was willing to bruise her purple.

"You can't know that." She didn't trouble to glance in his direction.

She spoke the simple truth, and the sense of helplessness that filled him was worse than any personal fear he had ever known.

"Once, I caught an echo of that great chorus from Your thoughts." Again Glennian invoked the malevolence. "Hear my mind. I will remember it for You." Shutting her eyes, she stood motionless.

Tradain supposed she must be singing inside. But it was probably more than singing—she was capable of internally reproducing the vocal swell of an entire chorus, together with the accompaniment of countless instruments. Whatever she was doing, it had drawn Xyleel's attention. For the first time since the Presence had manifested Himself, Tradain received a clear impression of detached interest, and his terror stabbed.

"*Stop.*" Catching her by the shoulders, he shook her hard.

He must have succeeded in breaking her concentration, for her eyes opened, and she spoke. "Great Xyleel, all of this music and more I offer unto You in exchange for this man You now own."

"I won't let you." He actually doubled his fist to strike her senseless. By the time she awoke, the matter would be settled, and she need never suffer the eternal consequences that her eager generosity never remotely conceived. Some huge force stayed his hand. It seemed that the Presence Xyleel desired to hear more, and Tradain's horror deepened.

"The decision isn't yours," Glennian told him.

"The decision was made long ago."

"Quiet," she commanded raptly. "He listens to my music of the mind. He hears, and He weighs. Now it is between Him and me."

"*No.*" The useless denial rang pitifully false. No good talking to her.

Tradain addressed himself to Xyleel. "The bargain was sealed, the conditions fulfilled. Nothing has altered, and now remains only the delivery of the promised payment."

No acknowledgment, no response.

His impotent little buzz lost itself in nothingness. He was powerless to control the events that he had set in motion, and the desperation that swept his mind and body heightened his awareness, sharpening receptivity. He caught the echo of Xyleel's sentience, through which quivered a hint of Glennian's melody. He could interpret the humanly knowable component of the malevolence's response, and his worst fears were confirmed.

The music of Glennian liTarngrav had caught the attention of the Presence Xyleel. He found her offer worthy of His consideration.

She is not part of this. Tradain shot the voiceless words with all the strength of his mind, and knew at once that the malevolence had excluded an obvious absurdity.

She was very much a part of it. She had insisted on making herself so, but the responsibility belonged to Tradain liMarchborg alone.

Intent upon his own purpose, he'd rushed at breakneck pace down the path to ruin. And he'd dragged Glennian liTarngrav along with him.

Every step that he had taken, every choice that he had made, had led to this place and this moment. His hatred and anger had driven him on, until at last he'd achieved his aim. He'd had his expensive, worthless vengeance that quenched no internal blaze. He'd sold himself for next to nothing, and ended by destroying the one being in all the world that he would willingly have died to defend.

He couldn't save her, or even help her, for he had nothing to offer Xyleel to compare with her music. She was damned, on his account. Such was the culmination of his great endeavor.

He thought he had known despair for half his lifetime. He had never known it until now.

A white-hot rush of grief and self-loathing seemed to duplicate or perhaps exceed the torments of the Radiant Level. He had no words to curse or plead with, and they would have been useless in any case, for tiny mortal yammerings scarcely touched the consciousness of the Presence Xyleel.

Something caught His attention, however. Perhaps the singular quality of the emotional emanation intrigued Him, or perhaps simply its extraordinary force. The regard of Xyleel shifted, and once again Tradain liMarchborg experienced the unhurried ransacking of his mind and all its contents.

He had suffered through it more than once, but never before had the scrutiny seemed so prolonged, so deliberate, so utterly unendurable. There was, this time, no shred of mental reciprocity. Xyleel vouchsafed nothing of Himself, but merely examined the subject's anguish at inconceivable length.

Tradain sensed his reason buckling under the strain. His thoughts blurred, one desire only retaining its strength and clarity.

"Take Your payment now, from me."

He spoke aloud into a psychic vacuum. Xyleel was elsewhere, gone, nonexistent. The intolerable pressure eased. He sagged, and caught the edge of the nearest table to keep himself from falling. His head and vision cleared, and he saw Glennian staring at him. Her lips moved, but he heard nothing, for the tiny respite had ended.

Once more, his intelligence trembled to an alien touch, and he whispered into the unknown, "The bargain was sealed, the conditions fulfilled."

The reply came not in words.

A power within himself, but not of himself, constrained him to draw the hourglass from his pocket. He regarded the glass, and doubted his own sanity. A single luminous granule glowed in the upper chamber; a lone, tiny quantum of sorcerous power. So long as it shone there, the debt was not yet due.

But it had not shone there, hours earlier. The supply had been exhausted. There could be no mistake about that. He was neither deluded nor mad, and the bright granule's existence admitted of but one possible source.

Tradain spoke aloud to the Presence Xyleel.

"Why?"

He knew he was heard, and yet, for a while, thought Xyleel too uninterested to reply. Then the effulgent voice reverberated through his mind.

It has all been meaningless. I did what I was impelled to do . . .

His own words, spoken not long ago. And there were more.

. . . hasn't given me what I wanted . . . The sum of destruction has brought little beyond . . . remorse, and . . . disgust . . .

"Why do You taunt me now with my failures?" There was no answer, and it dawned on Tradain that Xyleel, harboring no malice toward an inferior species, intended no taunt, but only explanation more or less comprehensible to a human intelligence. The implications were unexpected.

"You would question Your own purpose? You would choose to abandon it?"

No answer. No denial.

"You would spare Your own dimension?"

The sum of destruction has brought little . . .

The Presence Xyleel's voice suggested a certain finality, a preference to have done. There wasn't much time left for questions.

"What will You do?"

He had thought it the simplest of queries, but Xyleel's silent response suggested otherwise. A host of alien impressions buffeted Tradain. Most of it was incomprehensible, but a few words, a few concepts, broke all barriers.

Sentient Symbiosis.

He had heard that one before. He still did not know just what it meant, but the general sense could be inferred.

Autonn. Exiles. Anomalies.

Meeting. Communion. Exchange.

Information. Observation.

Contemplation. Consideration.

Reconsideration.

Sketchy, but decipherable.

"When will You know?" asked Tradain.

When . . .

He wasn't sure if he'd heard or imagined it.

"Where will You go?"

There was a reply, beyond understanding.

"You will return?"

Upon conclusion.

"And that will be—?"

This time, no reply, for the Presence Xyleel was gone, beyond the human conception of distance.

The magic bled from the workroom of Yurune the Bloodless. The sorcerous light expired, all save a single small ray beaming from the one granule contained within the upper chamber of the hourglass. Apart from that, the yellow beams of a mundane lantern furnished the sole illumination. The place changed character in an instant, and its mystery sank into shadow.

Tradain felt a light hand close upon his arm. He covered it with his own.

"Did you hear?" he asked.

"Most," Glennian told him. "I didn't understand everything."

"No mortal could." He turned to face her and, even in the dimness, caught the glitter of tears in her eyes. His own were not dry.

"Will He come for you when the light in the glass dies, or you do?"

"Perhaps, if He is still interested. He's entitled, but I don't believe He'll be back before His Sentient Symbiosis concludes. And time, as measured upon the interdimensional level, is an inconsistency, its seconds translating to hours, months, years, centuries, millennia, and back again, without clear pattern or predictability."

"What does that mean, for you? It's certain you've got a reprieve. How long will it actually last?"

"I have no idea."

About the Author

Born and raised in Fanwood, New Jersey, Paula Volsky majored in English literature at Vassar, then traveled to England to complete an M.A. in Shakespearean studies at the University of Birmingham. Upon her return to the United States, she sold real estate in New Jersey, then began working for the U.S. Department of Housing and Urban Development in Washington, D.C. During this time she finished her first book, *The Curse of the Witch Queen*, a fairy tale for children that developed into a fairy tale for adults. Shortly thereafter she abandoned HUD in favor of full-time writing. These days she is back in New Jersey, camping in condo with cat and computer.